BALANCE OF TERROR

Raves for
BALANCE OF TERROR

An intelligent and riveting thriller.

Dr. Lawrence Starkey
International Defense Consultant

I couldn't put it down....!

Larry Bond
Best Selling Author

Watch out Tom Clancy, Bern and Rob are coming

- Terry

BOOKS BY

BERNARD KEMPINSKI

nonfiction

Model Railroaders Guide to Steel Mill Modeling

Realistic Track Plans for Mid-Sized Layouts

ROBERT KEMPINSKI

nonfiction

Introduction to Bonsai

BALANCE OF TERROR

BERNARD KEMPINSKI & ROBERT KEMPINSKI

Mahogany Row Studio

Published 2010
Printed in the United States of America

Library of Congress Cataloguing-Publication Data

ISBN: 1452854491
EAN-13 is 9781452854496
Published by Mahogany Row Studio
Melbourne, Florida

www.alkemscalemodels.com

The authors would like to dedicate this book to their father,

Robert Peter Kempinski,

who loved story telling and inspired us by his example.
Thanks Dad.

"To be certain to take what you attack, attack where the enemy cannot defend"

-Sun Tzu

"The states must see the rod; perhaps it must be felt by some one of them. . . . Every national citizen must wish to see an effective instrument of coercion, and should fear to see it on any other element than the water."

- Thomas Jefferson, The Jefferson Papers

Author's Comments 2010

In 1990 the US was in the middle of the greatest transfer of wealth from one nation to the other. Thousands of safety and environmental regulations, selfish unionism, management emphasis on next quarter's financial results, militant consumerism and unabashed greed contributed to this imbalance. The nation watched blithley as first the steel industry shriveled, then the electronics manufacturers and others vanished or went offshore. When the market assault on the American automobile industry intensified everyone thought it had enough market size and inertia to survive the onslaught. From the viewpoint of 2010 we know it really didn't.

The September 2001 terrorist attack opened American eyes to another problem – militant terrorists. It shouldn't have been a surprise as Al Qaeda had conducted a steady assault on the nation, first with a car bomb in the basement of the World Trade Center, then truck bombs and even a boat bomb. While the attacks escalated, our leaders largely ignored the threat until the twin towers came down.

This book was written in the early 1990s before the Oklahoma City bombing and September 11th attacks and has only received only minor updates to reflect those events. Some of contemporary allusions have faded, but what is interesting is the premise of the book hasn't changed. What if some American's tried to take matters into their own hands to solve these problems? It could still happen.

Chapter 1

Fire Marshall Joe Nicca scanned the road ahead, his gaze drifting past the glare of the oncoming headlights. A stale taste reminded him of a half-finished cup of cold coffee wedged between his seat and the center console. He'd have to give up coffee - too much caffeine. He moved his eyes, absorbing the details and rhythm of a city coasting downhill into the dark night, when his eyes locked onto a woman entering a Taurus station wagon. His breath left him with a jolt. It was Joanne, his wife, wearing a red parka. He twisted his head to get a better look as he passed her car. The smile, the hair, the posture, it had to be Joanne. He strained to see inside her dark car when the impossibility struck home. He shook his head. It's not her - - Joanne was dead. Three years, tomorrow.

Nicca exhaled through clenched teeth. A bead of sweat dripped down his neck onto his blue Oxford buttoned-down shirt.

Willy Jones, Nicca's partner, threw a look from the driver's seat. "What is it, Joe?"

Nicca looked out the front of the car again. "Nothing. I thought I saw someone. Don't worry. It's nothing."

"Are you feeling all right?"

Nicca adjusted his moist collar with his finger and slowly scanned outside the car. "I'm fine."

"How about if we stop for a doughnut or something?"

"I'll pass, Willy. I'm not in the mood."

"Eh, I don't need one, either." Jones yawned. "It's been a quiet night."

"Not for long." Nicca lowered his eyes in the darkness. "I have one of those feelings. Can't say when. Maybe now, maybe a little later, but there'll be a scorcher. A bad one."

"Cut it out, Joe. You're giving me the creeps."

"It's been too long. Something about tonight. I can just feel it."

Jones pondered the last remark then raised his chin with recognition, waved his hand and smiled. "I get it. You do this to all the rookies: try to spook us as part of our initiation."

Nicca let his face relax and grinned at his new partner. "Maybe so, but don't discount your instinct. It can be your best weapon."

Jones shrugged and drove the sedan toward Livonia. Shadows flickered across the dashboard with a pulsing cadence while Nicca continued to scan the roadside, trying hard to forget the woman in the car and his premonition.

Two miles down the road, the dispatcher's voice crackled over the Motorola radio. "Code 10-24, 1600 block of Wilson."

Nicca listened intently.

The dispatcher continued. "Two alarm. One fatality."

Jones did a double take and stared at Nicca.

Nicca made a slight nod. "Keep your eyes on the road, Willy, and step on it."

On the notepad next to the radio, Nicca jotted the address while his partner reached up with his left hand and placed the removable emergency light on the roof of the unmarked sedan. Nicca grabbed the armrest as Jones flung the Ford into a sharp U-turn and headed for Wilson Avenue.

Detroit had lots of arson. On Halloween, or Hell Night, four hundred arsons lit up the downtown like a miniature Dresden. Roving gangs of hooligans ransacked houses, stores, or cars and used whatever they found handy to burn them. Even though the mayor's office, the police, and the FBI had cracked down, burned-out shells of buildings still littered the cityscape.

The last year or so, the situation had improved, and Nicca prided himself on his contribution to reducing the arsons, but at what cost? He was the last member of his academy class still with the Detroit Fire Department. The rest had either left the dangerous city for the safer suburbs or succumbed as line of duty victims of violence. In the three years since Joanne had died in the car fire, Nicca had done plenty of thinking, wondering more and more about his future as a Fire Marshall. Tonight, he figured the city got lucky. Their most senior investigator was on duty to handle an arson homicide. He'd give the city its money's worth, and worry about his career later.

Even before arriving at the scene, Nicca could smell the fire. Raised by the draft, smoke blanketed the neighborhood, laying a

14

surreal fog in the street light cast between battered row houses. The telltale odor, something like burnt pine, charred shingles, blistered paint and melted wires, made an acrid combination that etched itself on the inside of his nose. As his sedan approached the scene, he knew tonight, there'd be one more odor. One he couldn't yet sense, the putrid stench of charred flesh.

Nicca closed his eyes. He pictured a flash of light and dense black smoke, tinted orange around the edge of billowing cloud. Then like always, he saw her. Joanne clawing, screaming for the door, her car exploding into a fireball. Her face disappeared behind a wall of flame.

Nicca had been working when his wife had the accident, but in a different jurisdiction. The news seemed like a cruel joke, but after he had buried her, the irony hit every time he responded to a fire. He saw the same scene, grasped the same helplessness.

Nicca rocked his head sideways and opened his eyes. He saw no fire, only Jones turning onto Wilson Avenue. Nicca stuck his index fingers on his eyelids harder than he meant and rubbed his eyes. When he opened them, a cacophony of fire pumpers, hook and ladders, police cars and ambulances greeted him.

Jones parked the sedan behind a yellow Mack CF pumper. Nicca jumped out and strode over a tangled web of fire hoses and power cables, sizing up the smoldering fire as the uniformed firemen finished extinguishing the blaze. He straightened his tie and zipped up his leather jacket. A full head of hair and trim waist belied rapidly approaching middle age, but the lines surrounding his dark brown eyes projected a sadness beyond his years.

He turned his head from side to side and stuck out his chin inhaling the wafting fumes.

"Smell that?" Nicca turned to Jones.

"Smell what? The smoke?" Jones scrunched his face.

Nicca nodded. "You still got a rookie nose. Get a few years under your belt. You'll smell it."

"Smell what Joe?" Jones seemed confused.

"Gasoline." Nicca paused. "Arson."

"I don't smell any gasoline." Jones stretched his neck while wrinkling his nose.

"It's there. Let's get moving. I don't want to waste time. The judge isn't going to trust my nose. Get the camera and the sniffer. Start taking pictures and samples. I'm going to check the scene."

Jones headed for the trunk of the sedan while Nicca approached the porch where a policewoman peered under a sheet at a body while holding her nose.

"Who is this?" Nicca asked the officer while flashing his badge.

"Don't know. He's pretty well toasted." Her voice made a nasal sound as she continued to pinch her nose. "Judging by the shoes, I'd say pretty young. I haven't found any ID."

Nicca lifted the sheet and flinched when he caught a whiff of the remains. He'd never get used to it. The smell of burnt flesh turned his stomach. Nicca fought back the caustic taste of bile and inspected the body. He saw a tall, slim man, about six two, one hundred seventy pounds, in what looked like a Detroit Pistons jacket, shredded blue jeans and the remnants of Doc Marten boots. "There's your arsonist." He dropped the sheet.

The policewoman squinted. "What do you mean?"

"The body is badly burned, but really charred on the front. He must have been facing the source of the flames when they flashed. Now, take a look at the bottom of his boots." Nicca pointed at the blackened feet. "They're burned away to the skin. Rubber doesn't burn like that unless there's a catalyst. He must have been standing in the accelerant, probably gasoline. Nothing else on the porch has burned, except for him."

Nicca stood up and gestured to the inside of the house. "He's inside splashing gasoline. It backfires on him, flashing his front. He makes it to the front door but collapses here on the porch."

"You know, you could be right," said the crouching officer lifting her hat and running her hand through her hair.

Nicca twisted his lip. "Yep. One gang burning the enemy's hangout. I've seen this before."

Jones, returning with the equipment, started photographing the front porch. Nicca took the portable flame ionization detector and a flashlight. He entered the front room of the house. Embers crackled and steam drifted from the residue of the burned-out floor. A uniformed fireman selectively shot a stream of water at the few remaining glowing coals, while another fireman hacked at a wall with a fire ax making a tremendous racket. Nicca set up the portable detector on top of the charred wooden floor. With a shovel, he stirred up the ashes, hoping to release traces of the accelerant so the detector could sense it. The sniffer indicated hydrocarbons. Four more readings above the localized burn patterns on the floor confirmed gasoline.

"Don't need a FID for this one," he said flaring his nostrils. "A definite torch job."

He picked his way around the burned out floor, until he found the stairs to the basement. He shined his flashlight down the steps. The spotlight illuminated a foot.

"Ah, damn, not another one."

He descended the stairs, checking each step before putting his full weight on it.

At the bottom of the stairs, he found a crumpled body with the limbs splayed at impossible angles. Nicca shuddered when his flashlight lit up a head twisted around the torso of a young male. He crouched down for a closer look, careful not to disturb the body.

"Bullet hole right in the middle of his forehead and a broken neck too." He squatted on his haunches and rubbed his chin. "He must have been shot upstairs, then tumbled down the steps. Such a young kid."

With his light he searched the burned debris in the basement As he examined the far corner of the room, he heard a loud crash behind him. He ducked as a ceiling beam fell to the floor.

"Hey, take it easy up there." He yelled up the stairs. "We got another body down here."

Then he hustled up the stairs to the porch and motioned to the police officer he saw earlier.

"Did the coroner show up?"

"Any minute now," the policewoman said.

"Well, have him take a look in the basement. I found a body with a broken neck and a gunshot wound." Nicca pointed to his forehead.

Nicca noticed Jones talking to a civilian near the curb. Jones used his flashlight to illuminate the street. Nicca jogged over to see what Jones had in the spotlight.

"Hey, Joe, get this." Jones pointed over his shoulder to a man wearing a corduroy jacket over plaid pajamas. "This neighbor says he heard a car screech off around the time of the fire. I found these tire marks."

"Tire marks, huh. Get a couple of photos and fax 'em to Wilcox at the ATF laboratory in Phoenix. Maybe he can identify the brand."

"Got it."

By the time the coroner arrived, Nicca and Jones had collected more than enough evidence to prove arson. It was one hour past their shift.

"Hey, Joe, didn't you want to leave early today?"

"Damn, that's right. Doing this report, it skipped my mind. I can go later, I guess."

"Where you going? "

"Up to Greenlawn."

"Greenlawn, the cemetery?"

"Yeah." Nicca lowered his gaze and fiddled with his papers. "It's been three years since my wife's accident."

Jones furrowed his brow forming a deep crease between his eyebrows that continued half-way down his nose, "Oh, I'm sorry, Joe. I. ..er... Why don't you leave now?" Jones nodded toward the car. "One of the Blue and Whites can give you a ride back to the station. I'll finish up the report. It's all over."

"No, it's not over, Willy." Nicca slammed his notebook shut. "Once we identify the guy on the porch, we may have more luck with the tire marks. Somebody left in a hurry. I want to find out who."

"You don't give up."

"You never give up. Remember that." Nicca stared at Jones, making no effort to mask the fatigue from the long night on his face. His dark hair fell down in front of his brown eyes and he moved it aside with a slow motion of his hand. "You saw what I saw. Some guy or guys in a car got away. We don't stop until we nail 'em. Then we nail the next one and the next one until we don't have to do this anymore."

After leaving the arson scene, Nicca hitched a ride to his office at the station headquarters. He leafed through the mail in his in-box, then left, driving his own car ten blocks to his two-bedroom apartment not far from Interstate 75. By the time he got home he was stone tired, so he stripped off his pants and shirt and lay down on his bed.

A noise from a city garbage truck woke him a little past noon. After a shower and shave he felt better but still ill at ease. He flipped on his stereo and listened to a Beethoven sonata on a CD while he ate a sandwich.

The phone rang, interrupting his lunch.

"Nicca here."

"Hello Joe. This is Dr. Rachael."

"Dr. Rachael! What a surprise."

"Just called to see how you were doing."

"Not too bad. I had a rough night. An arson. Two fatalities. Two wasted lives. Like Joanne."

"Do you want to talk about it?"

"There's nothing to talk about." Nicca slumped on his couch. Dr. Rachael didn't say anything.

"Well, maybe," Nicca finally said. "I still see her, every time there's a fire."

"The same image."

"The same as always." Nicca leaned his head onto the back of the couch. "You know, maybe I'm getting too soft for this. Maybe it's time to find a job in the suburbs. Get away from the hate and violence of the city."

"Running away doesn't solve anything, Joe."

"I know that." The hair rose on Nicca's neck. He scowled at the phone. "I know why you called. You circled your calendar. 'Three year anniversary for Joe Nicca.' Well, I'm not counting. I'm getting over it."

"I know, Joe. You're doing fine."

Dr. Rachael's voice had its same soothing tone. Nicca slouched. "I'm sorry, Dr. Rachael. Look, I'm fine. Really. I'm dealing with it. It's just tough."

"Those feelings are natural."

"I'm heading up to Greenlawn. I'll bring some flowers. Joanne loved carnations."

"Sure. That would be nice." Dr. Rachael paused. "If you need to talk, please call. You have my number."

"Thanks. Thanks for caring."

At the cemetery Nicca placed two carnations by the headstone, then crouched on the grass. He sat there with his eyes closed, trying to think back to the good times with his wife. But he couldn't. Images of the dead bodies from last night flashed by him. He put his hand to his head to wipe away the horrible scene, but it came back.

The crime scenario replayed in his mind as if he had it on a VCR tape. Over and over it appeared. Each time he visualized more and more of the arson. Finally, he saw a pickup truck screech from the crime, the same truck he noticed driving past the scene at daybreak.

"That's it." He reached into his pocket for his cellular phone and dialed his partner, Jones.

"Willy, this is Joe. You're not sleeping are you?"

"Nah, I'm awake. Getting ready to eat."

"Hey, did you see a Chevy low-rider pickup drive past the scene around dawn?"

"No, I didn't."

"Well, run a make on a late model Chevy pickup, greenish, with a two tone paint job. Michigan plate. Starts with a 'WL'. I think our perps may have returned to check the scene."

"Really? You think they would come back?"

"Sure. Amateurs always want to check out their damage."

"Okay, Joe, I'll see what I can do."

Nicca shut his phone and looked at the headstone. After a second he said, "Well, honey, I have to go." The wind picked up and whistled through the trees, blowing early autumn leaves across the grave. Nicca swept them aside. He turned and brushed a tear from his cheek.

STERLING HEIGHTS, MICHIGAN

A brisk gust whipped a paper cup along the sidewalk. Chuck Holzer kicked an empty beer can as he pushed open the squeaky glass and chrome doors of the unemployment office and walked inside. He was late. Yesterday, the loan company had repossessed his truck, making the fifteen minute trip an hour and a half bus ride. The unemployment office had been open for several hours by the time Chuck arrived.

Long lines at every counter held silent people too ashamed to look up. Chuck, in his old Army jacket and jeans, picked the shortest line.

Chuck recognized the face of the man in front of him from previous visits to Michigan Employment Security Commission.

"How's it going?" the stranger asked.

"Hey, it's my Monday. Sixteen weeks since the last time. The

20

bureaucrats want to harass me 'cause I still haven't found a job."

"Yeah, me neither. This is your first time, right?"

"Yeah," Chuck deadpanned. "I don't know if they're ever going to call me back. Chrysler closed my plant. Managers got rid of everybody. Didn't matter if you were a worthless drunk or had a wife and kids to feed. Everyone got the pink slip."

"Yeah, but I bet you they got their bonuses."

"That's right. They got their money. We got the ax."

The other man looked at his feet. "The old lady has been bugging me to move south and work at a Japanese factory."

"What! And get half of what you make here? They got no union."

"Has to be better than this," the man gestured to the room around him.

"Not for me. I ain't going to work for no non-union rice burner company. They put me, no ---" Chuck paused and motioned toward the grim people in line, "us out of work."

When Chuck reached the counter the clerk told him he had to see a counselor. "Why?"

"Your benefits are about to expire. Sign in and a counselor will see you when it's your turn." She pointed to a drab waiting area and bellowed, "Next."

Chuck fumed on his way to the waiting area. Without my unemployment check, I'm in deep trouble. My savings are gone, my credit cards at the limit. I'm getting deeper and deeper into the hole and there's no escape.

He heard a loud voice call, "Mr. Charles Holzer?"

Chuck looked up and saw a rotund man in brown polyester pants, permanent press shirt and worn tie frowning at the group of waiting people.

"Yeah."

The man didn't introduce himself. Instead he said, "Come with me."

Chuck followed him to a desk in the back of the room and sat.

"I see from your file you haven't been able to find work for the past fifty-five weeks. You've already had two extensions."

"Well, I was hoping Chrysler would call me back."

Chuck could see the counselor shrug.

"Why did you drop out of career retraining?"

"I couldn't deal with it. They wanted me to..."

The counselor interrupted Chuck. "You could have lost your benefits just for that. Have you been looking for work?"

Chuck felt his face flush. "I tried, but I'm a shift supervisor. All I could find were jobs flipping hamburgers and..."

The counselor stopped him again, "Did you turn down an offer for employment? I could halt your benefits for that too."

"No," he shouted. "I didn't turn down a job offer at McDonald's, God damn it."

"There's no need to get angry, Mister, er Mister...," he looked down at the file, obviously forgetting Chuck's name.

"It's Holzer, you asshole. Charles W. Holzer." Chuck stood and grabbed the counselor by the shirt, shaking him and knocking off the man's glasses. "You're telling me what to do and you can't even remember my damned name?"

The counselor fell backwards when Chuck let go of his shirt. He landed on the floor with a loud thud. The counselor moaned and curled up on his side on the vinyl tile and put a finger to his lip, where a thin trickle of blood streamed from his nose.

Chuck slid around the desk and glared at the prostrate worker. "Just 'cause you sit behind a desk in this hell hole don't make you any better than me. You can't tell me how to live my life."

A security guard hustled to the scene. Chuck saw the guard and stepped back, brushing his blonde hair from his forehead while he regained his composure.

With an eye on Holzer, the guard knelt down next to the bleeding counselor and asked, "Are you okay, Mr. Thompson?"

"I think so," the counselor peeped.

Chuck started to leave when a middle-aged man of average size stepped in front of him. The man said, "Where do you think you're going?"

Chuck stopped, his anger gone. Who is this guy? The office manager. I can get by him, but what for? They know my address. They could get me whenever they want.

"Guard, watch him while I call the police," he heard the manager say.

22

Stay in control, Chuck thought as he balled his fists. I'll get my chance.

NEW TOKYO INTERNATIONAL AIRPORT, JAPAN

Yuichi Kondo felt the rain hit his face like a thousand points poking his skin. Before he could step off the portable aircraft-passenger stairs, the steady drizzle formed a light film on his wire-rimmed glasses.

"Miserable crowded airport," he mumbled. "Can't even use a covered jet way." He pulled on the plaid collar of his Burberry trench coat as if trying to protect his pinstriped business suit long since wrinkled from the tiring flight. Kondo stepped on the tarmac and crowded onto the articulated airport transfer bus for the short trek to the airport entrance. Once off the bus, he shuffled through the immigration counter, retrieved his luggage and picked the shortest customs line. At his turn, Kondo placed his well-used Louis Vitton suit bag on the customs counter while offering his red Japanese passport to the uniformed inspector.

"What is the purpose of your trip, Kondo-San?" said the courteous customs official in a light blue para-military uniform.

The question brought Kondo from his jet-lag induced trance. "It's automobile business," he replied, wondering the same question. Two days ago Teruki Takahashi, the Fuku-shacho, Sunon Corporate Vice President, had summoned me to Japan. Takahashi had said they needed to discuss the introduction plans for the newest Sunon model, the 500GSX. However, my staff and I had been developing these plans for months. We had no problems. Takahashi, in typical indirect fashion, wanted to talk about something else. Exactly what I pondered throughout the twelve-hour flight.

Appearing satisfied with Kondo's passport and entrance visas, the inspector politely nodded, "Go ahead. Welcome back to Japan."

As Kondo left the customs area, a small man in a black uniform suit came up to him. The man bowed at the waist, his head almost touching his knees. "I am Kobayashi, your driver. Please follow me, sir."

Kobayashi grabbed Kondo's suit bag and led him through the crowded lobby, past the airport limousine bus lanes to a double-parked Sunon Fredrick sedan. Kobayashi closed the door behind Kondo and put the bag in the trunk.

As they pulled into traffic, Kondo noticed the omnipresent gray police barricades. Police officers clad in anti-riot gear resembling medieval Japanese armor surrounded the airport, protecting against terrorist attack.

"Still these infernal barricades," muttered Kondo. "They've been here thirty years."

"No one wants to be the one to do away with them and then have an attack," said Kobayashi from the front seat.

"No terrorist attacks in ten years. I hear the real reason is the police union does not want to disband the large security force it has assembled."

"It is possible, Kondo-San." Kobayashi squirmed in his seat. "Things are not always what they appear."

"What a waste of resources," Kondo said. "These are not the forty-seven Ronin samurai waiting patiently for a moment when security is lax to launch an attack. Not today's Japanese. More likely they are drinking in some beer hall."

Kobayashi grunted and accelerated the Sunon Fredrick onto the Higashi-Kanto Expressway west to Tokyo.

When they were at speed Kondo asked in familiar Japanese, "Where are we headed tonight?"

"The Shizuoka Prince Hotel in Toyokawa. Your meeting tomorrow will be at the Shizuoka Parts Fabrication Plant." The driver stared ahead.

"Ah so," Kondo used the ubiquitous Japanese phrase for "I see." The Shizuoka Prince Hotel meant a full four hour drive, provided light traffic in Tokyo. Not meeting in Tokyo meant Takahashi wanted to talk in private. Takahashi must need my support. Why not talk over the telephone? I am president of Sunon's North American operations. They should not keep me in the dark. Yet, Takahashi surely earns his reputation for mysterious ways. No. Not mysterious, rude. Why not tell me?

As Kondo mulled the possibilities, the fourteen-hour jet lag overtook him and he fell asleep.

OLD EXECUTIVE OFFICE BUILDING, WASHINGTON, DC

The Old Executive Office Building stood at the corner of Pennsylvania and Eighteenth, next to the White House. Thousands of tourists visiting the White House each year ignored the gray stone building, yet most of the executive branch's action took place in the venerable building.

Jay Gait, or JG, as the President and everyone else called him, had a corner office on the third floor. His prestigious office came with the position as Chief Trade Negotiator for the President.

The intercom on Gait's desk buzzed. "Representative Pringle is here to see you, Mr. Gait."

Gait looked at his watch and put his papers away. "Oh sure, let him in."

Representative Pringle, from the Ninetieth Congressional District of Detroit, was a large man with a hard face that Gait thought made him look more like a UAW boss than a politician. He burst into Gait's office with a rush and shook hands. Pringle's hand felt like a bear paw as it swallowed Gait's smaller hand.

"JG, nice to see again," boomed the Congressman. "Look, I'm sorry. I don't have much time. They've called a roll call on the continuing resolution, but I have to talk to you about these upcoming trade talks with Japan."

"Oh, you'll like where we're heading." JG made a thumbs up motion with his hand. "The President is keeping up the heat. We're asking for precise measurements to follow up on our trade agreements."

"What, is that all? Meanwhile they continue to assault our economy to sell their cars. Look at this." Pringle tossed the latest issue of Autotrend on Gait's desk.

"Sunon is about to introduce a new sports coupe. This is the type of car the trade restrictions would have nailed. This car will put my constituents out of work. No sir, we have to do more than take some measurements."

"Wait a minute! We haven't given up on the threat of a tariff. It worked once. It will work again."

"No, that's not enough. I want something better. We have to really hurt them, then they'll see it our way."

"Congressman, these are delicate negotiations..."

Pringle pointed his finger, interrupting him. "That's exactly right. When you have a tough negotiation, you need leverage."

"We have leverage. We're the world's most important market."

Pringle wrapped his thick arm around Gait's shoulders. "Mr. Gait, my Daddy always told me. 'If you can't avoid a fight, make sure you hit first and hit hard.'"

"What do you suggest?"

Pringle let out a broad smile. "Let me worry about that."

Chapter 2

The 37th District Courthouse also held the Warren City Jail. Chuck sat in a holding cell with another man whom he ignored for the most part. Chuck didn't mind being arrested. It wasn't his first time. Losing his unemployment check worried him more. He wouldn't be able to get his truck back without the money.

The clicking heels of a police officer approaching the cell interrupted Chuck's thoughts. The officer said, "Holzer, come with me. The Public Defender wants to talk to you."

"When do I get my phone call?"

"Why does everybody always ask that?" The guard wagged his head back and forth. "Save your questions for the lawyer."

Chuck followed the guard down a hall and entered a small cubicle containing a gray table with two simple upright chairs. A man seated in one of the chairs rose while extending his hand, "I'm Marvin Felder. The court assigned your case to me." Motioning to the guard he said, "Thank you, that'll be all. I'll call you when we're done."

The guard exited. Chuck took a seat. The straight back dug into his spine as Chuck looked at the lawyer.

The public defender stared back. "You have a problem. You're being charged with a third degree felony, serious bodily injury. In fact, the man you assaulted..."

"I didn't assault him," Chuck threw his hands on the table. "I didn't hit him. Whose side are you on?"

Felder looked at the paper in front of him. "From the report here, you grabbed him with both arms and pushed him down. He fell. He claims to have broken his nose. This is a serious charge."

Chuck swallowed hard and glared at Felder.

"I can help you. Given the circumstances, I think we'll be able to resolve this without a protracted hearing. Your best bet is to plead guilty if we can get the DA to drop the charge to a simple summons. The judge will probably give you a fine and send you on your way."

"And what if I don't want to plead guilty?"

The lawyer arched back and responded mechanically, "Then you'll be arraigned. The judge will wait for the hospital report on Mr. Thompson. You could spend a night or two in jail awaiting trial. If found guilty, which is likely given the statements the police took from the witnesses, then the judge could sentence you to up to thirty days incarceration. A record of the felony charge will be placed on your yellow sheet."

Chuck shifted in his chair and sneered.

"Look, you're not a first timer. I have your rap sheet." The lawyer read from a computer printout. "'Drunk driving, enlistment in lieu of incarceration, grand larceny leading to dishonorable discharge from the Army.' This record is not going to help. With a summons, they add nothing to the yellow sheet. Do you want to risk it?" Felder leaned back and looked Chuck in the eye.

Chuck returned the cocky lawyer's stare. What am I going to do? What options do I have? After a few moments, Chuck dropped his head and whispered. "Nah, I just want to get out of here. Do what you got to do to get me out."

"Good decision. I'll see what kind of deal I can make with the DA." Felder picked up his papers. "In the meantime, is there anyone you would like me to call? You should be out of here by this afternoon."

"I don't have any family here. Maybe you could call my landlady, Mrs. Maddie Fischer. She might be able to find someone to pick me up." Chuck gave him her phone number.

"I'll call her." Felder grabbed his briefcase and called for the guard.

As the guard opened the door, Chuck's eyes locked on the young lawyer. "Hey, Felder. Thanks."

"No problem," said the lawyer without looking back as he ducked out the door.

"Yeah, no problem for you, asshole." Chuck muttered as the guard led him back to the holding cell.

The Cadillac STS turned off Fourteen Mile Road and entered a modest housing development. It slowed at each corner where Bob Cannon checked the street names. After three tries he found the right street and parked in front of a tidy white craftsman-style bungalow. The address matched the number in the phone book.

Cannon strode toward the front door. The porch steps creaked under his weight. An elderly woman answered his solid knock.

"Yes. Can I help you?" The woman said with the door cracked open but still chained to the jamb.

"I hope so," Cannon responded in his best sales voice. "I'm looking for Chuck Holzer. I found this address in the phone book. I'm an old friend from the Army. Does he live here?"

"Why yes, he does. He rents my garage from me. It's a converted apartment you know. He's such a nice fellow. I can't understand why he's in trouble."

"What do you mean?"

"Well ten minutes ago a Mr. Felder called. He mentioned the Thirty Something court and that Mr. Holzer was arrested but he would be released this afternoon and needed someone to pick him up. I was so upset. I haven't been able to think of anyone who could go and get him. I don't drive anymore, you know. Mr. Holzer has been such a good fellow, helping around the yard and house and all. I hope it isn't too serious."

"It doesn't sound too bad if he's being released. Where did you say?"

"The thirty something, oh you know, the Warren City Courthouse over on Van Dyke."

"I'll tell you what Mrs.--," Cannon stopped when he realized he didn't know the woman's name. "I'm afraid I didn't introduce myself. I'm Robert Cannon, but everybody calls me Cannon." He extended his hand.

The woman grabbed the fingers of Cannon's hand and said, "I'm Mrs. Maddie Fischer. Mr. Fischer died seven years ago."

"I'm sorry. If you don't mind, I can pick up Mr. Holzer this afternoon. I'm sure he'll be surprised to see me." Cannon smiled as he made the offer.

"Oh, that would be so kind of you. It sure would save me a lot of worry. I don't know who I could call."

"I'll head down there right now. Don't you worry Mrs. Fischer, I'm sure this has all been a perfectly innocent misunderstanding." Cannon waved good-bye and got in his car.

In the car Cannon chuckled to himself. "So Sergeant Holzer is in trouble again. Once a loser always a loser. Well, maybe he'll be more receptive to my job offer. This might work out after all." Cannon picked up his phone, auto-dialed his office and told the secretary he would not be in the rest of the afternoon. Then he turned off

Fourteen Mile Road onto Van Dyke toward the court house.

It didn't take long for Cannon to find the courtroom where Chuck's hearing would take place. He sat in the back and tried to spot Chuck in the crowd of people awaiting their hearing. After a half hour wait, he spotted a tall blond figure entering the courtroom from a side entrance under escort of a guard.

Cannon recognized him immediately. Chuck's appearance hadn't changed much from his Army days. He still had the rugged good looks of his youth, thick blond locks and swarthy skin. Cannon absently pinched his waist, regretting the thirty pounds he had gained since he last saw Chuck.

From the back of the room, Cannon watched the prosecutor and the public defender present the judge with a plea bargain. The judge agreed. He fined Chuck one hundred dollars and told him to stay away from the unemployment counselor. Chuck didn't say a word as the guard escorted him back through the side door.

Cannon walked up to the public defender and introduced himself as a friend of Chuck's. "Where can I pay that fine?"

"At the cashier's office down the hall. He'll be released shortly thereafter. Good luck."

The lawyer and Cannon walked in separate directions. Cannon paid the fine with cash and waited in the lobby of the building. A few minutes later, Chuck walked into the lobby and hesitated. Cannon stepped up to Chuck, offered his hand and said, "Good afternoon, Sergeant Holzer."

Chuck squinted at the face of the man standing in front of him. The years of soft living camouflaged the face as well as any disguise. Chuck could not recognize the man, but he took his hand and squeezed it hard. "Were we in the Army together?"

"You don't remember me, do you? Fort Devens, 10th Special Forces Group..."

"Jesus Christ, is that you Cannon? Damn! I wouldn't have recognized you."

"Well, I haven't been staying in as good a shape as you, but I never bought into that physical fitness craziness anyway."

"Right." Chuck laughed. "So what the hell are you doing here all gussied up in a suit and tie?"

"I'll tell you over dinner. Let's get out of here." Cannon grabbed Chuck's elbow and guided him out of the lobby.

Chuck stopped when they reached the outside steps, "Did you pay the fine?"

"Yeah, I took care of it."

"Thanks, but - but why? I ain't no charity case." Chuck searched Cannon's face for a clue.

"Would you believe a favor for an old friend?" Cannon beamed a smile.

"No way. Staff Sergeant Cannon always had an angle. You were the best wheeler dealer in the Army."

"Maybe too good." Cannon laughed. "We almost got busted over that generator deal. Getting kicked out of the Army was the best thing for me. It forced me to be an entrepreneur. Believe me, I'm doing a lot better now than I ever could have in the Army."

They got into the Cadillac and drove off. Chuck looked around the interior of the car. "You must be doing pretty well. Cadillac STS, car phone, Rolex watch. I'd say you were doing pretty well indeed."

"I am, and I want to cut you in on some of it."

"What do you mean?" Chuck turned toward Cannon. "First, you show up out of nowhere and bail me out of jail. Now you're talking about some kind of cut. What's going on? "

Cannon waved his hand. "Hey, I'm a legitimate business and family man. Wait. We'll talk about it over dinner. I know a nice quiet place. My treat."

"If you pay, I'll listen."

At the fire station, Nicca shrugged off his leather jacket and stood with his back to Jones while he poured a cup of coffee. "What did you find out about the pickup truck?"

"Based on your description, Joe, there are at least twenty-five trucks in the metro area," Willy Jones held up a sheet of paper. "I did some checking. Only two vehicles are registered within the same zip code as the fire."

"Good work, Willy. You took some initiative. Maybe there is some hope for you yet. Let me see that," Nicca reached for the list. He pointed to the first entry Jones had circled. "Nah, this one is too old. I saw a new truck, a Chevy, with a custom paint job." Nicca moved his finger down the page to the other circled entry. "Now this one. This could be it. It fits."

"Should we go check it out? It's a little late for interviewing."

Nicca looked at Jones with mock surprise. "Willy, it's never too late to nab an arsonist."

The restaurant Cannon selected recalled the golden years of the American automobile industry. Pieces of restored classic American cars formed the tables and booths. The maitre d' recognized Cannon and took them to his favorite table in the rear of the establishment. They sat in the back seat of a shiny turquoise fifty-six Chevy arranged to provide a private dining booth.

"I always loved this car," Cannon said as they got settled. "George, bring me a light beer. Anything for you, Chuck?"

"Sure, I'll take a Mich."

The waiter disappeared to fetch the beer.

Chuck looked into Cannon's beady eyes. What's going on? Cannon seems too relaxed. Finding no clues, Chuck opened, "So what's up, Bob? "

The waiter brought the drinks before Cannon could answer. Cannon picked up his, clinked it against Chuck's and raised it as if proposing a toast, "To my newest employee."

"What?" Chuck blurted. "What do you mean?"

"I've got a job offer for you, good buddy. It's not what you think. I've got a little problem. In fact, I've got a big problem. I think a man with your talents might be the solution I need."

Chuck inched forward on his seat waiting for Cannon's explanation.

Cannon looked at his beer, "When I got out of the Army, I was flat on my ass. I went to work for my uncle selling cars. Well, I had a talent for it. I've always been a fast talker. My uncle brought me in as a partner. I became the primary manager when he had a heart attack. Then we bought a dealership across town. One thing led to another. It got to the point you couldn't buy a car in the northern Detroit suburbs without putting money in my pocket."

Chuck sipped his beer while Cannon continued.

"I had to do something with the money, so I diversified. I bought a construction business, then some convenience stores. My accountants estimated my net worth at five million bucks. My wife, kids and I moved into a big colonial in Grosse Pointe. I drove new cars, drank the best Scotch. Man, the sweet life."

"So, you bragging or complaining?" Chuck slouched in his seat.

"I'm an unemployed bolt turner on the assembly line. What the hell do you need me for?"

"I know all about you, Chuck. I've been doing some checking. I know you're out of work. You never married. Listen, I got you out of jail. We've been through some tough times together, but let me finish my story." Cannon took a long pull on his beer, his mood somewhat more reserved and his voice almost a whisper, as he took a quick look around.

"Things went pretty well for awhile. Then the car business changed. The gas crisis, smog control laws and high interest rates really put the brakes on business. This was all small change compared to the real problem."

"And what was that?" Chuck was still not sure of Cannon's angle.

"The Japanese! They were cleaning our clocks. Even here in Detroit, the car capital of the US. So I figured if I couldn't beat them, I'd join them. I tried to swing a deal with Sunon. Back then they weren't squat. I figured they'd jump at the chance to have a solid established dealership on their side.

Cannon's expression turned sour. "I met with their corporate reps. I went to Japan to see their factory. I ate their stinking raw fish. All along I thought they were saying yes, yes, yes. When I got back to the States, I had no deal." He slammed his fist on the table.

"They set up their own independent chain of dealerships. Sunon put their Detroit dealerships in locations that I suggested. Naturally these locations are right in the middle of my territory. I know it, but I can't prove it, or I'd sue their asses in a heartbeat. Sunon screwed me. They're still screwing me. They're screwing you. They're screwing the country." Cannon raised his beer and drained it in a gulp.

"Tell me about it," Chuck moaned. "I've been out of work over a year now."

"I know. I want you to work for me." Cannon paused and squinted at Chuck. "If you don't want to take the job, then forget we ever had this conversation. Understand?"

"What kind of work is this?" Chuck tightened his grip on the beer bottle at the idea of work.

"I want you to run some special operations for me. A little like the old days."

A surge of electricity ran down Chuck's spine. He sat up straight. "What kind of operations?"

"I need a break. My accountants say if I can get two good quarters strung together, I might be able to save my dealerships. One more bad quarter and I'm looking at bankruptcy. The way I figure it, if I can close down some of those Sunon dealers in my territory, I might be able to pull it off." Cannon's eyes poured over Chuck.

"And how do you propose to close these dealerships?"

Chuck's interest appeared to calm Cannon. "That's your department, Chuck, planning or pulling off operations, the green beret stuff. Me, I'm just an old supply sergeant. You can do the operations. You sure ran enough of them in the Army."

"Some of the less than legal ones were for you," Chuck punctuated the reply with a pull from his drink. He wanted Cannon to know he remembered.

"That's right. Nothing really changes, does it?" Cannon glanced around. Then he leaned forward and whispered, "For each dealer you can take out, I'll pay you five thousand dollars plus another thousand for expenses." He reached into his jacket pocket and pulled out an envelope. "In this envelope is a list of Sunon dealers I want closed. There's also five thousand cash in advance for the first job. You take care of the details. Hire someone to help if you want, but no one except you is to know I'm involved. The rest I leave up to you. I know what you can do."

"What do you consider taken out?" Chuck fingered the envelope but didn't open it.

"What do you want, an Army five paragraph operations order?" Cannon laughed nervously. "They shouldn't be able to sell cars from that location. I need to get them off my back. Keep it simple."

"What kind of resources would I have?"

"Aside from the cash, nothing from me. I only want to know when to pay you." Cannon pointed to the envelope. "Inside there's a phone number and a location. Memorize them. If you need to contact me, call the number using the pay phone at that location. I will call the pay phone back fifteen minutes later."

Chuck opened the envelope. He saw a neat wad of one hundred dollar bills and two slips of paper. He looked at the number and the address on the small piece of paper. It said,

245-9752

CENTER PAY PHONE IN AISLE

ACROSS FROM ENTRANCE 7, EASTLAND SHOPPING CENTER.

Cannon continued, "If I ever need to contact you, I'll call you at your home. I'll ask for T.S. Cobb. You need to get to Eastland Mall in thirty minutes. I'll call the pay phone. Understand?" Cannon seemed quite serious now. Sweat beaded on his high forehead.

Chuck nodded. "Yes. What do you have in mind?"

"That's up to you." Cannon wiped his glistening brow with a handkerchief, "Torching them seems like a good approach, but the details are your business. I have only one ground rule. Don't hurt anybody."

Chuck didn't react to the last statement. He looked at the list of five Sunon dealerships. "How soon do you want this done?"

"I'd like to have them shut down in a month or two. I wouldn't mind seeing the first one down this week. Timing the rest is up to you. Do what you can to avoid the heat. I have faith in your abilities. I trust you."

"About as far as you can spit." Chuck searched Cannon's face to confirm the deal. He added quickly, "I'll do it."

"Good. Now let's eat." Cannon said cheerily as if they had finished discussing a football game. "This will be the last time we see each other for a while."

SHIZUOKA PREFECTURE, JAPAN

Kondo, wearing a subdued gray flannel suit and a crisp starched white shirt, contrasted with the other Sunon engineers and technicians wearing khaki uniforms. He was early for a meeting at the Shizuoka parts fabrication plant. A combination of jet lag and anxiety over today's meeting had made it impossible for him to sleep beyond sunrise. After a cup of coffee, he asked a manufacturing engineer to show him the factory floor.

"Please wear these." The engineer offered Kondo a pair of safety glasses and a hard hat with built-in ear muffs. "This helmet will protect you from the factory noise and enable you to hear me. It contains a miniature radio transmitter and receiver."

Kondo placed the safety equipment on his head. He followed the engineer as he pushed open the double doors to the factory floor. Beyond the door in the large fabrication bay he saw a bright yellow robot arm grab a raw steel sheet and position it between two matching tool steel dies. With a deafening crash, audible despite the hearing protection, two dies closed about the raw steel. A fraction of a second later, the dies retracted, leaving an elaborate three-dimensional shape. The robot arm retrieved the newly fashioned part and zipped it onto a pilotless cart. Kondo followed the progress of the cart.

The crash of an adjacent press drowned out the whirring snap of the servo controls as the cart accelerated across the factory floor.

"The carts always interest me. They look like they're moving at random. Each one is programmed where and when to go." The engineer's voice sounded clear over the radio.

Kondo watched as others stopped to let the cart pass. It arrived next to another yellow robot arm, which grabbed the part in its long tendril-like magnetic fingers. The arm buzzed and clicked as it moved the metal to a jig on top of a moving conveyor belt.

Kondo eyed the part moving along the conveyor belt. It ended in another manufacturing cell where a large, bug-eyed lens watched the piece as a robot arm moved and positioned it with an accuracy no human could match.

"It only takes two minutes for the robot to create a complete fender from raw stock. Very cost effective." A smug smile revealed the engineer's pride.

"It's true." Kondo nodded. "This plant has the most sophisti-cated assembly operation I've ever seen."

As Kondo tried to take it all in, he felt a tug on his arm. Juichi Mizuno, a tall, athletic-looking aide to Takahashi, had a bare head with no radio equipped hard-hat. Covering his ears with his hands, Mizuno motioned for Kondo to walk to an exit. When they left the fabrication bay, Mizuno bent at the waist in a slow but perfectly executed bow. Kondo removed the head gear and nodded his head to Mizuno.

"Kondo-San, Welcome to the Shizuoka Parts Fabrication facil-ity. I trust you had a good trip," said Mizuno.

"It was uneventful," responded Kondo flatly, trying to subdue his frustration about not being told of the real reason for the trip.

"As all trips should be," chuckled Mizuno. "Anyway, we must hurry. It is almost nine o'clock. Please follow me to the meeting room."

High above the factory floor in a soundproof viewing room, the melancholy strains of a traditional Japanese flute contrasted with the dissonance below. Teruki Takahashi sat deep in thought. Since this factory opened, he came to this room each morning where he sat crossed legged on a tatami mat, meditating on the ant-like scurrying of the robot carts. Takahashi thought how his robotic formicary represented the culmination of years of his hard work. Set in rural Shizuoka Prefecture, Japan, among the rows of sculpted tea hedges and terraced rice paddies, the plant represented the capstone of Sunon Automobile's modernization and world-wide marketing program.

From his commanding view of the factory floor, Takahashi recalled the effort he devoted to this work. The memories of past deeds took him to a dream-like state. He saw the robots as obedient ashigaru, foot soldiers, in his feudal empire. He, in full samurai regalia, for the factory below was as much his empire as that of any Shogun who reigned over ancient Japan, leading them to battle. The next thought brought a smile to his face. "Hai, business is war."

The images of battle jarred him to more contemporary thoughts. Today two of Sunon's chief overseas executives would meet with him to discuss and reach consensus on a new direction for Sunon's five year development plan. This new direction would show Sunon's board Takahashi should lead the company into the twenty-first century.

At exactly nine o'clock, a knock came from the door. Takahashi checked his Patek Phillipe designer watch. He nodded with satisfaction; his aide, Juichi Mizuno, had followed his instructions to the second.

"Excuse my intrusion Fuku-shacho, but Kondo-San and Watanabe-San are ready."

Takahashi grunted acknowledgment. He rose, gazed once more at the factory floor, and paced down the hall to the executive conference room. Mizuno walked to Takahashi's left, a half step behind his superior. While this traditional custom afforded respect to Takahashi, he appreciated that it helped conceal the difference in height between his five-foot stature and the taller aide. Mizuno swung open the door, revealing Yuichi Kondo and Kazuo Watanabe, Sunon's Jomu of European Operations, standing in the elegant, but minimalist, conference room.

Already standing when the door opened, Kondo bowed, his head lowered to afford the right amount of respect.

"It is my pleasure to see you again, Takahashi-San," Kondo stated using polite Japanese grammar.

Watanabe also humbly greeted the corporate executive. Takahashi returned the bow, keeping his head slightly higher than the others.

"Takahashi-San, please accept my grateful thanks for the encouraging support you have afforded our operations. We owe our continued success to your generosity and leadership." Kondo bowed again, following the protocol so important to Japanese society. Kondo despised the behavior, but it was too ingrained to ignore.

Takahashi said. "It is your efforts that should be recognized."

"Thank you for your generous praise."

Watanabe in turn offered his appreciation for past favors, following the example set by Kondo.

"Gentlemen, please take a seat."

The three executives waited in comfortable leather chairs around a lacquered cedar table. While they got settled, Mizuno strode directly to the end of the polished conference table where he sat. No one said a word.

After two minutes of silence, Takahashi subtly gestured to Mizuno. The young aide stood and walked to the far wall of the conference room. Pushing a button on a portable remote control unit he kept in his pocket, he activated the audiovisual equipment hidden behind a translucent screen in the far wall.

"Gentlemen, in a few weeks, Sunon will be introducing the 500GSX to both the US and European markets. This important event will be the crowning achievement in Sunon's past five year development and marketing plan." Mizuno pointed at the image on the screen.

Kondo watched the others listen impassively while Mizuno reviewed the market figures and projections. He had seen this same information several times from his own staff reports. How would Takahashi have Mizuno broach the actual subject of today's meeting? The aide never did, presenting only benign market figures and projections Kondo already knew.

After the presentation, Mizuno faced Kondo. "Gentlemen, any questions?"

Not sure what to say, Kondo waited for Takahashi's lead. After a few seconds, Takahashi said, "Very well, I want to emphasize how pleased we are with the 500GSX and how much it represents for Sunon in the worldwide market."

Kondo saw Watanabe nod in agreement.

"Now go and make Sunon proud." Takahashi rose. Kondo did the same. Then Takahashi did an about-face and left the room.

Mizuno closed the door behind him.

Kondo still did not understand. He threw a sideward's glance at Watanabe but his expression also revealed confusion.

Mizuno smiled and said, "Takahashi-San has invited all of us to dinner tonight at the Cherry Blossom Club. Please be ready promptly at six thirty. Our vice-president does not like to be kept waiting."

Around six o'clock, Kondo entered the factory lobby. A display of Japanese antique pottery decorated one wall. He bent over to examine one of the ceramic pots, acting calm and unconcerned. Phone calls to his contacts in Tokyo had given him no additional insight about Takahashi's intentions.

I am the North American Director. I should not be treated like this. He pulled his hand back to slash at a delicate vase sitting on a pedestal but stifled the urge. Say nothing. Do nothing. Wait until Takahashi makes his move.

DETROIT, MICHIGAN

"This is the place," said Willy Jones, stopping the sedan in front of an apartment building in a shabby section of Detroit.

"Yep, there's the pickup truck. Looks like the one I saw," Nicca opened his door.

Nicca and Jones left the car and entered the four-story apartment building on the corner of a block. They found the first floor apartment at the end of a dimly lit hall. Jones knocked while Nicca stood to the side of the doorway. The door creaked open and a young child appeared.

"Hello. I'm Fire Marshall Jones, Detroit Fire Department. Is .." Before he could finish, a gunshot rang out. Nicca sensed the bullet zing past Jones and the child. Reacting faster than Jones, he dove across the doorway tackling the child as he went down. Jones flopped to the other side of the door. Nicca heard another shot and the doorframe splintered.

"Are you all right, son?"

The boy shook his head yes, seeming unfazed by the gunshot. Then he heard a loud crash, like a window shattering. Nicca stole a quick look beyond the door, peering over the muzzle of his Smith and Wesson thirty-eight. Window blinds swayed at the broken front window of the apartment.

"Willy, cover me. Keep the kid back here." He yelled, and then bolted down the hall toward the building's entrance. Jones aimed his pistol in the open apartment.

Pushing open the door with the snub of his revolver, Nicca saw a man stumbling amid shattered glass on the sidewalk. Blood ran from the man's arms and face.

Nicca yelled, "Stop. Detroit Fire Marshall."

The suspect spun, fired wildly at Nicca and ran. Nicca ducked. A moment later he raised his own weapon and took aim, but the mark slipped between two parked cars. Nicca considered firing a cover shot when he spotted a city bus bearing down the street.

"Freeze, don't move," Nicca yelled, realizing what was about to happen.

The man ignored it. He sprung from between the parked cars into the path of the bus. Nicca could see the driver grimace as he slammed the brakes. The squeal of the bus' tires ended with the sickening thud of flesh against the front grill. The bus rocked to a stop and the body fell limply to the pavement.

Nicca shouldered his pistol and ran to the bus. The driver behind the wheel gazed in shock. Passengers screamed and cried, but no one seemed hurt. Nicca went to the body, bending to give first aid. He saw a crushed forehead, blood, and skin on the bumper. "Damn fool," he muttered, reaching for the wrist. No pulse confirmed the worst.

Jones rushed over, still clenching his pistol. "Is he alive?"

"No. He never saw the bus. He didn't have a chance."

By Japanese standards the Cherry Blossom Club dwarfed other business clubs. Japanese companies helped fund these establishments to give their employees an informal place to discuss and understand each other's point of view. After work hours, employees could be totally frank with their superiors. Companies used these clubs as an effective and traditional Japanese way of opening business communications.

Kondo arrived at the club in the same Sunon Fredrick sedan that returned him from the airport. He dipped his head to avoid the traditional banner hanging over the doorway, indicating the eatery was open for business. A hostess, clad in a beautiful lime green kimono with intricate woven patterns and a rust obi, bowed as he entered the door.

"Irasshaimase." The hostess recited the idiomatic expression for welcome. She slowly raised from her bow. "What party are you with?"

Before he could answer, Mizuno appeared from behind a Shoji screen at the far end of the entry hallway.

"Welcome, please join us," Mizuno said.

Kondo removed his shoes and donned slippers placed by the door. Another woman in a kimono whisked away the shoes, placing them at the foot of the shoji screen leading to their party room, next to a line of other shoes.

Takahashi already sat cross-legged at the low table in the party room. Kondo bowed. "Good evening, Fuku-shacho."

Takahashi acknowledged Kondo and said, "Make yourself comfortable." Turning to the door, he ordered, "Bring my friend a glass." As required by Japanese custom, Takahashi filled Kondo's drinking glass; Mizuno topped off Takahashi's.

After they finished the last course of sukiyaki, Takahashi leaned back contentedly, rubbing his belly, his face tinted pink from the alcohol. "These are great times for Sunon. They are also difficult times. One problem, the recent drop in the stock market has severely dried up capital like a river in a Hokkaido drought. For the first time in a long while we will be short of cash. We must carefully consider our investment choices."

Takahashi paused. Kondo put his hands together while studying Takahashi. Where is he going with this?

Takahashi kept a stone face and continued. "Another problem is we have been too successful. Imbalances with all our major trading partners may spring back and hurt us. Political events could erode all we have gained. We must address a means to counteract the rising political risk our company faces in the American and European markets." Takahashi straightened.

So that's it, thought Kondo. Takahashi's directness surprised him. The alcohol must have weakened his traditional reserve.

Mizuno took over for his boss. "Unchecked, we forecast the increased political pressure in our overseas markets will reduce our market share by five to ten points." Mizuno's eye twitched. "Each day we are losing market share to the rejuvenated Big Three. American politics are to blame. We must act to stop this problem now."

Kondo frowned and waved off Mizuno. "This is an old argument. Blame everything on America. The Japanese media makes such drivel popular. Don't you read our reports?"

Mizuno hesitated as if Kondo's interruption had broken his

41

rehearsed lines. "After considerable discussion, we have concluded Sunon must divert from the current course of increased overseas manufacture and start a major joint venture with both an American and European manufacturer."

"Excuse me," blurted Kondo, "but what has been decided? What about the many other options? I can't accept this decision. This would cancel all of our work in the US."

Mizuno turned bright red. With a lowered voice he continued to deliver the rehearsed lines. "Using a joint venture we gain access to the US and European markets while still achieving our long term vision of integrated global competitiveness."

Kondo felt his neck bulge and his face grow hot. His staff had briefed him on the possibility of the joint venture proposal, but in this obvious power play, Takahashi had acted as if Kondo's own opinion didn't matter. "Why do all this without consulting me? You can't ignore the operating officers from the most important markets. After the recession passes and the American economy picks up, America will continue to demand our automobiles. Then what does a joint venture give you?" He leaned forward, not giving Mizuno a chance to answer. "A joint venture with an American company will squander the name recognition we have developed and marketing inroads we have made over the last decade." A well aimed finger just short of Mizuno's face made him blink.

"We have been developing a manufacturing plan for the past seven years. This is working. If we have limited investment resources, we should continue to follow this plan. Now is not the time to embark on a new strategy."

His words came in a torrent, but after making his point, Kondo calmed down enough to recognize his serious breach of protocol. I must save face, he thought, for myself and the others in the room,. "Please excuse me, my comments are too strong." Kondo bent at the waist in as humble a bow he could do while sitting at the table.

Mizuno and Watanabe looked down in embarrassment.

Takahashi raged at Kondo's rude behavior. He has been in America too long! He has lost his respect for the harmony of the team. Even worse than Kondo's bad manners, Takahashi realized he had not obtained a consensus. Lacking agreement would prevent him from adding this item to the agenda for the board's five year plan meeting.

Takahashi hid his displeasure. Taking a slight breath before he spoke, the stone-faced Takahashi said "Yes, Kondo-San, your words have merit. We must continue to study the situation. No decision has been made. We value your input so we will ask you to study this issue with us. Mizuno will work with you to set up a study plan." Saying this, Takahashi clapped his hands; meaning discussion of the topic had finished. All turned to their drinks in silence.

Chapter 3

Chuck called the loan company first thing the morning after having dinner with Bob Cannon to find out how to retrieve his truck. Bought through the Chrysler employee discount program, getting it back cost a short taxi ride and twenty-four hundred dollars. By noon when the T-shirt clad Chuck put the keys in the ignition, the Dodge four-by-four belonged to him again.

He drove out of the loan office impound lot, turning left away from home, toward the nearest Sunon dealer on Canon's list. Using a map he had marked with the locations of the targeted auto dealers, he drove past them from several directions looking for clues on how to complete his mission. His eyes darted back and forth recording the landmarks approaching each dealership. Quickly but thoroughly he scanned each target for covered and concealed approach routes, vulnerabilities in the layout of the fences and lights, or security personnel.

It's like I never left the Special Forces, he thought. Cannon was right -- I am good at running operations.

After visiting all the locations, two things became clear. One, he'd have to do the jobs at night and two, he needed help. After a few minutes thought, Chuck smiled, he knew just the man to call.

Chuck returned home. He stopped to assure Mrs. Fischer, telling her the police had made a mistake. Then he walked along the grass strip running down the center of the driveway to his converted garage apartment in the rear of the yard. In the kitchen he looked at the analog clock over the stove.

It's almost five. Brian should be home by now.

Chuck dialed Brian Russo's number from memory.

"Hey Brian. It's Chuck. How ya doing man?"

"Usual aches and pains." Brian grunted. "I had a killer day."

"Well then, sounds to me like you need a beer. On me. You won't believe what has happened to me in the last twenty four hours."

Chuck hoped Brian would detect a special excitement in his

voice. The two had been friends since high school, and while their careers and Brian's marriage pulled them apart, they always seemed to get back together.

"Must have been a pretty bad piece of ass," Brian voice betrayed a twinge of envy,

"No, nothing like that. Tell you what. I'll meet you at the Victory Cafe in a half hour," Chuck said.

"I'll be there."

The Victory Cafe was a classic American blue collar bar. Friendly middle-aged waitresses served generous-sized sandwiches and burgers to a clientele of mostly male workers from the nearby auto and Army tank factories. Beer was cheap. The atmosphere was unpretentious, boisterous and friendly. It was the kind of place where almost anybody could be comfortable, from junior engineers and secretaries to retired UAW veterans.

Chuck seated himself at a corner booth. The TV over the bar blared the local sports report and the patrons watched with rapt attention. There was a rumor that the Pistons were going to make an important trade. Chuck finished his second draft beer when he spotted Brian walking in the front door. His short stocky frame did not exhibit the nervous energy normally contained within it. Even with his freshly washed and combed hair, Chuck could see Brian's face had a tired, haggard air of resignation.

"Man, you look beat," Chuck shook his friend's hand. Then, he shouted, "Quick, Maggie, a beer for the walking wounded."

"Just another day in paradise." Brian took a seat. "I got a letter from the queen bitch's lawyer. She wants me to pay my back child support or she's gunna have them break my probation."

Chuck frowned. How ironic. Brian used to be a great street cop. Smart and savvy, he could smell a crime going down on the next block. Twice he received citations for bravery. Some said he was crazy and feared him. Others respected him, but almost everyone left him alone. Several citizens had made police brutality complaints against him, particularly in arrests involving minorities. His outstanding record let him beat the charges. Then his intensity caught up to him.

Chuck shook his head as he recalled Brian's trouble. Brian's marriage soured but he ignored it, devoting himself even more to his job. Chuck tried to tell him to take it easy. He wouldn't listen. Coming home early one day after a line of duty injury, Brian found his wife in the arms of another man. He lost control, beating the half-naked man senseless with a golf club from the garage. It was one charge he could not shake. Facing criminal charges, the police force dismissed him. His conviction resulted in a six month suspended sentence and probation during which his wife divorced him and took their only son to Ann Arbor.

The only job he could find afterwards was as a roadway construction laborer. Brian told Chuck he liked the job, but Chuck knew better. Brian needed the excitement of the arrests, the camaraderie of the shared danger. The construction job didn't pay much. Before the layoff, Chuck helped Brian with some cash to make the child support payment.

"I got to get some money to pay her off. I can't break probation. If I go to jail, it might as well be a death sentence. Do you know how long I would last in prison when they find out I'm an ex-cop? "

Chuck didn't bother to answer.

Maggie arrived at their booth with the beer, "Here you go Brian, it's on the house. What's a matter, trouble with your wife again?"

Chuck waved her off. "Don't you have tables to wait?" he said in a good-natured but serious tone. Maggie took the hint and walked back to the bar.

"So what's the story with your last 24 hours stud? She must be some hot potato to get you excited," Brian sucked the foam off the top of the beer.

"Let's not talk about it here. Looks like the walls have ears." Chuck angled his head in the direction of Maggie. "Drink up and we'll take a ride. I brought a six pack with me."

The two friends got in the cab of the pickup and headed north on Mound Road. Chuck made it appear like he only wanted to get away from the cafe, but he knew exactly where they were headed. He fiddled with the radio and opened two more beers. Chuck took a swig from his bottle. He considered how to approach Brian about helping with the job. "What would you say if I told you could make a thousand bucks tonight? Off the books."

Brian remained indifferent, "I'd say what's the catch?"

Chuck smiled, Brian was interested. "I'll show you in a few minutes." They were quiet while Chuck drove north. Five minutes later, Chuck stopped at a traffic light and pointed across the intersection at a Sunon automobile dealership. "That car dealer is worth one thousand dollars to you. How much do you need to pay off the slut?"

"Twenty eight hundred dollars."

46

Chuck drummed the steering wheel with his thumbs while calculated, "So we do three of them and you get two hundred dollars spare change."

"What the hell are you talking about? You been smoking some of the funny stuff, man?"

"Remember when your parents said don't play with matches? Well here's one time they were wrong. All you got to do is light a little fire and the money is yours." Chuck then described the events of the previous day. He carefully omitted telling Brian Cannon's name although he made sure that Brian knew that their sponsor was a heavy hitter. After a pause he summarized, "Our client wants us to shut down the dealers. For each dealer we torch your cut is a thousand bucks. No fuss no muss. And the sooner the better."

Brian didn't take long to think about the proposal, "Go for it." He held out the open palm of his left hand and Chuck gave him a high five.

They spent the rest of the night driving to each of the dealers and checking them. The more they drove, the more animated Brian became.

"If you only want to hit and get out, you got about four or five minutes before a squad car can respond. Most of the alarms these guys use are wired to their company's central office. It takes them a couple of minutes to react." Brian rubbed his hands together, enjoying sharing his police knowledge with Chuck. "They have to figure out the location of the alarm, then they have to call 911 and get a police operator. The operator then dispatches a squad car. If we plan it right, the squad on duty for this area will be at a donut shop taking a break. That will gives us another minute or two. All we have to do is be in and out in two or three minutes and they'll never catch us." Brian raised his hand and snapped his fingers.

"I knew there was a reason I called you," Chuck smiled and slapped Brian's outstretched hand.

After visiting all the locations, Chuck selected what he thought would be the easiest target, the Sunon dealer situated on Eight Mile Road in Detroit. Brian agreed. The dealership sat next to an abandoned one story warehouse. The alley behind the warehouse would provide a good escape route. It made a right hand turn and would put them on Ryan Road a quarter mile away from the job.

"Our best bet is to keep the job simple. Hell, every night there are three or four suspicious fires in Detroit. If we don't do anything fancy, the police or fire marshals won't be looking too hard." Brian offered as they drove back to the Victory cafe. By the time they reached Brian's old Ford Escort, Chuck had made a plan.

Takahashi held a pragmatic view of religion. When appropriate he would practice either Shintoism or Buddhism. He even followed a few Christian beliefs. Like many Japanese, he had no problem simultaneously accepting different religions because in practice, his one true belief was in being Japanese. His devotion to Japan, developed since his early childhood years during the difficult post-war period, became his religion.

When local workers asked for permission to use a Shinto purification rite to bless the success of the first shipment of Sunon 500GSX's, Takahashi approved immediately. It was proper. He also saw it as an opportunity to build better team spirit, and for valuable publicity.

Assembled on a platform in front of the automobile transport ship, Honshu Prince, were Takahashi, along with Toshi Itoh, the Chief Executive Officer of Sunon, a Shinto priest, and Takahiko Izumi, the ship's captain. The roll on-roll off transport ship, called that because workers actually loaded cars on and off the ship by driving them, towered over the crowd of workers and families eager to send off the first shipment of 500GSXs. Its boxy structure clashed with the sleek lines of the cars it carried. Once a day, it or a similar ship left Japan delivering more than 2,000 cars to various worldwide markets, but the vast majority went to the affluent American market.

Takahashi took his seat. The ceremony started with welcoming remarks by the manager of the shipyard and the mayor of Nagoya. Polite applause followed each speaker.

The audience became solemn as the Shinto priest approached the looming hulk of the RoRo ship. His plain white and crisply starched kimono contrasted vividly with the black hull of the ten story tall ship. In his hand, he held a three foot long branch from a sakaki tree to which was attached a folded white paper ornament. The cleric moved the branch up and down while chanting an ancient prayer to cleanse the ship and its cargo. An assistant rang a melodious gong. After the echo of the gong faded, the priest swung a small censer with burning incense toward the ship. When done, the other men on the dais rose to participate in the ritual, a symbolic rite to ask for success of the voyage across the oceans. Takahashi, holding a branch with folded paper ornaments, rose and walked toward the back of the platform facing the RoRo ship. Bowing solemnly toward the ship, he held the pine branch close to his chest. Then offering the branch toward the ship, he ceremoniously tossed it into the water. Clapping twice and bowing, Takahashi returned to his seat.

Takahashi surveyed the scene and absorbed everything. This merging of the traditional along with the modern was as natural as could be to him. The sound of the gong, the brisk salt air, and the pungent fragrance of the incense each stimulated a different nerve. Emotion swelled within him as he appreciated the work of his staff and company. Wiping away a tear that trickled down his cheek, he felt his soul refreshed.

After the blessing Takahashi spoke to the assembled group of automobile workers, shipyard hands, government officials, and reporters. As he cleared his throat, he trembled slightly; not from nerves but from pride. Assembled in front of him were the best workers in the world. Productive, efficient and all oriented to the team, he saw a little bit of himself in each of them. It was an honor to address them.

"Today, we celebrate a great beginning," the words came out slowly. "This shipment of the new Sunon 500GSX represents a culmination of years of hard and persistent work by the great workers of Sunon and its valued partner companies. Your efforts place Sunon on the verge of its greatest success ever."

Takahashi felt his voice warming up. Despite his small frame he had a commanding voice. He was a master of Japanese style public speaking. Using the same techniques he practiced many times on the workers in his section and later in his factory, he captured the audience. They listened raptly. With each phrase and humble parable, the audience grew more and more stirred, heads moving as they shifted from foot to foot.

Nearing the end of his remarks, Takahashi sensed the emotional tide sweeping the crowd. "Please, industrious workers of Sunon, join me in singing the Sunon corporate song." The request was perfect. The audience jumped at the chance to show their enthusiasm.

The combined voices of the assembled mass resonated off the hull of the ship. With each echo, the audience grew more and more animated, until finally, the song ended in a resounding chorus.

Takahashi put his hands over his head and yelled, "Banzai." The crowd repeated the chant, "Banzai!" The sound was deafening.

"Banzai!"

"Banzai!" came the retort.

Swelling with excitement Takahashi once more yelled, "Banzai!"

"Banzai!" again the crowd roared, this time louder than ever.

Takahashi looked over the crowd. He said in formal Japanese, normally reserved for addressing a person much senior, "Thank you for your efforts. It is my honor to serve." Upon finishing this statement, a bell sounded. This signaled the end of the ceremony. Takahashi left the dais and shook hands with some of the visitors in the front row. The crowd remained abuzz with excitement. As people trailed off to the refreshment tents, they sang the Sunon song.

Itoh beamed at Takahashi. Itoh, as the elderly patriarch of Sunon, was a beneficiary of General MacArthur's purge of senior Japanese managers after the Second World War. MacArthur ordered the removal of the officers from over six hundred different Japanese industrial cartels, or zaibatsu, claiming the zaibatsus had contributed to the militarization of Japan. The dismissed managers, shayozoku, the "tribe of the setting sun," left a managerial void. Itoh was a young but bright clerk when this happened. In this void Itoh quickly rose to upper management. Now in his late seventies and having led Sunon for more than two decades, he was ready for full retirement. Years ago, Itoh secretly selected Takahashi as his protégé. He watched proudly as Takahashi grew, first as an engineer and then as a manager. The speech today confirmed Takahashi's suitability as his replacement.

Later that evening, Takahashi sat cross-legged on the tatami mat in his observation room of the Shizuoka Parts Factory. The exhilaration from this afternoon had subsided. Takahashi was tired. Mizuno sat quietly next to him. Below, robots attended to the task of building automobiles.

"Any word from the U.S.?"

"We expect to hear in a few hours, Fuku-shacho," Mizuno's face was taut in a solemn mask.

"Ah so." After a brief pause, in which he strained to find the right words, he continued. "We are indeed fortunate to work for such a great company, seito-chan." He used the familiar form of the word student. It couldn't hide the melancholy tone of his voice. "As a team we can do the impossible. Whatever must be done, must be done by whoever is capable. This is the key to our success."

Down below, Takahashi saw a red malfunction light go off. He watched the automated control unit sense this and temporarily stop the assembly line. Quickly a maintenance robot removed the broken unit and replaced it with a back up. In a few moments, the assembly line restarted.

Chapter 4

After his morning run, Chuck went to the local convenience store to purchase a six pack of bottled beer. He also stopped at separate hardware stores and bought two plastic five gallon gasoline cans at each. He filled the cans with gasoline purchased at four gas stations on his way home to insure that no one would remember a person buying a large number of gasoline cans or gas for them. Work gloves kept his fingerprints off the bottles or cans.

He went home, opened two of the bottles and poured the beer down the drain. Then he put the bottles in a tub of water to soak the labels. When the labels were soft he peeled them from the bottles and set the bottles aside to dry. Later that afternoon he went to Radio Shack and purchased a portable police scanner.

At midnight, Chuck took two bottles and using a funnel carefully filled them with gasoline. He then slowly poured powdered laundry detergent into the bottles packing in the granules that escaped over the top of the funnel. The laundry detergent mixed with the gasoline making homemade napalm. Chuck put the lids back on the bottles, and wiped them with a dry rag. Two ripped cotton strips from an old T-shirt became wicks for the Molotov cocktails. He went outside and picked up three old bricks from a pile under Mrs. Fischer's deck and placed them into a large gym bag with the Molotov cocktails.

Brian arrived fifteen minutes early.

"Everything's ready." Chuck announced.

"Good, let's load the truck," replied Brian looking tense.

"No smoking," Chuck joked.

Brian frowned and got in the truck.

They drove to the Sunon dealer. "Let's go over it one more time. I toss a brick at the window, then you," Chuck stated.

"We won't have much time after the alarm sounds."

"I know. While I light the wicks you toss the open gas cans into

51

the window. Then head for the truck. I'll toss the flames and follow you out."

Brian nodded and put a piece of gum in his mouth.

After a moment Brian asked, "Did you remember the lighters?"

"Two Zippos in the bag."

They approached the Sunon dealer. Chuck scanned the car lot for signs of activity and was relieved to see none. He parked in a lot across from the dealer and listened to the scanner.

"The local patrol car will report to the dispatcher when it's taking a dinner break," Brian said.

"Good, let's listen." The night was quiet and so were Chuck and Brian as the scanner remained relatively silent. At 2:15 a.m. they heard a patrol car report that they were 10-8, out of their car.

"That's our cue," Brian said.

After circling around the next block and driving into the alley, Chuck parked the truck, leaving the engine running. He looked at Brian, took a deep breath and said, "Let's do it."

Chuck got out first and headed to the glass window. Brian pulled his Detroit Tigers cap down on his brow, got out of the truck, grabbed the gym bag and swung it onto his shoulder. The bag smashed against the door rattling the contents. Chuck turned to Brian and threw him a startled look.

Brian closed the passenger door and checked the bag. He trotted over to Chuck and said, "No damage. Everything's okay."

Brian huddled in the shadows behind the garage next to Chuck while Chuck prepared the wicks. Opening both five-gallon cans, the former Green Beret dipped the rags with a seemingly practiced skill, soaking them in gasoline and stuffing them into the bottle necks. Brian kept a lookout until Chuck was done.

"Ready," Chuck whispered.

The two men moved to the glass wall. Chuck's whole being concentrated on the job at hand. His intense concentration left no time for fear or apprehension. He picked up a brick and threw it. It shattered the glass and bounced off the fender of a new Sunon sedan. The burglar alarm sounded. Brian threw his brick, intending to increase the size of the breach, but the first brick left little glass intact. The second brick sailed into the showroom.

Brian picked up the open can and heaved it through the window frame. Gasoline spewed out the spout as the can twisted through the air. He followed the first can with the second but aimed for a slightly different area. Then he ran for the truck. While Brian tossed in the cans, Chuck calmly lit his Zippo and put it to the wick of the first Molotov cocktail. It ignited into a bright yellow then orange torch. He tossed it as hard as he could towards the first five gallon can. It burst as it landed on the terrazzo floor. Flames engulfed the sedan already struck by the brick. Chuck tossed in the second Molotov without lighting it. He turned and ran.

The roar of the fire drowned out the burglar alarm. As he ran, Chuck could sense heat radiating his back. Man, that's hot already, he thought. He rounded the corner to see Brian frantically trying to open the door to the truck.

"What the fuck's wrong?" Chuck asked as he pulled up to the driver's side door. "We got to get out of here." Light from the flames illuminated the two men.

"The god damned doors are locked. I can't get them open."

"How the hell did the doors get locked?" Chuck tossed the gym bag into the truck bed. Then he grabbed the handle and pulled on it. "Shit!" The door was securely locked.

Brian tried to pry the window down with his hand but it wouldn't budge.

Chuck stepped back and looked around. He reached into the gym bag and grabbed the last brick, picked it up and without hesitation smashed the driver's side window. Reaching in, he hit the power door lock button. Brian and he both jumped into the truck. Chuck slammed the transmission lever into gear and floored the accelerator. The truck shot down the alley then braked hard to stop before turning onto the main road.

Chuck looked both ways. There was no traffic as he turned onto Ryan Road and drove away. A few minutes later he heard the klaxons of several fire engines and emergency vehicles. Approaching Eight Mile Road, a police car flew past, headed toward the fire scene.

Chuck spoke first, "I'll be damned. We did it." He hesitated "But how the hell did the truck get locked?"

Brian, smiling broadly said, "I don't know. Maybe I hit the damned door lock with the bag when I was getting out."

"What are you trying to do, give me a heart attack?" Chuck said slapping Brian on the shoulder. Both men started laughing.

They were still laughing when they arrived at Chuck's garage acting like they were returning from a night on the town. They went inside. Chuck tossed a bundle at Brian "One thousand dollars in cash. You earned it, Buddy."

Brian said, "You weren't kidding. You really had the money."

"Sure. Who's going to pay for the window? Huh partner?"

"You broke it stud, you pay for it. Here, have a beer." Brian reached into Chuck's refrigerator and pulled out two beers.

"Why don't you make yourself at home?" Chuck said.

"Don't mind if I do. That was something. What a rush. That was as much fun as busting a dope dealer. When do we do the next one?" Brian asked.

"I'll give you a call tomorrow. I gotta get the truck fixed right away. Let's plan on doing it again in two or three days."

"Right. "

The friends said goodnight and Brian left.

Joe Nicca and his partner, William Jones, received the call at 2:25 a.m. from the fire company that responded to the alarm. "We got a two alarm on 2456 Eight Mile Road. It's an occupied commercial establishment, a Sunon car dealer. The origin is suspicious. Request your office investigate."

"We'll be there in about 20 minutes." Nicca responded. "Hey Willy, we got a two alarm on Eight Mile. Let's go." Detroit fire marshals had a standing order to investigate any two alarm or higher fire.

Nicca and his partner arrived at the Sunon crime scene before 3:00 a.m.. Fire engines and ambulances, with spotlights and flashers blazing, cluttered the street. The fire fighters already had the fire under control and were now attempting to keep the police from stomping on the evidence so the fire marshals could examine it.

A police officer met Nicca as he got out of the car. "Pretty much looks like a torch job. We checked the area for suspects but couldn't find anybody. It looks like they went through the back window there, but no need telling you your job. That's about it. It's all yours."

"Thanks," Nicca replied. "If I have any questions, I'll call your precinct." Turning to Jones he said, "Let's check the point of origin."

At the rear of the building they found the broken window. The corner of the building where the fire started was heavily charred. Inside were two barely recognizable cars sitting on their scorched steel wheel hubs. All four tires were melted on one vehicle. It sat flat on the floor. On the other, the fire reached only the front two tires, making the car look like a jacked-up hot rod.

"Two cars burned, but not much damage to the building." Nicca observed out loud. "Not too much combustible material aside from the cars. Sprinkler system helped limit the damage."

After looking around, Nicca walked toward the broken window. "Look here, Willy. Glass fragments laying on the floor inside. I'll bet the window was broken from the outside. That explains the charred brick over there on the side of the car."

Willy pointed at intense scorched spots near the closest burnt car. "Fire originated about here."

"Yeah, Check the scorching right there. Some kind of accelerant.

"Yeah, What do you think? Gasoline?"

"Probably, but the cars could of had some in their tanks. Look for some bottle fragments.

Willy and Jones used their flashlights to search the room.

"Here they are, Willy. Brown glass fragments against the wall, including the top lip of a bottle. It's a Molotov." Nicca stood and motioned to the broken window. "It looks like a pretty simple MO. Break the window, douse the floor with gasoline and throw in a cocktail. Let's check outside."

The marshals moved outside and surveyed the area. After searching for ten minutes and finding nothing, a tall thin man interrupted them. "I'm Jake Curtis. I'm the manager. The firemen up front told me I needed to speak to you before I went in." He was dressed in jeans, pull over shirt and an expensive trench raincoat. He looked like he just woke up.

"That's right Mr. Curtis. I'm Investigator Nicca and this is Investigator Jones. We're with the fire marshal's office. Could we ask you some questions?"

"Sure."

"First, is there anyone that you believe could be responsible for this fire. Did you receive any threats, extortion demands? Any employees who could be disgruntled? Perhaps a recently fired employee? Anything like that?" Nicca asked the questions while Jones took notes.

"No. Nothing that I know of," the man said, sounding like he wanted to help.

"It looks like business has been good lately." Nicca used an indirect approach to disguise the suggestion that the owner set the fire for his own purposes.

"Not bad considering the recession. This dealership moves a lot of cars. I wonder how long we'll be down."

Nicca responded, "Probably not too long. I've seen a lot of fires. This one isn't too bad. The structural damage is light. You should be able to get the showroom cleaned up, repaired and back in business in a few days. The rest of the building looks untouched."

"Luckily only a few cars were damaged," Curtis added, surveying the packed parking lot. "Most of the money on this lot is tied up in the cars. Since the cars are undamaged, we can still sell them. When can we start cleaning up?"

"As soon as you want. We've seen enough to complete a report. I'm afraid there isn't much to go on. It appears like a quick slash and burn. Maybe a professional job. The perpetrators planned it pretty well. We found two bricks inside but we could not find any missing around here. They also used Molotov cocktails. So they definitely were prepared to start a fire. The only question is, why your dealership?"

Curtis replied, "I don't know, Investigator, I don't know."

Nicca sized up the man. Normally he would continue to ask the same questions over and over to ferret out some inconsistency in a suspect's story, but Curtis appeared genuinely upset at the damage to his business. "Here's my card. If you hear anything or anyone calls about the fire please let me know. I'll send you a copy of the report for your insurance claim. If I have any questions, can I reach you here?"

"Thanks. Yes. If I'm not in, leave a message." Curtis turned and walked through the broken window, shaking his head and clutching his face with his hands as he surveyed the damage.

Something troubled Nicca as he climbed back into the car. Only twenty percent of all structural arsons involved occupied commercial establishments. And those usually were older, less successful businesses. This was a thriving, modern auto dealership, not a typical arson target. Who would want a car dealership torched? Nicca felt reasonably sure that it wasn't the owner. From the MO it was either a professional torch or a very carefully prepared vandal. Since the damage wasn't too extensive, maybe they were trying to scare the owner. "Willy, tomorrow I want you to check with the employees. See if you can find out anything. I'm going to visit my buddies at racketeering, see if I can find out if there is anything going down with the Mafia or gangs. Something about this one I don't like."

Chapter 5

The spacious dining room of the Pine Lake Country Club gleamed with new wallpaper, paint, shiny brass light fixtures and carpet. Elaborately framed lithographs on the walls depicted scenes of eighteenth century golf courses. The club's understated colonial elegance tried to mimic that of the more traditional American clubs.

Kondo had called his secretary from the cellular phone in business class section of the jumbo jet arranging a meeting with his assistants at the country club.

Kondo arrived at the club before the others and showered in the locker room. He changed into fresh sport clothes, entered the dining room and looked for his assistants. He saw Yasuhiro Hara and Jack Shane sitting in a table near the back of the room. Hara returned the wave.

"Welcome home, Jomu. Did you have a good flight?" Hara asked testing Kondo's mood after the hastily arranged trip.

"Yes. The flight was good. The meeting was not." As Kondo spoke a waiter, clad in tartan plaid plus fours, asked Kondo if he cared for anything.

"Yes, a Chivas on the rocks," said Kondo in perfect English. His words had a slight California twang common among Japanese students of the English language.

"Make that two," said Jack Shane, Director of Public Affairs.

Kondo looked at the American, and his prototypical all-American good looks, dirty blond hair, tall build and a square jaw. Even at forty, Kondo noticed his regular exercise regime kept him fit and youthful.

"Takahashi is worried about the changing political situation in the states."

"Have our reports not been well received?" asked Hara meekly.

"Oh, they read our reports, but they seemed more interested in what the press has to say. Every day the Japanese press is awash with story after story about the souring relationship between Japan and the United States. This is what sells in Japan. It is getting ridiculous. Before I left yesterday, Nikkei Shinbun reported a story about how a small town somewhere in Maryland is organizing a Japanese-prohibited product zone,"

"Ha! I wonder how long that town can last - probably only until one of their VCR's needs replacement," chuckled Shane.

Kondo was surprised by Shane's comment, "This is more serious than you realize, Mr. Shane. Even if the story is a gross exaggeration, it makes everyone in the home office worry. There is tremendous interest in Japan in everything that happens here. Managers everywhere have tuned their ears to political events."

"Does that include Takahashi?" Shane's ice blue eyes locked on Kondo's.

"That's the bad news. Now that Takahashi's pet project, the Shizuoka robot plant is on-line and producing well beyond expectations, he is stronger than ever. He appears to have broadened his horizons. He's looking to show the board that he can manage more than the development of a high-tech plant."

"What does Takahashi have in mind?" said Shane.

"Takahashi proposed a whole new strategic thrust that includes scaling back expansion of our production to invest in a new joint venture with an American company. He made some excuse about not enough capital resources being available."

"Wow!" whistled Shane. "That could wipe out all that we gained in the last few years."

"How would the joint venture overcome political risk?" questioned Hara.

"Autos from a joint venture would use a different name from a Japanese manufacturer, even though all the major assemblies in the car would be made in Japan. This disguises the amount of Japanese content in the car. By giving the American public the impression that the cars are American, political tension should subside."

"Oh sure, Toyota and GM got together. Chrysler and Mitsubishi Motors had Diamond-Star Motors. These joint ventures do a good job blurring the national line, but in general, their cars have not done well," said Shane "It's too hard to merge the culture of two diverse metal benders."

"That's correct, I made the point about Chrysler and Mitsubishi in our discussions. I also emphasized the success we have had to date with our operating plan." Kondo twisted his lip in frustration and continued. "Takahashi realized that he could not obtain consensus so he agreed to study the feasibility of such a course of action."

"Excuse me, Kondo-San, but don't you think that Takahashi has a point? I think the political situation may have changed. This very week, my wife and children complained about hostile people when shopping at the Pontiac Mall."

Kondo raised his voice and in colloquial Japanese said "Hara, you think your family's maladjusted complaints are reason enough to reverse the course we have followed over the past five years?" Kondo turned his shoulder from Hara and in English said, "Takahashi's plan would divert the capital investment we need to continue to build our factory in Kentucky. Creating a joint venture at the expense of our factory will ruin what we have worked so hard to build here in America. Takahashi knew this. This is why he misled me about the real purpose of this trip. He wanted me off-guard." Kondo's dark brown eyes jerked backed and forth scanning the room like a poorly programmed robot. After a moment he continued looking right at Hara. "Surely Takahashi knew I would not agree. Without consensus, he can not take this concept to the board. The board will insist that he have complete agreement among the international managers."

Hara dropped his gaze to the tabletop.

"Could he have an another motive?" asked Shane deflecting some of the abuse from Hara.

"Perhaps," replied Kondo recovering from his outburst. He could see that despite working under him for a year, Hara was not accustomed to direct confrontation and criticism, especially in front of a gaijin, or non-Japanese, worker. "If there is, we must seek it out."

The waiter returned with the drinks. After taking a long pull, Shane said, "You know it all boils down to money. The simultaneous development of the Shizuoka plant and the 500GSX cost much yen. First the recession has used up reserves, then we start to lose market share. You know, Tokyo may only be able to afford one major market thrust. A joint venture proposal is going to cost a lot of yen. So does continued expansion of our factory. Something is going to have to give."

"You are very perceptive Mr. Shane," replied Kondo, "You have summarized the situation very well."

"What are we to do?" asked Hara weakly.

Kondo pushed back from the table and twisted his head. "For now, nothing!" He drained his drink and declared, "Let's play golf."

After golf, Kondo called his secretary at home and checked his calendar of events for the next day. "Cancel my morning meetings. I want to meet Shane in my office at 8:30 a.m." He finished another scotch and water and left the club.

It was already dark when Kondo reached his home in Grosse Pointe Park, a traditional enclave of the automobile industry executives. The neat lawn and immaculately landscaped yard in front of the impressive Tudor style home hid that Kondo lived there alone. His wife had left him more than three years ago. While she hadn't divorced him, she said she could no longer accept the detached and lonely existence in the U.S. Every time Kondo returned to his empty home he would relive the arguments they had.

"Your job, is it so important that you can never be home? Why do we live here with you when I would see more of you if we were back in Japan?" Kumiko would cry.

"Be quiet. Why do you care? You have what you need," Kondo would snap back.

"I have nothing, only my daughter."

"Ah, this is nothing?" gesturing to the large house, "It is always the same from you."

"You're right. There is nothing. There is no love, no passion- only your work."

"What else is there?"

"Oh, I hate this. You bastard." Then she broke down.

"Stop crying you old fool." Kondo reached back to smack his wife.

She slid backwards to avoid the blow. Her face took a twisted look Kondo hadn't seen before. She stopped crying "No. Stop. No more. No more abuse." Her veins bulged and her bloodshot eyes held fire. "I'm leaving."

"Huh?"

"Masako and I. We are going back to Japan. We are going tomorrow."

"You can't go. You are my wife."

"I have talked to my family. They understand. They will take us; love us."

Kondo looked up toward the direction of his daughter's room. He blurted, "Then go," and turned from his wife and left the house.

61

After spending the night and the next day at the office, he found the house empty when he returned after dark. It bothered Kondo most that he felt no remorse about their leaving. It was the way it was. It was the way he felt every time he returned to his house.

Inside, he hung up his jacket and unpacked suitcase leaving the dirty laundry for the maid. In the kitchen, he put some ice in a tumbler and grabbed a bottle of Chivas Regal. Two drinks later he fell asleep on his living room couch.

WARREN, MICHIGAN

Chuck and Brian met at the Victory Cafe the day after the job. The bar was crowded with people ready for Friday night. The TV had a Pistons game but the juke box drowned out the announcers with loud music.

"Did you see the paper?" Chuck asked.

"Nah," Brian said. "Was there anything interesting?"

"No. I guess we don't rate."

"That's cool. I don't need no publicity."

"I guess you're right." Chuck paused. He stared into his beer, disappointed that the fire didn't make the news. "I've been thinking about last night."

"Pretty hairy, man." Brian smiled broadly.

"Yeah, a little too hairy. We almost screwed it up royal like. Next time we got to be more careful. We need a better plan."

"I was thinking the same thing. I got an idea."

"What is it?"

"The mistake we made was we rushed too much. We need to take our time. We take our time, we do it right," Brian said. "If we could disable the alarm, then we could take our time when we're inside. That would give us a chance to really hose the place down."

"How do we disable the alarm?" Chuck asked.

"No problem. I've done it before for undercover stakeouts. I made a few calls. All the Sunon dealers use Winkler Security."

"How did you find that out?" Chuck was worried that Brian might have tipped their hand.

"I stopped by a Sunon dealer and saw the Winkler emblem on

the door. Then I called them saying I was from Sunon's bookkeeping section and needed to resolve a dispute with a bill. After a little chitchat, I got the clerk to tell me what I needed to know. First, all the dealers use Winkler. And they have telephone service interruption defaults. That means if the phone service to the place is cut, for whatever reason, the alarm trips. This type of system usually has a lot of false alarms."

"So what can we do?" Chuck was smiling now, impressed and pleased with Brian's initiative.

"We can fool it by putting a dummy load across the alarm leads right at the phone system interface box. The alarm company makes it easy for their repair guys by marking the right wires with white tags. We'll know exactly which wires to use. Once the dummy load is hooked up, the rest of the alarm system is useless. We can walk in, take our time, and get out."

"Are you sure this will work?"

"I've done it before. All the alarm companies are a little bit different. I've seen Winkler's system before. It's really old stuff, but it usually works. You got to be smarter than the system." Brian's face showed a sarcastic grin.

"We'll do it tomorrow night. Do you have everything you need?"

"I'll have it by tomorrow."

"I'll get the gas. You take care of the alarm."

The two friends raised their glasses and drained them. Brian got up to use the men's room. While he was gone, Chuck spotted an attractive, tall, red headed woman, good shape with a pretty face. Chuck wasn't sure if he knew her but she did look vaguely familiar. He had never seen her in the Victory Cafe. He approached her and asked her to dance. Her beaming face said yes.

After a few dances, Chuck walked over to Brian and said, "I gotta split. Debbie wants to get out for some fresh air. I'll see you tomorrow at midnight."

"Go for it dude. Judging by the looks I'd say you're in for a fun evening."

Chuck escorted the girl to his truck. She stumbled and Chuck caught her.

"I guess I had a little too much to drink," Debbie said. She made no effort to release Chuck's grip. Instead she smiled at Chuck and looked him directly in the eyes.

"Do you feel good enough to take a ride?" Chuck asked without taking his eyes from hers.

"Where are we going?"

"How about my place?"

Debbie didn't answer. She stood up, walked to Chuck's truck and got in the passenger seat. Then she said, "Let's go."

At eight thirty the next morning Kondo's secretary buzzed his office intercom and announced Shane. Shane strolled in and sat on the couch next to Kondo's desk.

"You had a rough day yesterday Kondo-San. I guess its tough to play golf with jet lag," the public affairs manager said.

Kondo ignored the comment, "Jack, we have a problem and we must move quickly. We must convince Tokyo that we have control. If we can create the right information, it will slow the discussion in Japan. Takahashi will have trouble starting a joint venture. Meanwhile, the recession will pick up improving the political situation and our market share. By then, our plant upgrade will be nearly complete."

Kondo could see Shane liked his decisive plan. And why not, the other Japanese managers in the plant would never have proposed such a plan without spending months developing a consensus.

"I want you to contact Mary Fielding, our chief lobbyist in Washington. We need some good press immediately, but it must have an American face. See if she can get some congressman to make a public statement about the importance of U.S.-Japanese relations. "

Shane smiled. "I think we can do even better. While you were gone, Mary phoned me. She finally cracked Victor Deaver, the famous Japan expert. It seems Victor is way behind on the payments on his condo in Maui. Victor would be willing to do some consulting for us for a fee. He might even make a public statement for us."

Deaver! What a stroke of good fortune, thought Kondo. Deaver had a worldwide reputation as an advocate of stronger political response to the American trade deficit. If he were to go to Japan and make some appropriate comments to the Japanese media, Takahashi and the others would be sure to notice. This could give the time needed to enact the other parts of the plan.

"Are you sure he will cooperate?"

"Fielding is good. She wouldn't say this unless she had him locked."

Kondo paced to the window. "How much will it cost?

"It depends on what we want him to say. If we want him to reverse his long held position, we'll probably have to buy his condo and set him up for retirement." Shane chuckled.

"That won't be necessary. Have him make some statement about the improving political situation in the U.S."

"Hey, what do you think about this? Deaver and the congressman make a joint statement," suggested Shane with a schoolboy's enthusiasm.

"I was thinking more of a press conference in Japan. Takahashi and the board would surely notice that."

"I like that."

"Make sure lots of Japanese reporters attend."

"Yeah, we'll have free food. Maybe sushi. That always attracts the sharks," sneered Shane.

Kondo returned to the desk. "Also, I want to beef up our charity effort. Where else we can donate money and get the biggest impact."

"Do you think we need more donations? Last year we donated over ten million to charity. Will extra money make a difference in the short amount of time we have?"

"Find me something with lots of bang for the buck." Kondo smiled for the first time in the meeting. He enjoyed using American slang. He had an upper hand on the American. He could speak Shane's language, Shane couldn't speak his.

Shane unwittingly returned the smile. "Is that it, boss?" He stood and readied himself to leave.

"There is one more thing, Mr. Shane. We need to improve our odds in the political arena."

Shane turned and leaned forward, his hands resting on Kondo's neat desk.

"What do you have in mind?"

"The political situation is too chancy. We can most directly influence Tokyo by influencing the political assessment." Kondo knew Shane had worked for him long enough to tell when the he was making an implied request.

"What are you saying Kondo-San?"

Kondo looked into Shane's eyes, hoping that Shane would catch on to his real meaning.

"We have been too frank in the past and may have overestimated the situation. The political risk assessment is our most important tool in persuading Tokyo that our course is the correct one." Kondo hesitated while searching for the right words.

"In light of the current problem, make sure their upcoming assessments say what they need to say. If you have to, fly down to Washington, visit our political consultants, and take care of it in person."

"A bribe? If Takahashi finds out it could be big trouble."

"This is why you and not one of the other Japanese managers has to handle this job." Kondo rotated his chair to face the window.

"Anyway, this is not illegal. We won't break any laws. We are tweaking the system."

"Understood. I'll get right on it,"

Shane opened the door behind him. Before he left Kondo wheeled around in his chair. "And Shane, don't worry about ethics. Worry about the business. About survival. Make sure you do this right."

Shane appeared shaken. "I'll take care of it. Don't worry."

Kondo watched Shane close the door. Shane is too smart, he thought crossing his hands in his lap. "He knows he's a tool, a gaijin. He has no where to go. Yet he works so hard for the company, no complaints."

Chapter 6

WARREN, MICHIGAN

The morning after meeting Debbie, Chuck awoke to the smell of coffee. Turning over, he noticed the sheets were pulled completely from the bed and clothes were strewn about the room, his clothes and Debbie's. He rubbed his eyes and checked his watch. As he focused on the hands, he noticed Debbie leaning in the doorway with a cup of steaming liquid. She was wearing one of Chuck's cotton oxford shirts. The unbuttoned blouse did little to hide her athletic build. The sight of her standing there reminded Chuck of the previous night. He wondered if the Richter scale went that high.

"So, tiger, do you take cream or sugar?" she asked. She too was smiling.

"No. Forget the coffee. Get back in here." Chuck motioned to the bed alongside him.

"I'd love to, but I got to be at work in half an hour." She walked over to Chuck and kissed him on the lips. " I can come back tonight." She raised her eyebrows above hopeful blue eyes.

Chuck smiled as he looked in her eyes. Then he thought about the job and frowned.

"Is something the matter?"

"Nah," he paused. "Well, I got a job, I got to work tonight. How about if I pick you up after I'm done?"

"Okay." She replied. "Can I take a shower?"

"Sure, I'll get you a towel."

Chuck stood there watching her soap up and rinse off. He resisted the urge to join her.

"What time do you get off work?" Debbie asked stepping from the shower.

Chuck considered how to respond. "Pretty late. Probably about three a.m."

"How about if I meet you here. My roommate might not like it if I disturb her that late."

"When do you get off work?"

"I have to do a double shift today. I won't get done till about eleven."

"Well, come here after work. I'll leave the key under the doormat. Make yourself at home. I'll be here by three A.M."

"That sounds great." Debbie moved over to Chuck and wrapped her arms around him, kissing him passionately on the lips. The towel unwrapped from her body and fell to the tile.

"I better get moving or I'll be late for work," she said.

Willy Jones met Nicca at the diner across the street from Fire Department Headquarters. The waitress was placing a cheeseburger in front of Nicca as Jones sat across from him. "What did you find out?" Nicca said as he salted his cheeseburger.

"Not much. Everyone seems to be pretty happy at Sunon. No one could even suggest a remote suspect. I don't know. This could be a random torch job."

"I couldn't find out anything downtown. No one's heard anything on the street. They said they'd run some checks but they couldn't promise anything." Nicca bit into his burger.

"What do you think, Joe? Think it was a joy riding pyro?" Jones asked as he glanced over the menu.

"I don't know. If nothing else happens, the guys that did this will probably get away with it. If we hear from these boys again, then maybe we'll catch them."

"What makes you think there was more than one?"

"Did you notice how there were two bricks, two cans and what appeared to be two cocktails. I'd say there were at least two guys, with maybe another driving the getaway car."

"That makes sense."

"Take the rest of the weekend off, Willy. I'll see you on Monday night. By the way, I asked the guys working tonight to call me if there's another case with the same MO. I'll call you if I hear anything."

Chuck arrived at midnight at Brian's apartment. Brian had his equipment ready.

"The target for tonight is the Sunon dealer on Gratiot Ave, near East Detroit," Chuck announced. "The car lot is on a wide street next to another car dealer on one side and several small shops on the other. The shops have security bars, but the car dealer doesn't."

"Sounds perfect," replied Brian.

Chuck drove to the Sunon property and parked alongside a row of used cars. His truck faced a side street exit.

"We'll wait for a while. Keep a look out for any sign of anyone in the building." At one fifteen Chuck was satisfied no one was inside.

"Let's do it. And don't hit the door lock." Chuck said.

Brian sneered, got out of the car and walked to the rear of the building with a small tool bag. A few minutes later, he stuck his head around the corner of the building and waved to Chuck.

Chuck moved quickly to Brian with the cans of gasoline and Molotov cocktails. "Did you do it?"

"Yeah, the alarm is useless. Let's go inside."

Brian showed Chuck to a door he had pried open. It led into a short hallway that connected the service bay to the showroom. Off to each side were sales offices.

"You do the parts supply room, I'll do the offices." Chuck whispered.

Brian opened the door and entered the spare parts sales area. Walking around the counter, he poured gasoline on the rows of cardboard boxes containing Sunon spare parts. He managed to splash fuel over most of the front half of the storage area. As he walked out of the room a hand reached out and covered his mouth, while another pulled him against the shadowy wall.

"Shhh," Chuck hissed, putting a finger to his lips. Then he pointed through the hallway to the front lot at a Ford Mustang parked with the headlights on and doors open. Two teenage boys were walking around, checking out the new Sunon sports cars. Chuck and Brian waited in the gloom. The men pressed against the wall as they watched the youths wander about. The smell of gasoline permeated the air.

"If there's a spark in here we're dead men," Brian muttered.

"Shhh. Wait."

One of the boys appeared to lose interest. He returned to the Mustang. The other came up to the showroom window and pressed his face against the glass. He peered into the display area, then turned around abruptly and got into the Mustang and the car accelerated away.

Chuck made sure that the car had left. Then he said, "Go get the truck started. When I hear the engine, I'll light the Molotov. Remember, be cool."

"As a cucumber," Brian said but the sweat on his forehead belied his bravado.

Brian left for the truck. Chuck heard him start the engine and after a quick glance, lit the cocktail with his Zippo lighter. Chuck tossed the firebomb into the open door and ran before it hit the ground. As he rounded the corner of the building a huge fireball lit the sky behind him. The showroom windows shattered, doors blew open and pieces of the roof and siding flew into the air. The building erupted into a total inferno.

Chuck climbed into the cab of the truck and Brian floored the accelerator. Chuck's clothes and hair were singed, but intact. Both men reeked of gasoline. The truck shot down the side street. Chuck looked back and saw flames and smoke climb into the night sky.

"Holy shit," he said in between deep breaths. "Scratch one car dealer."

Brian turned the next corner and drove from the fire at a legal speed. After a few moments, Brian said, "This is nuts. But I love it. Man, did we trash that place or what?"

Chuck, still panting, said, "Yeah we toasted it good." However, as the adrenaline from the excitement of the job wore off, he said. "We toasted it good, but we almost toasted ourselves. The delay in lighting the fire must have let the fumes fill the building. That's why there was an explosion. There's got to be a better way." Chuck took a deep breath and rubbed his forehead. "Let's go to your place. I'll drop you off. Tomorrow I'll see big daddy and get our money. He might be able to help us out with our next job."

"No sweat man. If you don't pay, I know where you live." Brian smiled.

At Brian's house, Chuck got behind the wheel, "I'll call you tomorrow."

"Want to have a beer?" Brian asked.

"Nah, I stink of gasoline. I got to change clothes. I'll call you tomorrow." Chuck drove toward his apartment. He wondered if Debbie would be there. If she was, what would he tell her about tonight.

The electronic ringer didn't interrupt Willy Jones' loud snoring. His wife picked up the phone.

"Willy? This is Joe," the voice on the phone said.

"Just a second," she rolled over and shook her husband. "Willy, wake up! It's for you."

Willy took the phone from his wife and said, "Hello" in a raspy voice.

"Willy, this is Joe. Get up. Grab a cup of coffee. I'll be by to pick you up in ten minutes. We had a four alarm at another Sunon dealer. Over near East Detroit. Willy. Willy, did you hear me?"

"Yeah, I heard you. I'll be ready."

"See you in ten minutes" Joe said.

Willy hung up the phone. He looked as his alarm clock, 1:48 A.M. "Damn, no sleep tonight." He put his feet on the floor and looked at his wife. She never had this problem. She had already fallen back asleep.

Nicca and Jones arrived in time to see many of the fire rigs responding to the alarm starting to leave. Willy whistled when he spotted the building. Nicca hadn't seen many fire scenes as impressive as this. The sheet metal walls bulged and buckled at the seams, shattered glass and charred chips of the building lay scattered around the parking lot. The interior of the building was gutted. The firemen had to use foam to fight the blaze and it created a smelly, sticky mess. The crews were wrapping up hoses and replacing their equipment. A white van with a satellite dish on top pulled alongside the street. The reporter, a tall, handsome black man, jumped out of the front door while a camera crew prepared their equipment.

"Let's find the night crew before that reporter does," Nicca said to Jones.

After a few minutes of searching they spotted their colleagues huddled around an electrical box at the back of the building. The senior night crew fire marshal, Darrel Robertson, spotted Nicca and waved him over. "Hey, Joe. Check this out."

Nicca walked to the box and examined it. He shook his head and then walked to the back door.

"What gives?" Willy said.

Robertson responded, "They rigged the alarm so it wouldn't go

71

off, went inside and soaked the place down. They probably used a Molotov to set it off. We found this laying right here." Robertson held out an evidence bag containing a broken beer bottle with a cloth rag stuck in its mouth. "Looks like some homemade napalm on the inside of the bottle. They must have dropped it."

Nicca came back to the group. "Looks like it could be the same boys from the other night. MO is pretty much the same. Maybe they weren't happy with the amount of damage they did on the other dealership. They sure wasted this place. What are you guys going to do with the bottle and those wires?"

"I was going to send them to the lab. See if we can get any prints. " Robertson said resignedly.

"If you don't mind I'll take care of it. I doubt anything will turn up. The smoke usually makes fingerprinting worthless. Still, we might find out something from the residual ash on the bottle. Did anybody get a witness, anybody see anything?"

"Nothing yet. We'll get the dayboys to scour the neighborhood tomorrow. Might find something." Robertson said.

"Willy, you organize that. I'm going to do some checking on Sunon. This is starting to have the smell of an inside job," Nicca said.

"It's your case if you think it's the same guys," Robertson said.

"I'm almost sure of it." Nicca replied, knowing Robertson would trust his own hunch.

The glare of a bright TV camera light shining to their right caught their attention. It was the reporter interviewing the fire captain.

"Let's get out of here before that reporter wants to ask us any questions." Nicca said to Jones. He ducked into the burnt building and exited from the shattered front door.

Chuck parked his truck in the driveway behind Debbie's old Chevy Nova. He saw a flickering blue light through the window of the kitchen. He opened the door and quietly entered his apartment. Walking through the kitchen, he saw Debbie, on top of the covers, dozing on the bed while the TV played an old movie. Chuck went into the bathroom, removed his gas soiled clothes and took a fast shower. Wrapping a towel around his waist, he piled the clothes on the front porch. Standing in the kitchen, he noticed that the dishes were all washed and the place straightened up. Chuck smiled. Then he went into the bedroom, turned off the TV. He laid down next to

Debbie and kissed her cheek. He kissed her again and she roused at the touch of his lips. "I'm home," he whispered.

"Hi," she said. "I must have fallen asleep." She put her arms around his neck and kissed his lips. Then she stood up, removed her clothes and crawled under the covers.

For a brief second, Chuck felt relieved that Debbie did not ask about the job tonight. His earlier concerns of the evening faded into oblivion as Debbie caressed him. Sensing Chuck's fatigue, Debbie took charge. Lying on his back, he was at Debbie's mercy, but she wasn't in a merciful mood. After several loud groans of delight, she moved alongside Chuck and fell asleep.

Chapter 7

The first light of day woke Chuck. He had difficulty sleeping. The excitement of the previous evening and the unaccustomed but enjoyable presence of Debbie in his bed woke him after a few hours of sleep. He turned on the TV but kept off the sound. Flipping through the channels, he found the news on the local NBC affiliate station. He propped himself on a pillow and watched the report.

Debbie rolled over and kissed Chuck on the cheek. She then started to nibble his ear when the news anchor introduced the fire story.

"Wait, wait, wait," he said, lurching forward to turn up the volume.

"What's the matter?" Debbie said.

"Oh, I want to see this."

She sat next to him and listened.

The reporter read from her notes, "Last night a four alarm fire destroyed a Sunon automobile dealership on Gratiot Avenue in Detroit. Witnesses said that flames from the blaze could be seen as far away as the Renaissance Center. The cause of the fire was described by Fire Captain Russell as suspicious."

The screen image changed to videotape filmed the night before. The view panned across the front of the shattered showroom window. Then the image cut to close-ups of damaged cars and office equipment.

The voice-over continued, "This is the second suspicious fire this week to occur at a Sunon automobile dealership in Detroit. Captain Russell said that Detroit fire marshals have no suspects and no arrests have been made. When asked if the two fires are related, the fire captain had no comment. Fire department officials continue their investigation."

The news anchor smoothly shifted to the weather report.

Chuck got up and turned off the TV. Then he looked at Debbie and smiled.

"What's so special about a car dealer going up in smoke?" Debbie asked looking puzzled.

"Oh. Nothing. I heard about it on the radio last night. I was curious." Chuck lied. He was thrilled.

"Well, it serves those bastards right. I wish they'd burn all those Japanese car dealerships right to the ground and ship the ashes back where they came from." Debbie's expression changed as she said the words. Her face seemed to age and grow grim. "They can take their Sunon shit boxes and put them..." Her voice trailed off. She looked at Chuck with a sad longing. "The hell with them. They aren't worth getting all worked up about."

The change surprised Chuck. So far in their brief relationship Debbie had been full of life, uninhibited, warm and friendly. This was a different side. What could make her change so rapidly? He placed his arms gently on her shoulders. "I'm sorry if the news bothered you. I was," he paused, "I didn't want to upset you." Then he hugged her.

"I'm not upset. Not at you. It's those Sunon bastards. Let's not talk about it now," she said, returning his hug.

"Sure," Chuck said to her, but his curiosity was driving him wild. He wanted to know what Sunon could have done to her to invoke such a reaction. "What do you want to do today? I don't have to work. Do you?"

"No. I'm off all day. I don't even have any plans."

"Why don't we take a drive and hit the mall? I want to stop by Eastland." Chuck said.

"The weather looks like it's going to be pretty warm, let's go to Belle Isle. I used to love going there to watch the sailboats when I was a kid." Debbie's face brightened.

"Sounds like fun. I haven't been there in years. I remember, a powerboat race in 1978."

"Let me get dressed." She went into the bathroom and closed the door.

They arrived at Belle Isle at eleven A.M. The air was crisp and clear. The sun glinted off the glass and chrome towers of the Renaissance Center. Chuck wondered if you really could see the fire from way down here. He parked the truck at a lot on the eastern side of the island then walked alongside Debbie on the stone embankment.

She stopped frequently to watch a sailboat or to examine something among the rocks. At a metal pipe fence that cordoned off a stone embankment Chuck paused. Debbie leaned against the fence, chatting about little things; the weather, the river and the boats. Then Debbie became quiet.

Chuck watched her as she looked into the bright eastern sky. Finally, Debbie said "My father used to bring me here when I was a kid. He would describe all the sailboats and tell me what all the parts were."

Chuck noticed Debbie knuckles turning white as she squeezed the metal fence post.

"He used to get so into it, but I could never remember the difference between a ketch and a yawl. He said that someday he'd buy me a sailboat and teach me how to sail." Debbie let go of the pipe and shifted her gaze downward.

Chuck put his arm around her waist and said, "Did he ever get you the sailboat?"

"No." She shook her head slightly side to side to seemingly to suggest it was all right. "He had his own business. He made parts for the auto companies like everybody else in Detroit. That sucked up all his money and his time. He put all he had into it." She reached for a small stone.

"At least he was his own boss," Chuck said. "I hated working for those jerks at Chrysler."

"He wasn't his own boss. The business owned him. He worked late every night and most weekends. My Step-Mom and I hardly ever saw him." She tossed the stone into the waves. "Then there was the Sunon deal. That finished him."

A bolt of electricity shot through Chuck. "What about Sunon? Tell me more."

"My dad had some kind of exclusive contract with Sunon. They insisted on it. He made some parts for their cars. Using American made parts allowed them to get around some import law." Debbie rubbed her toe in the pebbles, her blue eyes turning gray and detached.

"He had to use tools and machines Sunon supplied. American tools supposedly weren't good enough. He could only work for them but they guaranteed him a certain level of business." She bit her lower lip.

"Well, they never got things going. Sunon screwed him. The machines they sent over didn't work. The tools broke. He couldn't meet their schedule. When they did work, the Sunon would reject the parts. It all happened so fast."

Debbie seemed about to break down. Chuck reached for her arm.

"Then what happened?"

Debbie squeezed Chuck's arm. "I don't know. One day, Sunon called due his loans. The gave him no time too respond or to try to raise money. They forced him out and left him with nothing. It was almost like they set him up."

"Damn!" Chuck said. "What's he doing now?"

"He works for a dry cleaner in Lansing. His brother lives there. That isn't the bad part. He changed. He won't call me. He won't talk to me." Debbie pulled away and turned her back from Chuck. After a moment she said "I try to call but he never answers. My uncle says it's because he's ashamed. He says to give him time. Once in a while, I'll get a card from my uncle with some money. I guess it's really from my Dad. He's lost it. He put too much of his life into that business and Sunon snuffed it out like that." Her shoulders slumped.

Chuck reached for Debbie and turned her around. He looked at Debbie's face. Her eyes were moist with tears. She sniffled slightly. He squeezed her saying nothing as his brain raced. Chuck had never been in love before. He preferred the independence of bachelorhood. If he needed female companionship, he had no trouble finding it with no strings attached. Debbie was different. These last two days he couldn't take his mind off of her. He never felt like this for any woman.

Then there was Sunon. First they cost him his job. Now they cheated her too. She shouldn't have to hurt. He would protect her; avenge her. And Sunon would know his revenge. When he was done, everybody in Detroit would see how he was changing the balance - a balance of terror.

Chuck and Debbie made the ride to Eastland Mall in relative silence. Debbie sat in the middle of the seat and held Chuck's arm. Chuck turned off Interstate 94 onto Moross Road.

"Is this a shortcut to the mall?" Debbie asked.

"No, I want to check out something." Chuck looked at Debbie to check her reaction to the excuse. She smiled back. After a couple of lights Chuck turned onto Gratiot Road. Traffic was light, and in a few moments he reached the destroyed Sunon dealer. Chuck slowed as he drove by the fire scene. He was surprised to see lots of workers at the dealership moving about, busily erecting plywood to cover the broken windows or throwing damaged materials into one of several dumpsters on the site. In the area in front of the building other workers erected a large yellow and white tent.

"Wow, that must have been a big fire," Debbie said.

Chuck made no reply. "What were they up to?" he wondered.

Debbie looked at Chuck, "Is there anything wrong?"

"What? Oh no, I was thinking."

"Well if you ask me, somebody ought to burn the rest of those Sunon dealerships. Then they can start on all the Sunon cars. Wipe out every trace of the slime balls."

Chuck grinned and looked at Debbie. "Do you really believe that?"

"After what they did to my father? I'd light the match myself if I had the chance."

Chuck accelerated away from the scene. He considered Debbie's statement. Then he mumbled, "You might get your chance a lot sooner than you think," and laughed.

Debbie laughed uncertainly too.

At the mall Chuck parked as near to Entrance 7 as he could. As they walked through the doors, Chuck noticed the pay phones. Down the hall was the typical brass and wood entry to a franchised restaurant where a small crowd waited to be seated. Chuck said, "See if you can get us a table. I have to make a phone call. It might take a while. Order me a beer."

"Oh okay. "Don't be too long."

"I'll do my best. He kissed Debbie on the lips then squeezed her butt before walking back toward Entrance 7. He reached the phone. The hall was deserted except for some people walking toward the restaurant. He dialed the number Cannon had given him. He was surprised by the sweet female voice at the other end, "Hello?"

"Oh, is Bob there?" Chuck asked.

"One second please."

Chuck could hear her say, "Bob, it's for you!"

After a few seconds Chuck heard Cannon's voice, "Hello?"

"Bob, this is Chuck."

"Ohh," Cannon paused. "No I'm not interested in buying life insurance on a Sunday morning. Thanks anyway." The line went dead.

"What a slickee boy," Chuck mumbled to himself as he hung up the phone. Then he leaned against the wall and waited for Cannon to call back. Time seemed to drag but fifteen minutes later the pay phone rang. Chuck picked it up after the first ring. "Hello?" he said.

"Chuck? Is that you?"

"Nah, it's State Farm. Want to buy some fire insurance?" Chuck joked.

"I saw the news this morning. Good job. I'll pay you tomorrow night. We'll meet at the same place as last time. Say seven o clock."

"Right. We've got to talk." Chuck said.

"About what?"

"The jobs. They're too risky. I got some ideas. We need to talk."

"So we'll talk. I'll see you tomorrow." Cannon sounded annoyed.

Chuck hung up and turned around. Debbie was standing behind him. "What are you doing here?" Chuck blurted. His face felt flushed with blood.

"You've been gone so long, I wondered if you were okay. I'm sorry." Debbie seemed surprised by Chuck's reaction.

"Why were you snooping on me?"

"I wasn't snooping. I was worried. Chuck, what's wrong? What's going on? Are you in trouble?" She looked at him. Her eyes showed that she was hurt by Chuck's outburst.

Debbie's look disarmed Chuck. He couldn't stay angry at her. He stared, turning his tight-lipped grimace into a broad smile. "I'm not angry at you. You surprised me that's all." He paused, thinking about his next step. If she felt for him like he did for her, he had nothing to worry about. He looked around. They were alone. He continued, "This morning you said you'd light the match yourself. Were you serious? I mean could you really do it?"

"Chuck, what are you saying? I... I had nothing to do with that fire.

"I know. I know because I did."

"What? Are you serious?" She looked at Chuck. He tilted his head to one side, raised his eyebrows and smiled.

79

" Why?" she asked after a pause.

"Let's say it's a business deal. It's payback time and the Sunon boys got a lot of payback coming. After what Sunon put you through I figure you might want to get a piece of the action. Before we go any further, you got to remember no one gets to know about this. Nobody. Not your father, not anybody. This is serious stuff. But if you want to, I'll let you in. Understand?"

"Not really." She put her arms around his waist and hugged him. "I know one thing. I trust you. I'll do whatever you want if it's a way to get even with Sunon."

"Let's go get lunch. We got a lot to talk about." He put his arm around her shoulders and they walked to the restaurant.

CAPITOL BUILDING, WASHINGTON, DC

"You can sit anywhere you find an open seat," said the Capitol Police Officer in a hushed tone.

"Thank you" whispered Shane. He scanned the spectator gallery and found an aisle seat.

The room itself was impressive. Detailed crown moldings and raised mahogany panels recalled times when craftsmanship was a virtue and people genuinely cared about the quality of their work. The late afternoon sunlight filtering onto the massive leather chairs and the flags of the fifty American states gave the room a mysterious air of dignity. In front of the spectator gallery, a table faced a raised paneled dais where the members of the House Subcommittee on Foreign Trade sat like a stoic tribunal. The table, shrouded in a green cloth, held three microphones for the witnesses. On each side of the witness chair there was room for lawyers and handlers and between the two tables for photographers. None were there today. Testimony about the flat-panel computer display price fixing by Japanese companies had not caught the eye of the American public.

"The committee calls Ms. Mary Fielding," announced the chair into the microphone.

A well-dressed woman in her mid-forties rose from the spectator gallery and sat in the middle witness chair. Her appearance was attractive, her makeup convincingly hiding the wrinkles time had unfairly bestowed upon her face. Shane remembered how his last meeting with her ended. It would be interesting to watch her testify to Congress.

"Do you swear to tell the truth and nothing but the truth?" mechanically stated the sergeant at arms.

"I do," replied Fielding.

The committee chair started, "Ms. Fielding, on behalf of the House Subcommittee on Foreign Trade, we welcome you to our hearings. I understand you have prepared testimony that you would like read into the record."

"That's correct, Mr. Chairman."

"I move that Ms. Fielding's statement be officially read into the record by unanimous consent," said the chairman. There were no objections as only the chairman, Congressman Pringle and two of the other fourteen representatives were present. Such a parliamentary move was routine on Capital Hill as committees sought to enter testimony quickly into the congressional record. "We'll proceed with the questions. Will the gentleman from Michigan please take the floor."

"Thank you, esteemed Chairman," said Pringle. After adjusting his half moon glasses so he could read the papers in front of him, Pringle said, "Ms. Fielding, I understand by your statement that you do not support the placing of import restraints on flat panel displays."

"That's correct, Congressman."

"Yet as the former Chairperson of the International Trade Commission, you had an instrumental role in instituting these trade restraints."

"My tenure as Chair of the ITC five years ago is not germane to the current situation," responded Fielding flatly. "As I made clear in my written statement, the situation has changed. Since there are no longer any American manufacturers of flat panel displays, trade restraints on foreign flat panels will unfairly penalize American manufacturers of portable personal computers. It is the American consumer that will end up paying more."

"Yes, I've seen your written statement. Isn't it true that all the flat panel screens used by our heroic soldiers across the globe are from Japanese companies."

The Congressman was not pulling any punches, but Fielding seemed ready for such an onslaught

"That is true Congressman. However, the reason we have no major manufacturer capable of making flat panel displays has nothing to do with Japan. Rather it has plenty to do with the shortsightedness and poor management capabilities of the American flat panel manufacturers." Fielding paused calmly folding her hands in front of her. "Not able to look beyond the next quarter's profit and loss statement, the American panel manufacturers frankly did not make the right decisions, invested poorly and did not react properly to the market. They were out-managed."

" Pringle pulled off his glasses and sneered. "If that is so Ms. Fielding, why did the ITC find the Japanese manufacturers guilty of dumping and price fixing?

"As you will find in the records, Congressman, the ITC based its findings on an abstract administrative ruling. The ITC determined that the actual result of this ruling was so minimal, that the final penalty was but a mere token," replied Fielding, seemingly anticipating the question.

The representative glared. "Don't you think its time we start considering the viability of our nation's manufacturers?"

"With all due respect Sir, American companies must learn to compete, but not at the expense of the American consumer. That's the concept of free trade."

Shane listened to Pringle continue for eight more minutes trying to make his point. For each question, Fielding had a confident and well-reasoned response. When time was up, he yielded to the chair. Shane was glad that Fielding was on his side. He wouldn't want to go against her.

"Thank you for your time today, Ms. Fielding. The committee will adjourn for the evening," intoned the Chairman at the end.

Shane caught up with Fielding on the steps of the Capital Building. "Nice job in there, Mary."

"Shane, hello." Shane accepted her syrupy hug. "Yeah, normally I try to avoid testifying. Our lobbying efforts are much more effective when we work behind the scenes. Anyway, don't worry about that. Let's have dinner and find out what's on your mind. How does the Willard sound?"

"Great," replied Shane. "I haven't been there since they renovated it."

Inside the Willard Hotel at the Occidental Grill, Fielding and Shane had a lunch of rainbow trout with Julienne potatoes. Between bites, they gently recalled the days of their prior friendship. As Fielding spoke, Shane stared into her eyes reflecting on the intimate moments they had shared on their previous meetings.

Over their second glass of California Zinfandel Shane said, "Mary, we need you to arrange some support for our side. My boss is feeling some pressure from the Japan bashing that's in the press every day."

"How is Kondo-San?"

Shane titled his head to the side. "Oh, fine I guess, but he sure is sensitive about this latest one. He hasn't been this uptight since his wife left him. We need a good effort from you on this one."

"What specifically did you have in mind?"

"Well, for starters we could use some friendly words from a Congressman."

"How much do they need to say?" Fielding smiled over her wine glass.

"Oh, not much really. As long as the comments are well aimed. We want something positive about our operations in the U.S. Maybe praise the efforts of our Kentucky-based manufacturing. You know, mention all that we've done for the community where we've set up manufacturing operations."

Fielding put her finger to her temple. "I got it. We mention that Sunon has done a lot for the American economy and that we are very appreciative. I can arrange it. I have one or two targets in mind."

"How much will it cost?"

"Shouldn't be too much. My Congressmen need big bucks for reelection. They'll take anything, especially a modest PAC donation to the appropriate campaign funds."

"Good. Now what about Deaver?" asked Shane. Shane was anxious to hear what Fielding had to say. Deaver was a well-known advocate for managed trade between the U.S. and Japan. His foundation, really a consulting company, saw its mission to educate American industry about Japanese business practices. Because of his renown, Japan paid him heed.

"Ah, Deaver." She leaned back in her chair. "We've been working on him for a long time. You know he has been trying to unravel the details of our secret lobbying pact. Well, through our, shall we say, research, we found Deaver has a problem. Aside from trying to accumulate frequent flyer miles, he can't make the mortgage payment on his condo in Maui. Seems like his consulting business doesn't pay enough to maintain his lifestyle." Fielding rolled her head backwards with an evil smirk. "He's ripe for some consulting work."

"Great." Shane clenched his fists. "We want him to go to Japan and attend a conference. Have him say something positive about Sunon." Waving his hand in front of him he added, "Not something radical. We don't want him to lose credibility. If he says the right thing, we can cover his condo for the year. We'll even throw in a week layover in Hawaii on his return flight if he wants."

"I think Deaver will find that to his satisfaction."

"Then it's settled. You make the necessary arrangements." They raised wine glasses and clinked them together. "To Mr. Deaver. Cheers."

"When are you flying home?" asked Fielding afterwards, the rising eyebrows and twinkling eyes instantly conveying her intentions.

Shane too found himself again attracted to the self-confident brunette. He didn't mind mixing business and pleasure, after all that's what lobbying was all about. "I have a 9 p.m. flight."

"Any chance you can take a later flight? Perhaps we can have a drink and talk about old times."

"I can manage that," smiled Shane, knowing that it would be a long night.

Chapter 8

Chuck left the heavy rush hour traffic on Woodward Avenue when he entered Cannon's favorite restaurant. Alternating thoughts of Debbie and the up coming jobs racked his mind. Chuck scanned the mostly empty tables. Not seeing Cannon, he sat at the bar and ordered a beer.

Two beers and twenty minutes later, Chuck spotted Cannon's Cadillac pulling into the parking lot. He got up and met him at the door. "How's it going Cannon?"

"Fine," Cannon replied while looking at the maitre d'. "George, can we get a table? And have somebody bring me a martini."

George took them to the same-converted 56 Chevy table as the last time and then hustled away to place Cannon's order at the bar. Cannon took a seat across from Chuck and said, "I've had a rough day."

"That's too bad," Chuck said without conviction. "What did you think about the last job?"

"You did what I asked." Cannon frowned. "Would you believe he's open today and selling cars? From a tent! Rumor has it that it has been his best sales day ever."

"You got to be kidding me. After the damage we did to that place. I thought he was shut down for good," Chuck said, not hiding his disappointment.

"I'm not surprised. To hurt a car dealer you got to hurt his cars. The cars are his real assets." Cannon tugged at the skin hanging from his neck.

"We had a fire in one of my dealerships a few years back. Didn't slow us down much. Hell, if I had the right cars I could sell them from my basement." Cannon paused, "You did what I asked and that's all I want. They're getting the message."

Chuck squinted. Something about what Cannon said didn't sound right, but he couldn't put a finger on it. Thoughts of his own plans went in and out of his head. Then he said, "It's not enough. We need to put the hurt on them. They need a real lesson."

"What are you talking about, Chuck? I call the shots on this. After all I'm paying the bills. I said 'I'm happy' and that's all you need to know."

"Listen, champ," Chuck said, staring at Cannon's face, his voice barely a whisper. "That isn't all there is to it. My butt is on the line out there. You aren't taking any chances sitting in your fancy house in Grosse Pointe. Me, one mistake and I'm either a crispy critter," Chuck snapped his finger for effect. "Or I'll spend the rest of my life in jail. So don't give me any crap about who calls the shots. You pay the bills. I run the show."

"What's your problem? What do you want? More money?"

"You cheap bastard," Chuck said, and then laughed putting a finger to his cheek. "I hadn't thought of that, but now that you mention it, it wouldn't hurt. I had to hire a few hands to help pull these jobs off without getting nailed. Extra bucks wouldn't hurt. But that isn't what I want to talk about."

"So what the hell do you want?"

The waiter arrived with Cannon's martini. Chuck took the opportunity to sip from his beer and think.

Putting down his beer, he reached over, and patted Cannon on the shoulder, "Take it easy, Cannon. We're business partners, remember? I need to get some help from you. That's all. Those first two jobs were a little too hairy. We almost got nailed on the last one. Some twerps showed up right in the middle of our dousing the place. With a little more bad luck and we would have been roasted real good. We can't keep torching them. I need a better way."

"Do you have anything in mind?" Cannon's mood appeared to improve when Chuck said he wasn't asking for more money.

"You said you had a construction business. What kind of construction?"

"Roads, parking lots, a few buildings, why?" Cannon shrugged.

"Do they do any blasting?"

"Sure, they do that kind of stuff all the time. Except right now the whole thing's been going kind of slow. Most of my equipment is leased out. I only have two caretakers watching the yard and a couple of engineers and business types working a few bids."

"Do you think you could get me some blasting caps and TNT?" Chuck asked?

Cannon dropped his jaw. "Why do you want that kind of stuff?"

"Man. I told you that the arson jobs are too risky. With a small bomb and a timer, I can get the job done without taking too many risks."

"I don't know," Cannon said slowly. "It sounds too dangerous."

"Dangerous for who? Not for me." Chuck shot back. "You're so god damned concerned about hurting someone else, but you don't give a damn about me. I'm telling you doing a torch job and doing it right is too risky. Besides, the chances of hurting a bystander are about the same if we use a bomb or a Molotov cocktail."

Cannon ran his hand through his thinning hairline.

Chuck continued, "It's no big deal, man. I thought about a lot of different possibilities. A bomb is the easiest way."

"I don't know. Somehow a bomb seems like it's going too far," Cannon said, almost to himself.

"Look, Cannon," Chuck glowered. "I'm in this up to my eyeballs. And so are you. We can't back out now. We started this, and we're going to finish it. We got a chance to make a real impact. A chance to get even." Talking to Cannon like this energized Chuck.

Cannon relented, "All right, I'll see what I can do. I'll try to get you some TNT and caps. I don't know how much we have right now. I might not be able to get a whole lot."

Cannon's quiet tone told Chuck the employer-employee relationship between them had changed. Chuck was now in charge.

"Get what you can." Chuck picked up his beer and drained it. "Where's the money?"

"Here." Cannon reached into his jacket pocket and pulled out an envelope. "There's seven thousand dollars in there. One thousand for expenses on the first job, five for the last job and another thou for expenses. Is that all right?"

"Yeah. A deal's a deal. If we need more I'll let you know. When can you get me the explosives?"

"I'll let you know by Thursday. I'll call you at the mall to set up the pick up. Be there at 7:00 PM. Now if you'll excuse me, I got to go." Cannon stood up, threw a twenty on the table and left.

Chuck took the envelope and looked inside. The cash was all there. Putting the wad in his pocket, he stood up and mumbled, "You might have started it, but I'm going to finish it." Then he, too, left.

Chuck stopped at a pay phone in the restaurant's parking lot. He dialed Brian's number. Brian's deep voice said, "Hello."

"Hey, Brian. It's Chuck. Why don't you come over tonight. I got something for you."

"When?"

"Say in about an hour. One other thing, I got somebody I want you to meet."

"I'll be there."

Chuck hung up and immediately dialed Debbie's number.

Her roommate Liz answered. Chuck waited a few moments for Debbie to come to the phone. "Hi Debbie. My meeting ended early. Why don't you come over a little early tonight? I want to introduce you to a friend."

"Ooo, that sounds nice. I'm not doing anything. I can come over now."

"Great. See you in a few."

Chuck stopped at a liquor store on the way home and purchased a chilled bottle of champagne and a six-pack of beer. When he got home he took Brian's thousand dollars and put it into a separate envelope. He hid the rest of the money in a brown bag in the freezer. The booze went into the refrigerator.

Debbie arrived first. She greeted Chuck with a passionate kiss and tight hug. Then she said, "You look like you're in a good mood."

"I am," Chuck said. "I had a good day, plus you're here. What more could a guy ask for?"

Debbie smiled broadly and kissed Chuck again. "I knew from the first time I saw you that you were special. I was right."

"Do you want something to drink? Champagne?"

"What's the occasion? Other than I'm going to spend the night with you?" Debbie said with a twinkle in her eye.

"Do I need more reason?"

Debbie grabbed Chuck and pulled him into the bedroom. He feigned resistance until he heard a car pulling into the gravel driveway. Chuck looked out the window and said, "Look's like company's here. You're going to get to meet my partner, ah, excuse me, our partner. He's an old friend of mine. We go way back. He's a little on the strange side but I wouldn't want anybody else with me if I got stuck in a dark alley. He can play tough but don't let him scare you."

Brian knocked on the door. Chuck let him in and shook his

hand. "Hey, man. How's it going?"

"Pretty cool." Brian stopped abruptly when he saw Debbie standing in the kitchen.

"Brian, this is my friend Debbie." Chuck walked over to her and put his arm around her waist. She did the same to him. "Debbie, this is Brian. Brian and I are old friends."

"Hi Brian," Debbie said warmly.

Brian grunted, "Hi."

"Do you want something to drink, Brian? Here's your money." Chuck picked up an envelope from the kitchen table and handed it to him.

Brian slowly took the envelope, squinting at Chuck.

Chuck knew his friend and could read his thoughts, "Don't worry man. Debbie is cool. She's going to be working with us."

Brian put the envelope in his pocket. He glanced at Debbie. She smiled nervously. He looked back at Chuck. Chuck also smiled. Brian turned around, opened the fridge and got a beer. He peered for a moment at the champagne. Then he twisted the beer top and took a deep tug.

"Let's take a seat in the living room. We need to discuss the next job."

The word "job" seemed to dig into Brian like a razor blade. He threw his head to the side and said, "Chuck, can we talk outside for a second."

"We don't need to talk outside. We don't have to have any secrets from each other."

Brian twisted sideways, his body tensing almost as if he was taking a martial arts stance.

"Come on Brian, take it easy. Have a seat."

Brian looked at Chuck and then slowly sat on Chuck's worn armchair. Debbie and Chuck sat on the sofa.

"I know you're surprised Debbie knows what's going on. Don't worry, I told her about it. She's got plenty of reason to want to help out. Hell, she's got more reason than either of us."

Brian ground his teeth slowly.

Chuck motioned to Debbie, "Tell him about your dad."

Debbie tightened her lower lip. Then she took a deep breath and summarized the story of how Sunon cheated her father. When she

89

was done, she brushed away a tear.

Chuck said, "Like I said, she's got more in this than we do. Brian, you were a cop. You know about revenge. Debbie is with us." Chuck watched Brian for a reaction. Seeing none, he continued.

"We need to talk about our next job. I met with our client tonight. He's going to help us out with some supplies. In the meantime we got to check out these Sunon dealers. I found out that the last dealer we toasted had a fire sale in a tent. He sold a record number of cars."

"Yeah, I saw him on television this evening. Amazing, after what you guys did to that place," Debbie said.

"Yeah, well apparently it ain't enough to trash the buildings. You got to trash the cars too."

Finally, Brian broke his silence, "What did our client say about it? By the way, I presume that Debbie doesn't know who he, or she, is either?"

Chuck smiled recognizing Brian's question meant he had accepted Debbie. He needed Brian. Debbie could help out, but she wasn't necessary to finish the jobs. Still, having her involved would make it easier for him to spend time with her. Sharing the danger with her multiplied his excitement. He was building a team that was loyal to him. He hadn't the satisfaction of having a team working for him since he left the Army. This team was for real, not a bunch of guys playing around in camouflage fatigues. This was life or death with a purpose.

"Neither of you know who our client is. That's the way he wants it."

Brian looked at Debbie and raised his beer in a mock toast. She raised her bottle too.

Chuck continued, "Since that last job, I guess Sunon's going to beef up their security. We have to check on that. I want to get together again next Friday night. If we plan things right we might be able to pull the next job over the weekend. Any questions?"

Debbie shook her head while Brian appeared bored.

"Remember, you don't tell anyone about this. Understand? Keep your cool. We'll get it done."

"Where and when do you want to meet again?" Brian asked.

"Next Friday. We'll meet at the Victory Cafe. If we need to talk we'll take a ride."

"That's cool." Brian got up patting the pocket with the envelope. "I'm going to hit the road."

Chuck walked Brian to the door.

Before leaving, Brian hesitated and turned to Chuck. "I hope you aren't thinking with your pecker," he whispered. "You better know what you're doing man."

"Everything's cool Brian. It will work out."

The intercom on Kondo's electronic phone buzzed.

"Mr. Kondo, Mr. Shane is on the phone."

"Thank you, I'll take it in here." Kondo picked up the handset. He didn't want to use the speaker phone.

"Hello, this is Kondo speaking."

"Hi Kondo-San. This is Shane. I'm at the Detroit Metropolitan Airport. You said to call as soon as I got back."

"Yes that's right." Kondo paused. "Why don't we meet at the San Marino Club. I want a full debriefing on your trip."

"Can't wait till I get back, huh?" asked Shane.

"Timing isn't as important as privacy. These walls are as thin as the paper in a Shoji screen. I'll meet you in forty minutes."

"Right boss, bye."

Replacing his handset, Kondo hit his intercom, "Claire, please clear my calendar for the remainder of the afternoon. I'm leaving for an off-site meeting. I'll drive a Fredrick from the pool. Please have one brought up front."

"Yes sir."

Before leaving his office, Kondo took a swig from a bottle of brandy he kept in his desk drawer. Swallowing the spirit, he pondered Shane's success. He had directed Shane to interfere in his company's most important mechanism for accurate reporting of political information to Japan. If the board knew of this, he would surely lose his job - not so much for interfering, for if it was for the common good, everyone would understand. He would lose his job because he had acted for his own good.

Traffic was heavy on Metropolitan Parkway so Kondo tried a short cut. He turned right onto a side street he knew intersected a street parallel to Metropolitan Parkway. After a few blocks, he found the street closed by an accident. A wrecker was lifting the rear end of a smashed car blocking traffic both ways on the narrow road. Kondo turned his head so he could back his car from the accident scene, but he couldn't as a car had pulled behind him. Kondo turned to look at the smashed car. The car's trunk had been crushed and its contents strewn across the road. He couldn't tell the make of the car, but it wasn't a Sunon.

Kondo wondered where the other vehicle was when he noticed a lone little boy sitting on the curb next to the wrecker crying. A stream of blood coursed from his nose. Kondo starred at the boy and recalled his childhood when he had a bloody nose. Then a familiar voice surprised him. He turned to see his mother.

"Don't cry Yuichi-chan. You'll be all right."

"Why did those boys hit me?" Kondo started sobbing.

"Those boys are bullies. They don't need a reason to hit you."

"They said I was a show-off, that I was selfish."

Mrs. Kondo took a rough cotton handkerchief she kept in her drab gray smock and dabbed the blood streaming toward Kondo's lip. "You'll be all right son. You'll be all right."

Kondo choked back sobs. "I hate them, I hate them!"

"Yuichi-chan, don't be spiteful. Those boys don't mean ill. They don't understand. You are different. They know, but they don't know why."

"I don't want to be different. I want to belong," cried the young Kondo.

"You can belong, you must learn how to use your talents without offending anyone."

The words echoed in Kondo's head. Kondo knew he was different.

His mother said, "You must be like a fox. Clever. Don't flaunt your superiority, but don't follow the herd. Use your schoolmates to help achieve your end."

Kondo closed his eyes and time flashed past him. He heard his mother say "Yuichi chan, I am so proud of you. First in your class and headed for Tokyo University."

"Please mother, you'll embarrass me."

"Oh, stop it. Let an old lady enjoy the most special moment of her life. It seems like only yesterday, you were my little boy. Now you are off to college. The best college in Japan. How I will miss you."

"I will visit, you'll see."

"No! You must not. You must work even harder than ever. Don't relax. College is an opportunity to learn the ways of the world. Observe. Listen. Apply yourself. Don't worry about me." His mother started to cry.

Kondo brushed off his mother's selfless mood thinking she was sad, like all mothers when they realize a child has grown. She kept her cancer a secret. She died only a few months after Kondo left for college.

A dark sadness fell over Kondo. His eyelids became heavy and his stomach churned. He clenched his fists. Mother, you never told me about your cancer. How could you keep it from me? You didn't even give me a chance to help. If only you had told me. I would have saved you.

"Mother I'm coming," he yelled. "I'm coming!"

A car horn knocked Kondo from his trance.

"Hey wake up. Get moving mister, you're blocking the road."

A sideways glance to the right revealed a large and weary station wagon trying to squeeze between Kondo's car and the curb. The driver, craning his neck out the window like a heron searching for food, was sneering at Kondo.

The wrecker had left and traffic was coming in the other direction. How long had he been daydreaming? Quickly, Kondo put the sedan in drive and accelerated. The painter in the battered station wagon yelled more curses as Kondo pulled in front of him. The little boy was gone.

Kondo found Shane standing at the club across from City Airport. Off in the distance, a vintage Grumman Tigercat was doing touch-and-go landings on the runway. The plane's twin radial engines droned in the background.

Shane waved to Kondo. "Kondo-San, over here."

"Have you been waiting long?"

"Nah, I just got here. Let's go in and get a drink." Shane held the door open.

"Yes, a drink would be good."

Inside Shane ordered a draft beer. Kondo ordered a double Chivas Regal on the rocks.

"So tell me, how was your trip to Washington?"

"Very successful, not only did we make big gains with our lobbying, but our special project is off to a great start."

"Really, tell me about it," Kondo said rubbing his palms together.

"Well," said Shane, "First, Victor Deaver is all lined up. He's leaving next week for Japan. He's going there to look into the latest trade friction. We'll get some public statements that Takahashi is going to find hard to ignore."

"Excellent," said Kondo. "Deaver will score big points with the board for us."

"Right. Accompanying Deaver will be Congressman Shurr from Kentucky. Shurr's district is the one where two of our suppliers are considering erecting parts factories. He's itching to butter up the home front. He'll add the political side to the statement."

"Yes, that's very good. Few Japanese, let alone the board members, understand the individual nature of your Congress. When one speaks, they naturally assume that they are speaking for your government. Yes, Deaver and Shurr will have a big impact. Well done, Mr. Shane."

"Thanks boss, it was all in a day's work."

Lowering his voice, Kondo said "Now what about our special project?"

"Even better news. Using the appropriate grease." Shane winked. "I convinced our consultants that we need to have an input on their impartial political report. They will send the next draft to us in a few days."

"That's not good enough! We must be able to craft the report as we see fit. I personally want to see the final Japanese version so I can assure the Tokyo folks will read exactly what we want them to read."

Shane seemed taken aback by his boss' reaction. "Well that's what I meant. They'll provide us with a draft that includes all the raw data. They'll let us rewrite it however we see fit."

Kondo leaned back crossing his arms on his chest. "From now we must craft the words so that they read the right amount into them. What is not said is as important as what is."

Chapter 9

Nicca drove the unmarked Ford sedan down the pothole-marred street past a row of double-parked cars. He loosened his tie and ran his finger around the collar of his shirt. The air was stuffy from the unseasonably warm weather. Nicca stopped in front of the firehouse. Jones waiting on the front steps opened the passenger door and got in the car.

"Well, how did the house-to-house go?"

The rookie Fire Marshall shrugged. "All right I suppose. I got most of the day guys to help. We didn't turn up anything. Nobody saw or heard anything. Couldn't find anyone who was in the area at that time of night."

"I see. I had a meeting with the owner." Nicca pulled the car into traffic. "He didn't give me any leads. They had a few personnel problems in the past year but nothing recent. Since we got two different owners at two different dealers we'll probably have to expand the scope of the investigation. The torchers could be anybody in the Detroit Sunon organization. It might even be a disgruntled customer, but I think that's unlikely."

"Maybe we should check in with the Sunon corporate personnel. They might have a lead."

"That's a good idea. Why don't you work on that tomorrow. In the meantime, I want to check on that moving warehouse from last week. I got a tip this morning that the owner might have hired a local hood to pull it off."

Nicca turned the unmarked car onto Six Mile Road while rolling down the car window. "It has been a busy afternoon, Willy. This crazy weather - one day cold, one day hot, my body doesn't know what to think." The car phone ring startled him. He reached for the speakerphone button.

"This is Nicca."

"Joe Nicca, I'm glad I caught you," a voice crackled over the speakerphone. "Listen, we got a PR problem with the Sunon Car jobs."

"Who is this?" Nicca looked at his partner. Jones shrugged.

"This is Captain Wilson."

"Captain Wilson," Nicca hunched. "Sorry, I didn't recognize your voice."

"Anyway, like I was saying, remember the Sunon arson jobs?"

"Sure I remember them, similar MO, break in, spread some gasoline and let it go."

"Well maybe so, but Sunon's top manager in Detroit got wind of the problem. He's demanding to know what's going on. The mayor personally called me on this one."

"We haven't caught anyone yet, if that's what they want," the hair on Nicca's neck started to rise. Obviously, the Fire Captain was about to stick his nose into his investigation. "If you ask me Captain, it looks like either an inside job or extortion, maybe organized crime."

"I'm not asking for the torcher yet. This Sunon bigwig wants information. It seems Sunon is about to introduce a new sports car model and he wants to know if there will be more..." The Captain paused, as if he was searching for a word, " ...problems."

"What does he think, I have a crystal ball?" blustered Nicca. "There were five suspicious fires last night, ten the night before. Yeah, there'll be more."

"Well that's not what you tell him. I want you to go see this guy and give him a run down on the case. Hold his hand if you have to. I don't need any more calls from the mayor. He plays golf with these guys so he wants us to treat them well."

"Jeez Captain, I got a plateful of investigations. I can't spare the time to brief every Tom, Dick and Harry that wants to know about a torch job."

"Who said you have a choice. Do it!" The Captain's tone told Nicca the conversation was finished. "I'll transfer you to my secretary, she'll give you the address. Now get over there and don't make waves."

Nicca rolled his eyes as he disconnected the phone.

Jones, busily writing down the address said, "Maple Road in Troy, west of I-75. That's in the other direction but we can get there in about twenty-five minutes."

"Well how do you like that," said Nicca tasting bile in his throat. "The mayor of Detroit plays golf with the Sunon big shots. Isn't that a hoot. He calls the Captain. The Captain calls us. We got forty other cases, but all of a sudden this one is top priority. The Captain never gave a shit about our other cases but one call from the mayor and we're all jumping through hoops for a Japanese car dealer."

Jones seemed surprised by Nicca's bitterness. "Er, Joe, weren't we going to talk to Sunon anyway? Maybe we can learn something from the executives."

"Damn, you're right. I'm sorry. These high visibility cases always aggravate me. You get all kinds of help - most of it not helpful. It's extra bullshit. Why do you think there's no other senior Fire Marshals around?" Nicca raised the car window. "When you get to be my age Willy, maybe you'll understand."

At the Sunon Headquarters building, Nicca and Jones found Kondo's suite. Nicca adjusted his tie and leather jacket as Kondo's secretary led him into Kondo's office. "Please have a seat, Mr. Kondo will be here shortly."

Taking a seat, Nicca scanned the office. He was surprised to see Spartan furnishings. He always figured mahogany paneling and ornate marble would surround the president of an automobile division. Instead, Kondo had a simple modular metal desk with only a phone and two plastic folders on top. Even the decorations were plain. A simple plaque hung behind the desk with the Sunon logo. Along the far wall was a series of neatly arranged loose-leaf binders with Japanese characters on the edge. As Nicca scanned the room, three well-dressed men entered from a side door. Two rather short Japanese and the third guy could have been a male model straight from an Esquire advertisement.

One of the Japanese men moved in front of the others. "Hello, I'm Yasuhiro Hara." He extended a business card.

Nicca stood and said, "I'm Investigator Nicca, this is my partner Inspector Jones." He took Hara's card, then fumbled in his coat pockets, "Ash, I don't have any cards today."

The other man reached for Nicca's hand "Hi, Jack Shane. Good to meet you."

"Please sit down," instructed Hara.

Hara and Jack Shane sat across a low coffee table from Nicca and Jones. The other Japanese man, who hadn't said anything, sat at the desk.

"Investigator Nicca, you are investigating the recent fires at two Sunon dealerships?" questioned Hara in a tone of voice that sounded like he already knew the answer.

"Yes, that's right."

"Could you please tell us about your investigation?" Hara's question sounded more like a threat than a request.

"There's not much to tell. Both jobs had a similar MO."

"Excuse me, MO? I'm not familiar with this term."

"Sorry, MO means modus operandi. It's how the arson jobs were done.

"Arson! So the fires were deliberately set." Hara leaned back in his seat.

"Yes. This particular MO is pretty simple." Nicca threw his arms out in a circle. "Spread gasoline and throw a Molotov cocktail to ignite the gasoline from a distance. It's somewhat risky, so not what we would consider a professional job. Unless of course the professional wanted to try to throw us off track." He purposely omitted the fact that the arsonists disabled the alarm system in the second job, certainly something a professional could do. No sense telling them everything.

"Do you have any suspects?" queried Hara.

"No, not yet, of course our investigation is in the early stages. Unless we get a lucky break, we'll never bust the torchers."

When Hara seemed to not understand the response, Shane jumped in. "When do you think you will catch the arsonists?"

"Catch them!" Nicca blurted, "We get hundreds of arsons a month. Only a handful of the criminals are ever apprehended. Unless these guys get caught in the act of doing another one, we probably will never find them."

"So there's more than one."

"We think so," grimaced Nicca realizing he let that information slip.

"Do you think they'll strike again?" Hara said dourly searching Nicca's face.

"Your guess is as good as mine." Despite his annoyance at their questions Nicca wanted to lead them on. If these guys were involved in an inside job, he wanted to learn as much as possible. He asked his question quickly, before the executives could ask another of their own. "Has anyone made any threats? Is there anyone you would suspect?"

"No." Shane retorted. "If there were we would have told you."

"How about your competitors, anyone want to see Sunon go up in flames?"

"I have no knowledge of anyone, but then again, there are probably quite a few people who wouldn't mind some bad luck falling on Sunon." Shane winked.

"Anyone you would suspect?"

"You name it - the big three, the UAW. We have some friends and some enemies - like any big company."

While Shane answered Nicca's question, Hara had turned to the man behind the desk and said something in quick Japanese.

The man nodded.

Hara turned to Nicca and Jones, "Thank you very much for your time. Please keep us informed of any developments. You have my number on the card."

Nicca felt his blood pressure rise. "Wait a minute, we came to talk to Mr. Kondo. We have some questions for him. Where is he?"

"I am Kondo," said the executive from behind the desk. "We have no information to add to your case."

"Let me be the judge of that. I have some more questions."

"Detective Nicca, we have told you all we know. If you have something to add, please tell us. Otherwise, we are finished."

Nicca rose from the chair. "Listen here, Mr. Kondo."

Before he could say anymore, Jones interrupted. "Hey Joe, I think we have enough. Let's go." Jones sounded like a sheepish schoolboy trying to avoid trouble.

Nicca glanced at Jones. He didn't like to be pushed around by automobile executives, particularly Japanese ones, but Jones was right. Don't make trouble. "Yeah, that's it, Willy." Turning to Kondo he said, "You will be available if we have further questions?"

"Of course Investigator Nicca, we will cooperate as much as possible. Unfortunately, we know even less about this than you."

Nicca looked right into Kondo's dark brown eyes. The executive glanced down.

"Please follow me to the door."

Outside the office in the parking lot, Nicca walked toward the car. He popped a piece of chewing gum in his mouth. "Thanks partner, I was about to tell that slick SOB how I felt."

"Yeah, I know! Then we'd be explaining more to the Captain and maybe the civilian complaint review board."

Nicca used his key to open the door. "Well, what did you think about what they said? How do you size up the situation?".

"I think they're being up front. Sounds like they don't know much."

"They don't know much, but they know more than we do," Nicca looked over the top of the car at Jones, "and what they know has them worried."

"How do you figure?"

"Think about this, two arson jobs at two separate dealerships, both done by the same clowns. The dealers are doing well. The owners are annoyed. Nothing fits the typical arson scenario. Then we get a call to go see these big shots."

"Okay, so nothing fits."

"Nothing," Nicca curved his index finger and pointed at Jones, "Except why meet with us?" Nicca paused to give Jones a second to consider the question. "Someone is putting the pinch on them. They needed to find out what we know. Why didn't they ask about security or other preventative measures?"

"So you think it's extortion?"

"Maybe not your everyday extortion, but definitely a pinch job. My bones tell me so. Now all we have to find out is who is doing the pinching." Nicca slid into the car seat. Jones did likewise. "You know partner, this case became a lot more interesting."

After the detectives left the conference room, Kondo turned to Shane. "Mr. Shane, would you please tell us your opinion about the policemen's report."

"Well, the police do not seem to be too concerned. They have lots of arsons in Detroit. Without any hard evidence or an inside tip, I doubt they'll be able to find the arsonists."

"There are more than one arsonists. This concerns me," stated Hara. "It could be evidence of some sort of conspiracy targeting our dealers. Perhaps we should set up security guards at our dealers and factories. These criminals could strike again."

"Let's hold on, consider the options." Shane made a stop motion with his hands. "If it is a disgruntled customer, chances are there won't be any more arsons. The amateurish MO tends to point that out. Security guards would cost money. I'm not sure our dealers would want to do that. More importantly, if it is an organized group, perhaps one of our competitors like the detective suggested, they could want us to beef up security. If the media gets hold of it, it could set the wrong image to our customers. We don't want to give the impression that our dealerships are unsafe. You know, like an armed camp. It would keep the customers away. Let's stay calm and let the insurance cover the losses."

"Perhaps we should ask Tokyo for assistance."

"Ask Tokyo?" Kondo practically yelled at Hara. "That is the last thing we will do. Tokyo does not understand our situation. If we tell them about this minor incident, it will help reinforce their ideas that the political situation here has changed."

"It is standard procedure to report unusual incidents to the home office," he offered meekly.

"This is not an unusual situation. It is a fire at two dealerships. There will be no report to Tokyo. We will let the police handle this matter." Kondo turned away from his subordinate. "Mr. Shane, it is important that the media not blow this story out of proportion. We do not want any negative publicity before we unveil the 500GSX."

"That's a good point. After all we spent to publicize the 500GSX, we don't want to be preempted by these fires. I'll talk to my friends at the Detroit Mirror. I'm sure I can convince them they are not really interested in these two fires."

After dinner Chuck and Debbie drove to the remaining Sunon dealers on the target list. Chuck made Debbie point out all the relevant security related points of interest. The effort confirmed the dealers had not stepped up security.

They were back at Chuck's apartment by one in the morning. They spent the night together. The realization Debbie was not only his lover but co-conspirator intensified his attraction for her. Chuck let down his guard. Debbie seemed to respond in a similar way. He made love like never before, transferring his energy and excitement from the arsons.

In the morning, Chuck got up while Debbie took a shower. He took five hundred dollars out of the bag in the freezer and put it in an envelope. He walked to the bathroom and leaned against the door. "Here's your first pay check sweetheart. You'll get the second half after we do the job. You did good."

"When, last night or the night before?" She smiled as she watched Chuck's face in the moist mirror.

Chuck laughed, "Both. I'm going to meet with the man tonight. Let's meet with Brian at the Victory Cafe tomorrow night."

Debbie turned to face Chuck. "Can't I stay with you tonight?" she asked coyly.

Chuck had a hard time refusing her. She stood naked in front of his sink. Her wet hair pulled back and skin covered with beads of water made him think of the previous night's passion. "If you put it like that, sure. I'll meet you here tonight."

Debbie stopped by her apartment after work to pick up a change of clothes. Her roommate, Liz Kessler, and Liz's boyfriend, Alex Gustav, were there. Liz was a high school friend of Debbie's. Unlike Debbie who waited tables at an elegant restaurant, Liz had a job as a regional representative selling women's makeup at local department stores. Debbie started rooming with her when her father left for Lansing. Alex was an unemployed welder and mechanic. Liz and Alex had been dating since high school. Alex was serious but Liz didn't want to get married until Alex had a steady job.

Debbie said hello to both of them and walked into her room. After a few moments, Liz came in and gave her a lecherous smile. "Spend the night with Chuck again?"

"Yes. He's such a hunk. You know what's funny? I've spent practically the whole week with him and I don't even know his last name."

"You're kidding. Geez, girl. Get your head out of the clouds before you get hurt. Don't you think you're taking this one a little too fast. You just broke up with Ken. You know what they say about being on the rebound."

"I don't care. You know what it's like when you meet someone who fits all that you ever wanted in a guy? An answer to all your prayers?"

"Yeah, he's sitting outside," Liz said with a laugh. "At least I know his last name."

"Good one. Hang on a second. I got the money I owe you." Debbie grabbed her purse, counted out three hundred dollars and handed it to Liz. "Thanks for everything."

The money surprised Liz. For months, Debbie had been barely able to make ends meet. Now all of a sudden she pays off her debt. "Where did you get this from?"

"I got a letter from my uncle," Debbie lied. "Anyway, I've got to hurry. I'm going out with Chuck tonight, and tomorrow night too."

Liz didn't see any letter for Debbie in the mail but she let it go. Instead she said, "Wow. You two are a hot item. Is he really that special?"

"Liz, you won't believe this guy. You'll get to meet him one of these days. Then you'll see. Got to go. I'll see you tomorrow. Bye." She walked to the door, but she didn't see Alex. "Good bye Alex," she shouted as she closed the door.

Chapter 10

Chuck was standing beside the phone at Eastland Mall Entrance 7 at 7:00 PM. No call came in. He waited a few minutes and decided to call Cannon. He started to dial when he felt someone tap his shoulder. He turned around to see Cannon standing beside him.

"I got here a few minutes ago. Come outside. I got what you wanted."

The two men walked to Cannon's Cadillac in the parking lot. Cannon opened the trunk and picked out two boxes. The cardboard one was the size of a briefcase, the other was a plastic box as big as a pack of cigarettes. "This one has the demo," Cannon motioned to the bigger box. "The little one has the caps. They're electric blasting caps. This is all we had."

Chuck hefted the bigger box; "There can't be more than ten pounds in here. Is that all you could spare?" Chuck knew Cannon was lying. This wasn't enough demolitions to blow up a small boulder.

"That's it. It's old stuff. We don't do much of this anymore."

Chuck looked in the smaller box. There were ten electric blasting caps inside. Chuck put the box of caps in his oxford shirt pocket. Then he looked at Cannon and said, "Breaking the rules again. Huh, Cannon? Don't you remember? You're never supposed to transport caps and demo together. You could have blown yourself sky high getting here."

"The hell with that," Cannon said. "What are you going to do with this stuff?"

"I'll let you know. Have the money ready. We'll probably pop the next one within the week. You'll know about it."

Friday afternoon, Alex walked into the restaurant where Debbie worked and took a seat in the corner. Debbie noticed him after a few minutes and made a beeline for his table. "What brings you here, Alex?" Debbie asked as she took the extra silverware settings from the vacant seats around him.

Alex was not the smartest of men, nor was he comfortable in front of women other than Liz. He was big and strong and devoted to Liz. Debbie liked him. At times she pitied him because she knew that Liz would probably never marry him no matter how much he loved her.

"Debbie, I, uh, don't know how to say this. But, uh..."

"What's up Alex? You can tell me."

"Well, uh, Liz told me about the three hun'erd dollars."

"So? I owed her the money. I paid off a debt, " Debbie replied somewhat casually.

"Come on Debbie I ain't stupid. Where could you come up with that much money?"

"I told Liz. I got it from my uncle."

"She don't believe you and I don't either."

Alex's comment annoyed Debbie. "So what do you want?"

Alex looked around. Then he spoke in a whisper, "Liz thinks that your new boyfriend is a sugar baby..."

"Don't you mean sugar daddy?" Debbie interrupted.

"Whatever. But I don't think so."

"And what do you think?" Debbie said with amusement.

Alex paused. "I think you're doing something illegal. I think I know what it is."

The shocked expression of disbelief on Debbie's face gave her away.

Alex continued, "I think you're dealing drugs. Don't get me wrong. I'm not going to squeal or nothing. I want in, that's all." Alex looked at his silverware. "Look, I ain't worked in months. If I don't make any money, Liz will never want to get married. If I could get a little money, then I can set up my own shop. You know. Then maybe Liz would go for it. Plus I can help you out. You can trust me."

Debbie took off her apron and sat on a chair. She looked at Alex. He raised his eyes and looked briefly into hers. "Alex, I'm not dealing drugs. Don't you know me better than that? I've never even used drugs."

Alex remained silent.

Alex must really be desperate to think up such a plan. She felt sorry for him. She decided to take a chance. "I'll tell you what Alex. I am involved in something on the side. It's a little risky but I'll introduce you to my," she hesitated, "my boss. If he says it's cool, then you're in."

"I don't want Liz to know anything about this."

"Right," said Debbie. "In fact, you better not tell anyone about this."

"I swear. Thanks Debbie."

"Meet me at the Victory Cafe tonight at seven PM. Do you know where that is?"

"Yea, I think so. I'll be there."

Judging by the crowd at the Victory Cafe, one would not get the impression that Detroit suffered as much as it did from the economic recession. Cars filled the parking lot and the surrounding street. Chuck was fortunate that he arrived early. Brian showed up next. The two men leaned against the bar in the far corner.

"So what did you find out?" Chuck asked Brian.

"I think we're going to have trouble on these next jobs. The dealer in Troy has some security guards. Even though they're a bunch of bozos, they will definitely complicate things."

"That's pretty much what I saw at the dealers I checked out. I think we are going to have to change our tactics. I met with our client yesterday. He gave me some interesting stuff." Chuck smiled at Brian.

"What kind of stuff?"

Chuck lowered his voice, "Ten pounds of TNT and a bunch of electrical blasting caps."

"Hmmm. That changes things. Is that enough to do the jobs?" Brian asked. His police experience did not include any demolitions training.

Chuck, on the other hand, was well versed in demolitions while in the Army Special Forces. "No, not really. Especially when you consider that blowing up the dealer's buildings doesn't do much good. We got to get the cars. Individually a car is an easy target. How do you take out a bunch of them?"

"I don't know," Brian responded. "It would be too much of a hassle trying to do each one."

"Yeah, that would never work. We got two choices, we either use a big bomb or we have to change targets,"

Brian said, "You said we had ten pounds of TNT. Is that enough for a big bomb?"

"No. That's hardly enough for a firecracker. There are some ways to make it stretch." Chuck stopped in mid sentence when he spotted Debbie walking into the cafe. She appeared to be escorted by a big, plain looking guy.

Debbie scanned the bar. She spotted Chuck and Brian and pointed them out to Alex. Then she and Alex walked over to the bar.

Chuck and Brian stopped talking. Debbie approached Chuck and gave him a kiss.

Brian gave Alex a brief nod.

Debbie said, "Chuck, I want to introduce you to my friend, Alex."

Chuck extended his hand. Alex grasped it in his huge paw and gave a hard squeeze. Chuck squeezed back and said, "How ya doing." Both men were impressed with the strength of the other's handshake.

"Alex was interested in helping us out," Debbie said without reservation. "I told him I'd have to ask you."

Chuck couldn't believe what he heard. Brian immediately frowned and turned to face away.

"Let's go outside. You too Brian." Chuck spoke in a quiet terse tone. He was barely able to control his anger. The four walked outside. Brian gave Chuck an icy stare. Chuck looked around and said, "Let's go over there, behind that dumpster."

Debbie looked at Chuck. She could tell Chuck was upset but she didn't know what to say.

When the four of them reached the dumpster Chuck said, "Brian you keep a look out. I'll handle this."

Brian smiled. "You better man," he said emphatically.

Chuck turned and looked directly at Debbie. He could control his temper no longer. He yelled, "What the hell is wrong with you? Don't you remember what I told you?"

Chuck's anger frightened her. She stuttered, "I'm sorry honey. I was trying to help."

"Don't give me that crap. I told you not to tell anyone about this..."

Alex interrupted, "Hey man, don't yell at her. I asked..."

"And who the hell do you think you are? I don't know you from Adam. What did she tell you?

"She said that she was involved in something but she had to ask you first."

"Involved in what?" Chuck asked.

"She didn't say but I think it's drugs. Look man I need the bucks and I ain't gunna rat."

"You're god damned right you ain't gunna rat because I'll kill you first." Chuck looked at Debbie, "If I have to, I'll kill both of you." Chuck paused. He noticed tears forming in Debbie's eyes. Now he regretted the last comment. He looked at Debbie, "What the hell do you think we're doing? Playing cops and robbers? One little screw up and we can all get canned. And let me tell you something right now, I ain't going to jail because some dumbshit don't know how to keep his mouth shut."

Chuck could see from Debbie's face fight back tears. His words had their intended effect. He looked at Alex, "Listen Alex. None of this ever happened. Do you understand what I'm saying?"

"Yeah. I keep my mouth shut."

"Right." Chuck said.

"But," Alex bit his lip. He wasn't afraid of Chuck but he was afraid for Debbie. "Look man. I can keep my mouth shut. I asked her to get in. She didn't say nothing. I took a guess. I can help you out. I can steal cars. I can fix anything. Man, I need the bucks."

Brian returned from his lookout with a wry smile. He heard most of the conversation but he kept silent.

Chuck said, "Is that right? You're a regular gangster. What do you think Brian? Think we could use him?"

Debbie and Alex looked expectantly at Brian.

Brian looked at Debbie then Alex and said, "I say we ice both of them right here, right now."

A look of horror grasped Debbie's face. Alex gulped.

Chuck weighed the alternatives. He really didn't have a choice. Debbie was in too deep to get her out. Short of murder there was no way to make sure Alex kept quiet. If they got rid of Alex they would have to get rid of Debbie. Although Chuck threatened her, he could never go through with that. He decided to give Alex a chance. "I don't know Brian. That could be kind of messy. Maybe we ought to try him out. See what he can do."

Brian shrugged.

"Debbie what are you doing this weekend?"

"Not much, I'm supposed to work Monday."

"How about you Alex?" Chuck asked.

"Nothing man. I'm free."

"We're gunna go on a trip tomorrow. We're gunna see if you two are ready to be real troopers. Let's say it will be your initiation. Remember what I said. If a word of this leaks out you'll answer to me."

Alex and Debbie shook their heads in acknowledgment.

"Brian, meet me at my place tomorrow at six a.m. Pack a bag because we're probably going to stay overnight."

"Alex, we'll pick you up tomorrow morning. Be ready at six. Debbie, do you know where he lives?"

Debbie shook her head up and down.

Chuck continued, "Remember, don't tell anyone where you're going or for how long. If anybody asks, tell them that you're going fishing. Now get the hell out of here. I want to talk to Debbie and Brian."

"Right. Uh, thanks," Alex said and then headed for his car.

"Debbie, give me a minute with Brian. I'll meet you by my truck."

"Sure," she replied, still shaken by the events of the evening.

Chuck waited until Debbie left.

"Brian, I want to go up to my uncle's old farm in Grayling this weekend. I got an idea on how to make that explosive go a little further."

"Okay. What about them two?" Brian asked.

"We'll see. Debbie I trust, except for her inexperience. I'm going to have to keep an eye on her. Alex, I don't know about. We could use the help, but it's risky. We'll feel him out this weekend. If he looks cool we'll let him stay. If he screws up, then we'll deal with that when the time comes."

Brian nodded, "We don't need anymore people in on this."

"I know that," Chuck said curtly. "What choice do we have?"

Brian frowned.

"One other thing. Do you still have your gun collection?"

"Nah, I hocked most of it. I have a few pistols left. Why?"

"We're gunna run a mini boot camp this weekend. Can't have a boot camp without marksmanship training." From Chuck's army experience he believed that you can tell a lot about somebody when you put a gun in their hand and put them on a firing range. "Bring up three pistols and some ammo with you this weekend."

"You're gunna give them guns?" Brian asked in disbelief.

"Like I said Brian, it will help us check them out. You'll see."

"I'll see you tomorrow," Brian said as he walked away shaking his head.

Chuck walked over to his truck and joined Debbie in the cab. She looked at him. Chuck returned her gaze and said, "Look, what happened out there. I'm sorry. I lost my temper..."

"Don't apologize, Chuck. It was my fault. I shouldn't have said anything to Alex. I was trying to help."

"When this is over, we'll laugh about it," Chuck said.

Debbie looked at Chuck through tight lips, then smiled and leaned toward her. His lips found hers and the two kissed with passionate abandon. Debbie pulled her head back slightly and said, "Let's get out of here. We've got to make an early start."

Chuck repositioned himself in the driver's seat and said, "Do you want to go to your place?"

"Only long enough to pack a bag," she responded.

"Sounds good to me," Chuck said as he drove away.

Chapter 11

D riving to Grayling took several hours. The cool temperature, overcast sky and leafless trees were more like winter than autumn and cast a somber mood. Alex rode with Brian in the Ford, while Debbie rode with Chuck in his truck.

Chuck was absorbed in his plans for the weekend. He wanted to accomplish much in the next two days. The first priority was to test his idea for expanding the amount of explosives they had. They couldn't keep on doing simple arsons. They did not cause enough damage; at least, not enough of the right kind of damage. Plus, arson was too risky. He knew that after the first two missions almost went awry. He was convinced that they needed to switch tactics. Using a bomb was the perfect approach. They could build the bomb, set the timer and get out. An hour later, the job is done - no high-speed getaway, no getting spotted at the scene.

He remembered a few techniques from his Army days on how to make expedient explosives, but he never put them into practice. Back then, there were always plenty of government demolitions available to do the job. He wasn't sure the idea he had would work. He needed to run a test and his uncle's farm seemed like the perfect place to do it.

After a stop for early lunch, the group arrived in Grayling at fifteen minutes before eleven. "Let's stop in town to pick up some supplies," Chuck said. "Debbie, you go to the grocery store. Take Brian with you. Tell Alex to come with me. We'll meet you back here in thirty minutes."

Chuck drove Alex to the other side of town to an agricultural supply store. Chuck and Alex wandered through the old barn-like structure examining various bags of fertilizer. Finally Chuck found what he wanted. He crouched alongside a pile of fifty-pound bags of fertilizer and carefully read the label, "Ammonium Nitrate Prills."

"Yep. This is it. Alex, grab two bags of this stuff. I'll meet you at the cashier."

Alex appeared eager to demonstrate his usefulness to Chuck.

He grunted as he lifted two bags onto his shoulders. Alex's apparent great strength surprised Chuck. Though Alex was big, he looked flabby, but he handled the bags as if they were merely two five pound bags of sugar. Chuck gave an approving nod and wandered off to another aisle. Later he appeared at the counter with a small fuel can and an empty garbage pail where he paid for the supplies. On their way back to the grocery, he stopped at a gas station. He filled the truck with gasoline but pumped two gallons of diesel into the fuel can.

They met Brian and Debbie at the grocery store. Debbie got into the cab with Chuck while Alex returned to Brian's car. Brian followed while Chuck drove north from town. After ten miles they turned onto a dirt road, driving another mile before pulling onto the driveway of an old farmyard.

"This used to be my uncle's, and before that my grandfather's farm." Chuck explained as he drove up the dirt path. "I came up here a lot when I was a kid. Technically, the farm belongs to my aunt, but she lives in Florida and I don't think she's been here for five years. I come up here a couple of times a year to take care of the place."

Chuck parked the truck and used a key to open the front door. Inside, the only furniture in the parlor was a sofa and chair covered with drop clothes. Next to the sofa was a pile of old magazines. The kitchen had a table and chairs. The cabinets were bare except for some paper plates and cups. A few canned goods lined the cupboard.

"I haven't been up here for awhile." Turning to face Alex and Brian, Chuck said, "Let's unload the bags and get to work."

"So what are we going to do, Chuck?" Brian asked.

"First, we'll unload the vehicles. Then we'll do some target practice."

When Chuck reappeared in the kitchen he saw Debbie had opened the kitchen window and was cleaning up the accumulation of dead flies and dust that gathered on the sill. Chuck approached her. She turned to face him and she reached out to hug him.

"Chuck, this house is so cute. It's adorable. I love it."

Debbie's enchantment with the quaint farmhouse surprised Chuck. He hadn't considered that under other circumstances a visit to the farm could be a romantic getaway. His attention had been focused on the business planned for the weekend. However, he had noticed that Debbie perked up when they reached the farm. He smiled as he realized that there would be more to do than business this weekend. He put those thoughts aside, "Finish up what you're doing in here. I want you outside with the rest of us. We're going to have our first training session this afternoon."

Debbie kissed him quickly and said with mock seriousness, "Yes, sir."

"Hurry up and meet me outside. I need to get my stuff."

The four assembled in front of the barn. Debbie and Alex looked expectantly at Chuck. Brian was casually leaning against the barn door. Chuck set his gym bag down and stood facing the others.

"I wanted to come up here for a couple of reasons. We'll take care of the most important thing later this afternoon. Now I have something else in mind. If we're going to finish this job without getting killed or arrested, we got to start acting more like a team. We've got to be professional and level headed. We can't have any more screw ups with security or running our mouths. We're about to get involved in some serious shit." Chuck gazed at each of the people standing in front of him.

"It's not too late for anyone to back out." No one said anything, although Alex shuffled his feet.

"From now on we're going to run things like a Special Forces A team. I'm the team leader. Brian is my assistant. You do what you're told. If Brian or I tell you to do something, do it. Is that clear?"

No one said anything. Chuck repeated, "I said, 'Is that clear?'"

This time Alex and Debbie both responded, "Yes."

"Good. Brian, give them the guns. We're going to carry these guns with us all weekend to get used to them."

Brian entered the barn and returned with a large duffel bag. Packed between his clothes and shaving kit were three handguns in their holsters and several boxes of ammunition. He handed the first holster to Debbie as he said, "This is a Smith and Wesson Model 36. It's a standard .38 caliber pistol. Undercover dicks like to use it because of its small frame."

He handed the second pistol to Alex. "You'll get this Colt Police Positive slash ten. Both of these pistols fire .38 special ammo. Before we load them though, take them out of the holster and get the feel of them."

Debbie and Alex did what they were told. Brian watched them. Both seemed familiar with handing weapons. "Have either of you ever fired a gun before?"

"Oh sure," Debbie said. "My father used to take me target shooting. Most of the time I used a rifle, but I fired his pistols a few times. I'm no expert, but I know what I'm doing."

"How about you, stud?" Brian tossed his head toward Alex.

Alex shook his head and said, "Yeah, I fired a gun before. I've gone hunting."

Brian squeezed his lips "So you've both fired guns before. Hah. You've never had to fire at another person." Brian pointed at the two trainees with sudden seriousness. From the sound of his voice both were convinced that Brian not only shot at, but also probably killed, people in the past.

"It's a lot different when the target can shoot back. Anybody can shoot a deer because the deer can't shoot back. We don't have that luxury. Our targets can kill us as easily as we can kill them. Since you've both handled guns before I'll skip the safety talk." Brian continued to lecture his two pupils on how to operate the weapons.

Satisfied that Brian could handle the task, Chuck left the group and entered the barn. He found a sheet of old plywood. Using a broken piece of plasterboard, he drew three crude human torso silhouettes. He placed the target panel against an elevated dirt berm about fifteen yards from the barn. He walked over to the group and asked, "Well Brian, are you ready to bust some caps?"

"I am. How about you two?" Brian asked Debbie and Alex.

"Go for it," Debbie replied looking nervously at Alex.

"Yeah I'm ready, too."

Brian handed each of them a handful of rounds. Then he reached into his duffel bag and withdrew his weapon. It was a larger, and a more sinister looking, .44 Automag semiautomatic pistol. "This bad boy was my favorite piece. It's a little big but it's got as much firepower as those two pistols put together and then some." He loaded seven rounds into the magazine and instructed the others to do the same. Chuck took a position behind the firing line formed by the three marksmen. "Ready on the firing line. The firing line is now clear. Firers, aim at the silhouette to your front. Fire when ready."

Almost instantly, Brian fired. The blast from the .44 Automag shattered the country quiet. He fired his remaining rounds in quick succession. The initial muzzle blast startled Alex and Debbie, but they began shooting before Brian could empty his whole magazine. The slugs tore through the plywood sheet. All of Brian's bullets found their target. Debbie and Alex didn't do as well. Some of their rounds missed the wood panel completely.

"Cease fire, cease fire." Chuck yelled. "Clear your weapons." He peered at the target panel. The impact of all seven of Brian's high-powered projectiles shredded his assigned silhouette. Alex and

Debbie scored one hit each on their silhouettes. The rest of their shots missed the target or the panel. "Alex and Debbie. Reload, and this time, fire each round slowly. Take your time and try to aim each shot.

They did as Chuck said and the results were more promising. All the rounds at least hit the panel if not the silhouettes. Alex and Debbie smiled broadly, "Piece of cake," Debbie boasted. She gave Alex a high five.

Chuck squinted at the two would-be marksmen. Although their cockiness irritated him, he answered, "Good. Now reload. Fire these rounds as fast as you can while trying to be as accurate as possible." While the two reloaded, Chuck waved Brian over to him. He whispered to Brian, "Stand behind me." Then Chuck reached into his jacket and drew his pistol, a match grade Colt .45 Double Eagle. "The firing line is now clear. Firers, on my command, open fire."

Alex and Debbie were staring intently at the target panel. They did not see Chuck raise his pistol and aim it between them. "Ready,... aim," he never said fire. Instead he pulled the trigger on his .45 and let loose three quick rounds. The bullets zinged over Alex and Debbie's heads and smacked into the woods beyond. Neither Debbie nor Alex fired a round. Alex fell prone to the ground and covered his head with his free hand, Debbie hunched her shoulders, squatted and dropped her pistol to cover her head with her arms. After the echoes from the shots faded Chuck yelled, "Fire, damn it. Make that target pay."

Alex looked at Debbie. She had her eyes closed and was shaking slightly. He reached out, aimed and fired from the prone position. The first bullet went wild and kicked up dirt to the side of the target but the rest found their mark. The crack of the pistol to her side made Debbie open her eyes. She saw Alex firing. Steeling her nerves, she knelt down, picked up her revolver and also began to fire. The firing from behind startled her, but now she was angry with herself for dropping her gun. As she fired, the anger flowed from her. She had trouble keeping her hand steady but two of her five shots hit the target.

"Cease fire, Cease fire." Chuck said. "Clear your weapons. That stunt was to make a point. We ain't training for the Olympic pistol team. We're here to learn how to kill somebody that's going to kill us if we let him get the chance. Remember that the next time you get cocky on a mission. This ain't a kiddy game." Chuck paused to let his words take effect.

"Reload and we'll do it again." Chuck waited as the two trainees slipped new rounds into the cylinders of their revolvers. They tensed and looked at the target panel when they were ready. "The firing line is now clear, at my command open fire. Ready,... aim, ... fire."

The instant the fire command rolled past Chuck's lips, Debbie opened up as fast as she could. Alex fired a second later. Chuck again fired three rounds over the trainees' heads, but this time it didn't faze them a bit. Bullets hit and ricocheted wildly around the target panel, but most found their mark making it difficult to tell who was getting a hit.

"Cease fire, cease fire. Clear and holster your weapons. We're done target shooting for today. You did well. When you're under fire you need to shoot back, even if you can't aim. You want the other guy to duck, to get his head down. That gives you time to think, time to plan your next move. Now it's time for demolitions training." Chuck reholstered his pistol under his jacket. Then he said, "Alex, you bring the fertilizer, Debbie, grab the garbage can. Brian, you bring the diesel. We're going for a little hike into those woods over there."

Alex and Debbie, both looking somewhat frazzled, sprang to obey Chuck's orders. Brian looked at Chuck and said, "Man, you are one crazy dude."

"I don't care. We don't have a lot of time to break these 'cruits in so we have to bust a few rules here and there."

"Hey, man. It's cool. You do what you got to do but don't mess with me."

Chuck smiled, "It ain't you I'm worried about. Take the supplies and tarp up that trail into those woods. I'll catch up with you in a minute."

Chuck caught up to the rest of the group by jogging briskly along the trail. He carried a shovel in one hand and his gym bag in the other. The group hiked together for fifteen minutes until they reached a small clearing in the woods. A junked pick up truck lay rusting on the far side of the clearing. "This is the place," Chuck said. "We'll dig the hole by that truck."

The group followed Chuck as he walked across the brown grass meadow. He stopped by the truck and said, "Debbie, bring the garbage can over here. I want to see how big to make the hole."

Debbie gave Chuck the can and he placed it on the ground next to the truck. He marked the outline of the can's bottom. Then he said, "Alex, dig out this hole about a foot deep."

Alex dropped the two bags of fertilizer and took the shovel.

Brian and Debbie watched Alex dig the hole.

Chuck used a pocketknife to cut the corner of one of the fertilizer bags. He poured some of the white pellets into the garbage can until a layer about three inches deep lined the bottom.

"Brian, let me have the diesel. We'll need two quarts of diesel for each fifty pound bag."

Brian handed the fuel can to Chuck. Chuck poured the fuel onto the white pellets judging the amount by eye. He then added another layer of fertilizer and stirred the contents with a tree branch he found nearby. Repeating the process, adding diesel fuel to layers of fertilizer, resulted in a sticky mixture.

"We'll have to let this soak for about an hour, but I don't think the time is too important. In the meantime we'll set up the firing circuit."

"Chuck, what are we doing?" Debbie asked. Alex stopped digging to watch Chuck. The looks on his and Brian's faces were equally perplexed.

"We're going to set up a single electric firing circuit. I don't have enough caps to go dual, so we'll take a chance. If it misfires, I'll change caps." Chuck said nonchalantly.

"If what misfires?" Debbie asked.

Brian interjected, "What he meant to say, is that we're making a bomb."

Chuck smiled at Brian and said, "That's right."

"Alex, you done with that hole?" Chuck asked.

"I don't know. Am I?" Alex said looking at the hole.

"It looks deep enough. Come over here and I'll give you your first lesson in demolitions."

When Alex joined the rest of the group Chuck began to explain, "What we're about to do is make a field expedient explosive. This here mixture is basically the explosive. The fertilizer contains ammonium nitrate, which can be explosive under the right conditions. The diesel fuel acts as an oxidizer. Mix the two together and you make a pretty good explosive. This is the same stuff those guys used in Oklahoma City."

Alex, Brian and Debbie took a half step away from the can. "Don't worry," Chuck waved his hand, "It won't go off. You could probably shoot it with your pistol right and nothing would hap-

117

pen. It's what they call 'non-cap sensitive.' That's why we'll need a booster charge. We'll use a TNT block with an electric blasting cap as the booster. I'll take care of that."

Chuck turned toward a spool of wire. "Brian and Debbie, I got a job for you."

Brian stepped forward "Yeah, what is it?"

"Take this wire and run it as far back along the trail as it will go. Leave one end here, I'll hook that to the cap leads. Come back here when you're done. Make sure you don't disconnect the ends of the wire on the far end."

"Why's that Chuck," Brian wrinkled his brow.

"Because I don't want to get killed," Chuck colored. "Both leads have to touch each other in a dead short. That will prevent static electricity from setting off the thing in my face. Understand?"

Brian and Debbie quickly nodded and started unrolling the wire.

Chuck supervised them for a few moments then looked to Alex and said, "Hey, help me put this can in the hole you dug."

Chuck and Alex lifted the can. The plastic sides bulged under the weight of the slurry. They placed it in the hole. Then Chuck said, "Pack some dirt around the can so it fits in there nice and tight."

Alex gingerly put dirt in the space between the can and the side of the hole. He was careful not to touch the can with the shovel. Chuck noticed his hesitancy and said, "Alex, let me have the shovel for a second."

Alex handed Chuck the shovel. Chuck took the tool, and stepped up to the can. Taking a big back swing he whacked the side of the can with the back of the shovel. Alex jumped back, his eyes bulging with terror. He looked at Chuck dumbfounded. The can dented and the contents vibrated, but nothing else happened. Chuck reassured Alex, "Like I said, it's not very sensitive. So don't worry. It's not going to blow in your face." He handed the shovel back to Alex saying, "Finish packing the hole."

While the rest of the group did their jobs, Chuck prepared the booster charge. He took a one-pound block of TNT from his bag, and using a Phillips screwdriver he gouged a hole into one end of the block. Then he took a plastic box out of his front jacket pocket. He opened the box. Inside were ten electric blasting caps in a piece of matching molded plastic. He gingerly extracted one of the caps, closed the box and placed the box back in his pocket.

"This is the only sensitive stuff out here. Even though this cap isn't any bigger than a cigarette, it has enough pop to take off your hand."

He carefully inserted the cap into the hole in the TNT and then gently squeezed the block around the cap. "Alex, back off from the can. Once I put the booster in the can, the bomb is armed."

Alex stepped back.

Chuck used a stick to make a cavity in the fertilizer and fuel mixture. He placed the booster into the hole and carefully packed the mixture around the booster. Then he used some duct tape to secure the blasting cap wire leads to the can. He finished taping the wires when Brian and Debbie returned.

"The wire is run," Brian said.

"Good. Everybody be careful because the bomb is armed." Chuck nodded toward the bucket.

"I got to check the wires and we'll be ready to go. While you two were running the wires, I made the booster charge. There is a one-pound TNT kicker in the can with an electrical cap initiator. When the cap goes off, it will detonate the TNT. That will make enough heat and shock to set off the fertilizer. We should see the equivalent of a one hundred pound bomb when it goes off. It won't be the same as a hundred pounds of high explosive, but it should make a nice hole in the ground."

"Why do we have to use fertilizer if we have TNT?" Debbie asked.

"Good question. We don't have enough TNT to make anything more than a few booster charges. We have to make our own expedient explosives if we want to make a decent size bang. There is only one problem. I'm not a hundred percent sure it's going to work. That's why I wanted to come up here, to test out the idea."

Chuck knelt alongside the can. He tested the firing wires with a small voltmeter to insure they were shorted. Then he unwrapped the shorted leads of the cap and connected each to one of the firing wires. "That's it," he said. "We're out of here."

He picked up the gym bag and coolly stuffed his tools in it. His calm demeanor was as much a sign of confidence instilled through previous training, as it was an attempt to provide a good example for his trainees. Alex grabbed the shovel and the four walked to the other end of the wires.

At the firing point Chuck said while he prepared the batteries, "I don't expect you all to be demo experts. But I want you to know the basics in case you have to take over for me. Is everybody ready?"

119

Then he shouted, "Fire in the hole, fire in the hole." He laid down on the ground and the others did likewise while also covering their ears. Chuck unwrapped the two firing wires and placed one on each terminal of the battery. Nothing happened. He scrapped the wires against the terminals to make better contact.

Through the trees they saw a bright orange flash and then black oily smoke. Scant seconds later the shock wave ripped over Chuck and the other prone figures. It shook Chuck bodily. The most noticeable effect was the thump felt in his chest. For an instant his lungs resonated with energy from the explosion. Then dirt, bits of leaves and small rocks rained upon him pelting his clothing and skin. Larger chunks of earth spun slowly through the air making an odd whush-whush sound. There was a loud crashing noise about twenty feet to their left. A piece of the abandoned pick up truck that was thrown by the blast smashed into a tree.

"Sheee-it," Alex exclaimed. He was closest to the falling object.

When it appeared that the dust and debris had settled, Chuck stood up. His ears rang from the blast. "Can anybody hear me?" he shouted.

The rest of the group shook their heads up and down.

"Let's go check the crater," Chuck said.

WASHINGTON, DC

The Chevy Caprice of the Yellow Cab Company jerked to a stop at the 1921 Club on Massachusetts Avenue in Washington D.C. A doorman in a gaudy uniform with braided epaulets dodged raindrops as he opened the rear passenger door of the cab. Behind him a couple sought refuge from the rain under the awning in front of the red brick restaurant.

"This is it," said Sam Gould to the taxi driver.

"Hey man, no tip," called the taxi driver as Gould and his guest scurried out of the cab.

"That's right," Gould yelled back. "Next time get me here in eight minutes and you'll get a tip."

The doorman shut the cab door as the driver uttered an Arabic obscenity.

Inside the two-story lobby of the 1921 Club, Gould approached the Maitre D' standing at a podium next to the entrance to the dining room.

"Good evening, I'm Sam Gould. I'm meeting Ms. Fielding."

"Ah yes, she is expecting you," said the Maitre D' with a pompous air like he was trying to dignify his position. "Please follow me."
The Maitre D' led him under the curved arch of the entrance into the
dining room.

Gould caught sight of Mary Fielding sitting across the room.
"Good evening Mary, you look great."

"Thanks, Gould" said Fielding. "Have a seat."

"So what's the latest on HR-5840? I hope you guys have
smoothed out the wording," she said looking over the top of the
menu.

Gould carefully spread a napkin on his lap. "I had the wording
worked out between House and Senate. There was going to be no
problem. On the surface, the bill looked tough, but in reality we gave
industry plenty of room to maneuver." Gould seemed to enjoy telling
Fielding about his influence. "Then the White House had a few comments, and the whole thing fell in the crapper."

"What do you mean crapper?" Fielding's tone betrayed a slight
annoyance.

"You know, the Chief of Staff is trying to link the compromise
wording on this to his other diplomatic initiatives. Everything this
day has to be synergistic with everything else."

Fielding put down her menu. "Gould, I thought we had an un-
derstanding here. HR-5840 will really hurt. It's not diplomacy we're
talking here. We're talking the real prospects of a trade war."

"I know Mary, that's why the Senate will never go for serious restrictions. I think the conference committee report will be in the best
interest of everyone. We are working closely with the White House
to hammer out some good words." Gould tried to sound earnest He
didn't want the bad news to ruin his free dinner.

"If anything close to what the President is saying in public gets
into this bill, there is going to be some ruckus." She threw him a
skeptical look. "You know how Japan will respond."

"We know, but politics doesn't always follow the straightest
path."

"This is risky." Fielding adjusted her seat. "How do the votes
look? My clients are very concerned."

"Don't worry. We can handle Executive on this. Let the President have his popularity ratings and let us handle the resolution."

"Rhetoric inflames the situation. Take Sunon for instance."

"Yeah, what is this about Sunon? Everyone seems so interested in them."

"What do you mean?"

"Well, a guy I jog with is a staffer for Pringle from Detroit. Pringle has him doing all kinds of background research on Sunon Corporation."

"Why?" Fielding leaned forward and turned her head.

"I don't know. Pringle is working closely with the White House on these trade restrictions. I think they may be trying to work the backfield really hard."

"I don't follow," said Fielding reaching for her PDA.

"They may think by pressuring some of the big transplant companies, they could exert back pressure on the Japanese government, kind of like a safety blitz in football. You have one of your defensive backs suddenly charge deep into the opponent's backfield."

"Can't be. If they were working Sunon, I would know about it."

"I know. That's what is so strange. My office mate says Pringle has a real creative technique on this one. It may have something to do with the UAW. Even you have to admit Sunon has a bad record when it comes to the unions."

"I'll admit nothing of the kind," Fielding almost joked but Gould could tell the wheels were turning in her head.

"Does Sunon have a big announcement or something coming up in the near future?"

"Yes, they are about to announce a radically improved sports sedan. Don't you read Autotrend?"

"I don't care about that. It's that my running buddy says Pringle is trying to time his effort to coincide with some big announcement. Pringle thinks he'll make lots of political capital on this one. The timing though has to be right."

"Really, this is strange. Sunon is already jumpy. This political attention may force them to embark on a radically new strategy, and that's the last thing the U.S. needs. With the strong yen and resurgence of the big three car manufacturers, Sunon and the other transplants are off balance. Give them a rallying point and a new business approach and it won't be long before the big boys in Detroit are up to their butts in the swamp again. And that includes Mr. Pringle."

"Wait a minute, what do you care?"

"My multinationals pay me and your boss a lot of money to make things go their way. Let's make sure they do."

Gould picked up his drink in a mock toast. "To our way."

"Cut the crap, Gould. We're going to have to turn up the heat on our coalition."

"How's that?"

"First, get the damn wording on HR-5840 turned around. Talk to the guys who have been taking my money. Remind them. Then get your boss to say something good about Sunon. Make it a public statement. I'll make sure the clippings get to the right people."

"And..." Gould's voice trailed as if he were asking a question."

"And we make a $10,000 contribution to your PAC."

"You got a deal."

Later that evening Shane's phone rang.

"Shane, Fielding here."

"Hi Mary, I'm riding my exercise bike. I could use ..."

Fielding cut him off. "Have you been on the level with me?"

"What do you mean?"

"I mean, what's going on? Are you guys getting heat from someone in Washington and you didn't tell me?"

"Washington? Huh, what are you talking about?"

"It seems Sunon is the target of a one Congressman Pringle."

Shane's face frowned in disgust as he wiped his brow with a towel. "Pringle. I haven't heard anything about him lately."

"Well, I hear he's trying to arrange some rain on Sunon's parade."

"Mary, we don't have any parades planned, at least none that I know about." He threw his towel across the room as he tried to figure out what was bothering Fielding.

"Yeah, but you do have the introduction of the 500GSX." Fielding's voice said checkmate.

"The 500GSX. He's going after that, huh."

"That's right."

"What's he going to do?"

123

"I don't know exactly, but a reliable source says that he is already running a safety blitz."

"Come on Mary, this isn't football. This is business."

"You're wrong there. This isn't business. This isn't even football. This is war."

"Then war it is." Shane paused. "What did Sun Szu say? If you can't beat them, buy them."

Fielding chuckled. "That's what I like about you, Shane. There's not a serious bone in your body."

"I am being serious."

"You mean Pringle?"

"Yeah."

"No way, he's solid Detroit. He's got more Big Three and UAW money than you could believe. Supposedly he has gotten real creative. He's running some kind of angle."

"Well you haven't seen it and I haven't."

"If there is anything…"

Shane interrupted, "I know, I'll let you know. Shoot, I would never pass up a chance to talk to my favorite lobbyist. Now, is there anything else?"

"Why yes. It's looking good on turning around HR-5840. The conference report words should be favorable."

"Great. Anything else?"

"One last thing. I did get you some good press from another influential person. Watch the papers in the next two days. It will get the attention of your friends back in Tokyo."

"Really, I can't wait."

"You won't have to for long. Anyway, if you hear anything about Pringle or a safety blitz let me know. Good night."

"Sure. Good night," replied Shane and he hung up the phone.

What the heck does she mean by a safety blitz? I didn't even know she watched football. She is really something. Shane shook his head and continued riding his exercise bicycle.

Chapter 12

Brian shrugged, "So, what are we going to do tonight? I'm feeling kind of antsy."

"We got to clean the weapons," Chuck replied. "After that I don't know. Just cool out I guess. I got a lot to think about."

"Is there anything to do in town?" Brian nodded outside.

"Not much. Town is over thirty miles away. There are a few redneck bars. I think there's a dance hall. It used to have a bar. I haven't been in a long time."

"I wouldn't mind just staying here. This house is so..." Debbie almost mouthed the word "romantic" but instead said, "Well, it's kind of cozy." She finished the dishes and was drying her hands.

"Hey Alex, do you want to go to town or stay here?" Brian yelled toward the living room.

"Don't matter." Alex rose from the couch. "I guess I'll go to town."

"First get the weapons cleaned," Chuck scowled. "Then you two can head to town. Remember, don't tell anyone about why you're here. You're just spending the weekend in the country with your friends. Got it?" Chuck stared at Alex and Brian.

Alex shook his head. Brian appeared to ignore the chiding. "I'll get the cleaning kits," he said.

At nine o'clock Brian and Alex started their drive to town. "You two be careful. Watch what you do and say," Chuck warned as they drove off.

The Grayling dance hall was converted from an old brick storefront. The interior decoration reflected the simple country tastes of its clientele. Pine board paneling, rough trim surrounded a bar adorned with scores of beer manufacturers' promotions. Along the rear wall, a DJ spun a mixture of country and easy listening tunes.

Brian quickly scanned the room as he and Alex entered from the cold. "So this is the hot spot on Saturday night. Let's get a drink." He ambled across the uncrowded room to sit at the bar.

Brian ordered a double shot of Jack Daniels with a beer chaser. He quickly downed the drink and ordered another. Alex ordered a beer and nursed it. After a minute or so Alex broke the awkward silence, "That Chuck. He's really something."

Brian glanced from his glass to Alex's face, "Chuck is cool. Strung a little tight, but he's cool. Let's not talk about that here."

Alex winced at the rebuke and didn't reply.

Brian broke into a broad smile, "Hell, a few more of these," gesturing to his drink, "and I'll be ready for some pussy. Let's see what the market will bear." He turned his back to the bar and scanned the crowd. Alex did the same. "Now there's some hot poontang." He angled his head toward the table where three girls sat. He gazed at one of the girls, a pretty brunette, for a few moments. She looked toward the bar, caught his eye and quickly looked away. Brian smiled and said, "I'll bet you with lips like that she could take the chrome right off a trailer hitch."

Alex smiled at the crude remark but didn't say anything.

"Drink up dude and we'll see if the ladies could use some company." Brian turned around and downed his second whiskey and then the beer. Alex took a swig but didn't finish his beer. "Are you ready stud?" Brian asked.

"Nah, I don't think so. I got a girl back in the city. Kinda my fiancée."

"Hey man, my lips are sealed," Brian put his finger to his mouth with mock seriousness. Alex blushed and he looked down at his feet. "Ah, all right. You hold down the fort and watch the master at work."

Alex watched as Brian walked up to the girls, said a few words and sat down. The three girls smiled weakly but appeared uncomfortable with Brian's presence. Brian's interest in the brunette was obvious, even to Alex across the room. After a few minutes of talk, Brian laughed uproariously and put his arm around the girl.

She shrunk under Brian's arm and looked thoroughly relieved when Brian removed it to pay for a round of drinks. He chugged his quickly. One of the other girls got up, excused herself and walked towards the pool room.

"So what do you say you and me get some fresh air, huh sweetheart?" Brian's voice was slightly slurred by the effect of three double whiskeys.

"I'm sorry but I'm married and my husband..."

"Don't worry about your dammed husband," Brian patted her shoulder. "He'll never know a thing. I can be very discreet"

"Please. I'm here with my husband. I don't want any trouble."

"That's the problem with you bitches, you never want any trouble."

"Is there something wrong?" A short but athletic looking man asked as he quickly walked to the table. Three other men followed close behind.

"It's none of your business," Brian said as he stood to face the stranger. His feet automatically assumed a Tee stance taught in police martial arts training and practiced many times. "I was just trying to get me a piece of ass but the bitch here says she's married. That never stopped my old lady."

"Listen mister, that's my wife you're talking about so you better watch your mouth."

Brian could see the man tense the muscles on his small frame. Brian stared into the man's face. His lips formed a contemptuous sneer but his eyes never lost their ice-cold calculation. "What are you going to do, chump? Punch me out? Be a hero in front of the old slut?" He no sooner finished his sentence than the stranger took a wild right. The alcohol had loosened Brian's tongue but had comparatively less effect on his reflexes. He ducked to his right and grabbed the oncoming forearm with his left hand. He twisted the arm and as momentum took the husband forward, he lost his balance and crashed to the floor. The three buddies moved up. Brian kicked one in the knee and he crumpled to the floor. However, the other two wrestled with him in an attempt to get him down. One landed a good hook to Brian's right ear.

Brian struggled to let go but the two held him tight. The husband got off the floor and lunged at Brian. The pile of bodies smashed into the table and then fell to the floor. Brian tried to wiggle free but the two men held. The husband got on one knee and threw a jab into Brian's gut. Brian laughed because the punch had little impact. One of the friends grabbed Brian's hair and pulled his head back. "I think you ought to apologize to the ladies," he said.

Brian winced at the pain but he forced himself to relax. When he felt the two assailants ease their grip he shouted, "Screw you!" and tried to squirm free. The effort almost worked except that the husband grabbed him by the waist and held him down. Brian was panting heavily when suddenly the husband let go and went sliding across the floor. He saw Alex pick him up and throw him like a sack of potatoes. Alex then leaned over and sent a powerful jab into the man who held Brian's hair. The punch landed solidly on his nose and knocked him

127

out cold. His grip went slack.

"Let him go," Alex said to the third man. The man complied and Brian squirmed to his feet. "Let's get outta here," Alex said.

"What for?" Brian drawled out between breaths. "I'm just starting to have fun."

"You two better clear out of here before I call the cops," threatened the manager from the gathered crowd. Neither he nor the two bar tenders appeared anxious to bounce them from the dance hall.

"Let's go." This time Alex insisted and he grabbed Brian's elbow. Alex had a vise-like grip but Brian managed to shake his arm free and grudgingly said, "All right we're out of here."

The two men slowly backed out the door.

"I better drive," Alex said as they reached the car.

Brian laughed and tossed him the keys, "Stuck-up bimbos. That'll teach them. We cleaned some house back there, didn't we?"

"Next time you pick a fight you could at least let me know beforehand," Alex said with a grin. He put the car in reverse and pulled away from the dance hall.

"Ah, if you can't get any pussy you might as well fight. What a crazy high." Brian slapped Alex on the shoulder. "Hell, what else is there to do in this hick town. Let's stop and get some beer at that store over there."

As Alex drove the car to a mom and pop grocery, Brian rubbed his ear. "Man, you handled yourself pretty well back there."

"I don't normally take on the whole place by myself but I been in a few brawls in my time." Alex said with macho pride.

"You must be some cock-strong dude. Did you see the way that slut's little husband flew across the room? Damn, that was something else. Give me five, man."

Alex slapped Brian's hand and the two men laughed.

"That should do it." Chuck had thrown the largest of the logs into the ancient wood stove. "The fire should burn for a few hours."

"It's nice and toasty here," Debbie purred. "Since Brian and Alex left for town, I'm going to take a bath."

"Have a good one, you earned it." Chuck smiled as Debbie walked up the stairs. He went to the kitchen getting a beer from the refrigerator. Back in the living room, he took off his sweater and plopped on the couch. The sound of Debbie's bath water coursed through the plumbing. He imagined the sight of her upstairs, bathing in the same tub he used many times as a child - her body, barely covered by bath bubbles. He rose to join her when he spied the freshly cleaned pistols neatly slung in their holsters by the front door. The spotless weapons reminded him of his original purpose for visiting the farm.

The test had been a success. We don't need lots of dynamite - the ammonia nitrate works better than I thought. I guess those Oklahoma City terrorists knew what the were doing. An eerie chill shuddered through his body. Until now, the idea they were terrorists did not occur to him. They were hired hands doing some corporate dirty work. Somehow that changed. The risks, the planning, the danger, and then the success with the early missions had a catalytic effect. All along, the Japanese car companies were fighting a war with America. It was an economic war and the other side was winning. Nobody in America would admit it. His job, Debbie's father, his buddies at Chrysler, all were casualties in this economic battle. Even Detroit looked like a bombed out war zone.

Now the enemy was vulnerable. They could be beaten. The first two missions showed that. Today's test showed that they had the tools to do the job. They just needed the right target.

Chuck tugged at his chin. Cannon hired him to take out the dealerships. That wasn't going to work. There wasn't any good way to destroy all the cars at the dealer. Plus, why pick on the little guys? Sure, they sold out to the Japanese, but what choice did they have? It was either that or welfare for most of them. No, they needed a better target. One that would have a real impact.

"Hi Chuck," Debbie interrupted his thoughts as she descended the stairs.

Wearing an olive drab tee shirt and jeans she looked every bit the part of an urban terrorist. Chuck could make out the outline of her athletic body through the thin fabric of the tee. He could picture her standing with a machine gun in her arms and an ammo belt across her shoulders. Her face contrasted with the exotic image. The rosy red cheeks, a product of the fresh country air, and the clean scrubbed skin with the faintest touch of freckles exuded childlike innocence.

"What are you doing? You have a funny look on your face," she said as she sat next to him on the couch with her feet folded under her legs. She propped her right elbow on his shoulder. "Hmmm?" She sighed as she looked in his eyes.

"I was thinking. Well, fantasizing really."

129

"About what?"

"You, actually."

"Anything you'd care to share?" She asked as she wrapped her arms around his neck.

"Not right now," he whispered before planting a wet, hard kiss on her lips. He leaned over and Debbie toppled backwards on the couch. Chuck followed her over and lay on top of her. The herbal scent of her shampoo wafted from her hair as he stroked his fingers through it. Her warm breasts rubbed his chest. The temptation was too much. He grabbed her shirt and tried to pull it off. Instead it ripped. Debbie groaned at the sound. Chuck smiled and pulled faster, tearing off most of the shirt. Debbie laughed and then moaned as Chuck nibbled at her neck and shoulders. She pulled on his shirt. Chuck cooperated by kneeling up and removing it himself. Then he picked up Debbie by the waist and placed her on the rug near the stove. The warmth of the stove glowed over his body as he grabbed her clothes. Debbie groped in return. He kissed her with force and she seemed to want more. The time passed quickly as Chuck sought and satisfied his urgent desires, forgetting about the bomb and Sunon.

Afterwards, Debbie rolled over and sat up. She found Chuck's shirt and put it on. Then lay her hands on Chuck's chest. "You know. I really love this house. It's like I lived here all my life. It's funny because I never lived on a farm before."

Chuck took a drink from his can and nodded his head.

"Chuck, I've been thinking," she paused

"And?"

"Well, I realize that we've only known each other a short while, but it doesn't seem like it." Debbie's eyes flickered. "I feel like I've known you forever. I can hardly remember what life was like before I met you.

Chuck searched Debbie's face as she spoke but said nothing.

"For the last few years nothing's gone right in my life. Since I met you, I have a sense of hope. I have a chance to settle the score and get on with my life." She stopped talking and looked into the grating of the wood stove. "One thing's bothering me."

"What is it?" Chuck was surprised by the tone of his question and his own genuine concern for Debbie. Man I'm in too deep, he thought.

"I don't know. I guess last night made me think. Where is this going? How do we get out when it's over?" She looked at him with wide, worry-filled eyes."

Chuck put down his beer and took Debbie's hands, "You don't have to get out when it's over."

"What do you mean?"

"Look Debbie, we have to finish a few more jobs. We got to put the hurt on them. We got to do something with an impact. Something to wake up America. If we're careful, then nothing will happen. We'll get our money and that will be it."

"What about you and I?" Her eyes dropped to the floor.

"What about you and I?"

"Wasn't tonight and the last couple weeks something special? Didn't you feel it?"

Chuck looked at, but beyond Debbie. He had to admit that he did. Debbie was in love with him. What scared him was he was in love with her. Finally, shaking his head he said, "Yeah, I felt it. I shouldn't have gotten you involved in this."

"No, Chuck." She squeezed his hand. "I'm glad you did. I want to be involved. I want to do my part. For the last few years, all I could think about was how those scheming Sunon bastards ruined my life. I was so angry. I wanted to lash out but there didn't seem to be any way. It was futile." Debbie pursed her lips. "Think about it. What can a poor struggling waitress do to settle the score with a Japanese megacompany?"

"I can think of a few things," grinned Chuck.

"I know. That's what's so incredible." She put her face up against his. "You're like my knight in shining armor."

Chucked looked down at her head "You know Debbie, this is going to get really intense before it's all over."

"It's intense right now. Look," Debbie sat up and faced Chuck squarely. "I love you. I'm in this until the end, bitter or sweet."

Chuck smiled, "Are you sure?"

"One hundred percent."

The next morning Chuck found Alex asleep on the couch. Brian was in the kitchen. He sat on a chair, his elbows resting on splayed knees. He cradled a coffee cup in both hands. His black hair, slicked back after a shower, and his dark Mediterranean skin and two day stubble contrasted sharply with his fresh white T-shirt. He appeared completely recharged from his night on the town. He looked up and smiled, "Coffee's ready."

131

"Thanks." Chuck said cheerfully. "We got to talk about our next mission."

"What's the plan?"

"We got to change targets."

"What does the man want?" Brian emphasized the word "man."

Chuck poured himself a cup of coffee and considered how to answer Brian's question. "He doesn't care. He wants us to put the hurt on them big time. Doing the dealerships ain't working."

"So how do we do that?"

Debbie walked into the kitchen as Brian finished asking his question. "Good morning," she said cheerfully. She gave Chuck a kiss on the cheek before opening the cupboard to retrieve a plastic cup. "Don't let me interrupt."

Chuck spoke as he poured Debbie a cup of steaming coffee, "I don't know. It's got to be some kind of corporate thing. Not another dealer. Someplace where they keep their cars. Something like that."

"Sunon doesn't have much in the Detroit area. There's that building in Troy."

"Yeah, that's their corporate headquarters." Debbie said. "I've been by there."

Chuck laughed, "That'd be nice, but it might be too hard a target."

"How about the parts warehouse?" Debbie suggested. "I visited it one time with my Dad. It's somewhere in Sterling Heights. I think. It's on a side road in an industrial park. Near some railroad tracks. It's kind of isolated."

"What's it like?" Chuck straightened his back with interest.

"It's a real big, plain looking warehouse. God, it's about a city block square. Inside is row after row of parts. Tires, fenders, engine parts. You name it. If I remember what my Dad said, it's the distribution point for repair parts for the whole country east of the Mississippi. I remember how proud Dad was about being affiliated with it. That was before they screwed him, of course." She added the last remark almost as an afterward.

"That sounds like it has potential. We'll head back to Motown today. Tomorrow we'll meet at my place at eight o'clock. Then we'll go out and recon these two targets. See what we can find out. All right?" Chuck asked and looked at Debbie and Brian.

They both nodded.

Chuck pointed at Alex, "Brian, wake up sleeping beauty so we can get some chow. I'm going to take a shower."

When Chuck found out that the feed store in Grayling was closed on Sunday, he changed plans. He had Brian drive Debbie to Warren on Sunday afternoon. Alex and he remained at the farm until Monday so they could buy twenty fifty-pound bags of fertilizer from the feed store. The load made his pick-up sag to the rear but they made it to Warren as the sun was setting. Alex helped Chuck unload the bags into the storage shed next to his garage apartment. There was no sign of Mrs. Fischer. Chuck drove Alex home.

"I'll see you tomorrow night," he said as Alex leapt out of the truck.

"Right. You'll pick me up at eight?" Alex sounded somewhat tentative.

"That's right. Remember, man. Not a word to anyone."

"I got it. See ya."

The prospect of the next mission loomed as he drove away. From Debbie's description the parts warehouse seemed like an ideal target. He decided to drive to Sterling Heights to try to find the building and learn the local area. He found a phone book at a pay phone in a restaurant. There he copied the warehouse's address on the margin of the Detroit map page of his Rand and McNally Atlas. Finding the warehouse was a simple task.

It was pretty much as Debbie described. A large one story building made of several rows of concrete blocks below vertical metal siding. There was no indication of the occupants except for a relatively small sign at the entrance to the parking lot. Its carved and painted wood face simply read, "Sunon." Truck loading ramps and doors lined the side of the building to the right of the main entrance. The rear was adjacent to a rail siding that also had several portals to access trains. Sodium vapor lamps illuminated these three walls. The north side of the building was a long expanse without any doors, windows or lights. Weeds and litter piled against the building hinted that this area was rarely used. The utility service entered at the corner of this wall and the front. Several unmarked semi-trailers were neatly parked there. Four cars were parked on the other side near the main entrance.

"This is looking good," Chuck whispered to himself. He left the Sunon facility and drove up and down the adjoining street. The neighboring businesses appeared closed. Most of the parking areas were empty. A few trailers were scattered about. There was no sign of people or workers.

133

A tractor-trailer rig pulled into the Sunon warehouse when Chuck passed on his way home. So there is some activity here at night, he thought. We'll have to find out when they shut down.

When Chuck returned home he called Brian to confirm the meeting on Tuesday night. Then he called Debbie. Two rings later Liz's electronically distorted voice told him that no one was home. He hung up without leaving a message on the machine.

Although he was tired, he went back to his storage shed and began rummaging through the boxes in the back. In one of the boxes he found a copy of an old Army manual on explosives and demolitions.

Back in the house, he made himself a cup of instant coffee and began skimming through the pages. It was a long time since he last looked through this book, as the musty smell and yellowing pages could testify. With his memory refreshed, he did some crude arithmetic. After an hour of scribbling and scratching he believed he had the answer. He went back to the shed and stared at the fertilizer. In his head, he formulated the designing of a bomb.

Chapter 13

Chuck was busy the next day buying the materials needed to construct the bomb. Later at his home, he fashioned the timer mechanism. "This will be the most likely thing to screw up," he thought. "Got to keep it simple."

He took an old-fashioned wind up alarm clock and taped two electric wires to the hands such that when the minute hand passed the hour hand, the two wires touched. Moving the hands with his index finger, the contact closed the electric circuit.

"Pop goes the blasting cap," he blurted then smiled. Methodically, he reassembled the modified clock and tested it several times. After each trial he adjusted it to insure it worked smoothly. Finally, satisfied with the way the timer operated, he placed it aside.

"Now we need a plan," he thought as he ground his teeth slowly.

Later that evening, Brian and Alex arrived followed soon by Debbie. They sat in the small living room, eyes flickering at each other but not saying much.

After a few moments, Chuck entered from the kitchen and faced the others seated in the room. He began. "This is the plan. We're going to use a car bomb. Actually, it will be a truck bomb." He held up a piece of paper,

"I did some figuring last night. A Fifty five-gallon drum filled with fertilizer and diesel slurry weighs about 200 pounds. If we use two of these, they should make a twenty foot crater in the ground."

Alex ran his finger around his plaid collar and Debbie squirmed in her seat while Chuck continued.

"If the truck is parked close to the wall, the crater will extend into the building's foundation. That should do a number on the wall and breach it. If the blast gets inside the building, which it should, the place will get pretty well scrambled."

"Whose truck will we use?" Debbie eyes blinked with concern.

"We'll steal one. Didn't you say you could steal cars, Alex?" Chuck stared at Alex.

Brian jumped in, "Hell, any kid who grew up in Detroit can steal a car. No problem."

Chuck raised his eyebrows. "Brian was sticking up for Alex. Good teamwork," he thought. Then he said to Alex, "Well?"

Alex smirked, "No problem. I can steal a truck."

"Cool. I have everything else we need." Chuck started pacing back and forth. "We have to pick the time and day. We need to case the place to find the best time for the hit. We'll up there tonight together to check it out. Then we will set up a watch." He stopped and motioned toward Debbie. "I'll team with Debbie. Brian teams with Alex. We'll watch the place for a few nights to find a time when no one, or at least the fewest people, are around. Got it?"

Brian, Debbie and Alex nodded in unison.

"Let's go."

They arrived at the warehouse at nine thirty P.M. While they sat in Brian's car, they noticed several semi-trailers pull into and out of the warehouse.

"It's definitely too busy to hit at this time of night. Brian, you and Alex come back tonight after midnight. Debbie and I will do it tomorrow. We'll get together Thursday to work up the final plan."

Brian pulled out of the parking lot and started home. "You know," he said almost as an aside, "this is going to get a lot of attention."

"What do you mean?" Chuck asked while he scanned the exit route.

"Well, you set off a couple hundred pound bombs and people start to get interested. The fire department, police, ATF and maybe even the FBI will be swarming over this place like flies on honey. We got to be careful. This is a big time felony, dude."

Chuck didn't reply. Alex stretched his neck as if Brian's comment didn't phase him. Debbie gulped slightly.

"It don't bother me none though," Brian continued. "As long as I get my money and don't get caught, I'd shove a stick a dynamite up the mayor's ass. Heck, I might even do that for free."

They all laughed.

"You're right, though," Chuck stopped laughing and his face grew grave. "We got to be real careful. No screw-ups. But I don't mind the attention. Didn't you always want to be famous?"

"Yeah, the mad bomber of Detroit. That's me. Right up there with Mrs. O'Leary," joked Brian.

"What do you two think? Anybody getting cold feet?" Chuck said as he turned to the rear to face Debbie and Alex.

Debbie put her hands on Chuck's neck and gently massaged his muscles, "Not me."

"Me neither," said Alex.

"Alright. Let's go for it."

Brian took Alex to his house after dropping off Debbie and Chuck. He prepared a pot of coffee and made a couple of bologna and cheese sandwiches. "Got to have something to munch on when you're doing a stake out."

Alex hunched his shoulders, "Sounds good. Say, Brian. I never asked Chuck but...," he paused.

"But what? Come on boy, spit it out. What's on your mind?"

"Well, I'm like you. I'm in dis for the money."

"So. What else is new?"

"Well, no one ever told me how much I'm gunna get," Alex dug his hands in the pockets of his blue jeans and lowered his gaze, embarrassed by his apparent greed.

"Hell, I don't know. Why don't you ask Chuck?" Brian retorted. "I don't even know how much he's getting paid. If Chuck hasn't said how much, I'm sure he has a reason. Do the job and don't worry about it." Brian chose not to mention his previous payments.

Brian and Alex returned to the warehouse after midnight. They noticed that traffic into the warehouse had slackened. It was quiet by one A.M.

Chuck and Debbie observed the same behavior the next night. On Thursday, the four met to develop the final plan. Brian and Chuck discussed most of the operational factors. Debbie occasionally asked a question. After a few hours Chuck said, "All right, let's go over the basics, Brian and Alex will get the truck tomorrow evening and bring it here."

Brian smiled at Alex and gave him a thumb's up.

Chuck continued, "In the meantime, Debbie and I will prepare the bomb. When you get here, we'll load the truck. Brian will drive while I ride shotgun. Alex and Debbie will follow in the car. You wait for us down the street. I'll arm the bomb. After five minutes you come and pick us up and we split. We wait at my house. If the bomb goes off, I'll give you your money and we go home. Any questions?"

Chuck waited, but no one said anything. "I'll see you tomorrow night. Oh, one last thing. Debbie and Alex, have either of you ever been fingerprinted?"

"Not that I know of," Debbie was taken aback.

"Me neither," shrugged Alex.

"Are you sure? Never been arrested?" Chuck said looking at Alex.

"Nope. Never."

"See you tomorrow."

"Why did you want to know that?" asked Debbie after Brian and Alex left.

"Just background information. I'd like to know some things about the people I'm working with."

"Me too," said Debbie. Then she hugged him and gently pushed him towards the bedroom.

LINCOLN COUNTY, KENTUCKY

The fresh air, rolling hills, and farms of Lincoln County, Kentucky, made Kondo uncomfortable. The hardwood forests and bluegrass pastures outside window of his chauffeured Sunon sedan were beautiful, but to Kondo they were alien. He might as well have been on the moon. He didn't belong here. Look at the faces of the people; they knew it. The land knew it. Worst of all, he knew it. Both the simple country dwellings and imposing farms made him anxious and lonely. It was the same loneliness he had when he learned his mother had passed away.

"Driver, please speed up, I'm in a hurry."

How could it be that the longer he lived in the United States the worse he felt about venturing from his own home and office? America was so grand, so expansive, so varied. Why could he not find some place that would make him comfortable? Every time he saw a tree or a grassy field, he felt like an intruder; like a voyeur.

Yet Kondo had no longing for Japan. He had emotionally and physically detached himself from there long ago. Each day that he was separated from Japan, the more alienated he felt. It was as if all the facsimile messages and telephone calls to and from the corporate headquarters stretched the Pacific Ocean wider and wider.

"I can never return to Japan. It would be unbearable," he muttered. "This is the largest and most important market for Sunon and Sunon's North American operations are mine. I created it. I deserve it."

He recalled when he first learned he was selected to manage Sunon's North American operation. Sunon was in trouble in the home market and needed to copy the success the other Japanese automobile manufacturers had in the U.S.

"Kondo-San, I am pleased to announce that you will head our North American manufacturing operations. You will thrust the corporate banner of Sunon onto the mainland of North America," spoke Toshi Itoh, the Chairman of Sunon Corporation. "America is a great market and we must have a presence."

"Shucho, I am grateful for the chance to serve the company," humbly replied Kondo hiding the bubbling sensation in his stomach.

Looking at the Chairman, he said, "This will be an extreme challenge. I will devote body and soul to the task. Sunon must develop the American market." Kondo hoped the words sounded sincere and masked his enthusiasm. Kondo knew he was the youngest Sunon executive to be given the responsibility for an overseas operation; not any overseas operation, but the North American operation. He felt an inner pride, like a sumo wrestler strutting off the dohyoo but it would send the wrong impression if he let anyone else know it.

Itoh continued speaking to the other board members. "Kondo-San will have the responsibility for establishing Sunon's first manufacturing facility in North America. Sunon will soon be able to say our high quality cars are made in USA. This will let us overcome our very small export allowance under the new trade restraint." Itoh's flat voice hid the irony.

"Kondo San deserves our confidence. He will do his best to earn it."

That's right, Kondo thought. The board of directors had finally recognized his potential. It was only right. He was the one who advocated expanding the manufacturing base to the United States. The others were too blind to see it. They wanted to continue to improve domestic manufacturing to achieve economies of scale and cost advantages but they didn't anticipate the small export allocation that MITI would give them. Overseas manufacture was the key to Sunon's success. This was a way to skirt the Japanese government's self-imposed automobile export restraint. Besides most of our competitors had done so already.

"Five years, that's all it took - now we have a manufacturing powerhouse in this rural countryside," he mumbled under his breath. "How could Takahashi expect me to agree to a plan that would tear down all that he had worked so hard to build in America? Take this away and I am nothing." His voice rose.

"What was that Mr. Kondo?" the driver of the Sunon sedan glanced in the rearview mirror.

"Huh, oh, oh nothing. How much longer?"

"Almost there, Mr. Kondo."

Kondo's sedan approached the factory entrance. In the distance the sun glinted off silver trim of the maroon brick factory walls. The executive glanced at his watch. He had only five minutes until his scheduled meeting. As the sedan drove up the driveway to the entrance, Kondo's portable phone buzzed. Kondo removed it from his jacket pocket.

"This is Kondo speaking," he said in a clipped tone.

"Mr. Kondo, this is Claire. We received a FAX from Panama. The Honshu Prince is there."

"What about it? I'm in a hurry."

"Well, the ship has a mechanical problem. It is going to be delayed."

"Delayed? How long?"

"It will need a few days to get repaired. Something called the main shaft seal failed and caused minor flooding in the engine room."

"Damn, this will interfere with our plans to introduce the 500GSX," Kondo thought out loud. "Claire, have Mr. Shane contact me today. Let's see," he looked down at his schedule for the day. "Have him call me at 12:05 p.m. Kentucky time. He can reach me on my cellular phone."

"Yes Mr. Kondo, I'll tell Mr. Shane. Is there anything else you would like?"

"No."

"Have a nice day and have a safe trip back. Good-bye," came Johnson's cheerful voice.

Kondo grunted and hit the disconnect button on the phone. So the ship is delayed, Kondo thought. This is the first time a ship has been delayed in over two years and with the first shipment of the 500GSX. What bad luck.

Kondo entered the conference room that was at the center of the modern plant. As was everything in the plant, the architecture and layout were carefully planned to complement the Sunon management style.

Jim Greer, the plant manager, an affable man in his mid-fifties with a middle age paunch rose to greet Kondo. Greer, like the others in the room, was wearing the khaki Sunon uniform jacket over a white shirt and club tie. He shook Kondo's hand. "Kondo-San, how's it going. Have a seat. We're ready to get started." Greer gestured to a plain but new conference chair.

Kondo shook Greer's hand and nodded his head to the other managers in the room.

"The first item on the agenda is a review of the month's production figures."

"I have already seen the report," interrupted Kondo. "Are there any changes?"

Greer looked over at the production manager who moved his head to say no. "No, the report is accurate."

"Good, then let's talk about the union situation."

"I'm a little concerned about this. When we first started here in Kentucky we successfully thwarted a unionization attempt but this time the situation is somewhat different," Greer frowned.

"How so, Jim?" Kondo looked over his glasses.

"Well, when we started here we were a new quantity and we had no established UAW presence in Kentucky. It was easy for us to bring in a bunch of workers new to the auto industry."

"Well, that is still true. That's why we picked Lincoln." Kondo leaned back in his chair and crossed his arms. "There is no union tradition there."

"As you know, GM brought the UAW into Tennessee with the Saturn plant. After failing to organize the Toyota plant in Georgetown, the Kentucky local turned their eye to our plant. Since our arrival they have been running a disinformation campaign against our plant."

"Disinformation. What do you mean?"

"Oh, sort of a propaganda campaign. It started out when the union ran an ad or two in the local paper. Once the seed of doubt was planted some of the employees began to think that the grass was greener on the other side of the hill."

"I see."

"This is similar to the tactic that the UAW used at other Japanese transplant sites," chipped in Ellen Bronsky, the Manager of Human Relations at the plant. "Union organizers try to make it sound like the just-in-time system puts too much stress on workers. Well, once the leaflets appeared, we noticed an increase in lost time."

"Yeah, that's right. Thanks, Ellen, for reminding me about that." Greer motioned toward the west. "The organizers have set up a small office downtown and are trying to collect enough signature cards to bring a union vote to the factory floor. Now, there are rumors that the UAW has sponsored a pro-union group of our workers. Supposedly a group of employees are excited about the prospects of a union. They have loosely organized themselves. Shoot, they even call themselves 'The New Horizons.' I don't know how far they've gotten but the rumor on the floor is that if they keep growing they may get enough people interested again in a union vote."

"Well, how serious do you think this is?" Kondo trusted the advice of the practical plant manager.

Greer twisted his lips. "It can get pretty serious. This past week, a quality action team asked to look at the accident data for the whole plant over the past five years."

"Certainly our employee relations haven't dropped to the point where the union could win." Kondo's eyes searched Greer's face and the others in the room.

"I don't think so, but I'm worried about the counter-productive effort we will have to do to keep the union out. My concern is that now, they have found gullible employees to believe them."

"Your concern is warranted, but remember we must avoid the derisive adversarial relations that the UAW encourages." Kondo's stiffened his back. "We must have a satisfied work force. Do what it takes to improve working conditions. We need a content, but hard working labor force."

"We have a plan that we should finalize next week. We would discuss it at your convenience."

"Good," Kondo both hands flat on the table in front of him. "I'll eagerly await your recommendations. Is there any more discussion about the unionization attempt?" No one spoke so Kondo continued, "Now what about this afternoon?"

Bill Ketchum, the Lincoln Plant's public relations representative rose and adjusted his jacket. "We're all set at the Community College over in Wintrop. There'll be a small presentation and a reception following. The college is very excited about the donation. That robot equipment will rocket them into the next century. There's been lots of good press about it. Why heck, even the governor is going to be there this afternoon."

"Oh really," Kondo leaned back in his chair and smiled. "To refresh my memory, please summarize what we are giving them."

"Sure Mr. Kondo," said Jim Greer. "As you know, we recently upgraded our subassembly lines with new robots similar to the ones over in the Shizuoka Plant. The surplus equipment, what was it? Three Naehi Vorg welding units and a Tokico Finishing unit - they were still in pretty good shape. We didn't need it, so, with a little refurbishing, we donated it to the Community College at Wintrop. They'll be able to use the equipment to set up a whole new curriculum on robot technology and maintenance."

"That sounds good."

"It is in lots of ways," said Greer sounding proud. "We can write off the equipment and we help guarantee a stream of partially trained robot technicians for the future."

"There should always be synergy in activities, particularly those that involve our relations with our outside community. How far is Wintrop from here?"

"Oh, it's about a 35 minute drive."

"Then we have time to walk the plant and have lunch."

After lunch, Kondo and Greer left the sedan parked in front of the college laboratory when Bill Ketchum came running toward the car. Greer could see the concern in his face.

"Jeez, Bill, what's going on?"

Still panting, Ketchum blurted, "It's the union," he gasped for air, "They set up a protest at the ceremony. The media is all over them."

"The union, what the hell are they protesting here?" Greer looked incredulous.

"It's the New Horizons, they are trying to grab some publicity."

Kondo broke in, "Have the police escort them away."

"We can't, the police guarding the governor say they have a permit. They're within their rights. So far there hasn't been any trouble, but they are getting a lot of press attention."

"Well, let them protest, it ain't going to do them any good," Greer pointed indignantly toward the protesters.

"No, we can't let them upstage our publicity," Kondo fumed. "This affair is critical to our public relations campaign. Mr. Ketchum, I want you to talk to your media associates. Tell them to ignore the protest."

"I can try Mr. Kondo, but they don't always respond."

"Then talk to the editors. Threaten to pull our advertising dollars. Use our leverage, damn it." Kondo turned and glared at Greer. "Do I have to get Jack Shane down here?" The icy stare added to the threat.

"No, no, I understand." Greer made a stopping motion with his hands. "I can take care of it"

"Good," said Kondo as he pulled down his coat jacket and buttoned the front. "Let's get inside."

After the ceremony at the school, the Board of Regents sponsored a cocktail party at the new robot laboratory.

"Kondo-San, how good to see you again," said the Governor of Kentucky, vigorously pumping Kondo's hand. Kondo had grown used to the custom of shaking hands, but he never liked it. It implied a degree of closeness that he would never actually allow.

"Yes, Governor Jones, it is nice to see you again."

"I must say, your plant has been a bigger success than we all imagined."

Kondo replied, "We have worked hard. Together we will continue to prosper."

"Ha, that's my boy, keep on plugging, the old Japanese way." Jones' delivery had a good old boy sound to it. Kondo recognized the unintentional defamatory comment, yet he did not respond.

"You know Kondo-San, the state and the county are grateful for the selection of a new manufacturing facility in their area. If Sunon has any expansion plans we would be glad to help you in your efforts."

"Your offer is gratefully acknowledged," replied Kondo knowing the real impact the Sunon factory had on Kentucky. By locating Sunon's plant there, the local government was guaranteed the arrival of a host of other new business and that meant votes for the governor. "We are still working on improving the Kentucky plant. We have no definite expansion plans."

"I'm sure we could make some sort of satisfactory arrangement."

"I appreciate your consideration, Governor. Sunon values our good relations with your office."

"Okay, Kondo-San, but if you need anything, give me a call."

WARREN, MICHIGAN

Once Brian knew they would need to steal a van, he kept his eye open for one. He took Alex to the area where he had previously identified a likely candidate. It was an early eighties Chevy van. He told Alex, "There it is. Been there a couple days. If it starts, it's an easy steal - jimmy bar on the door and slide hammer on the ignition. If anyone shows up or I got to split, come and get me. If I get it started, follow me to Chuck's house, but don't get too close."

"I can handle it." Alex voice quaked.

"Hey, man. You look nervous. Mellow out. This is a piece of cake," Brian grabbed his tool bag and walked away. "Just be cool."

Brian walked nonchalantly to the van. The street was deserted. Walking past the car, he checked to make sure it was unoccupied. He turned and walked up to the driver's side door. Using gloved hands, he slid a long thin piece of metal between the window and the door and made a slight upward motion. The door popped open.

Alex saw the van's brake lights glow. A few seconds later, the exhaust let out a gust of smoke and the engine growled to life. He followed the van to Chuck's house.

"God damn van needs gas," Brian said as he walked into Chuck's apartment. "How's it going with you guys."

"Pretty good. We got the drums filled with the slurry. We'll load them into the van, put the booster charges in each can and set up the firing circuit. That shouldn't take too long."

The van was loaded and bombs primed by ten o'clock after which Chuck said, "Let's relax. We'll take off at eleven thirty."

LINCOLN COUNTY, KENTUCKY

It was too late after the reception for the aircrew of the Sunon Corporate jet to go back to Detroit so Kondo took a room in a hotel to wait for the start of their next work day. The hotel, near the Lincoln County airport, was a modest but comfortable Holiday Inn and it had a good restaurant. Kondo went straight to the bar after checking in. Still feeling the effects of the drinks he had at the reception, he none-

145

theless ordered a double Black Velvet.

"A little nightcap to help me sleep," he made a motion of putting a drink to his lip. "What else is there to do is this sleepy town."

The bartender nodded and gave Kondo the drink. After a quick swig Kondo turned absentmindedly examining the other patrons of the bar. A small group drinking and laughing in a booth near the bar's TV caught Kondo's eye. They were wearing Sunon factory uniforms. Kondo stared over his shoulder at one of them, a stout man he didn't recognize drinking a beer. The man laughed at something, slammed his drink on the table and pulled a redheaded woman close to him. The man kissed the woman fully on the lips. She didn't resist. He then groped her, his hand squeezing her breasts. She laughed and kissed him again.

Kondo turned and stared at his drink. Kondo mulled the couple in love. I never felt a love like that. I can't even remember the last time I was with a woman. It was well before Kumiko left me. She had had a difficult pregnancy. We stopped having sexual relations for medical reasons. After Masako's birth, we never resumed.

I should have had a normal family life but Kumiko wouldn't make the sacrifice of supporting a career man. Masako's birth should have changed that. It didn't.

At 11:30 p.m. Kondo staggered to his room, an almost empty bottle of scotch in his hand. Unsteadily he unlocked the door and nearly fell flat of his face when it swung open. Catching his balance he jerked toward the bed, pulling on his tie and kicking off his shoes. He took another drink from the bottle of scotch. The liquid had no taste to him as he blacked out on the bed.

At the appointed time Chuck gathered the group in the kitchen. He passed out their weapons. "Lock and load. Safeties on."

Chuck watched the others prepare their weapons. Brian handled his without a second thought. Debbie and Alex were clearly not accustomed to carrying a loaded weapon, especially in the city of Warren.

"Don't think about why you need them. Carry them and be ready," ordered Chuck.

At five minutes before midnight, Chuck and Brian pulled into the Sunon parts warehouse lot. Brian drove slowly to the north corner. He parked near the wall. "How's this?" he asked Chuck.

"A little closer."

"You won't be able to get out of your door."

"I'll get out on your side. Okay. Stop here." Chuck spoke with clipped tones. His voice was steady and calm. "Turn off the engine. I'll arm the bomb. He climbed into the back of the van. He removed his black leather gloves to reveal a pair of surgical rubbers. Moving deliberately he placed the electric blasting caps into the kicker charges. He connected the wires to the firing circuit, which he had previously laid out.

"That's it. I'll connect the wires to the battery when they show up."

Chuck watched out the rear window of the van. Despite sitting next to the bomb he felt safe.

After a couple of minutes, Brian spotted headlights in the rear view mirror. "That looks like them. Right on time."

Alex pulled the Escort to the curb. Debbie looked apprehensively at the van through the passenger window.

Brian craned his neck to look up and down the street. "Everything looks clear."

"All right. Get out. I'll be out in a second," Chuck ordered.

Brian jumped out. He climbed into the back seat of the Escort.

Chuck connected the two wires to the firing batteries. He stepped out of the van. He calmly closed the door and checked to see if it locked. Then without looking back, he joined Brian in the back seat. "Home, James," he said with a grin.

"How'd it go?" Debbie creaked from a dry throat.

"Just peachy," Chuck smiled. "Now let's hope it goes off like it's supposed to."

The group arrived at Chuck's converted garage in Warren. Chuck looked at his watch. "Any time now," he said. The four entered the garage and took seats in Chuck's cramped living room.

"Anybody want a beer?" Brian asked opening the refrigerator. He took out a six pack and passed cans to the others.

"What do we do now?" Debbie's eyes grew wide with worry.

"Nothing. We wait. Give me back the guns. I'll keep them."

"Think we'll hear the explosion down here?" The pop of Brian's beer punctuated the question.

"I don't think so. We'll watch the tube. If it goes off, I'm sure

147

we'll see it on the news before long." Chuck pushed the television remote's "on" button. David Letterman had started his monologue.

The wind-up clock ticked its final second. The shiny contacts of the lead wires met surging electric current through the circuit, instantly heating the wires in the sensitive blasting caps. Their explosion initiated the carefully planned sequence of events. In a fraction of a second the small caps set off the kicker charges that, in turn, detonated the fuel-fertilizer mixture. Chuck and his group would have been surprised by the intensity of the explosion. The steel drums provided much better containment for the mixture than the plastic can used at Grayling resulting in an explosion that thoroughly consumed the can's contents.

The van disappeared in the expanding fireball. Chunks and shards flew through the air gouging the ground and walls of neighboring buildings. The blast wave ripped into the pavement, shattering it, then reflected back, as if it had had enough of the hard earth and sought the easier air through which to travel. The shock wave expanded outward knocking over three semi-trailers. It reached the wall of the warehouse, whose broad sheet metal surfaces were only designed to withstand slightly more than hurricane winds, tearing the metal to pieces, like autumn leaves off trees. The violent blast pulsed through the warehouse and blew open doors and windows on the far walls. Parts boxes, steel frames, and building insulation flew through the air.

The blast twisted and ripped the utility lines serving the building. The gas main whooshed. Sparks from the bared lines set off the volatile pressurized vapor creating a bright blue flame that roared out of the crater and angled into the building. Once neatly stacked boxes became pillars of fire. In a few seconds, the raging inferno spread from the corner of the warehouse down the aisles of the building.

Electronically controlled servos would have normally engaged the sprinkler system to rain water on the fire. They couldn't because the bomb crater destroyed the water mains and interrupted power to the building. The sprinkler system sat useless while the fire raged.

The image on Chuck's television segued to a local car dealer's advertisement for no-money down, zero percent financing. The television spokesman's strident voice obliterated any chance for Chuck to hear the dull boom. By the time the noise from the blast reached Warren it was not discernible from the sound of city life.

148

Nicca and Jones were on duty at the fire department headquarters. Nicca was on his way to the bathroom when he noticed an excited commotion from the radios in the main dispatcher's office. He side-stepped there to see what was the matter.

The radio speakers on the walls were blasting in simultaneous confusion. The night dispatcher had two phones up to her ears and was shouting instructions to her assistant, also on a phone.

"What's going on?" Nicca directed his question at the assistant, a harried looking rookie in a blue work uniform, as she hung up the phone.

"There's a real cooker up in Sterling Heights. It might be a gas explosion in a warehouse. They've called down here for assistance. She's trying to figure out which companies to dispatch up there. It hasn't been busy tonight, then all of a sudden all hell breaks loose."

"What kind of warehouse was it?" Nicca scanned the computer screens flashing in front of the dispatcher.

"I don't know. Sterling Heights asked us to send up our Hazmat emergency response team." A radio call from the hazardous material team asking for directions to the fire interrupted her.

"Ten-four," she nodded. "The address is 42106 Greystone Circle, Sterling Heights. The location is one Sunon automobile car parts warehouse. Suspected hazardous chemicals on site. Possible gas leak caused the fire. How copy? Over," the dispatcher released the key button on the microphone.

"Good copy," crackled the speaker. "Have an escort meet us at the Rochester exit of I-75. We'll need to know where they want us."

"Roger," she turned to pick up the phone to call the Sterling Heights fire department.

Nicca didn't hear the rest. He hurried back to his office. Grabbing his coat and briefcase he shouted, "Willy, get your coat. We're going up to Sterling Heights. There's a multiple alarm up there."

"What for? That's not our jurisdiction."

"I know. It's a Sunon building!"

At the scene in Sterling Heights, fire fighting rigs and every other kind of emergency vehicle blocked Mound Road north of Metropolitan Parkway. Local police were detouring the late night traffic south away from the scene. The magnetic blue gumball on the roof of Nicca's unmarked car served as a pass through the chaos. Jones parked the car in a lot near Greystone Circle. Nicca dismounted and with his hands on his hips scanned the scene before him. The whole warehouse was ablaze. Flames roared a hundred feet into the air.

"Hey Willy," he yelled over the whop-whop echo of two helicopters hovering above. "Remember this one. Its a biggie."

Jones whistled.

Nicca approached two fireman laying water hoses for pumper trucks to bring more water to fight the blaze.

"What's the story, fellows?" waving his badge.

"Hell if I know. This one's a handful," replied one of the men between gasps of air. "We got here an hour ago, but they told us to hold up, the place might blow again. We had to wait for the gas company to shut off the line. By then it was out of control."

"Yeah, we had a lot of trouble finding a damn hydrant that worked," added the other wiping his brow with a towel. "I guess the explosion ruptured a water main. We've had to pump water from everywhere."

"Who's in charge up here?" Nicca looked for a command vehicle.

"I don't know. We're from Troy. Probably somebody from Sterling Heights. Try over there," he said pointing toward a group of parked official sedans.

"Thanks a lot guys."

Nicca hustled toward a group of men near the fire cars and after a few questions, located the fire captain in charge.

"Hello, Captain. I'm Investigator Nicca and this is Investigator Jones from the Detroit Fire Department. We're..."

"Detroit? No time to talk, gentleman. I'm up to my ass in alligators right now. Excuse me," he said as he turned around to talk on the radio.

Nicca hid a reaction to the curt response.

"You two fire marshals from Detroit?" came a voice behind Nicca.

Nicca turned to face a tall, uniformed state police sergeant. The trooper was thickly built and wore a Smoky-the-Bear style Ranger's hat on top of a closely cropped hair. He had a sharply chiseled chin with a distinct cleft and clear blue eyes.

"That's right. I'm Investigator Nicca and this is Investigator Jones." Nicca flashed his badge.

"Sergeant George Denzer," the trooper extended his hand. "I'm with the Michigan State Police Arson squad. So what brings you guys up here?"

"A hunch, sergeant." Nicca glanced from Denzer to Jones. He knew that most of the suburbs surrounding Detroit didn't have their own arson departments and had to rely on the State Police to handle their investigations. "This might have something to do with a case down in Detroit."

"An arson case?"

"We've been looking into two at their automobile dealerships. I think there's a connection."

"We're not really sure if this one is arson yet. So far, the line doggies say it was a gas leak and explosion."

"What do you think?" Nicca's eyes poured over Denzer's face. He'd decided he liked Denzer.

"Don't know yet. The fire's been out of control since I got here. We'll have to wait and see what we can find out once we get inside."

"That might be awhile," Nicca motioned toward the fire blazing behind the sergeant.

"If you want, you can tag along with me. I'll stick with the captain. Once it's under control we can go in together."

"Good. Willy, stay with the car and listen to the radio. If they need us back in the city let me know."

"Roger, Joe," said Jones sounding disappointed with his assignment.

"So what's with that captain anyway?" Nicca asked Denzer when they were alone.

"I don't know him that well. He's probably overwhelmed with such a big burn." Nicca watched a television news crew shine a bright light on the captain while a reporter prepared to interview him.

"Yeah, he looks real busy," Nicca sneered.

"The bomb should have gone off by now," Chuck glanced at his watch. "I wonder how it did."

"Maybe we could take a ride up there and check it out?" offered Debbie.

"Big mistake," Brian sat forward on his chair. "Never go back. Easy way to get nailed."

151

"Brian's right. If the bomb worked we should hear about it soon enough. Hey, what about the scanner? Maybe we can pick up something." Chuck opened a closet and looked for the scanner.

Debbie watched him and then returned her gaze to the television. The station cut away to a special news report. "Hey guys, here it is. Look!" She pointed at the screen.

A news anchor read a statement, "MICHIGAN STATE PO-LICE ANNOUNCED TONIGHT THAT A LARGE EXPLOSION DESTROYED A WAREHOUSE IN STERLING HEIGHTS. NO ONE HAS BEEN REPORTED KILLED OR INJURED BUT ONE HUNDRED HOMES HAVE BEEN EVACUATED AS A SAFETY PRECAUTION. FIRE FIGHTERS CONTINUE TO BATTLE THE BLAZE. LIVE REPORT COMING UP..."

"Holy cow. Look at those flames." Debbie's face whitened.

"We did it!" shouted Chuck, smacking his hands together. "Get me another beer to celebrate."

"What started the fire?" asked Brian.

"Who knows." Chuck shrugged while smiling. "Maybe something inside. This is great. I can't wait to see the report."

The fire fighters finally got the blaze under control. While they sought out and extinguished scattered smoldering remains, Nicca followed Denzer as he circled the building. Nicca stopped when he spied the crater at the north corner. Powerful lamps from several fire engines lighted the area.

"Jeez, look at that," said Denzer, pointing to the crater. A fireman and an ANR, the Gas Company, representative were standing on the edge. They shined a bright flashlight into the five feet deep and twenty feet wide hole.

Nicca circled the crater, a gaping hole, about ten feet from the building.

"Denzer, there was a big explosion here. And look, it doesn't extend into the building." Nicca crouched to get a better look at the cavity. "The edge stops at the concrete foundation."

"Hmm," Nicca considered the evidence as his eyes followed the spotlight in the hole. "This explosion happened outside the building." He twisted his head sideways. "What could have happened? A gas pocket in a sewer, maybe."

The gas company man stiffened his back and said, "Nah. No way. The gas line here ran straight through the dirt. Then it turned up and came out right along the wall, where there used to be a meter. There's no way we could have had an explosion out here." He pointed to the center of the crater, which was clearly outside the building.

"He's right," Nicca stood and using his flashlight searched the area around the crater. In less than a minute he found the twisted and burnt remains of an automobile door. He bent over and inspected the door without touching it, then waved toward Denzer.

"You better seal off this place."

"I was thinking the same thing." A grim look crossed Denzer's face.

Nicca shined his flashlight at the crater. "Look at the way the crater lines up with the gas line and wall. No place for the gas to accumulate. If the line exploded under ground, we should have had a deeper crater. No, ANR is right. This wasn't a gas explosion. Something exploded above ground, here." He stomped his foot.

The Sterling Heights Fire Captain drove up to the crater. He and three other men exited the car and walked to Denzer. "So Sergeant. What do you figure caused this mess?"

"I don't know. We'll have to investigate. I think we should set up a cordon around this crater here."

"What for?" the captain said impatiently. "Wasn't this a gas explosion?"

"Sir, pardon me, but I'm with ANR," the gas company representative sounded nervous. "We would rather you not make that claim until an investigation can be conducted."

"I understand your concern for bad publicity, but this had to be a gas leak. What else could have caused an explosion like this?"

"A bomb," replied Denzer.

"A bomb," the captain's jaw dropped. "This isn't Beirut, Sergeant. People don't bomb buildings in Sterling Heights."

"That's what Mario Cuomo said," Denzer paused. "Right after the World Trade Center bombing. And he's not governor anymore."

Nicca noticed Denzer kept his voice flat. He was making a point, not trying to antagonize the captain.

"Pardon me, Captain. I need to have a word with you." said one of the men who got out of the captain's car. He was dressed in an expensive trench coat over what appeared to be a tuxedo. His face had blanched when Denzer had made a reference to a bomb. The captain stepped aside and spoke in quiet tones with the man. Nicca saw the captain shake his head up and down several times.

"Who the heck is the guy in the penguin suit?" Denzer crooked his thumb.

"A Sunon rep.," Nicca dug his hands in his pockets. "I met him a couple of days ago. I'm not sure what he does, public affairs, advertising or something, but he's some kind of big shot."

The captain returned to the crater. "Cordon off the area and conduct your investigation. There'll be no release whatsoever about the cause. If anyone asks if it was a gas leak, say that it's under investigation. No mention of a bomb is to be made to anyone, especially the press. You got that?"

Denzer shook his head up and down. The captain and the Sunon representative returned to their vehicle and drove to the other side of the building.

"I'll seal off the place. We got to get the lab people out here," said Denzer.

"Can I make a suggestion?" Nicca said.

"Sure, what is it?"

"Get the ATF or better yet, the FBI forensics lab. They have the best chance of figuring out what caused this."

"That's a good idea. I'd like to get the FBI, but we'd have to convince them this is a federal case. Sure would be nice to get them out here while the trail is still fresh." Denzer made some notes on a pad. "The captain sure got agitated when I said it could be a bomb."

"Sure, you know why." Nicca winked. "That Sunon guy asked him to downplay the whole thing. As it is, it will probably be on every TV channel in the morning. Maybe even FoxNews and CNN. I'll bet you that Sunon doesn't want the word to leak out that someone is burning and bombing their facilities."

"Hey, Joe," a voice called out.

"What is it, Willy?"

"We got an auto fire down in East Detroit. They want us to check it out."

"Oh, I'll be right there." Nicca turned to Denzer, "Here is my card. If it turns out to be a bomb, then we might be working together on this one."

"Right. Thanks for your help."

As promised the live report came on in fifteen minutes. Chuck stood transfixed as they watched an aerial view from a news helicopter. Then the screen jumped to the face of the Sterling Heights fire captain. He released a brief statement.

"What caused the explosion?" the reporter asked.

"It's under investigation." he replied.

"Some say it was a gas explosion. Can you confirm that?"

"That's possible but the cause is officially under investigation. I have no further comment," replied the obviously harried fire captain as he bulled his way past the reporter.

The reporter signed off and the program returned to the late movie after the Letterman show.

"Whew, that was something," Brian wiped his brow with a beer bottle.

"A gas leak. What makes them think it was a gas leak?" Debbie asked out loud.

"What else are they going to say?" Brian said as a statement more than a question. "They can't really say anything that would affect the investigation."

Chuck stood and faced Brian and Debbie, "Yeah, well I wonder. People got to know it was a bomb."

"Why's that?" Brian sneered. "Who cares what people think?"

"That's the whole point, Brian. We got to let the average Joe know that there is a way to get back at these guys."

"What the hell are you talking about? I'm not on some crusade. I only want my money." He threw down his beer.

"Brian, there is more to this than money." Chuck felt his neck veins bulge. "We got a chance to get even with these dirt balls. Somebody's got to do something. Why not us?"

"Look, don't give me any politics What's gotten into you, man? If you want to get your rocks off on this thing that's fine with me. I don't give a rat's ass. You give me my money, I'll do what you say, but don't give me no politics."

"All right god damn it." Chuck trembled as she stood there. "You want your money." Chuck backed up and retrieved three envelopes from the desk. "Here's your money." He tossed the envelopes on the floor in front of the sofa. "But don't tell me this ain't important."

"Oh Chuck, come on," Debbie jumped between Chuck and Brian. "Let's not fight among ourselves. We did good tonight."

Chuck glared for a moment, then smiled "Yeah, we did do good. That warehouse is history." He put his arm around Debbie then turned to Brian. "You are one cold mother. Only interested in money. That's cool, but don't give me anymore shit."

Brian made a mock salute.

"I'll give you all a call in a few days to set up the next job. Good work tonight. A couple more and we'll be all done."

LINCOLN COUNTY, KENTUCKY

The hotel's wake up call at 6 a.m. pulled Kondo from his drunken slumber. He saw the message light next to his bed blinking as if it were in time with the throbbing in his head. After stumbling through a shower and shave, his body started to recover from his pounding hangover. He dialed the front desk and got Shane's message. Quickly, Kondo punched Shane's mobile number into the phone. He had to do it two times, as his shaking hands kept hitting the wrong numbers.

"Yeah, this John Shane."

"This is Kondo" rasped the executive.

"Kondo-San, we tried to reach you last night, right after it happened but we couldn't get through."

"I turned off my cell phone, I needed some sleep." The lie didn't faze Kondo. "What do you mean 'it happened?"

"Oh hell, we had a big fire, no, I mean explosion at the parts warehouse in Sterling Heights. I've been up all night coordinating the public affairs effort."

"Did you say explosion?"

"That's right, they think it was a gas line, but it could be arson. The investigators are still checking out the scene."

"I must get up there right away. How much was destroyed."

"The place is toast."

"Huh?"

"Everything burned up."

"Everything?" Kondo rubbed his temples.

"Maybe the walls are standing. I was at the scene with the Fire Captain. I gave him the proper instructions."

"Could this be related to those fires at the dealerships?'

"Don't know, one good thing is so far they haven't found any

156

bodies. We're not missing anyone."

"Oh," Kondo paused. The full impact of the fire had not become apparent to him. "What's your take on the situation?"

"Bad, the logistics guys say we will really have to scramble to meet the routine parts deliveries in the north central area but they are already working on a plan to iron out the parts flow."

"I will return right away. Have a car meet me at the airport."

"Yes Mr. Kondo. There's not too much left to do but we'll have a full briefing for you when you get back."

"Yes, I want to know everything." Kondo hung up the phone.

He then called the front desk and asked for the pilot's room. The pilot had finished shaving when Kondo called.

""Good morning, Smith here."

"Captain Smith, this is Kondo, how soon can the plane be ready?"

"Ah, we're scheduled to depart at 9:30."

"I must leave for Detroit right away, how long will it take to get ready."

""Well, we have to file a flight plan, preflight the aircraft. Probably take us an hour."

"Good I will met you at the airplane in 50 minutes, be ready to go."

When Kondo entered the Sunon Headquarters building in Troy he sensed uneasiness in the air. Bursting into the executive conference room he saw Shane still wearing his tuxedo but with the tie loose around his neck like Cary Grant in Bringing Up Baby.

"What is the latest situation, Mr. Shane?" Kondo put down his briefcase and took a seat at the middle of the table.

"Well, the fire is out. Amazingly no one was hurt or killed. There was a big explosion but so far the fire department doesn't know the cause. The fire captain tells me they suspect an arsonist."

"Dame desu," Kondo uncharacteristically issued a Japanese epithet. "An arsonist! What is happening here?"

"We don't know. Anyway, the damage was extensive to both the building and the material inside so we've been working since 2 a.m. on a contingency plan. Hara and Kawasaki will be here in a few minutes to discuss the preliminary plans for working around the damage."

157

"Good, I want a full report, then I want to visit the site."

When Hara and Ryoichi Kawasaki, Sunon's North American marketing director entered the room, Kondo was sitting at the end of the table, a scotch on the rocks in his hand.

"Good! You are here, let us start. I want a full assessment of the situation in Sterling Heights and how it will impact our North American operations. Mr. Shane, since you were at the scene, you start."

Shane stood and paced in front of the conference table.

"Right, last night right after the Museum Benefit, I got a call from the Fire Captain that there was a major explosion at our warehouse up in Sterling Heights. When I got there the warehouse was in flames. I'm talking a major league fire here. The building was totaled and almost everything inside was destroyed. Well considering the strange fires at the two dealers I convinced the Fire Captain that we had a sensitive situation so he agreed to keep a lid on any announcements until they had a chance to clear it with us. In the meantime, we had them announce that it was probably a gas leak. Oh course it could still be. So far they haven't figured out the cause.

"I want to meet with the investigators and hear their report."

"I can arrange that." Shane brushed his hand through his tussled hair.

"Now, what will be the impact on operations?"

"As far as the introduction of the 500GSX goes, I don't see any impact. In fact, I've been thinking about how to turn this fire to an advertising coup. We should get our advertisers to come up with something. After all we got a lot of free publicity out of this."

"Good thinking, there may be a way to use this publicity to our advantage."

"Precisely, I'll look into it later today."

Kondo sat back in his chair crossing his arms in front of him. After a moment he said, "the fire is not such a disaster after all." Kondo savored that last point with a long tug from his drink.

Hara, silent until now, leaned forward in his chair. "Excuse me Kondo-San. What about the fire? There must be a reason. A link to the other fires could cause concern about a degrading political situation."

Shane answered while Kondo placed down his drink "I don't think so. According to the investigators no one has taken credit for the fire. This has the cops thinking this is not a political situation. Terrorists usually call in to take credit for an attack."

158

Kondo made a twisted look. "Shane is right Hara-San, there is no reason to make more of this than necessary. We have no evidence yet of any wrong doing. This could be an accident. I will go to the scene and make my own assessment, meanwhile, Kawasaki-San, you are to estimate the parametric effects of the fire on sales and market share and on the repair parts sales. I want a report by this afternoon."

"Wakarimashita, I will have it ready then." Kawasaki bowed deferentially to his boss.

"Shane, I want you to figure out a way to capitalize on this fire. Meanwhile, work hard to keep the cause of fire under wraps. Regardless of the cause, we don't need any more distractions from the introduction of the 500GSX. It was bad enough the ship is delayed in Panama."

"Understood," Shane looked weary, the effects of his sleepless night hung under his eyes.

"And Shane, try to catch a few hours sleep and change your clothes. You look ridiculous sitting here in a tuxedo with droopy eyelids."

Everyone managed to laugh at Kondo's small joke.

Chapter 14

N icca had been asleep two hours when the phone rang. "Hello," his voice cracked.

"Nicca, is that you?" came a curt reply.

"Yeah. Who is this?"

"This is Captain Wilson. Did I wake you up?"

"Yes, sir, you did. I worked the night shift..."

The captain interrupted, "What the hell were you doing up in Sterling Heights last night?"

"Oh." Nicca paused, "I was checking on a lead to the Sunon case."

"Don't we have enough work for you down here? You know I only have twelve investigators to cover the whole city. I don't need you looking for extra cases."

Nicca was wide-awake now and the hairs on his neck rose as he expected a tongue-lashing. "I was checking on a lead for the Sunon case. There was a major fire up there and I wanted to see if it tied into the two fires down here..."

"Yes, yes, yes. I never understood you arson investigators anyway. Well, you must have made quite an impression because the commissioner called me to request that you represent the Detroit Fire Department on a special task force to investigate these Sunon fires. Apparently the mayor's office is also following this quite carefully. You report to the FBI's Detroit Field Office at noon today. Your point of contact is Special Agent Mike Gunston."

"What about Jones?" Nicca asked.

"He stays at headquarters. Hell, I can't afford to give up you, let

160

alone another guy."

"Yes, sir. I'll be there."

"Good. I want you to report back to me anything you find out. I want to know what's going on before the mayor does. Is that clear?"

"Perfectly."

"Wrap this up as fast as you can, Nicca. I need you back here. As much as I hate to admit it, you're the best we've got."

"Thank you, sir. I'll do my best."

Nicca put the phone back in its cradle and looked at the time. Ten thirty. "There goes another day off." He staggered into the kitchen, put on a pot of coffee and then headed into the shower.

Across the city, another telephone rang. Chuck was already awake and answered it.

"Holzer? This is Bob. I saw the news. Did you do that?" Cannon was clearly excited.

"Oh, um. Hello. Are you sure you don't want me to call you back?"

"What? Oh, forget that spy bullshit. Did you do that?"

"Sure did. Not bad if I say so myself."

"You must be out of your mind. I never told you to do something like this." Cannon paused to catch his breath, "That's it. No more. The job's over."

"Now hold on Bob. The job ain't over. First of all, you owe me money. Since the last job went so well, I think that we need to double the fee..."

Cannon cut him off, "No problem, I'll double the fee, but that was the last job..."

"No, Bob! I'll tell you when it's the last job." Chuck pressed the phone close to his mouth saying the words slowly and firmly. "We started this. Now we're going to finish it. I don't think our customer has quite got the message."

"I don't want anything to do with this. I'm out."

"Sorry Bob." Chuck meant to sound icily calm. "You can't back out of this now. You're in this as deep as we are. Deeper."

"You watch me."

"Now hold on a second. Put your thinking cap on." Chuck smiled as he turned the tables on Cannon. "You've got a lot more to lose than I do, Bob. I can disappear. I ain't leaving anything behind. You, on the other hand, have a few roots in the ground. I don't suspect you'd be willing or able to up and leave. Particularly if someone started poking around asking questions."

"Screw you, Chuck."

"Now, now, Bob. Let's not get nasty. One or two more jobs is all it will take. Then it will be over. You'll have what you need. I'll have what I need. Do you understand?"

"Yeah, I understand. You're a god damned maniac."

"You knew that when you hired me." Chuck's laugh pierced the phone line. "Why don't we meet for dinner? How about your favorite haunt? You can give me the money you owe me."

Cannon was silent for a moment. Finally, he said with resignation, "Meet me at five tonight at Dave's place. I can't stay for dinner. I'm going to the Detroit Symphony tonight. I'll meet you in the parking lot."

"Now you're thinking smart. See you at five."

Chuck stared at his own handset imagining Cannon shaking and sweating as he disconnected the phone. "I call the shots now. Don't forget it."

Nicca had been to the FBI field office before, but never in circumstances such as these. He showed his badge to the guard at the front desk and asked for Special Agent Mike Gunston. The guard dialed a number and announced Investigator Nicca's arrival.

"Someone will be down to pick you up in a few minutes. In the meantime, you might want to fill out a form so you can get your own entrance badge."

Nicca had finished filling out the form when a man of average height and build dressed in a dark blue business suit approached. "Investigator Nicca?"

"That's me."

"Pleased to meet you. I'm Special Agent Mike Gunston. Why don't you come upstairs and we'll get you to meet the rest of the team." Gunston's suit was a classic Brooks Brothers cut, starched shirt with matching Italian silk tie. His tasseled wing tip loafers glistened.

Nicca adjusted his open neck sport shirt, tugged on the bottom of his leather jacket, and pulled up his wrinkled khakis as he followed Gunston to the elevator.

Gunston and Nicca got off the elevator on the third floor, and walked through a large bay jammed with desks to a small conference room. Nicca recognized Sergeant Denzer from the previous night and returned his nod. Gunston said, "Investigator Nicca, this is Special Agent Laura Snell. She and Sergeant Denzer are also assigned to this special task force." Nicca and Snell shook hands.

Snell was tall and thin. Her light brown hair cut short and casually styled around her plain girl-next-door face complimented a dark gray suit with a red paisley scarf and black pumps. She looked more like a young MBA from General Motors Finance than an FBI special agent.

Gunston continued, "Let's get settled and we'll start." He looked at Nicca, "You're probably wondering what you're doing here. As you know, last night a powerful bomb destroyed an automobile parts distribution facility in northern suburban Detroit. The Michigan State Police requested FBI forensic assistance in analyzing the crime scene. We've already dispatched our local lab people and have requested a contact team from the FBI Headquarters Laboratory. They should be on the way to the scene, as we speak."

Gunston spoke quietly with the slightly nasal accent Nicca recognized as native to Detroit. Nicca guessed he was ten years older than Gunston, but he immediately respected and took a liking to him. Snell, on the other hand, acted bored and impatient with the briefing.

Gunston walked to a white board at the front of the room. "Later this morning, the SAC, that is the Special Agent in Charge, my superior, received a call from the Mayor's office requesting we look into a possible link between this incident and two earlier arsons committed at Sunon automobile dealerships. After he and I discussed the situation with Sergeant Denzer, he decided the Mayor's and the Michigan state police's requests for forensic help could be better facilitated by the use of a special task force. Considering the nature of last night's crime and the possible international repercussions if these crimes continue, it is imperative this investigation be concluded in as expeditious a manner as possible." Gunston leaned forward with both hands on the conference table. "You should realize domestic counter terrorism is the highest national priority program for the FBI. I've been assigned to head the special task force. However, we are here to work together to nail the persons responsible for these acts." He paused to look at each task force member. "And to ensure that no further acts are committed. We can bring the full assets of this field office or, if necessary, the entire FBI to bear. Sergeant Denzer is the liaison with the Michigan

State Police." Gunston turned to Nicca. "Investigator Nicca is the representative from the Detroit Fire Department. You come highly recommended by Sergeant Denzer."

Nicca looked at Denzer and smiled.

"Anybody have any questions?"

Denzer raised his chin. "Why did the mayor request FBI assistance?"

Gunston shrugged, "I'm not sure."

Nicca said, "That's an easy one. The Sunon execs are buddies with the mayor. Hell, after the second arson, my boss ordered me to brief some Sunon corporate types on the progress of the case. They say Japanese managers consider all angles. These guys are no different."

"That's right." Denzer snapped his fingers. "Didn't you say that one of the executives was at the fire scene last night?"

"Uh huh. I recognized him. He was riding herd on the Sterling Heights Fire Captain."

Gunston looked at Nicca, "Well, Investigator Nicca, since you have the longest experience with this case, perhaps you could lead off by briefing us on the progress you've made so far. Give us whatever level of detail you have. We know how you local guys have a knack of adding up the little details." At this suggestion, Snell opened a notebook to a clean page.

Nicca took a deep breath, and exhaled, "So far, I don't have much to go on. Most of what I know is what this case isn't. The two cases in Detroit don't add up. If you'll indulge me I'll go through the possibilities and you'll see what I mean."

"Please do." Gunston grabbed a seat, listening closely while Nicca spoke.

"Let's see," Nicca stood, gesturing with his hands. "The most common reason for arson in Detroit is revenge, lovers quarrels, that sort of thing. But those are usually amateur jobs and this work has the mark of a professional. Most arsonists are losers. Contrary to popular belief, a professional arsonist is rare. Second," Nicca held up two fingers. "This wasn't arson to conceal another crime like murder since there have been no bodies or evidence of robbery or other crimes, at least none that we've found.

Walking around the table, Gunston and the other's eyes followed him. "Third, there have been no suspects that fit the hero syndrome or vanity fires. They're usually done by bored security guards. That

164

leaves profit motive or terrorist arson, both of which could involve professionals. Both of the torched businesses were thriving and successful. Insurance covered most of the damage but the fires cost the owners money, so it definitely wasn't for the owners' profit."

In front of the white board now, Nicca turned and wrote with a red marker - 'TERRORISTS.' "Either extremists or international narcotics traffickers. There have been no extortion demands nor any claims. At least none that anyone has admitted."

"What do you mean by that?" Denzer scanned Nicca. "You suspect something?"

"Well, the Sunon big boys are feeling heat from somewhere but I can't put it together."

Snell scribbled furiously at Nicca's last comment.

"No one has taken credit for the arsons or the bombing!" Gunston tapped a pencil on the table.

"No one, so far," Nicca replied and looked at Denzer. Denzer also shook his head.

"Are you sure these were arsons?" Gunston queried.

"Absolutely. At least the two fires at the dealerships. In both cases the perpetrators used gasoline accelerants. When an arsonist uses gasoline he or she might as well put a sign that says, 'Arson here.' Gasoline never completely vanishes in a fire. Both times I could tell even before using the hydrocarbon sniffer because of the obvious smell. The puddle patterns and glass fragments on the floor indicated Molotov cocktails. Multiple points of origin. Alligation patterns. Everything indicated arson. Also, in the second fire, the perps disconnected the alarm system so they could get inside. These are some rare birds. They know what they're doing. I haven't had a similar MO in the last ten or so years."

"What do you mean by alligation pattern?" Snell furrowed her forehead.

"It means the crackled pattern a piece of wood gets when it burns very intensely. It usually indicates the point of origin of a deliberately set fire using some kind of accelerant."

"Thanks," Snell nodded.

"Any eyewitnesses?" Denzer flipped a page in his notebook.

"None," Nicca frowned, "but they're hard to come by at three A.M."

Denzer shook his head in acknowledgment.

Snell put down her pen. "Do you have any files on these cases we can study?"

Nicca looked at Snell and raised his eyebrow. "I don't have much time for paperwork but I have a few reports back at my office. I can get them later."

"If the first two fires were arsons set by professionals, then it follows that they might know about and have access to explosives. That makes me think that there is a better chance these cases are linked." Gunston turned to Denzer. "Sergeant Denzer, could you brief us on your case?"

"Yes, sir. With Investigator Nicca's help, our initial investigation seems to indicate that at approximately one twenty a.m. an explosive device was used by persons unknown to destroy the Sunon," Denzer checked his notebook, "Eastern Division Parts Distribution Center located in Sterling Heights. I have no eyewitnesses or suspects as yet. I've not received the report from the bomb units. Damage to the building was extensive. No injuries or casualties were reported. Apparently the building was unoccupied when the bomb went off. No one called in a warning or has attempted to take credit for the explosion. According to the warehouse manager, this distribution center supplies the whole midwestern portion of the country. Its loss will put a big dent in Sunon's repair parts resupply system. The manager believed it would take several weeks to get the other parts centers to handle the increased load."

"Have there been any other acts of sabotage or violence targeted at Sunon related businesses?" Gunston's voice had an air of authority.

Nicca replied, "I checked with the Detroit Police Racketeering and Organized Crime Units. They had nothing in their files. Nobody I've checked with heard anything on the street."

"I see," Gunston paused his eyes internally focused deep in thought. Then he continued, "Let's go over what we have. In the last two weeks, out of the blue, two Sunon automobile dealerships, professional arsonists torch thriving businesses. Then a large bomb destroys a Sunon warehouse. There are no warnings or threats. No witnesses or suspects."

Scanning the room Nicca saw the grim faces of his fellow team members.

Gunston continued, "We don't have a lot to go on. We'll have to start with the basics. First thing is to see what the lab unit finds out. Hopefully the perpetrators left something useful at the bomb scene. In the meantime, we need to see if we can figure out why Sunon is the target. Who stands to gain from this? Laura, I want you to do a search for all violent crime relating to Sunon and its employees. Also, get a list of all Sunon facilities in the local area. Nicca, you might be able to help her with that."

"Right," Nicca raised his eyebrows. A female partner.

"I want to inspect the bomb scene personally. Sergeant Denzer, could you accompany me up there this afternoon?"

"Yes sir."

"I appreciate it. Laura, leave a message with me when you get something. Let's plan on meeting back here tomorrow at eight a.m. to go over what we've found. We should have something from the bomb analysis then. Nicca, I want to visit the arson sites?"

"I'll take you to them."

"We'll do that tomorrow. Everyone get cracking."

Before they could get up, a secretary entered the room, "Mike, a message for you. The mayor has asked that you brief the President of Sunon on the status of the investigation."

"All right, Snell, Nicca and I will handle it. Schedule an appointment."

Gunston and Denzer left the conference room to drive to Sterling Heights. Snell picked up her papers and said, "We might as well get going on the searches. Come on. The terminal is in the other room."

Nicca followed her to a small cubicle containing a new personal computer, modem, and stacks of manuals. They took chairs facing the screen.

Snell reached for a piece of paper in her Daytimer, "I have to check the password to get started."

"I haven't much of a knack for these things," Nicca motioned toward the computer. "My partner Jones, he is a whiz with them."

"I've been using a PC since high school, but every system has it's own quirks. The FBI system has several security wickets you have to get through to log on." Snell booted up the computer.

"How long have you been with the FBI?"

"This is my third year. Although, I've only been in Detroit for six months. Before that I worked CI-3 in the Washington field office."

"CI-3?" Nicca scratched above his ear.

"That's the counterintelligence section that tracks Soviet, oops, I mean the CIS spies. It used to be one of the biggest field divisions in the FBI. When peace broke out, they reassigned us to other field offices. I picked Detroit because it had the most action but wasn't too far from DC. My fiancé is a defense analyst with a consulting firm in Northern Virginia."

"What did you do before the FBI?"

"Hold on a sec. Let me log on to the Domestic Threat Warning System." Snell typed in a seven-digit password.

"I went to law school at Georgetown and did my under grad at Stanford."

"Impressive schools. I'll bet the big law firms were after you."

Snell laughed. "No, not really. I didn't want to sell out and bill thousands of hours on insignificant and boring corporate mega-mergers. Even if it was for big bucks. Working for the FBI looked a lot more interesting. At least some of the cases are."

"What do you mean? Too much FBI computer work?"

"Counterintelligence was a lot more exciting. We were up against professionals. They were good. It was like a game; there were rules to play by. So far in Detroit I've only dealt with white collar crime, and some petty bank robberies."

Nicca pushed back his chair and interlocked his hands behind his head. "Well this case could get exciting."

"Maybe, but I doubt it. I don't have much sympathy for the victims. The Japanese had it coming to them the way they've been buying up American businesses and taking over neighborhoods. When I was in Stanford, you could see it happening. One time I was jogging on campus and got mugged by a bunch of punks from an oriental gang." Snell creased her forehead. "Ever been to California?"

"No. I usually take vacations around here, fishing, that sort of thing."

"You'd be surprised by the things are going on. A friend of mine works environmental law in LA. She says the Japanese are quietly buying up all the water rights. Ten years from now if there's a drought, California will be in deep trouble." Snell stopped and turned her head to the terminal as it flashed the response to her query. "Hmm, this is interesting."

"What is it?" Nicca stared at the blinking icon on the screen. "I don't see anything."

"There's nothing to see. The search came back negative." She touched the screen above the data. "None of the U.S. intelligence agencies have anything on terrorism against Japanese targets in the U.S. Usually, even the smallest tidbits of information get put in the

DTWS. It's weird. Nothing shows up. Nada." Snell leaned back in her chair.

"Is there anything else to try?"

"Let's go with some other keywords and see what comes up. We'll also query the NCIC. Also I think we should check the Canadian Security Intelligence Service files. They could be operating out of Windsor."

Nicca snapped his fingers. "Good idea."

"A lot of criminals and terrorists can't resist that four thousand mile border between us and Canada. They don't realize how closely we cooperate and share information."

Although they tried several different approaches they didn't have much luck. After two hours of searching all they could find were reports on Japanese gang violence in Los Angeles and a case where an American worker threatened and then stabbed a Japanese executive in his home in California.

"See -- what did I tell you about California?" Snell smirked at Nicca.

"Hey Laura," Nicca paused. "I can call you that?"

Snell nodded. "Sure, we're going to be partners. I reserve 'Special Agent' for interrogating."

"It's a crazy world, but California doesn't have any lock on it. Ever been here on Devil's night? One thousand fires in a four-hour period. The city looks like Dresden during World War two. Makes you wonder. I guess that's why we have our jobs. To keep a few of the crazies under control."

Nicca looked at Snell. Her skin was young and smooth. She could be my daughter, he thought.

Snell tilted her head. She seemed to detect the sadness in Nicca's face. She smiled and waved her hand. "I guess you're right. You'll have to pardon my bad mood. I was supposed to go to the Michigan game today with some friends."

Nicca stood. "I know what you mean. You hungry? I know a good place in Greek town. They make a great mousaka."

"Sure, let's go. I'm getting tired of carrot sticks and yogurt."

Chuck spotted Cannon's Cadillac entering the small parking area alongside Dave's restaurant. He got out of his truck and walked to Cannon's car. Getting in Chuck said, "Evening partner. How's it hanging?"

"I have your money for the last job. Double the fee." Cannon forced a smile and handed an envelope to Chuck. Chuck opened it and counted the thick stack of hundred dollar bills.

"That's it, Chuck," Cannon said. No more jobs."

Chuck finished counting before replying, "Why? Aren't you happy with the work we've done?"

"Look Chuck. You've done more than I asked. Way more. It's too much for me." Cannon opened and closed his hand around the steering wheel. "It could backfire. Somebody could get hurt. People might get the wrong idea."

"What people? Didn't you see the news today? Seems like most of Motown agrees with me. Take out the bastards. If the government won't take action why not us?"

"What's going on with you?" Cannon's voice quaked. "I hired you to take out a few dealerships. Now you want to take out the whole Japanese car industry."

"That's right man. These scumballs think they got it made. Well they're wrong. Dead wrong. America has got to fight back. They've been screwing us over for too long. Look at Debbie. The Japs screwed her and her father royal."

"Who's Debbie?"

"Never mind," Chuck pursed his lips and jerked his head sideways. "She's a friend."

"All right. Calm down. Calm down. Let's be reasonable. You've made your point. How much would it take to make you stop?"

"What are trying to do? Buy me off?" Chuck put his hand to his chest.

"I want to put an end to this madness. I don't know whatever possessed me to do it in the first place."

"Why do you give a shit about them anyway? They screwed you like they've screwed everyone else."

"Yeah, yeah," Cannon mumbled. "How about fifty thousand? Will that get you to stop?"

"I got one more job to do. We made a deal. You're going to live up to your end of it."

"Look Chuck. Fifty thousand and we both forget all about this. Think about it."

Chuck popped open the car door. "I'll be in touch."

The intercom on Gunston's desk buzzed. The task force had just concluded a staff meeting.

"Mr. Gunston, Mr. Kondo is here to see you."

Gunston motioned to Nicca and Snell as they were leaving the room. "Nicca, Snell, I want you two to stay and listen while I talk to Mr. Kondo. I'll do the talking. You watch and listen."

"That's fine with me," Nicca moved against a window wall. "I think you'll find Mr. Kondo very interesting."

Gunston buzzed back "Send him in."

The Japanese executive followed a uniformed officer into the room. Kondo wore a finely tailored pinstriped suit with a white shirt. Below jet-black hair, his brown eyes were bloodshot and his face slightly flushed.

"Mr. Kondo, I'm Special Agent Gunston. It's a pleasure to meet you, although I wish it were under better circumstances."

"Yes, so it seems."

Gunston raised his arm towards Nicca and Snell who were on the other side of a gray metal conference table. "This is Agent Snell and Fire Marshall Nicca. They are assigned to the special task force investigating the bombing."

Nicca reached over the table to shake hands "We've met before, Mr. Kondo. Nice to see you again."

"Yes, I remember," Kondo nodded without shaking Nicca's hand and turned toward Gunston. "You said investigating a bombing. This was an accident, a gas leak?" Kondo's speech was slightly indistinct.

"I'm afraid not. That's what the Fire Captain announced but we are almost certain some sort of bomb caused the explosion and subsequent fire."

"What evidence is there of a bomb. I visited the site. It looks like a gas line exploded to me." Kondo looked at each officer like he was trying to confirm his comment.

Gunston walked to his chair, taking time to respond. "The evidence hasn't been confirmed but by the physical arrangement of the crater we believe it was an above ground explosion. Pieces of a demolished automobile were found in the crater. This all points to some sort of car bomb."

"A bomb, it doesn't seem possible. Here in Detroit."

171

"I am sorry Mr. Kondo," Gunston sounded sincere.

"Do you have any idea who did this?"

"We don't know yet. A bomb makes a big mess but it leaves lots of evidence. It's our job to collect that evidence, put it together and have it tell us what happened and hopefully who did it. Our investigative team is very experienced. We should know more in a few days."

"I must be kept informed of the investigation's progress."

"I'm sure you are concerned Mr. Kondo, but we have a lot of work to do. We can give you an update in a few days."

No, I will assign someone to your team. I must know what's going on."

"Wait a minute." Gunston made a stop sign with his hands. "I understand your concern but we don't assign civilians to special investigative teams."

"I must be assured the criminals will be caught and that no word of a bomb is released. This is imperative."

Gunston folded his hands in front of him and spoke slowly. "It's our policy to keep our investigations confidential. There is no need to worry about any information leaking out. We already have told the media that the investigation is routine."

"It must be solved as soon as possible. And there must be no word mentioned about a bomb until the criminals are caught."

"Mr. Kondo, we can't make any promises," Gunston swiveled his chair. "It will take time, if we solve it at all. A bomb might leave a lot of evidence, but we will need some good breaks if we hope to catch the perpetrators. The odds aren't with us. At least half of the major bombings go unsolved. So, please leave the investigation to us. We will brief you as developments occur."

Nicca watched Gunston handle Kondo. Gunston's years in Washington must have trained him well for dealing with a foreign dignitary.

"As far as keeping a lid on this case, no publicity suits our purpose too. We are better off not letting the perpetrators know what we know."

"All right Agent Gunston, I will let your investigation progress, but I insist that your office provide me with daily progress reports."

Gunston's eyes flicked upward. After a moment of silence Gunston said. "We can do something like that. We will give you a copy of the case file in three days."

"Very well. Now who do you suspect?"

"We don't have anyone yet, but my hunch is that we are dealing with some sort of hate crime here. We are checking out that angle. We'll keep you posted." Gunston rose to shake Kondo's hand.

"I expect you to work hard. Find the lawless bastards that did this." Kondo backed up a few steps ignoring the Special Agent's hand. "You have my card. You know where to contact me." He turned and left the room.

Nicca waited for Kondo to leave the room. "Well, what do you think about Mr. Kondo? Makes you want to go out and buy a Sunon doesn't he."

"No kidding," added Snell. "What arrogance, wanting to assign one of his people to our team."

"Hey, I think either one of you would be pretty upset if some of your property went up in a ball of flames."

"I don't know. He's a typical big-time Japanese executive -- used to getting everything his way," Snell said.

"He's an big shot." Gunston sat back in his chair. "We'll give him what he asked for. We don't need him uptight and messing in our knickers."

"Uptight," Nicca said. "I wouldn't say uptight. I would say he was drunk."

"Drunk?" Snell furrowed her brow.

"Oh, he was definitely polluted and in the middle of the afternoon. I'd say Mr. Kondo is taking this harder than one would think."

"Maybe so." Gunston rubbed his chin. "I found it strange he came here by himself. That's unusual for a Japanese top executive. Anyway, let's give him a way to save face. Send him a copy of our report."

"Excuse me sir!" Snell blurted. "We can't give him a case file. That's sensitive material."

Gunston dropped his chin and looked at Snell over the top of his reading glasses. "Look, I've been involved in these types of cases before. This guy has clout - shit already the mayor, and the Director have called me on this one. Maybe the President will be next. Give him the report. That should make him happy and with his clout we need him happy and on our side. Who knows, he may even prove useful."

Chapter 15

Joe Nicca arrived at the Detroit Federal building at seven forty Sunday morning wearing a paisley tie over a blue button down shirt. The guard recognized his name, gave him a temporary photo ID with his picture on it, and he passed through the security doors without an escort.

Upstairs, he found his desk in the array of cubicles stuffed in the interior bay of the drab government building. He sifted through the papers in the in-box while he sipped a cup of black coffee.

After a few minutes, Snell entered the bay. She carried a stack of computer printouts under her arm. Denzer, wearing his State Trooper uniform, was behind her. She smiled, "Good morning, Joe."

"Morning," Nicca dipped his head.

Gunston stepped out of his office. "Looks like everybody's here. Let's use the conference room."

The members of the task force sat around a scratched and worn conference table. Gunston said, "Good morning everyone. Since this is Sunday I'd like to make this quick. First, this is Supervisory Special Agent Winslow Logan." Denzer pointed to a tall thin man, with balding gray hair and wrinkled but friendly looking face. "He's the Unit Chief from the Headquarters Lab Division, Explosives Unit. He's going to brief us on the results of his investigation at the bomb scene. Win."

The man that stood to brief carried the calm and confident demeanor of an FBI veteran. "Good morning," the words dragged in a Southern drawl. "My team arrived here yesterday afternoon. We were on the site at two seventeen PM. The local lab crew had already determined the crater was caused by some kind of bomb. I concurred. We're definitely dealing with a felony." Logan lifted a photograph of the bomb crater.

"Judging by the size of the crater, we are talking somewhere around five hundred to one thousand pounds of explosive. A bomb that big probably was planted in a car or truck, We started searching for pieces of the bomb or the vehicle it was carried in."

Nicca's eyes met Denzer's.

"We noticed a mangled car door near the crater." Nicca said.

"We looked at it." Logan nodded. "One of the search team found a charred license plate, Michigan. We ran a make on it. It's a Chevrolet van registered to an Elizabeth Johnson, of Warren, Michigan. I believe the Michigan state police checked up on her." Logan glanced at Denzer.

"Right," Denzer opened a note pad. "Two state police officers interviewed her last night. She has an alibi for the night of the explosion. We'll check her story."

"We haven't seen any indications the van was stolen, but we've only recovered about a third of the vehicle. As for the bomb, we've collected samples from the fragments found on the site." Logan held up a black and white photograph of a jagged piece of steel. Nicca edged forward in his seat and squinted.

"I've sent them to the SOG for analysis. We also found some unusual fragments of heavy gauge steel. Too heavy to be used in auto body construction."

After a sip of coffee, Logan pointed to a area of the photograph. "There were microscopic white crystals imbedded in the metal. High speed particle penetration, a high order explosion. The steel fragments also have ablation craters left by the hot gases. These fragments were in direct contact with the explosive, most likely the bomb container."

The analyst made a circular motion with his hands. "The bomb was contained by a heavy gauge steel drum. Something like a standard industrial fifty five gallon drum. If we're lucky we might be able to identify the drum as we put more of it together."

Denzer and Snell jotted down Logan's last comment.

"Any idea what kind of explosive they used?" Nicca said.

"Don't know yet. The samples I sent back to DC will tell us. Given that the bomb was placed in a large steel container, I would say the explosive was some type of free flowing material. Not plastic. Some type of construction blasting agent. We'll know that for sure in a couple days."

"How about the trigger mechanism? Any leads?" Nicca looked

up from his notepad. Logan bit the inside of his mouth before answering.

"We've found lots of wire and other electronic components. It might be useful if an engineer from Chevrolet could help us to identify any parts that don't belong in their vans. That could help us figure out the trigger mechanism. If we get enough parts we can use a Special Projects computer to reassemble the bomb and truck. From there we can identify the bomber's signature."

Nicca whistled. "With resources like that in Detroit I could take a vacation."

Denzer rocked his head in agreement.

"I'll take care of the Chevy engineer," Gunston made a notation. "Anything else?"

"We've dusted for fingerprints, but no luck so far. I'd like to get as many fragments as possible to the lab so we can check them with the laser."

"What about the gas explosion?" Nicca said. "I saw a sharp blue flame at the site."

"The truck exploded on top of the gas, electric and water lines to the building. The gas line ruptured in the initial blast, ignited and burned. However, I don't see any evidence of a secondary explosion."

"So we can rule out an accidental gas explosion?" Gunston looked at Logan for confirmation.

"Most definitely. All the evidence points to a bomb. Any other questions?"

The group was silent.

"Thanks, Win." Gunston patted Logan on the shoulder. "You and your guys have accomplished a lot in a short time. You're welcome to stay and listen to the rest of the meeting or you can get back to the lab. Your call."

"I think I'll listen in on what you all have found so far."

"Laura, what did you and Investigator Nicca find out yesterday?"

Snell flipped the pages in her notebook, glanced at it and then said, "We didn't find much. We searched NCIC, DTWS and the Canadian Files. We didn't find anything that looks like it's connected to this case. However, I did compile a list of anti-Japanese hate crimes. I'm in the process of sorting them so I can send requests for further information to the originating offices." Snell paused to consult her notes.

"Oh, one more thing. I've sent a request to the CIA liaison to check DESIST to see if they've any rumblings about anti-Japanese activity. It might take a few days to get an answer, but you never know what they'll have."

Gunston took a deep breath and leaned back in his chair. The morning sun filtered through the blinds and reflected off his trim haircut. He cupped his hand in front of his mouth. After a moment he said. "I don't want to waste a lot of manpower tracking the owner of the stolen car but we need to follow up on it." He leaned forward and stretched his fingertips on the table. "The owner didn't report the van stolen until the next morning, right? She says she doesn't use it every day. Maybe she has a boyfriend or something. Let's see if we can put her under electronic surveillance. Denzer, can you handle the request for a wiretap?"

"Yes sir. I'll also do some checking on her in the neighborhood."

"Good." Gunston marked a check in his notes. "Let's discuss the public affairs approach. I don't want to release any information regarding the forensic investigation. It might spook our bombers, cause them to change tactics or go under ground. No leaks! Got it?"

The team members nodded.

"Nicca do you have anything to add?"

"Yeah. I got a feeling. Two quick arsons and a bomb says to me they'll strike again, and soon."

Gunston nodded. "Could be. I wonder if the behavioral unit could help here. I'll check with the SAC."

Nicca dug into his briefcase for a piece of paper, "I put together a list of Sunon facilities in the metro area."

"Make sure everybody has a copy. Chances are the next target is on that list. We need to get Sunon to beef up their security."

Nicca shook his head. "I doubt it. The Sunon people seem to want to down-play the whole thing. They don't want bad publicity. We'll have to talk to their executives."

"I'll get the secretary to see if we can track them down today. Nicca, you should come along." Gunston looked at Nicca.

"Sure," Nicca smiled. "I'll mind my manners,"

"Anybody else have anything?"

No one replied.

"Let's get going. We'll meet tomorrow morning at eight A.M. In fact, we'll have daily task force meetings until further notice."

177

Nicca was at his desk Monday morning at eight working his way through his case material when Snell bustled into the cubicle. She had her khaki trench coat slung over her arm.

"Come on, Joe. Gunston got called away for a meeting with the mayor. He wants us to talk to Sunon about increased security."

"Do you have an appointment?"

Snell nodded, put on her coat, and tied the belt into a knot. "Let's go. We got thirty minutes to get over there."

Nicca looked her over, taking in her trim legs and cute face. "You're mighty chipper this morning. Have an exciting evening?"

She leaned her head back, frowned, and then dashed out of the office. Nicca reached for his leather jacket and gloves and followed her.

A light rain dappled the windshield on the way to the Sunon headquarters. The wipers squeaked as Nicca adjusted the defroster. He had just recounted his last meeting at the Sunon headquarters as they pulled into the Sunon parking lot. Nicca parked the car in a reserved spot.

"Joe, that's a reserved spot."

"So. This is FBI business." He tried to look serious. "Plus we have an appointment."

Snell burst out laughing. "They broke the mold with you."

Claire Johnson, Kondo's secretary, ushered them into. Kondo's sparsely furnished office. Kondo sat behind his desk, engrossed in a loose-leaf binder with Japanese Kanji writing, Shane in the couch diagonally opposite from the desk.

"Mr. Kondo, Agents Snell and Nicca are here." Johnson announced then shut the door behind them.

Kondo grunted, while Shane rose to shake their hands.

"Any news on the warehouse?" Shane made a broad grin, then winked at Snell. Her pleasant smile disappeared as she turned from Shane to face Kondo.

Snell smoothed her gray flannel suit then cleared her voice. "Well, the initial lab tests confirmed a bomb. Of course the investigation continues, so we can't say anything else on that, but we did come here to talk about security."

"Security?" Shane returned to the couch. Snell, standing next to Nicca, turned again to face Shane.

"Considering the spate of attacks, the Bureau recommends you increase the security at your facilities."

Shane glanced at Kondo. Kondo barely nodded, still looking at his report. "I'm sorry Ms. Snell. We can't do that."

"It's in your own best interests."

Shane leaned back and spread his arms on the top of the couch. "Not really. We're in the business to sell cars. No one wants to buy a car from a police station."

Snell's face started to turn red. "Mr. Shane, this is the FBI's recommendation!"

Shane made a mocking smile and shrugged as if he had no other explanation.

Nicca stepped forward. "The pattern of the previous attacks suggests there could be another one. Soon."

"I don't agree. Do you have evidence of another threat? I mean this could be a fluke. Whoever did it probably is beating out of town.

"All right Sunon. That's your call. It's your business but think about it. If you have a change of heart, let us know." Nicca turned to face Kondo. "Mr. Kondo, thank you for your time. If you learn anything, please give us a call."

Kondo raised his head and his eyes locked with Nicca's. Nicca stared into the blank and inscrutable brown beads.

After a moment, Nicca motioned to Snell, "Let's go."

Back in the privacy of their car, Snell steamed. "Those guys. What creeps."

"Yeah, makes we wonder if we're on the right side. I mean look around. Maybe Detroit would be better off without Sunon."

"After dealing with those guys, I might agree."

Nicca started the car, then dropped his hand from the ignition. "Hey, what the heck are we saying." Nicca faced Snell. Her cheeks were red from either the cold or anger, Nicca couldn't tell, but he liked what he saw. He felt his face turning red, and not from the cold. "They may be stubborn, but they don't deserve bombs. We'll find the bombers and maybe they'll find some humility."

179

"I don't know, man," Brian said to Chuck in a quiet voice back at the garage apartment. "I think we should lay low for a while. They brought in the FBI. This is getting heavy."

Chuck, propped against the kitchen table, stared at Brian. "They got nothing on us. We need to do the next job as soon as we can. We got to keep the pressure on."

"Why's that?"

"We're trying to send a message to Sunon and the rest of the Jap car dealers. They got to know we ain't gunna take it anymore."

"I told you before, Chuck, I ain't into politics," Brian slapped the refrigerator. "We're supposed to do a job for the man, make some bucks, then disappear into the crowd. If you want to make this some kind of personal crusade, you can count me out."

"I can't count you out. I need your talents." Chuck paced the room.

"It's not a crusade. Look, I met with Cannon, I mean our sponsor, last weekend. He wants us to do one last job. He's doubling the fee. If we pull this off, we're in fat city." Chuck faced his friend. "What do you say?"

Debbie spoke first, "I'm up for it. I can handle another job."

Chuck turned toward Alex. "What about you?"

Alex's eyes darted toward Debbie and Brian. He shrugged, "Go for it, I guess. I could use the money."

Chuck turned to Brian.

"I don't know." Brian walked to the window. "This doesn't feel right." Then he spun around to face Chuck and the others. "I ain't no quitter, man. I groove on this stuff more than any of you. I just don't like taking chances. I got to be careful."

Chuck opened the refrigerator, pulled out a beer, and handed it to Brian. "Here. I'll tell you what. Why don't we scout out the next target together? You look it over and tell me what you think. If it looks too risky, we'll can it and look for another. I've already checked it out and it looks good, but I want you to be satisfied that everything's cool." Chuck popped a beer for himself.

"That sounds like a good plan to me," Debbie said and glanced at Brian.

"Okay," Brian grunted, "But you yard apes better not screw up."

Debbie shot back with indignation, "We've done fine so far, haven't we?"

"So what's the next target?" Brian put the beer bottle to his lips.

Chuck smiled, "The Sunon HQ in Troy."

Brian coughed and spit beer across the room. "Blow up their headquarters! That's what I call keeping a low profile. Every god damned Fed in the country will be looking for us if they aren't already."

"Chuck, isn't it too risky?" Debbie's eyes tightened.

"What! You suggested their headquarters back at Grayling, Debbie. Don't you remember?"

Debbie blanched. She hunched her shoulders as if she didn't want to contradict Chuck.

Brian eyed Debbie. "No, she didn't. I suggested it."

Chuck blinked at Brian. "Doesn't matter. It's the best target we got without leaving Michigan. If we do it right they'll never have a clue."

"There are always clues," Brian said. "The trick is to make sure they don't lead to us. Why not leave Michigan? It could throw off the investigation."

"Because the boss man doesn't want it that way! Got it?"

"We better get more than last time."

"Two thousand each." Chuck swallowed hard.

"Homicide ain't worth two thousand," Brian threw up his hands in disgust.

"Who the hell says there's going to be any homicide?"

"How're you going to avoid it if you blow up a building full of people?" Brian turned his back to Chuck and grabbed another beer from the refrigerator.

"We wait until the people are gone. We do it at night, on a weekend."

"There'll probably always be somebody in the building, even at night," Debbie said as if she was thinking out loud.

"Brian's right, man." Alex edged forward on the couch. "I don't want to kill anybody."

"I got you covered," Chuck smirked. "Before the bomb goes off, we phone in a warning. We give them fifteen minutes to clear the building."

There was silence, and then Brian spoke. "I guess that'll work." He rubbed the stubble on his chin. "We got to be careful with the phone though. It could be an easy clue for the Feds. Better let me figure out how to do it. If we plan it right it could lead them down a dead end street."

"All right, Brian. That's what I like." Chuck turned to Debbie and Alex. "I checked out the area last night. It won't be hard. You'll see tonight. They've got a fence around the perimeter, but there isn't any gate. The place has a huge parking lot. I think the loading dock is the best place to hit. Let's head up there and take a look."

Sunon's North American Corporate Headquarters, unlike the high rise Ameritech building across the interstate, lacked a mirrored glass facade and huge neon letters on top. Energy efficient fixed double pane windows punctuated the plain two-story brick facade, the only ornament a gold "S" inside an inverted triangle depicting the Sunon corporate logo over the entry doors. A narrow traffic circle surrounded the building. Inside the circle ten reserved parking spaces occupied the southwest corner. A loading dock, screened by large junipers and azaleas, bisected the east wall of the building. The main entrance occupied the southern wall near the reserved parking spaces. The true size of the building was difficult to gage because of clever landscaping but it covered half a city block perched like a green-mantled island in a concrete sea of parking spaces.

Brian pulled through the main entrance and into the parking lot, to the left and around the traffic circle. He slowed to examine the empty reserved parking area.

"Look at that man, all Japanese names. They'll end up control-ling everything from Japan, like GM and Ford used to control every-thing from Detroit," Brian said.

"I ain't worried about who gets parking spots or who gets a key to the executive john." Chuck squeezed to the right and looked up and down the driveway. "What I can't believe is that they haven't beefed up security. What's on the other side of the building."

They slowed as they rounded the east wall and passed a loading dock.

"Hmm. This looks good," Chuck's blue eyes darted back and forth taking in the details of the site.

"Yeah," Brain motioned toward the wall. "We'll be able to get the truck right up close to the building. Plus it's nice and dark. These trees do a good job of blocking the view."

They continued around the circle and exited the lot the way they entered. Brian spoke as he drove, "It's not as simple as the warehouse, but it looks doable."

Chuck turned his head to watch the building as the car pulled away. "They have a guard desk inside the main entrance but none outside. You can't get in the building without a badge. I guess they were more worried someone might steal their plans. The outside is wide open." Chuck laughed. "My A-team could have waxed that building in a heartbeat."

"Right, Chuck." Brian sneered. "This ain't the Green Berets, and the guards could be a problem. What do you have in mind?"

"Same as last time. We get a stolen truck; make up two drums with the explosive. Park it by the loading dock. Fifteen minutes before game time we call and give them a warning. That should give them plenty of time to evacuate but not enough time to find the bomb."

Brian nodded as he upshifted onto the highway. "Sounds simple. Now we need a pay phone. Out in the boonies. Someplace where we won't be spotted or remembered. Anybody got a suggestion?"

"I don't know, let's look around. Let's go this way," Chuck gestured to the west. "Somewhere in Birmingham. Maybe they'll think it's some rich suburban brats."

Brian laughed, "Good idea, bud." He raised his hand. Chuck smacked it in salute.

"I know."

In Farmington Hills Chuck selected a pay phone after rejecting several others along the route. Outside an older and partially occupied suburban shopping center, they could park in the shadows and be only twenty yards from the phone.

Brian pulled out a handkerchief and used it to pick up the phone. He dialed the weather to insure it worked. "That settles that. It works. What next?" he said as he returned to the driver's seat

"Let's head back. You can drop Debbie and I off at my house."

Brian drove onto I-696 East. "When do we do it?" Brian's thin lip cracked a smile.

Chuck looked at his watch. "Let's go for next Sunday night. We need a truck. Brian can you handle that?"

"No problem. Alex and I can take care of that. We'll get one on Sunday evening and bring it over to your place."

"Good, I'll work on the drums Sunday afternoon. We'll load the truck Sunday evening. Then we'll drive to Troy, park in the loading dock, arm the drums, switch to the car and drive to the phone. Fifteen minutes before it blows we'll call the guard desk."

"What will you say?" Debbie's eyes glimmered.

"I don't know."

Brian tilted his head from the driver's seat. "How about, Hey asshole, you got fifteen minutes to get the hell out or you're toast."

"Nah, no good. They got to think we're some kind of big time operation. We need a name." Chuck knitted his brow. "How about Take America Back. TAB?"

"Are you kidding?" Brian sneered at Chuck. "I got a better one. People of the United States Shooting," he hesitated, "Yuppies! That spells PUSSY."

"Get serious, Brian. If we give ourselves a name it could throw off the FBI."

"You are dreaming man. There will be fifty lunatic groups calling in when this one goes off. The Feds will ignore it."

"Someone calls before, they don't ignore that. Which makes me wonder why no one took responsibility for the last bomb."

Debbie leaned forward putting her arms on the back of Chuck's seat. "Maybe somebody did, but we didn't hear about it."

"I don't know. If we claim responsibility for the bomb like a real terrorist group we might have more..." Chuck's voice tailed off as he saw the reaction on his partners' faces to his remark. "Well, that's what we are. What's wrong? Debbie?"

"I'm a little surprised. That's all." She slumped into the rear seat. "I hadn't thought of it that way."

"I prefer to consider myself a mercenary," Brian said. "Just doing a job for money."

"Well, whatever we are, I'm trying to think of a way to get the most out of this and throw out a false clue."

"Actually, you could be right. If we make it look like some Arabs..."

Chuck cut off Brian, "No! They got to know it was Americans. This is us against them."

Brian thought for a moment. "I'll go along with it if we never use the name again and no one ever mentions it again. Deal?"

"Deal." Chuck blinked. "We'll use the name only in the phone call and never again. I'll think of a good one before Sunday."

Chuck and Debbie had already finished the bomb when the Brian and Alex backed another stolen van into the driveway. Chuck inspected the van. "It looks acceptable. Can we cover up the name of the business on the door. I don't want anyone to remember seeing a carpet van in this neighborhood."

Brian kicked the side of the truck. "Damn." Brian kicked the side of the truck. "I should have thought of that. You got any spray paint?"

"Not the right color. Why don't you go up to the hardware store before they close and get some white spray paint? First, help us load the drums."

Chuck waited for Alex to park Brian's car and walk to the garage. "All right, let's load these drums onto the truck. Then I'll finish the firing circuit."

Grunting and groaning the three men placed the heavy drums into the truck. "Brian, you get the paint. I'll rig the charges."

By nine the bomb was wired and the doors painted. "Let's go in the house and go over the plan."

In the living room, Chuck sat on the edge of the chair and motioned to the others.

"Brian and I will drive the truck into the loading dock. I'll rig the timer. Give us about five minutes, then you two will drive in. When we see you in the Escort, I'll set the timer for one thirty. Brian and I will get in your car and split. We head to Farmington Hills. At one fifteen we'll make the call."

"Maybe we should give ourselves some more time to get to the phone," Brian said.

Glancing at Brian, Chuck dipped his head. "We'll set the bomb for two A.M. That gives us an extra thirty minutes. Did I forget anything?"

No one spoke. Chuck took a deep breath, "All right. Why don't we get some rest." Chuck looked at his watch, "We'll leave at midnight. Debbie, come with me. I could use a neck rub."

"Would you like a wake up call?" Brian said.

"Nah, we won't go to sleep," Chuck said as he closed the door to the bedroom.

At twelve ten Brian drove the van from Chuck's driveway. Alex and Debbie followed in Brian's Ford Escort. The drive to Troy took half an hour. Brian pulled into the Sunon parking lot and proceeded around the traffic circle. As they passed the entrance, Chuck did not see anyone at the door or guard desk.

Inside the front entrance Bill Grabowski and Pete Kodurba, the security guards on duty, were watching an info-mercial on a black and white portable TV. Kodurba adjusted the antenna as the TV blared about the merits of a new lose-weight fast diet plan.

"Look, my brother-in-law had a great diet, he worked out, he didn't smoke and he still died of a heart attack at age forty-three," Kodurba flicked the antenna with his finger. The crackling snow on the screen continued.

"Sure, but that's one case. You got to look at the averages. I'm telling ya, that fast food is going to get even with you someday."

"I don't eat a lot of junk food."

"What did you have for dinner today?"

"I don't know. I don't remember." He avoided Grabowski's stare and watched the security television monitor connected to concealed cameras distributed throughout the building. The cameras, sensitive to visible and near infrared light, worked in day or night and fed images to the single monitor on the guard's desk. Grabowski had used the keyboard to command the software to split the screen into four views, enabling him to watch four outside views at once. The software in the system could save any scenes with recorded motion. When that scene flashed on the monitor, the guards could tell if anyone or anything was near the building since the last scan by the computer enhanced shapes on the screen.

The monitor showed a truck approach into the loading dock area.

"What's that van doing there?"

"What?" Grabowski spun in his armchair.

"Look at the monitor. That truck just pulled in there."

"We expecting any deliveries tonight?" Kodurba said.

"Not that I know of. The supervisor didn't mention any."

Ryoichi Kawasaki walking through the door diverted their attention from the monitor.

"May I sign out please?" Kawasaki's sport shirt and blazer still looked fresh even after six hours at work.

186

"Sure, Mr. Kawasaki. Here's the sheet. Another long day?" Grabowski asked as he handed a clipboard to the executive.

"Yes. I had a telephone call with Tokyo. I'm not sure they realize the time difference." Both men smiled. "Good night." Kawasaki bowed slightly as he returned the clipboard to the guard.

"Good night, sir."

Grabowski shifted his attention to the monitor.

"It looks like they're sitting there," Kodurba said.

As they watched, Alex and Debbie drove up. They could see the car on the edge of the screen. Next, they saw one man exit the van on the driver's side. Several seconds later they saw another get out. Both men boarded the car and it slowly drove off.

"I better go check this out. You hold down the fort." Kodurba picked up a portable radio and flashlight and exited the front door. He walked to the southeast corner of the building as the car rounded the corner. He held out his hand to stop the car.

Chuck was sitting in the back seat behind the driver. He tapped Alex on the shoulder and said, "You better stop."

"Chuck, he'll see us. Let's split," Brian said with clenched teeth.

"No. Stop. We'll play dumb. Maybe we can talk our way out."

Debbie looked at Chuck with wide eyes. Chuck noticed her and said, "Just be cool."

Brian bit his top lip and reached in his jacket for his gun.

Alex stopped and the guard tapped on the driver's window. Alex rolled it down. "What's wrong, officer?" Chuck leaned forward and said from the back seat.

"Did you park a truck back there?" He pointed toward the loading dock.

"No sir. We're lost and we're trying to turn around." Chuck leaned forward and spoke into the open window. Alex and Debbie looked away while Brian stared at the guard.

A frown crossed Kodurba's face. "May I see some identification please?" He shined his flashlight on Alex.

Alex opened his jacket to retrieve his wallet. The light beam clearly illuminated his shouldered pistol.

The guard spotted it. In surprise, he lurched back and drew his own weapon from his hip holster.

From the back seat of the car a terrific shot rang out. Brian had drawn his gun, aimed between the door pillar and the headrest and fired once. The .44 Automag bullet slammed into the guard's abdomen and drove him back five feet. As the guard fell he fired one round before he hit the ground.

Brian opened his door and moved at a crouch behind the rear fender. He spotted the moaning and writhing guard on the ground. He coolly walked toward him. He looked at the guard and shook his head slightly from side to side. Without a word he fired one round into the guard's head. The large caliber bullet pulverized the guard's brain. The body lurched and stopped wiggling. The moaning ceased.

"Let's get out of here," Chuck yelled from the back seat. Alex didn't respond. The noise from the blast must have deafened or stunned him, so Chuck shook Alex's shoulder. He felt a warm wetness. He grabbed Alex's shoulder and yanked on it. Alex upper body flopped over the stick shift. Visible in front of Alex's left ear was a small hole. Blood trickled from it.

Brian looked into the driver's window and said, "What's wrong?"

"Alex's been hit."

"What?" Debbie screamed.

Her scream was punctuated by the sudden appearance of vehicle headlights shining through the back window of the Escort. Brian looked up and Chuck turned around to see behind them a large Sunon Fredrick sedan.

After leaving the guard desk, Kawasaki drove his company car from the reserved parking area, around the traffic circle to side of the building. Kawasaki noticed the guard on the ground. He looked at Brian and saw the large pistol hanging from his hand. Their eyes made contact. Kawasaki was instantly afraid. He attempted to shift to reverse but he was too late.

Brian quickly raised his gun and fired three times. The first bullet shattered the windshield and slammed into the headrest, but the second and third bullets found their mark hitting Kawasaki in the shoulder and chest. Brian walked to the sedan and jerked open the door. He aimed his weapon at the wounded executive. He fired until he was out of ammunition.

"Brian, Get back here and help me get Alex out of the driver's seat," Chuck yelled.

Brian opened the passenger door and told the sobbing Debbie, "Get in the back seat." She complied. He then crawled into the car and helped lift Alex. Chuck dragged him to the back door and stuffed the limp body into the rear seat next to Debbie. Alex's wallet fell from his hand and the contents spilled to the ground. Chuck hastily scooped up the wallet and papers and threw them in the back seat with Alex.

"My god. He's dead," she cried.

Chuck slammed the door. He got into the driver's seat while Brian got in the other side. Chuck floored the gas and drove out.

"Cool it, man. Drive normally," Brian ordered.

"You're right. You're right. Shit, Shit, Shit." Chuck pounded the steering wheel. "Why did you shoot that guard?"

"He saw us, man. We were dead meat."

Chapter 16

DETROIT, MICHIGAN

The sound of Vivaldi's Winter drifted from the stereo in the living room to the kitchen where Nicca was reading the paper over a cup of coffee. He hummed the music to himself, lost in the pleasure of the piece's dynamic range. The soft chords at the start of Vivaldi's final movement had started when Nicca heard the electronic ring of his phone. He lowered the stereo volume. "Nicca, here."

"Joe. Joe. Laura. This is Laura." She was out of breath.

Nicca tensed. "What happened?"

"The terrorists struck again. I just got word."

"Where?"

"Up in Troy. The Sunon Corporate Headquarters. It sounds like an assassination."

"Did they use a bomb?"

"No, they shot up a Sunon executive. Gunned him down in the parking lot."

"Where are you now?"

"I'm home."

"Where do you live?"

"In Dearborn."

Nicca glanced at his watch, 1:05 a.m.. "I can get there before you. Where's Gunston?"

"At Headquarters for a meeting. I left a message at his hotel."

"Call Denzer and then meet me at the scene. The Sunon Headquarters, you said right?"

190

"Right. It's off Crooks Road in Troy."

"I'm on my way." Nicca slammed the phone. We should have known. He ran out the door, struggling to get his arm through his holster and under his leather jacket. Vivaldi's frenetic winter theme built to crescendo as he took the steps two at a time.

He reached his car and sped out of the parking lot. Why did they change tactics? Something doesn't add up. Is this the same group or some other opportunists? No, it has to fit.

Nicca arrived on the scene at one thirty-seven. A dozen police cars and ambulances had parked haphazardly around the entrance to the building. Getting out of his car he flashed his badge at two Troy police officers stretching a yellow plastic police line across two barricades. They let him through and pointed out the location where the bodies were found.

He approached two plain-clothes officers who were questioning a seated figure. As he approached Nicca could tell that the person was a security guard. Showing his badge Nicca said, "Hi, I'm Fire Marshall Joe Nicca. I'm working with the FBI task force investigating the Sunon bombing cases. Mind if I listen in?"

"Fire marshal, huh?" the more senior looking of the two detectives said. "Looks like you're out of your element here. This is pretty much a gangland style hit. Only problem is one of the security guards happened to walk right into the middle of it. Poor guy. His brains are scattered all over the pavement over there." The Detective motioned to his left at a lump under a white sheet.

"Who else got hit?" Nicca asked.

"A Mr. Ryoichi Kawasaki. He was a big shot with Sunon. Apparently, he was working late. He signed out with the guards. He got in his car and drove around the service road. When he got here," the detective pointed to the corner, "a gun man, or gunmen, unknown, let him have it. He had at least four holes in him. They were pretty nasty. Looks almost like rifle fire. The windshield was blasted out, but they must have wanted to finish him off because they opened the door and fired some more. Brazen as hell. Classic gang hit. We found six shell casings on the ground there and there," the detective held up a plastic evidence bag with the Automag cartridges, "next to the Sunon sedan."

Nicca scanned the scene as the detective spoke. "Why was the guard out here?"

Nicca and the two detectives looked at the seated guard. "Mister Grabowski, did you hear the question?"

"No, ... "No, I didn't."

"Why was your partner out here?" The detective crouched in front of the guard.

Grabowski looked up. "He was checking on a delivery. I mean, we weren't supposed to get any deliveries, so he was checking on it."

"What do you mean by delivery?" Nicca's pulse quickened. "Did someone call?"

"No. No one called. We saw a delivery van on the monitor. He went to check it out. That's all. He went to check it out." He started sobbing.

"I know this is hard...,"The detective started to offer Grabowski a handkerchief, but Nicca interrupted.

"Where was this van?" Nicca barked.

"At the loading dock." The guard's face awoke with realization. "Hey, we weren't supposed to be getting any deliveries."

"Where's the loading dock?" Nicca braced his legs like a sprinter reading for the start.

"Over there, around the corner."

"Did anyone check this out?" Nicca looked at the detectives. They didn't respond.

Without another word, Nicca bolted in the direction the guard pointed.

"Go with him," said the older detective.

Nicca sprinted the couple hundred yards toward the loading dock. Could it be another car bomb - and it hasn't gone off. Rounding the corner marked by a large pine tree, he saw the van. In the dim light as he neared the vehicle he could barely discern the logo of the company.

"King's Carpet." He crouched by the door and ran his finger over the obscured letters. "It's been painted over, and pretty sloppy too." He heard the Detroit PD detective approach. "We got a problem here. Start to evacuate the area. And get the bomb squad."

The detective said between pants, "Uh, right." He turned and ran back the way he came.

Nicca stood up and looked into the driver's window. In the darkness, the truck appeared empty except for a shapeless mass in the rear. He tested the door but it was locked. He looked across the seat and noticed the passenger door was unlocked. He quickly shuffled around the front of the van and grabbed the door handle. The idea that the door was booby-trapped caused him to hesitate for a second. Then he pushed the button and opened the door. The dome light weakly illuminated the interior. He took a deep breath and climbed into the van. Squeezing between the two front seats he was confronted by a large plastic sheet. Over his panting he could clearly hear a clock ticking.

"Oh my god."

He gingerly lifted the sheet and looked under it. There was the bottom of a fifty-five gallon drum. Continuing to lift the plastic revealed the rest of the drum and another behind it. On the top he could see wires entering the drum.

He followed the wires from one drum to the other. They ran down to the side of the second drum to a partially disassembled alarm clock. Other wires went from the clock to a car battery. Both the clock and the battery were crudely attached with duct tape to the second drum. The hands on the clock read five minutes to twelve.

"There's no time for the bomb squad. How do I stop this thing?"

He stared at the wires. A lump formed in his throat and he felt the urge to vomit as he remembered a picture he saw of a Detroit police bomb squad officer who accidentally set off a bomb while trying to defuse it. "Okay, Okay. It looks pretty simple," he said to himself to steel his courage. "It's got to have power. Disconnect the power and it should be safe."

The hand of the clock moved one minute closer to twelve. "Which wire? Which wire?"

Grabbing the wires leading to the battery terminal, he closed his eyes and yanked hard. He expected to be blown to bits but instead all he heard was the tick of the clock. Then he ripped the wires from the clock.

"I hope that does it," he said retracing his steps out of the van. Once near the brick wall of the loading dock, he leaned against it, slowly sunk to his knees, exhaled a deep breath and grunted, "I'm going to nail these bastards."

Chuck pulled into his driveway and doused the headlights. The three hadn't said much during the drive home. "Let's get Alex in the house. Then we got to figure out what to do with his body."

"Let's put him in the trunk," Brian said.

"Chuck, we can't do that." Debbie's eyes were red and her voice weak.

"What the hell are we supposed to do?" Brian shouted as he supported Alex on his shoulder. "Man, this guy is heavy."

Mrs. Fischer opened the door and stepped onto the back porch. "Is something wrong Chuck?" she asked.

Hearing Mrs. Fischer's voice, Chuck slackened his grip on Alex's body. The body slumped and Brian grunted to keep it from falling to the ground. Chuck turned his upper torso to face the voice. "Uh No. uh, nothing is wrong." He paused, "Old Alex had a few too many to drink tonight. He'll be all right."

Mrs. Fischer looked at Chuck but shifted her gaze to Debbie when she heard her sob slightly.

"Are you sure everything is all right?"

Chuck regripped Alex's arm and lifted him. " Everything is O.K. Mrs. Fischer. We'll get Alex inside and sober him up."

"I don't think he should drive home," Mrs. Fischer said.

"He won't be driving anywhere," Brian mumbled.

Chucked glared at Brian then turned back to Mrs. Fischer.

"Don't worry. Mrs. Fischer. I'll make sure he gets home all right. You can go back to bed. Everything's cool," Chuck barely controlled his voice.

Mrs. Fischer seemed satisfied. "I see. Well, good night."

"Good night," Chuck waved limply with his free hand.

Mrs. Fischer went back in the house.

"Keep your damn voices down," Chuck said to Brian. "We'll get Alex inside. Then we'll figure out what to do with his body. Come on Brian, give me a hand. Debbie, get the door,"

Inside the converted garage, Alex's body thumped on the kitchen floor. "Man," Brian exclaimed between heaving breaths, "That's one heavy dude." Debbie let the door slam shut and then ran to the bathroom. Brian watched her go and then looked at Chuck, "She's going to be a problem."

"I'll take care of her. Shit," he exhaled loudly. "What a god damned mess."

"So what are we going to do?" Brian leaned against the frame of the kitchen doorway.

"I don't know, let me think." Chuck rubbed his chin then ran his hands through his hair.

"Better get a sheet or something to cover his body." Brian turned, opened the refrigerator door, and reached for a beer.

The sound of Debbie's sobbing leaked past the bathroom door.

Brian wiggled his thumb at the bathroom. "You better go talk to her. Calm her down."

"No. Not yet." Chuck paced the floor, "We got to have a plan first. She'll take it better if it looks like we have things under control."

"All right, but I ain't worried," Brian said again with an air of complacency.

Chuck gave him an icy glare, "Bullshit. You kill two guys and we lose one of ours and you think it's another night on the town."

Brian slammed down his beer. "Look man. It wasn't my idea to get him and her involved in the first place. I liked Alex. He was a tough guy. But he made his choice. It could have been you or me. Or all of us could have gotten nailed. Anyway, we can get out of this. We got to lay low for a while. None of that terrorist crap. They ain't got nothing on us. They don't know that Alex is dead. If we get rid of his body and chill out for a while it will blow over."

Chuck stared at Brian while his hands quivered by his side. Chuck closed then opened his eyes and shook his head trying to clear his thoughts. He shuddered and the acrid taste of resignation crept up his throat. We screwed up. We almost got caught. Yet Brian seems calm, unconcerned. He shut his eyes again. Get control. Push it aside. Concentrate.

"You're right," he said as he stared out the window. "We got to keep cool." He took a deep breath and threw back his shoulders. "I'm back. What do think we should do with the body?"

"We got to bury it. Someplace where it won't be found. Want a beer?"

"No, not now. We can't bury him around here."

"We could dump him in the river, but that's too risky."

"Hey," Chuck snapped his fingers. "How about the farm? We could bury him there."

"Yeah," Brian ran his finger across his upper lip. "That should work. Plus, we can chill out there for a while until the smoke clears."

"Smoke! Oh shit. We forgot to call in the warning." Chuck gaped at Brian.

"It's too late now. What happens, happens," Brian took a long swig of beer.

"You better give me a beer. No, wait a minute I better go check on Debbie. Cover him up for me. I don't want Debbie to see him again. There are some sheets in the closet." Chuck knocked on the bathroom door and entered without waiting for Debbie's reply. He saw her sitting on the toilet seat with a balled up towel against her face.

"You okay?" he asked quietly.

Debbie acknowledged by nodding her head without looking up.

Chuck kneeled and put his arms around her. "I'm sorry about Alex." He paused. "Everything will be all right. We're going to take him to the farm and bury him there."

Debbie dropped her hands and said quietly, "What about Liz? What will I tell Liz? She has to know."

A flash of impatient anger stiffened Chuck's back. "No, Debbie. She can't know about this. Not now or any time soon. Someday maybe, but not now."

Anguish seemed to crease Debbie's face. She gazed for a moment at Chuck and then sighed, "I guess you're right." She straightened her shoulders and stretched her neck. Then she looked Chuck in the eye, "It's not my fault," she beseeched, " Is it, Chuck? I mean, he wanted..."

"You're right, Debbie. He had his chance to bail out. He took the risk. It's too bad it didn't work out."

"Why did Brian shoot that guard? Why did..."

Chuck interrupted, "He didn't have a choice. The guard went for his gun. I don't know. Maybe he saw something or it was something Alex did. I don't know. We'll never know."

"I didn't want to kill anyone," she began to sob and hugged Chuck.

"No one did." Chuck pulled her tight but his eyes focused across and beyond the small room. "Hell, I don't have any sympathy for that guard. No one forced him to work for Sunon. And who cares about that dude in the car."

Chuck patted Debbie's neck. And I don't care about Alex either, he thought. I have to escape, survive. I want Debbie to survive with me, but you have to cooperate.

"I'm going back out to talk to Brian about what we'll do. Will you be okay in here?"

"Yeah, I guess so. Give me a little time. I'll be out in a bit." She paused for a moment and then added meekly, "I guess I'm not cut out for this type of thing."

Chuck smiled at her. "Don't worry. Everything will work out."

Debbie emerged from the bathroom a half hour later. Her red eyes and haggard expression showed the effects of crying. She cringed when she saw the crumpled sheet in a pile on the floor. Brian and Chuck were sitting at the small kitchen table watching the TV.

"How do you feel, Debbie?" Chuck said as he stood and took her hand.

"I'll be fine. Do you have any tissues?"

"I don't know. Will a napkin do?"

"Sure, thanks," Debbie tried to broach a smile. "So now what do we do?"

Chuck looked at Brian and then said, "We've got a plan. We're going to take Alex up to the farm. There's some isolated woods where we can bury him. Then we'll stay there a while to see how things go. If everything is cool, then we'll come back here. If there's trouble, we'll contact the man and see if he can help us get out of town. Brian thinks that there shouldn't be any trouble. Still, we got to be careful."

"Can we bring some clothes?" Debbie asked.

Chuck put down his beer. "Sure," he nodded. "I'll pack up tonight. We'll go to your place tomorrow when Liz isn't there. You can grab some clothes and leave her a note. Tell her you're going with me to Florida to visit my aunt. We'll leave tomorrow morning as soon as you can get your things."

"Tomorrow," She replied distractedly. Then hesitating she asked. "Chuck, What about the bomb?"

Chuck looked at Brian and said, "We haven't heard anything on the tube. I don't know."

The bomb squad arrived at the Sunon Headquarters building and a plain-clothes officer escorted it to the loading dock. After defusing the bomb, Nicca got the local police to seal off the area and move the spectators and reporters back. He didn't want word to get out that there was bomb in the area to avoid a panic. He was relieved when the bomb squad specialists said that the bomb was completely disarmed and posed no danger.

He looked up to see Snell approaching with a notepad. "Hi, Joe. I checked out the shooting location. Pretty ugly isn't it?"

"It could have been a lot worse," Nicca frowned. "Any word from Gunston?"

"I reached him at his hotel. He's taking the first flight out tomorrow morning. I guess I'm the senior Bureau representative on the scene." She hesitated, "To tell the truth, I'm not that experienced with violent crime scenes. If you have any suggestions or questions, let me know."

Nicca studied Snell's face. She tried to act composed but the slight quiver in her voice gave her away. "Don't worry, you'll do fine. Did Gunston have any other instructions?"

"No, he didn't, except that he felt that we should keep a lid on the bomb for now."

"I was thinking the same thing. It wouldn't be a good idea to release the news about the bombing attempt. Like Gunston said a couple of days ago, we don't want the bombers going to ground."

"What about the bomb squad truck? Everybody saw it come in." Snell motioned to the black police vehicle with the hump-shaped trailer.

"If anyone asks we'll say it was a precaution only. No bomb was found. We better get the word out to our people and the Troy police soon before someone slips up."

"Right," Snell rubbed her forehead.

Nicca asked, "Did you get statements from the security guard and the cops and detectives that initially responded to the call?"

"Not yet. Their lab people are working the scene. I don't think our lab people will appreciate that, but I requested a Bureau forensic team come up here as soon as possible anyway. They like to analyze undisturbed evidence."

"Great. The lab guys should have a field day with all the stuff in that van. Talk about bomb signatures. These guys practically left their life histories. They didn't expect the bomb not to go off. Think how many more could have been killed if it blew." The memory of those few seconds in the van shuddered through Nicca. He raised one finger and waved it for emphasis. "We're going to get these guys and real soon." Nicca turned to leave, but hesitated. Looking back into Snell's eyes, he added "Let the Troy police work over the shooting scene but only the FBI forensic team is allowed in the van."

"Got it. I'll keep an eye on it until they show."

"Right. I'll go talk to the captain to make sure he gets the word about the bomb. Where's Denzer?"

"I couldn't reach him at home. He must have gone away for the weekend. I left a message on his machine."

"That's right. He told me was going to visit his daughter in Kalamazoo tomorrow. Says he didn't have a day off in two months. I wonder, can we get anymore FBI people up here to go collect evidence?"

"I can't, but Gunston could." Snell's blue eyes flickered.

"Damn, we could use the people now."

Snell pondered for a moment, "I can call the SAC and see if he'll authorize some help."

"Good idea."

Snell grabbed her cellular phone and dialed FBI headquarters. She asked for the SAC's home phone number. After verifying her identity, the operator gave her the number. Snell flipped a button on her portable phone turning to the unsecured mode. Then she dialed the SAC at home. "He's not going to appreciate being disturbed at this hour," she winked.

"Comes with the job," Nicca ran a finger around his collar. "I'm going to see the captain."

Fifteen minutes later, Nicca found Snell and they compared notes. Snell briefed Nicca in front of the Troy Police Captain, "I got a hold of the SAC. He's mobilizing a couple of additional agents to help out. He also wants to meet with Gunston and us tomorrow, Err, I guess I mean today. He's going to have public affairs release a statement at that time. He agreed that we should keep a lid on the bomb."

Nicca exchanged glances with the Police Captain.

"What about the van. Did anyone run a make on it?" Snell asked.

"Yeah. It's registered to some carpet outfit in Farmington. It was clearly stolen. Our guys used a slide hammer on the ignition lock. It's the same type of van as last time. Interesting, but wait until you check this out. One of the Troy detectives found this on the ground by the murdered executive's car." Nicca grinned and handed a plastic bag to Snell. Inside the plastic bag was a business card. It read:

Elizabeth Kessler
Sales Representative

Artemis Total Skin Care Products
6739 Woodward Detroit, Michigan
(513) 565-3468

Snell examined the card. "How do you think it ties in?"

"Don't know yet. It could be a lucky break or it could only be a business card that somebody dropped."

"We'll check into it." Snell transcribed the name and address to her notebook.

Nicca noticed pale streaks of red lightening the sky in the east. "Damn, it's sunrise already," he mumbled. He had been on the scene through the night watching the FBI team sort through the van. Now, he absently leaned against the door while a photographer flashed picture after picture of the vehicle. He rubbed his eyes to wipe away the fatigue. When he opened them again he saw Snell standing next to him. Seeing her try to cover a sleepy yawn he said, "It's been a long night."

"Yeah, I sure could use a cup of coffee," she nodded.

"I could use some breakfast. When is Gunston due?"

"He should be landing at seven. Figure forty five minutes to drive up here. Probably around eight. The SAC wants to meet with all of us at ten, so that gives us about an hour to brief him on the case."

"Let's see, it's almost five-thirty now. Hmm, I should have enough time to drive home, shave and get some breakfast."

"I don't have time to make it to Dearborn and back," Snell sighed.

Nicca smiled, "Just come to my place. You can freshen up. There's a good all-night diner near me. We can discuss what to brief Gunston over breakfast."

"I'm not sure I should leave the scene."

"Don't worry about it. The lab boys don't need us to baby-sit them. Let's go get some chow before it's too late. We have a long day in front of us."

The morning traffic on I-75 was still light and they arrived at Nicca's apartment in fifteen minutes. "Make yourself at home," Nicca offered as he walked into his bedroom, "I'm going to take a quick shower and change. You can use the hall bathroom if you want to freshen up."

Snell looked around. The apartment was large but sparsely furnished. There were few knickknacks and other touches that per-sonalize a home, yet for some reason she felt comfortable there. She stopped to examine a set of pictures on the stereo cabinet shelves.

"That was my wife," Nicca said as he walked up behind her. "Here's a new toothbrush if you want to brush your teeth. There are some towels in the bathroom."

"She's attractive. I'm sorry," She didn't know what else to say.

"Thanks." He looked at the photos with a familiar longing, "I really miss her sometimes. We'd better hurry if we want to get something to eat. I'm afraid I don't have much to eat here."

"You know, I'm not that hungry anymore. Every time I think about those two bodies, it depresses me. It gives me this lump in my stomach. " She shifted her gaze to the window. It wasn't the murders that made her lose her appetite. It was also Nicca. He was tall and thin with a naturally dark complexion. He was also kind and considerate of her without being condescending like many of her other male compatriots. He seemed to understand her better than any of the other agents she had worked with in the bureau. He made her comfortable, safe and secure. For a moment she felt awkward. Standing next to him in his apartment watching the sunrise slant through the window blinds was an experience that she had previously shared only with lovers.

Without thinking, he put his hand gently on her shoulder. "I know how you feel. It isn't easy getting used to this senseless kind of violence. But, take my advice, you'll be a lot better having after something to eat."

She looked at him and smiled, "You might be right."

Nicca looked into her eyes and he sensed some of what she felt but he wasn't sure what he was feeling. Maybe it was because he wasn't accustomed to working with a woman partner. He knew he couldn't afford to get emotionally involved during such an important investigation. The attraction was there and he couldn't deny it. He dropped his arm and said, "Let me take a shower and change and I'll feel a lot better. It will give us a better outlook on the case. Sometimes I do my best thinking in the shower," he said almost to himself as he walked back to the bedroom.

"Is that right?" Snell replied while watching him leave the room.

Nicca and Snell returned to the scene at seven ten. Both had benefited from the break. They found Denzer talking to the senior lab technician. He said, "A guy can't even visit his grandchildren around here."

"I thought you went to your daughter's house today?" Nicca asked with a smile.

"I did. For some reason I decided to check my messages this morning before I hit the road. When I heard Snell's message, I drove straight here," he explained.

"Anything new since we left?" Nicca asked. Snell took notes while Denzer went over the latest results.

"That should be good enough to brief Gunston when he arrives," Nicca concluded. "Laura, do you want to brief him?"

"Sure, I guess so," she haltingly replied.

Gunston arrived at eight seventeen accompanied by the SAC. By that time Nicca, Snell and Denzer had put together a thorough briefing. First they took the two senior agents to the murder locations and then the van. After looking over the scene, the two men moved to the side. They talked privately for a moment and then the SAC left. Gunston turned to his task force and said, "Team, you've done well up here. It looks like we have a ton of evidence to sort through. The SAC wants a progress briefing at noon today back at the Field Office. Let's leave the lab boys up here to wrap things up. I want to do a dry run brief at eleven. I'll handle the noon brief but I want you three there for backup. It's been a long night but I think we have some good stuff here. We should get something solid out of this. We've got to put an end to this case. "

At twelve precisely, Gunston and the remainder of the task force entered the SAC's office. Seated at the table were the SAC, the public affairs officer and a secretary. The SAC spoke first, "Mike, everyone, please have a seat. Before you begin the briefing I want to bring you up to speed on the latest from Headquarters. I spoke with the deputy director this morning. This case is getting hot. He got a call from the Attorney General. Apparently she received calls from the Secretary of State and from the White House Chief of Staff. There is some top level concern that the publicity from these incidents could put the wrong spin on the President's new get tough trade policy. State is concerned about the reaction in Japan. We need to break this case and quickly. The problem is everybody expects us to do another World Trade Center miracle." The SAC looked expectantly at Gunston.

"Well sir, I can't promise a miracle but we've got a lot more to work with than before. All the lab results aren't in yet but we have a pretty good picture of what happened last night. As you will see in a few minutes, we have enough leads that it's a matter of time. It's going to take a whole lot of solid investigation but we'll piece it together."

"So you don't think we've got the smoking gun?" the SAC asked with a touch of disappointment.

"No sir, not yet. Let me go through what we do have. I think you'll agree we have some solid leads."

"Mike, let's go. I wish we had something good to tell the director."

"Yes, sir. You've been to the scene so you know the layout. As best we can figure, the terrorists arrived around one a.m. in two vehicles. One was the van with the bomb, the second was the getaway car. We ran a make on the van and it was stolen. We have investigators checking that out. We'll know more tomorrow. We have not been able to identify the second car. The guards saw it on the video but could not see enough of it to clearly make it out."

"Do we have it on tape?" the SAC asked.

"No, sir. The security system at the Sunon building does not record video. It relies on a short jump scan memory feature which only alerts the guards to movement and break-in attempts."

The SAC nodded while Gunston continued, "The guards saw two men exit the van. One of the guards, Peter Kodurba, went to check on the delivery. He walked out front and probably encountered the getaway vehicle. There was shooting. The guard fired one round. Then he was struck by two rounds; one in the abdomen and one in the head. The bullet fired into his head lodged in the ground underneath, indicating that he was shot while he lay there. That was the fatal shot."

"We've identified the other victim as Mister Ryoichi Kawasaki, a Japanese National. He was Director of Marketing for Sunon North America. He apparently worked late..."

"On Sunday?" the SAC interrupted.

"Yes, he told the guards that he had a telephone conference with his office in Tokyo. It's Sunday here but Monday there."

"I see," said the SAC. "So you don't think this was designed to hit him then? After all, he's a fairly high ranking executive."

"No sir, I, we, do not. We believe he left his office and inadvertently encountered the terrorists. They killed him because he saw them. Admittedly he was killed in an execution style, but then why did they need a bomb if this was supposed to be a hit? We believe that the terrorists wanted to destroy the Sunon building in a manner similar to the warehouse bombing. Only this time something went wrong. The fact that the guard fired a round indicates that he detected some trouble. We haven't been able to establish if his shot hit anything."

Gunston took a sip of water and continued, "We have a wealth of forensic evidence to sort through. Thanks to Fire Marshall Nicca's cool thinking and courageous act, the bomb was defused five minutes before detonation. Our lab people have dissected the bomb. We're trying to identify the blasting caps and kicker charges. Then we can trace them to find out where they were sold and to whom. This is potentially a big break, unless of course the demolitions were stolen. This should give us a list of suspects with access to these particular demolitions."

"We also found six shell casings on the ground. They're from a rare type of gun, a .44 Automagnum. The shells are essentially modified rifle ammunition. Very powerful. We've got a list of all registered .44 Automagnums in the area. There are only twenty-five names on the list. If we cross check this list with the other list we might be able to narrow down the search. We'll need brick agents to shag each one down."

"Right, make a note, Margaret," the SAC said to his secretary. "Go on," he said to Gunston.

"Preliminary autopsy results indicate that both men were killed by the same gun. It's hard to say but it looks like the guard was killed first and then the executive. Anyway, I think the van and the bomb present the best opportunity for evidence. There are hundreds of fingerprints all over the vehicle. However, the prints on the steering wheel and door handles are smeared. We found none on the bomb itself. It looks like the terrorists wore gloves. The lab is doing a fiber analysis but the results aren't in yet."

"Anything else?" the SAC asked.

"Yes, we're not sure if it's related to the case but we found a business card with the name of a local cosmetics sales representative at the scene. It was lying on the ground near the guard. It appears to be in pretty good condition, no water damage or tire tracks on it for example. So it hasn't been on the ground long. There are some prints on the card but we haven't been able to identify them. The lab wants us to send the card to headquarters for laser analysis. The terrorists, the guard or Mr. Kawasaki might have dropped it. We'll have to run that down. My gut reaction is that it's related, but we're not sure how."

The SAC nodded in agreement, "Well. You have your work cut out for you. Let me know how many more people you need. If necessary, we can request help from headquarters. In the meantime, I agree that we should keep a tight lid on this case. Bill will handle the press." The SAC looked at Bill Wesson, the public affairs officer. Then he continued, "The best policy now is to not comment on the bomb. This isn't only to keep the terrorists off guard. Earlier, I received a call from the Detroit Mayor's office. They want word of the bomb kept as quiet as possible. Sunon is very sensitive to the reaction back home and they appear to have some well-placed friends in the Mayor's office. All right?" he asked. When no one replied he said, "Seeing how well this is going makes me wish I was back on the bricks. Mike, I want a brief tomorrow morning first thing."

"Yes sir," Gunston tersely replied not fully appreciating the attention.

"One other thing. Fire Marshall Nicca, I'm going to put you in for a citation for defusing that bomb. You risked your life but it might end up breaking this case wide open. Unfortunately, official recognition will have to wait until later since we need to keep quiet about the bomb. I hope you understand."

"No problem, sir. I didn't expect anything special," Nicca said with genuine modesty.

"Good, then get home and get some sleep. That goes for you too Snell."

"Yes, sir," she replied.

"Bill, stick around. I want to talk about the press statement," the SAC said as the others got up to leave.

Outside the office Gunston said, "Everyone's done a great job. Nicca and Snell, do as the SAC said and get some sleep. I want to have a meeting at eight tonight. I want everybody there."

GRAYLING, MICHIGAN

It was dark by the time Chuck and Brian finished digging the hole for Alex's grave. Debbie sobbed quietly while the two men lowered the body, still wrapped in the faded sheet, into the ground. The burial site was located in the same clearing where they tested the bomb. All three stared into the hole. After a few moments Brian started back filling the hole.

"Wait a minute, Brian," Chuck interrupted, "Shouldn't we say something first?"

"Oh, sure," Brian thought for a brief second and said, "Alex, it's too bad I didn't know you that well but you're a tough dude and they better watch out wherever you're headed." Brian looked at Chuck.

"Debbie, do you want to say anything?"

Through her sobs Debbie weakly said, "Good bye, Alex." She added softly, "I'm sorry."

Resting his hands on the handle of the shovel Chuck said, "Well,

Alex. I'll say this much. The motherfuckers are going to pay for this. You won't go unavenged." Then Chuck started piling dirt into the hole.

Both Debbie and Brian were surprised by Chuck's comment. During the long ride to Grayling, Chuck silently contemplated the turn of events. He gradually came to believe that they would survive this mishap. He didn't know what happened to the bomb but it didn't concern him. He knew that he was careful. There were no fingerprints. If they defused the bomb, they wouldn't find anything incriminating. There was nothing that he could see that could lead to them. They had to keep Debbie under control.

As he became convinced that they would not get caught he began to develop more of a sense of rage. His anger became more and more focused on Sunon than ever before. They cost him his job and his self-esteem. They cheated Debbie's father out of his life's work. They were screwing Cannon. Now he had lost one of his people and it was their fault. Sunon was the cause of all his woe. Patriotism and economics were no longer the issue. It was he against them. He became determined to seek revenge in a final significant and if necessary, desperate act. What that would be, he didn't yet know. But he vowed he would get revenge.

Chapter 17

Artemis Cosmetics was a retail outlet situated in a small office building off Woodward Avenue. Nicca wearing his leather jacket and Snell in a business suit with tan trench coat entered the store past a glass door plastered with beauty product ads. The clerk smiled at them from behind the counter as they entered. "Can I help you?" the clerk asked.

Nicca nodded. "I'm Fire Marshall Nicca with the Detroit Fire Department and this is Special Agent Snell with the FBI." He flashed his badge. "We would like to speak with Miss Elizabeth Kessler. Is she here?"

The clerk's face tightened and her eyes widened. "Is there something wrong?"

"There's nothing to be alarmed about. We're investigating a case and we need to ask her some questions," Nicca waved his hands in front of him. Snell nodded.

"She's in the back office. I'll page her." The clerk lifted the phone next to the cash registered and called Kessler. A few minutes later Nicca spied a young woman enter the room. She wore a stylish Anne Klein dress with matching purse and high heel shoes. Several layers of makeup, making her a walking demonstration of the product line, embellished her plain, broad face. Although the effect looked overdone, Nicca found her attractive. He threw a glance at Laura and then decided he preferred the agent's more natural appearance.

"I'm Elizabeth Kessler. Can I help you?" she smiled revealing perfectly white teeth. Too perfect, Nicca thought, obviously result of a bleaching treatment.

Nicca rose to greet her and extended his hand. "I'm Fire Marshal Nicca. This is Special Agent Laura Snell, from the FBI. We have some urgent questions to ask you."

"About what I can't imagine," Liz exclaimed, casting a glance at the clerk.

"It's routine for now. Do you have an office where we can talk privately?"

"Sure, this way." Liz led them past the cosmetic displays to a small office in the rear of the building.

Liz sat behind her desk. "Mind if I smoke?" she asked and without waiting for a reply, opened the desk drawer and retrieved a cigarette from a crumpled pack. She took a deep drag and said, "I'm trying to cut back, but I'm afraid your visit has me a little nervous. No, not really nervous, worried..." She pulled on the hem of her Ann Klein dress.

"Miss Kessler, Special Agent Snell and I are assigned to a special task force investigating a series of related crimes. Perhaps you heard on the news about a double murder in Troy last night?" Nicca watched Liz's reaction.

"Murder, double murder?" Liz tightened her shoulders then stammered. "No. No, I didn't hear about it. I'm not a fan of the news. What does this have to do with me?"

"Well, Miss Kessler we don't know exactly. That's why we're here." Nicca looked at Snell.

She took the lead, "Your business card was found at the scene of the murder..."

"Excuse me?" Liz questioned.

"We found your business card at the scene," Snell repeated.

"What! I don't...." her sentence drifted off. She stood with her hand to the cigarette, taking a deep drag. "How did it get there?"

"We don't know," Snell said softly. "We thought you might shed some light on it."

Liz gave them a blank look. She gestured with her hands slightly as if to say I have no idea.

Nicca asked, "How often do you give out your cards, Ms. Kessler?"

"I don't know. I guess I go through a lot of them. I keep a stack on the table out there. I give them to clients, suppliers, friends, you know."

Nicca waited for a second, then asked, "Are any of your clients Japanese?"

208

"I don't think so. No, I don't think any of them are."

"Do any of your clients or friends work for Sunon Corporation?"

Liz's eyes widened at the mention of the word Sunon. She turned her back to the investigators and squashed the cigarette in a clean ashtray on her desk.

"Is something wrong, Ms. Kessler?" Nicca threw a quick look a Snell.

"Oh, no, nothing's wrong. I'm a little nervous. I've never been questioned like this before. By the police, I mean. It's kind of nerve wracking." She exhaled then smoothed a fold in the fabric and continued, "To answer your question, no, I don't know anyone like that." Her voice quivered.

"I see. Well thank you for your time." Nicca reached into his leather jacket and removed a business card. "Here is my phone number. If you think of anything that could help, please give me a call."

"Sure. If I do, I will."

Nicca and Snell walked to their car.

"What do you think?" Snell titled her head toward Nicca as he pulled the sedan into traffic.

"She'll never be a poker player. You could read her like a book. She knows something."

"That's what I thought "

"We need to keep an eye on her. We don't want to bring her downtown for questioning although I'm sure she'd crack if we kept at her." Nicca sucked in air over his bottom lip. "No, it's too obvious. Our guys would find out and lay low. We have to be more covert. We don't have much to go on, but I'd like to tap her phone. I wonder if we could get a judge to go along."

Snell let out a deep breath, "It won't hurt to try. She's been linked to material evidence found at the scene. They might go for it. The only problem is it usually takes so long to get Title III court authority."

"If what Gunston says about the case getting top priority is true, maybe we can get it expedited."

"You could be right. I'll ask him." Her cell phone's ring interrupted the thought. Snell flipped it open, "Hello, This is Special Agent Snell."

Snell listened for a second. "Hold on. Let me put you on speaker." As she reached for the speakerphone button, she said "It's Denzer.

The lab found something interesting." Snell pushed the button, "Go ahead, Joe's in the car with me."

"Hello, George," Nicca called out, "What's up?"

"They found three different types of blood at the scene. Two of the types match the victims. There's a third type that doesn't match. It looks like someone else has been bleeding at our crime scene."

"The guard's shot...," Nicca blurted.

"That's right. I had the same idea."

Nicca's eyes darted back and forth. "Have you checked with the area hospitals? Doctors?"

"Not yet, but I'm working on it. One other thing, Gunston went to talk with one of the Sunon execs. He wants you to meet him at the Sunon headquarters at one o'clock."

"Got it. Anything else?" Nicca asked.

"Nope, that's it. I'll see you this evening."

"See you later."

Snell broke the connection. "This could be the big break."

"We'll see. Let's get something to eat."

NORTHWEST FLIGHT 12 ENROUTE TO TOKYO, JAPAN.

"Yes, Sir, may I help you," said the attractive flight attendant in her overseas work smock.

"Bring me another double scotch," Kondo replied.

"Yes, Sir," she said as she headed back to the business class galley of the Northwest flight to Narita Airport. At the galley, she snidely remarked to her co-worker, "We got a drinker in 28K. We're not even airborne an hour and he's already on his third double Ballentine."

"Well, keep an eye on him," said the senior flight attendant. "Try to cut him off at four drinks. On my last flight to Japan, we had to have the paramedics waiting for us on the taxiway. A Japanese passenger in first class collapsed in the aisle. We thought he had a heart attack. Turns out he was only drunk. He kept refilling his glass from the self-serve bar. We don't need that on this flight."

"Yeah, no kidding."

When the flight attendant returned to Kondo's seat, she could hear him talking in Japanese to the man sitting next to him. From the tone of his voice, she could tell that the drinker was agitated.

210

"This is ridiculous, Hara-San. Traveling to Tokyo for Kawasaki's funeral. We have a business to run," fumed Kondo.

"It is an unusual situation; murder of our co-worker. We should pay our respects to the family."

"Oh shit, Hara-San," Kondo blurted in English. "You know as well as I do why they want us back in Japan. The board will grill us. They will try to consider all possible angles to explain this violence. Even Takahashi will try to turn this to his advantage."

"Jomu please don't make more of this terrible situation than it already is," replied the junior executive in the most humble Japanese he could use.

"Hah," Kondo grunted. "Don't be naive. Everyone will try to use this incident to his own advantage. This is political." He took the refreshed drink from the flight attendant and downed it in three successive swigs.

"I need another," Kondo said gesturing toward the aisle but the attendant had already returned to her workstation. Turning back to face Hara, Kondo continued "Then there's the press. They will feed like vultures on the bones of Kawasaki."

Hara cringed.

"The press will cover the funeral. They will interview the widow and ask her about the situation in the U.S. as if she is some sort of expert. Her sobbing will be all over the TV. She'll end up a victim too. After they've used her, they'll dump her like they'll dump us."

"We have our press plan prepared by the public affairs office," Hara meekly replied. "We say that it was a tragic circumstance. A freak situation. The media won't expect more from us than that, will they?"

"It's not the media I'm concerned about. It's Takahashi. This damn situation fits right in with his plan to discontinue our work in favor of a joint venture." Kondo paused. "I need a better approach for the board meeting." The alcohol blurred Kondo's vision so he shut his eyes and tried to think of a way to handle the upcoming meeting in Tokyo. The drinks had the desired effect. He fell asleep.

TROY ,MICHIGAN

Nicca and Snell waited in the lobby of the Sunon Headquarters. The room was eerily quiet in contrast to their previous visit when police lines surrounded the area and detectives scoured the scene. Now the police barricades were gone and there was no one searching the

211

bushes. To outward appearances, the office was back to normal.

Nicca was pacing the floor when he spotted Gunston approaching the front door. Nicca eyed the man over. It was evident that Gunston's tours in the nation's capitol had a polishing effect on his image. The traditionally cut suit looked more expensive than it was and his tassel loafers and paisley tie completed the east coast power look. He certainly didn't look like a Midwestern detective working a homicide.

"Hi, Joe, Laura. Looks like you beat me here." Turning to the guard he said, "We have an appointment with Mr. Kondo. Could you call his office please."

"Yes sir. Are you with the police?" the guard asked politely.

"No, FBI. I believe he's expecting us."

"Hmm, that's funny. I thought Mr. Kondo was in Japan. I'll call his secretary." The guard spoke quietly on the phone. "Someone will be down to pick you up in a few minutes," he said to Gunston.

A conservatively dressed middle-aged woman walked into the lobby. She saw the three investigators and said, "Are you here to see Mr. Kondo?"

"That's right," Gunston said as all three rose to their feet.

"Well, Mr. Kondo is in Japan right now. He went with Mr. Hara to Mr. Kawasaki's funeral. Anyway, Mr. Shane will see you. He is the Director of Public Affairs. He's waiting for you upstairs."

They followed her up a short flight of stairs and down a long, plain corridor. At the end they entered Shane's spacious office. Unlike Kondo's Spartan decor, Shane's office held all the normal trappings of American executive success. Pictures of classic cars and golf scenes hung on the walls and a golf putter and two balls conspicuously occupied one corner. Shane rose to greet them. He quickly shook hands with Gunston and Nicca, but made an exaggerated display when he shook Snell's hand. "It's very nice to meet you," he said with emphasis on the word "nice."

Slightly embarrassed, Snell nodded and withdrew her hand. In the corner of her eye, she thought she saw a frown cross Nicca's face.

Nicca, impatient with Shane's apparent interest in Snell, started, "So Mr. Shane, I believe we met a few weeks ago. As you might know, the FBI is investigating the case now. Special Agent Gunston is heading the special task force."

"That's correct. I wanted to meet with you to go over some of the details of the case," Gunston added.

"Please take a seat. Is there anything you would like? A cup of coffee perhaps?"

"No thank you," Gunston replied. "I have a few questions..."

"I'm sure you do," Shane interrupted. "Believe me, we need to get to the bottom of this for a lot of reasons. We'll do everything we can to cooperate."

Shane's assurance sounded less than sincere to Nicca.

"I can appreciate that," Gunston said. "One of the problems I have with this case is the apparent lack of motive. Why would anyone want to single out Sunon? Can you give us an insight into this?"

Shane raised his eyes to study the ceiling for a moment and then shifted his gaze to Snell. He looked at her as he said, "I have a theory but I don't have any proof."

"What's that?" Nicca interjected.

"Well," Shane exhaled. "I hate to open this can of worms, but," he paused. "We've had a lot of trouble with the union lately. It's no secret that Sunon is a right-to-work shop. We don't want the union. Our workers don't want it. They tried and failed once before. Now they're trying again."

"Did you have any trouble with them before? Any similar acts of violence?" Gunston asked.

"No. All we have is some hate mail."

"Do you have that available?"

"Yes. We keep all customer complaints on file for a certain period."

"If there are any developments with the union, let me know. Meanwhile, I want to have an agent check these files against our suspect list. One of our agents will stop by tomorrow to start. Whom should he ask for?"

"Have him or her," he smiled at Snell, "call me when he arrives. I'll take him to the customer service section. You'll get our full cooperation."

After the agents left the room, Shane rose and paced back and forth. The agents' visit had temporarily distracted him from his earlier deliberations on how to approach Mary Fielding about his idea for a weekend trip. He wasn't sure if their relationship was ready for it plus the murder and bomb cast a somber mood over everything. Shane thought it over and decided he needed company so he sat down and dialed Fielding's office number.

"May I speak to Mary Fielding, please? This is Jack Shane."

After a brief wait, a breathless Fielding answered, "Hi Jack. I was getting ready to leave. What's up?"

"I wanted to hear your voice," Shane said.

"Come on, Shane. What's really up?" Fielding replied.

"Well, I did want to ask you something. I don't know how to say it." Shane paused but Fielding remained silent.

Shane continued, "How would you like to go on a cruise up the Chesapeake Bay?"

"Hmm? What do you mean? On a sailboat?"

"Oh, not quite. I have something a little different in mind but as romantic. Basically a get-away for the weekend."

"It sounds good so far, Shane. What and when do you have in mind?"

"Well, that's the sticky part. I'm not exactly sure yet."

"Shane, sometimes I don't get you."

"No, it's really simple. Well, okay, not that simple. Here's the story. I have to attend a special ceremony and reception in Baltimore two weeks from now. We're going to have a ribbon cutting ceremony at the Port of Baltimore for the first shipment of 500GSXs. We've got the Mayor of Baltimore and maybe even the Governor lined up. I'm representing the corporate office for Sunon North America. They'll be a bunch of other local dignitaries there. The local Sunon dealers will be putting on quite a show. I was thinking about taking the ship up to Baltimore instead of flying in the night before."

"What ship?" Mary's question betrayed her intrigue.

"The car transport with the first 500GSXs is due in Baltimore Saturday night or Sunday morning. It will be entering the Chesapeake some time Friday. I'm flying to Norfolk to wait for it. When it enters the bay, it will stop briefly to pick up a bay pilot. I've already made the call and we, that is if you want to go, can meet it then. We would take the pilot boat to the ship. Then we can spend Friday night and Saturday cruising up the bay. The ceremony and reception won't be until Monday morning. By the way, this is a first class operation. I reserved the owner's cabin on the ship. I hear that it is quite plush. What do you think?"

"Shane, it sounds wonderful. I could catch a commuter flight to Norfolk and meet you there."

"Great. Fax me your flight information and I'll pick you up at the airport."

"Say, this is a pleasant surprise. You do know how to make my day. I'll call you tomorrow."

"Mary, it's going to be a blast. Oh, by the way, did you ever find out what Pringle was up to?"

"Pringle," Mary scanned her memory. "Oh yeah, the safety blitz. Ah, don't worry about that. He's only a Congressman."

ANA HOTEL, ROPPONGI DISTRICT, TOKYO

Kondo awoke at sunrise and looked out the window of the seventeenth floor of the ANA Hotel over the tiled rooftops of Roppongi. The frantic atmosphere of Tokyo bustling with cars, trucks and people was strangely absent. The city had not yet risen. Through the morning mist, he could see two gaijins, probably Americans from the US embassy compound, jogging on the empty streets below. He wistfully watched the joggers. You are more at home here than I am, he thought. He rubbed his eyes. A combination of jet lag and the whisky from the trip made his head ache. Today was the funeral and tomorrow his meeting with the Sunon Board of Directors.

"I dread this, this funeral," Kondo muttered. He could not admit to himself the reason was that the ritual would remind him too much of his mother's death. How he did not have money to spend on a lavish ceremony, instead sending off his mother with a simple Buddhist prayer service and cremation.

He went over to the mini-bar in his room and poured a can of orange juice into one of the hotel glasses. He then emptied a small bottle of vodka into the glass. Sipping on this, he looked into the mirror over the dresser. He scowled at his reflection as he pondered his bad fortune turning his mood even sourer. He took another sip from the drink despite the bloodshot eyes, hollow stare, and pallid skin staring back at him in the mirror. Kondo yelled into the ghastly image, mocking himself.

"Oh sure, the Kawasaki's. Yes, they will have a nice affair. A complete send-off for their departed father and relative. God damn," he said and flung the drink across the room.

GRAYLING, MICHIGAN

"I'll take care of the dishes," Debbie sighed.

"Are you sure?" Chuck said.

"Yeah, it will give me something to do".

Brian and Chuck rose from the table and walked into the living room. Chuck tended the wood stove while Brian stared out the window. Then he joined Brian by the window. Brian glanced at Chuck but said nothing. Both men stared at the darkening winter sky.

Finally Chuck said, "I want to show you something."

"What is it?" Brian asked without removing his gaze from the winter sunset.

"I read an article this morning that gave me an idea. I want to show it to you to see what you think."

"What's it about?"

"Take a look." Chuck moved to a haphazard stack of old magazines near the couch and picked up an old copy of Time Magazine. "I was flipping through this magazine this morning when I saw this story about Honda shipping motorcycles to Vietnam during the war."

"Yeah, so," Brian appeared uninterested. He took the magazine and scanned the article. When he finished he said, "So what? I don't get it."

"What did it say about the ship?" Chuck asked as if he was a teacher quizzing a student.

"Let me see," Brian looked back at the article. Putting the magazine down he recited, "If the Viet Cong had managed to hit one of the ships that were delivering motorcycles as they were waiting in the Saigon River, Honda would have gone under. They took the chance and kept on shipping motorcycles to Vietnam."

"Right." Chuck pointed to the magazine article. "Losing a ship full of motorcycles would have ruined Honda. Made them bankrupt."

"So, what does that have to do with us?"

"It might be our ticket out of this. If we can strike one more time. One really big hit, we might be able to win this thing after all."

"What are you talking about?" Debbie entered the room while wiping her hands on a towel.

"How do all those Sunon cars get over here?"

"By ship I guess," she shrugged.

"Right, they ship in most of their cars. But think about it. What if we were able to hit one of them? That would really put the hurt on them."

"What? Are you saying that we blow up one of their car carrying ships?" Brian moaned.

216

"Yeah. That's exactly what I'm saying." Chuck slammed a fist into his other open hand. "Look, if Honda would have went under if the VC nailed one of their motorcycle shipments, think how bad it would hurt if Sunon lost one of their shipments. Do you know how many cars they put in one ship?"

Brian and Debbie shook their heads.

"Two or three thousand at a time. Man, we'd have to blow up a hundred dealerships before we could do that much damage. That's like sixty million dollars worth of cars. Boom, in one shot."

"Chuck, how can we sink one of their ships?" Debbie asked.

"It shouldn't be that hard. Ships sink all the time. I'll look in my SF stuff."

"When I was on the force," Brian added, "I remember hearing about an IRA attack on a British cargo ship. They kidnapped a pilot boat and boarded the ship. I think they used explosives to sink it."

"That's one way. But I don't think we have the manpower to board a ship. I'll figure out a way. What do you think?"

Brian took a deep breath, "Well, if we aren't on the top ten list now, we certainly will be after that. What do we get out of it?"

"I'm sure our sponsor would come up with some cash."

"It better be a lot of cash, because we won't want to stay in the US after this. Some place like Brazil or South Africa would be much better."

"Let me work that problem. I'll give the big man a call. This could be the answer. We nail Sunon, avenge Alex and get the heck out of Dodge. I've always wanted to go to South Africa."

"I don't know Chuck. Would we ever be able to return to the US?" Debbie flopped into an armchair.

"Maybe. If everything blows over, sure we could return in a couple of years, none the worse for wear."

Chapter 18

Kawasaki's funeral, arranged at the Shinshoi Temple, where there was enough room for the expected visitors, had a fake and prefabricated quality to it. The attention the Kawasaki family normally would have paid to balancing austere color and design disappeared in the pall of the tragedy. Garish colors and a jumbled mixture of religious and cultural artifacts contrasted terribly.

Kondo entered the vestibule of the temple and noticed a round short man in a morning coat.

"Ohayo gozaimasu" said the rounded gentlemen using polite Japanese. "I am Minamoto, Funeral Director." The mortician bowed deeply to Kondo.

"I am Kondo of Sunon," replied Kondo reaching in his pocket for an envelope, "Please take this."

"Hai," responded the funeral director. He gently took the envelope and cradled it with care. "Please enter and have a seat, Kondo-Sama, the service will start soon.

Kondo picked a seat in the last row on the far right. Kondo caught a scent of the incense; the smell made him clammy.

I need a drink, he thought. He looked to the rear of the room to see where the beverages were but froze in his seat when he saw the diminutive Takahashi enter the room. Takahashi quickly took a seat on the other side of the room. He did not seem to notice Kondo.

The room filled with other mourners. Above the quiet shuffling of feet Kondo listened to the sobs of the widow. Kondo stared glumly at his hands folded in his lap. He sat motionless, his mind trying to clear itself of the memory of his mother's funeral.

Kondo heard a sound at the rear of the room and turned his head to see a Shinshu priest and his assistant, both wearing spotless black outer kimonos, enter the room. The priest made eye contact with Kondo. Kondo stared back. The priest's eyes had a glistening shine; a shine that could see through Kondo, see the pain, the confusion, the fear he felt. After what seemed a long time, Kondo dropped his gaze from the priest. He could no longer bear to look into the man's eyes.

The priest carefully tied an intricate knot in a richly woven obi, and sat lotus-style in front of the altar and started reciting the death poem. As the priest repeated over and over each verse of the sutra, beseeching Kawasaki's soul on its journey, Kondo felt a chill shudder through his body. Images from his mother's funeral reappeared in his head. Sadness dampened his face as he recalled the frustration he felt about her illness and her death. He sighed while the chanting continued. Figures of his wife and only child appeared in front of him. The images had no faces. He put one of his hands up to move the figures from his mind but his mind flashed forward to the prospect of his own death. He could not fathom it and a wild confusion raced through his body. His pulse quickened and his blood pressure rose. Pained and flushed, he shook his head.

What am I doing? I must focus on the present. My plan is working. We had made progress in countering Takahashi's move for creating the joint venture. The political misinformation had worked and Deaver's press conference had more impact than expected. Now, Kawasaki's death. How would this change the plan? How would the board react? Would they relate this to the other bombing? Would this be enough to convince them the political situation in the US was different? They had to side with Takahashi.

Kondo swung his head from side to side trying to deny to himself what he surely believed was true.

I've lost. They will dismantle all that I've built. His face paled. He felt faint.

The walls felt like they were closing in on him. He rose and left the service. At a bar table in a room adjacent to the vestibule he grabbed a bottle of Suntory Scotch and filled a plastic cup. He gulped half the drink. The liquor, a respectable copy of a venerable Scottish blend, burned his throat as it went down. He didn't feel better.

I have no recourse. In Japan I am helpless to solve the problem back in the United States.

A familiar voice from across the bar table pulled him from his thoughts. "Kondo-San, it is good to see you again."

Kondo looked up to see Mansuru Hayashi, a former classmate from TODAI, Tokyo University, grinning at him. Hayashi was non-descript wearing a dark gray suit, white shirt and black tie. He looked like all the other mourners. "Hayashi-San, it has been a while," Kondo said.

"Kondo-San, you don't look well."

"Oh, I need some fresh air. It smells like death in here."

"Please, let me help you outside." Hayashi took Kondo's arm and led him through the doors outside the Temple. "Such a terrible circumstance to meet again, old friend,"

"Terrible in more ways than you can believe."

"What is happening in America?"

"Senseless violence, senseless violence."

"America is a dangerous place."

"No, it's not that. Some thugs have decided to wage their own war against Sunon. It is at the most inopportune time."

"Thugs, what do you mean thugs?" Hayashi's voice raised as if he had developed a different level of interest in what Kondo had to say.

"Kawasaki's death wasn't happenstance. Thugs murdered Kawa-saki. Thugs who think because we sell cars we are an enemy. They would like to destroy Sunon North America if they could."

"Do you know who these thugs are?"

"Those incompetent American investigators may. They are not sure. They believe they are disgruntled workers, racial supremacists, something. They think they know who they are, but they can't find them. No Detroit policeman is going to go out of his way to help Sunon Corporation."

"The police know who did this?"

"Yes... No.... I don't know." Kondo shook his head pathetically.

Two men dressed in sport coats rushed over to the old classmates. One of the men stuck a microphone in Kondo's face.

"Are you Kondo-San of Sunon North America? Is there any truth that the Sunon shooting was racially motivated? Is the murderer a member of a Japanese hate-cult?"

The other's camera flashed in Kondo's face. "What precautions is Sunon taking to protect its other workers in America? Is America too dangerous for Japanese workers?"

Kondo stared blankly at the reporters. Hayashi could see the pain and trouble his old friend was experiencing. "What are you doing?" Hayashi yelled at the reporters, "Have you no decency! We are trying to pay our respects. Get away from here." Hayashi put his arm around Kondo and pulled him from the reporters.

The first reporter asked again "What will Sunon do about the shooting?"

Hayashi sneered back at the reporter. "Please, let us be. We have no statement." He turned his head and said to Kondo "Come Kondo-San, let's go to my car. Let's get away from these rude reporters."

"I can't leave, the funeral is still..."

"No one will say anything. They know the stress you are under. Besides, we have already left. I'll take you back to your hotel." Hayashi ushered Kondo to his car. "What hotel are you at?"

"The ANA in Roppongi," Kondo whispered.

Hayashi told his driver, "ANA Hotel, let's go."

After driving a few minutes in silence, Hayashi looked into Kondo's face. "Kondo-San, how would you like to relax at my club."

"I'm afraid I'm not quite in the mood for that."

"Oh, come now old friend, it will take your mind off this terrible business. Besides, this is the Koganei Club, the best near Tokyo. "

"The Koganei Club." Kondo paused as he considered the merits of the club in his current mental state. "I suppose you are right. That might be a good idea. I have nothing scheduled for the rest of the day. I need to get away from this." Kondo briefly recalled the morbid images that haunted him inside the Temple. The flashback reinforced his decision. "Yes, I would like that. And a warm bath would help a lot."

"Good, why don't you grab a change of clothes at the hotel. We can drive in my car and still have time to play eighteen holes."

The exclusive Koganei Club on the northern outskirts of Tokyo catered to Japanese corporate clientele. Hayashi's company, the Inoman Bank, purchased several corporate memberships for its senior executives. More than executive perks, the memberships could be bought and sold at the going rate like financial securities. Hayashi could sell his membership for one million dollars, but he would never dream of doing it. The status and privilege of a Koganei membership was worth every bit of the money to him.

As the chauffeured Sunon sedan drove through the twisty narrow roads leading to the clubhouse, Hayashi said, "The course is spectacular. Many say it is one of the top five in Japan. I believe you will enjoy playing it."

"I appreciate your hospitality, I hope I can enjoy a round of golf right now."

"Just relax, old friend."

Kondo did. After a few holes, he had forgotten completely about his upcoming meeting with the Sunon board. Instead, he concentrated on his game and on soundly trouncing his old classmate.

After the round of golf, Hayashi and Kondo retired to the bathhouse.

Behind the clubhouse cleverly shaped concrete and stone made it look like a naturally flowing underground spring rose from the rocks into a frothing pool. Pine trees mixed with bamboo screens surrounded the pool leading to a hut with a thatched roof for the locker room. Elderly female attendants helped tired golfers relax in the soothing water. The bathing experience was sublime and many patrons felt it overshadowed the championship golf course. At Koganei Club the outdoor setting for the spa contributed significantly to the desirability of the membership.

Kondo sat on a traditional low wooden stool and scrubbed his body at the water taps in the washing room. Recalling his years bathing in public baths, he scrubbed every pore as if he were a surgeon preparing for an operation. Satisfied that he was clean, he filled the traditional wooden pail with cold water from the tap. By repeatedly dousing himself with water from the wooden pail, every trace of soap rinsed from his body. Using a small wash cloth to cover his groin, he then rushed naked to the outdoor spa where he sunk his body into the steaming water. Luxuriating in the deliciously hot bubbly water, the steam condensed on his face and dissolved his concerns. While he sat there with his eyes closed, Hayashi slid alongside him.

Hayashi whispered, "Old friend, I may be able to help you with your problem."

"Huh," Kondo opened his eyes.

"Let me say that in my contacts with the bank, I have some associates that may be able to solve your problem in the states." Hayashi reached for a pack of cigarettes lying near the pool.

"Bank contacts, what are you talking about?"

"I know of your appreciation for directness but please bear with me." Hayashi lit his cigarette. "You say the police know who the thugs are that are terrorizing your facilities."

"I believe they know." Kondo splashed water on his face.

"Yet, they are reluctant to move."

"Perhaps, it is more likely they are incapable of moving. It's either incompetence or racial prejudice."

"Let me be delicate then." Hayashi studied his cigarette, and then continued. "Like you I have learned how to be successful. I have learned of the difficulties that lie on the path to success. That path sometimes requires special consideration." Hayashi hesitated puffing on the cigarette, looking carefully at Kondo's face over the glowing tip. "You know, I have many duties at the bank. One special one is to deal with certain elements that some would frown upon. Yet, these elements can provide a valuable function when there is no other recourse."

"What do you mean elements? Say what you mean Hayashi-San," Kondo's voice grew impatient, his grammar coarse.

"You know of the ties we have with men that have the capability to deal with unsavory situations."

"What are you talking about?"

"Old friend, you have a situation where there is a gray area between the law and the corporation. When in the gray, it is sometimes necessary to walk closer to the dark side. Especially to accomplish business that is in the best interest of the company. Perhaps, I can arrange for one of my contacts to go to the states and erase your problem. It's not all that unusual. We have many similar cases here in Japan."

"Hayashi-San, do you know what you are saying? This is not Yokohama or Osaka. You are talking about Detroit. Michigan. In the United States! Your so called professionals cannot deal with such a situation."

"Like Sunon, we are a multinational corporation. We have many contacts in the states. This is not that unusual." Hayashi blew out a stream of fetid smoke.

"You are serious," Kondo blinked.

"Through my contacts, we can arrange for a suitable action either here or in the states or in Europe for that matter."

Kondo knew of the business' tie with the Yakuza, Japanese organized crime, he had no idea that members of his own keiretsu were involved. "You mean the Yakuza."

Hayashi seemed to draw back at the mention of the Yakuza. "No. Not gangsters. Professionals." Hayashi moved close speaking directly

223

in Kondo's ear. "The viability of your operation is at stake. Serious matters like this require action. You must move. You can not rely on the incompetent gaijins to solve a Japanese problem."

Kondo colored. "I will not associate myself with such rubbish. Enough of this."

"Please, Kondo-San. As one old friend washes another's back, let me help you."

"Stop with this talk." Kondo splashed the water in front of him. "You are making me upset."

Hayashi backed away. "As you wish old friend, but I leave the offer open. If you need help let me know."

"Thank you," Kondo scowled and quickly exited the pool for the locker room. Hayashi watched him go, his face expressionless as he rubbed out his cigarette on the tile.

When Kondo finished dressing he went to the bar of the club. Hayashi was already there. Hayashi showed no evidence of their prior conversation. Kondo still felt agitated.

"I hope you enjoyed your experience at Koganei."

"Yes, thank you. I did," replied Kondo staring away from Hayashi. "I will take a cab back to the hotel."

"It is a long way, I will drive you."

"Thank you, but that's not necessary."

"Kondo-San, here is my meishi." Hayashi extended his business card while bowing slightly. "Call me anytime if I can help you,".

Kondo bowed slightly. "Good night."

Kondo returned to the ANA Hotel around 10 P.M. Before going to his room he stopped at the bar and had a brief western-style supper and two drinks. During his meal he mulled over Hayashi's offer. The utter preposterousness of it made him mad but as he considered it, he could envision the offer working. If done correctly, perhaps he could correct the small aberration and thwart other threats to his U.S. operation. The risk that was a problem. If found, he would lose everything. At the end of his meal, he said under his breath, "It's a wild idea, it would never work. I need another strategy. What could it be? What?"

When he returned to his room, he looked at a text message on cell phone screen

To: Kondo@sunon_america.com

From: JShane@sunon_america.com

"Please call right away."

Kondo glanced at this watch and mentally calculated the time back in Detroit. "Nine ten, Shane should be in his office." He dialed his secretary's number.

"Good morning, Sunon North America," came the cheerful voice of Claire Johnson.

"Good morning Claire, this is Kondo."

"Mr. Kondo, its good to hear from you. We were wondering why you didn't call yesterday."

"Claire, Is Mr. Shane in?"

"Yes, Mr. Shane is in his office, I'll connect you right away." After ten seconds, Mrs. Johnson was back on the line. "Mr. Shane will be right with you. By the way, Mr. Kondo, Mrs. Kondo called from Japan yesterday. She said she needed to talk to you. She said she's hired a lawyer."

Kondo frowned. "A lawyer?"

"I told her you were headed to Japan. She may call you."

"Thanks, Claire, but she hasn't called yet," Kondo mumbled. "Was there anything else?"

"No, that's it. Oh, here's Mr. Shane. Good-bye, sir and have a good trip." Johnson hung up her phone.

"Hello, Kondo-San. This is Shane."

"Hello, what is it?"

"Bad news boss. First, I have heard from our sources in Washington that the President is about to announce a new get-tough trade policy. The word is that this will be about one step short of full protectionism. There are several facets to it, but the big one is the President is going to ask for massive auto restrictions, and not only on imports. His trade negotiator has concocted a complicated formula to determine the U.S. content of automobiles. Autos not fitting the formula will face a hefty tariff. Our Kentucky plant is sure to fail the test."

"Such a proposal will never pass Congress."

"You're probably right. We have lots of friends there, but such a high visibility announcement is sure to give Takahashi some ammunition in his joint venture proposal."

"True, is there anything we can do to change the President's mind about this?"

"I'm working on that right now. We may be able to get through to one of his close advisors, but it's going to cost us. It looks like the President may be trying to find him an external enemy so he can rally the voters and get some of his other initiatives through. So far, he hasn't done too well."

"Damn, this is bad news. If Kawasaki's murder hasn't given Takahashi enough to convince the board a change is needed, then this might."

"Yeah, that's the other bad news. It's getting really hard to hide that there was a truck bomb on the scene of the murder. Those nosy reporters have pretty much been piecing the story together."

"Shane, if that gets out, there is no doubt about the outcome. Do whatever it takes, but keep them off that story."

"Understand boss. I'll keep you posted."

"Is there anything else?"

"The only good news is that the Honshu Prince is steaming again. Introduction plans for the 500GSX are going smoothly."

"Good, but the trade policy has me concerned. Keep up on this. I'll do what I can here."

"Got it, good bye."

"Good night." Kondo hung up the phone. His head was splitting like it was unraveling along with all his plans. With a shaky hand, he reached for a bottle of whisky in the mini-bar in the room. Twisting the small cap off the shot-sized bottle he put it to his lips. The strain of the day, the jet lag, the possibility of his wife's call at any minute, all showed in the lines of his face.

"Things were getting out of control," he said to phone. "Ever since the meeting at the Shizuoka Parts Plant, my organization is deteriorating around me. Tomorrow I am sure to lose it all."

He rolled his head from side to side. I need sleep. A fresh look at this tomorrow morning will clear it up. He reached in his shaving kit and found his sleeping pills. He knew he should not mix the pills with alcohol but he could never sleep after an overseas flight. He washed down the pills with the remainder of the whisky in the shot bottle. Turning out the room light, he allowed his head to fall backwards to the pillow.

In the dark, Kondo thought through the possibilities like a child with a TV remote control that flips from channel to channel. His feverish mental state delayed the effect of the sleeping pill. A scenario started to take shape. What if the terrorists disappeared? The value of what Hayashi was proposing became evident to Kondo. Like older Japanese companies used the Yakuza to quell labor riots in Kyushu, these gangsters could surreptitiously wipe out the thugs that were attacking Sunon's buildings.

"It could work. No, it will work," Kondo muttered out loud. He jumped up and retrieved Hayashi's business card from the hip pocket of his jacket. He fumbled at the blurry numbers on the phone. There was a ring, and then a voice on the other end said

"Moshi, Moshi, Hayashi desu."

"Hayashi-San, this is Kondo." Kondo slurred the words. "Thank you for the great day at Koganei."

"It was my pleasure old friend."

"Hayashi-San, remember after college, how we worked together to build that company? How we worked as a team. How we built something from nothing."

"I have fond memories of that."

"Let's work together again." His words slid together, hiding their meaning from Hayashi.

"I don't understand?"

"You know, your offer Let's work on it."

"Ah sono koto desu ne! That thing. I understand. I can arrange everything. I will need some information. I need the identity of the people causing the problem. Can you provide that? If you don't have their identity, it will take a bit more work."

"I don't know. I have access to the authorities' case work. Surely, there is enough there to track them." Kondo's speech was becoming more indistinct.

"Yes, that would be fine. Our contacts are not bound by normal investigative procedures. They can be quite resourceful. Provide the information, the identities, and the problem would be solved."

After a pause Kondo replied, "I can do that." He almost felt gleeful. The idea of this burden lifting from his shoulders changed his outlook. The drugs were also making him giddy even though his eyelids were heavy. "If you can do this Hayashi-San, it would indeed be a great favor."

"It is my privilege to help. We are together my friend. We are Japanese."

Kondo replied in formal Japanese, something he rarely did, "Thank you very much."

Chapter 19

THE GINZA DISTRICT, DOWNTOWN TOKYO

At night the roof tops of the Ginza District come alive in flashes of neon. Multicolored logos -- Panasonic, Konica, NEC -- burst from two and three story tall computer-synchronized light banks burning kilowatts in blatant disregard of the country's lack of natural energy resources.

On the street below, Mansuru Hayashi picked his way through the hustling passer-bys as they scurried to and from clubs looking to burn energy faster than the lights above. Hayashi raised his head scanning for the sign that announced the Royal Bunny Club. The flashing neon lights reflected in the lens of his glasses making them look like miniature television sets. He double-checked the map of the club's location on the back of the business card. There, above a busker with a mandolin, on the second floor overlooking the street he saw the distinctive bunny sign.

An attractive hostess, dressed in a pink playboy bunny outfit complete with puff tail, greeted him at the entrance to the club. After announcing himself she nodded her head and led him to a small room in the back of the main room. There he found his guest already waiting. The hostess bowed and said, "Here is Mr. Sato."

"Ah Hayashi-San, good to see you again," said Wahei Sato bending at the waist in a deep bow. Sato, a tall but slim man, wore a fashionable European style double-breasted suit with a crisply starched mustard-colored shirt. His curly hair cropped short at the sides, obviously the result of a permanent wave hair treatment, conveyed a handsome appearance despite his crooked and discolored teeth.

Hayashi bowed slightly and replied in crisp Japanese, "Thank you for meeting me on such short notice."

"It is always a pleasure to see you Hayashi-San."

Hayashi nodded satisfied with Sato's deferential grammar, appropriate for addressing a superior. Although Sato claimed to descend from aristocratic clan of Samurai, Hayashi knew he understood his place. Hayashi was his client. Sato provided the service - even if you could not find it listed in the Tokyo phone directory.

The hostess took Hayashi's overcoat and helped him squat at the low table. She then knelt at the foot of the table and poured him a drink of whiskey. After she topped off Sato's glass, Hayashi gruffly waved her away. Sato's eyes followed her with a leer as she backed away from the table while maintaining her bow.

"Don't want some fun tonight? She is very good, one of my favorites," Sato used more familiar, masculine grammar. Hayashi said nothing. Sato shrugged. He picked up his glass and offered cheers.

"Kanpai. To the Bunnies."

"Kanpai," responded Hayashi.

They sucked their drinks with the customary gusto. When Hayashi put his drink down he looked into Sato's face.

"I have an interesting challenge for you Sato-kun." Hayashi used the familiar and masculine form of address.

"I relish the interesting."

"You have no doubt heard about the savage murder of Ryoichi Kawasaki of Sunon Corporation in the US."

"Who has not! It curdles my blood."

"This was not a random act of violence in the US. Kawasaki-San's murder was a premeditated act against the company - against Japan." He paused for effect. Sato's face remained inscrutable; Hayashi expected as much. Carefully choosing his words, he continued, "American authorities are not capable of resolving this crime. At best they will create all kinds of unwanted publicity." He paused again. "Certain circumstances have presented themselves as an opportunity. We can do something about this that is in the best interests of the company."

After a few moments of silence, Hayashi said. "You are to go to Detroit. Check into the Townsend Hotel on one hundred Townsend Street in Birmingham, Michigan, next Monday night. There, you will find an details identifying the targets. Make the vermin disappear without trace." Hayashi pulled an envelope from his coat pocket and slid it across the low table to Sato. "This will cover your immediate expenses. Your consulting fee will follow our normal procedure."

Sato broke in a broad smile revealing his malformed teeth. "Hai, wakarimashita. Consider it done."

DETROIT , MICHIGAN

Gunston walked into the FBI's small conference room and placed a stack of papers on the table. Snell, Denzer, and Nicca sat at the table. Logan and some other agents sat around the periphery of the room. "I'm going to brief the SAC this afternoon. I need an update on how everyone is making out. Winslow, why don't you start? What have we learned from forensics?"

"Not the whole story, but quite a bit actually. First, we're certain that the same group made the two bombs. We compared components from the unexploded bomb to the fragments from the first bomb. Take a look at these slides." He flipped on the switch to an overhead and put on a color view graph.

"This is an enlargement of a fragment we found at the scene of the first bomb. We identified it as a piece of an Acudet Mark V delay blasting cap made by DuPont. We found the same exact type of cap in the second bomb. That cap was obviously intact, including the lot number. We're checking with DuPont now to try to find out where this lot was sold. The downside is that the Acudet cap is extremely common. The list could be long."

"Why a delay cap?" Nicca said. "Does it point to a motive."

"I don't know. Normally delay caps are used to shape an explosion. My guess is that it was what they had available."

"The caps could have been stolen?" Denzer offered then turned a page in his notebook.

"Possibly. We should be able to check that out. If any of the dealers with that lot number reported a theft then we could be back to square one. We won't know until we get that list of dealers."

"Exactly," Gunston added. "It's something we'll have to shake down. I'll add it to the action list. What else did you find?"

"Well, the explosive was a homemade mixture of ammonium nitrate in a fertilizer base with a roughly five percent diesel fuel oxidant. Not much help there. Stuff's available in almost any farm supply store. The booster charges were a brand of dynamite, DuPont Red Cross Extra. No lot numbers on the packaging. It also is a common blasting agent. Farmers and construction guys all use it. Again, not much help there. The rest of the firing circuit was pretty generic."

Logan held up the slide with the blasting cap. "Right now the best lead is the lot number on the caps. We might be able to cross check the cap lot number with the Red Cross Extra to see if that gives us a unique list of dealers. Red Cross Extra is so common, I'm afraid it won't lead anywhere. We'll know in a few days. I sent an agent to Martinsburg, West Virginia to meet with the DuPont people and go through their records."

"Anything else?" Gunston turned in his chair.

"Not really. We need to run down all of the bomb hardware to see if anything sticks out. It's all pretty common stuff. We'll dig through it. That's all I have for today." Logan turned off the overhead projector.

"Thanks. Laura, what did the Sunon hate mail show?"

"So far nothing solid. We cross-checked the list of names from Sunon with the list of registered Automag owners in the metro area. That was a blank. I also checked the gun owner list against Sunon employee roles. Nothing there either. Joe and I want to interview the Automag owners."

"That's a good idea too. What else?"

Denzer cleared his throat. "We found three different blood types at the scene. Two match our known victims. The third is unknown, male, blood type A positive. The lab report indicated the unknown blood was probably from a head wound as there were traces of bone and brain tissue in the blood. There were no gun shot wounds admitted that night to any area hospitals. If the suspect was shot in the head, chances are he's in bad shape or maybe even dead."

"We can't take that chance. We need to keep an eye on the local hospitals to see if anyone checks in."

"I already have some troopers checking on that," Denzer replied.

"Good job. Anything else that I should know?" Gunston scanned the room.

"Yes sir," Snell added. "We received approval from the judge to do a Title III tap on Elizabeth Kessler's phone. The wire and pliers crew are going in this afternoon to install the bug."

"Great. Keep me posted on that. Daily briefings will continue as normal. Keep me posted on the DuPont results. That looks like our best lead. Next, the gun owners. Right now everything has led to dead ends but something has got to break soon."

"One thing we got to consider." Nicca rubbed his chin and leaned forward. "Will they hit again?"

Gunston gave Nicca a long look, then leaned back in his chair. "I don't know. If one of their guys has been taken out it could spook them."

"It could also provoke them," Nicca raised his eyebrow.

"You're right. Laura, call the behavioral unit at the academy and see what they think."

"Yes sir."

"I'm going to prepare for the SAC brief. See you tomorrow."

Outside the conference room Nicca leaned against the doorframe. "Well Laura, what do you think?"

Snell slouched and folded her pinstriped jacket over her arm. She looked directly into Nicca's dark brown eyes. "I don't know. I think Gunston is right. Everything keeps turning into dead ends. I thought for sure that finding the bomb intact would crack this wide open."

"Yeah. We got to keep," Nicca changed his voice to a pompous tone, "pounding the bricks as you Special Agents would say."

"You should know. You've been at this a lot longer than I."

"Actually, I'm pretty well caught up right now. I was thinking about taking tonight off."

"Really. I could use a night off too."

"Care to have dinner with me?"

"Nah, I see enough of you around here," she said with a wide grin. "I'd much rather pop a Budget Gourmet in the microwave and watch TV."

"Suit yourself."

"Just kidding. What time will you pick me up?"

"I want to stop by my office. Check my messages and mail. How about seven o'clock. I'll think of a good place between then and now."

"That should give me plenty of time to call Quantico. Sounds good. I'll see you then."

TROY, MICHIGAN

Kondo pushed open the oak door to the conference room in Sunon's Troy Headquarters. Hara, who had returned the day before from Japan, was sitting at the conference table reading the Mainichi Shinbun, a Japanese language daily newspaper, his tie pulled down from his plain white shirt. When Hara saw his boss enter, he jumped up, knocking the papers to the floor. He bowed humbly and said in Japanese. "Kondo-San, you are back. Good evening."

Kondo nodded and threw his briefcase on the nearest seat. In English he said, "Where is Shane? I said I wanted a staff meeting as soon as I get back."

"Oh yes, we know. Shane is downstairs in the gym working out. We heard your plane was delayed so he went to take a break"

"Get him."

"Hai, Jomu," Hara backed out of the room.

Ten minutes later Hara returned with Shane. Shane wore a dark blue warm-up suit with Nike cross trainer sneakers. A white towel wrapped around his neck sopped up the sweat from his head.

"Good evening boss. Nice trip I hope." The rising tone of voice made Shane sound enthusiastic.

Kondo, still wearing his dark blue suit from his trip, looked up and smiled at Shane, "You are looking casual?"

"Well, at my age, the pounds seem harder to take off."

"We are well aware of the problems with your age Mr. Shane." Kondo chuckled as not to admit he was more than a decade older than Shane. "Anyway, would you care for a drink?" Kondo reached for the bottle of Jack Daniels Black bourbon and topped off his half-full drink.

As he poured, Kondo looked at Shane and Hara. "I believe I have good news gentlemen."

Shane glanced quickly at Hara and raised his eyebrow. "Well, how did the board meeting go?" asked Shane.

"Surprisingly well. First of all, I think we may have over-reacted to the unfortunate Kawasaki incident. It seems that with all the violence in America, the board accepted Kawasaki's death without any link to our business operations. In the formal board meeting, no one mentioned Kawasaki. Discussion centered solely on the deployment of the new 500GSX."

"That's great." Shane said. "If you ask me that's the way it should be. Hara-San was telling me that there was only muted reaction to the shooting.'

"Oh, the reporters tried to make something of it. What do you call it, 'muckraking,' but with the other murders of Japanese citizens in the US, the Japanese have become almost as bored with the incidents as Americans have."

Kondo took a sip from his drink. "America doesn't have the stomach to fix crime. You are content to let your weapons industry influence the government until everyone will be shooting everyone else and no one will care as long as they think they are safe locked up in their house." Kondo stepped across the room seemingly in thought. He wheeled toward Shane and Hara. "The same people have made the police impotent. Take the Kawasaki incident. There is no way the police will solve this crime. Even if they do, the jury won't convict an American for killing a Japanese. No, these police, they will never solve the crime; like they'll never find who set fire to our dealerships."

"Well, you're probably right. There's not much we can do." Shane wiped his brow with the towel. "So what else happened at the board meeting? Did anyone mention the joint venture concept?"

"Takahashi was silent about that. The sole agenda item was to review the 500GSX plans. The board wants the introduction go as planned. The 500GSX represents a major step in our continued plan to secure the high technology performance market. With it, we will be able to boost our market share in the sports sedan segment. Even better is that the board endorsed the concept of US manufacture of the 500GSX."

"Wow, this and no mention of the joint venture. Takahashi must have been steamed."

"Perhaps, but he is in a weak position. With the devaluation of the dollar and a strong yen, Japanese built products are too expensive in the US. The quicker Sunon can transfer content to North America, the more competitive our cars will be. The quickest way is to transfer manufacture to our plants. The joint venture would take too long to implement."

"So we won that one," gloated Shane.

"Don't be hasty, Mr. Shane. There are still some loose ends to resolve."

Sato's jumbo jet left Narita airport on Saturday night. Crossing the International Dateline, Sato arrived in New York before he left Tokyo. Only slightly tired, he recognized Akira Sugai at the exit of the immigration counter. Sugai bowed deeply to Sato. "Sato-San, Welcome to New York. It is my honor to work with you again. I have made the arrangements as you requested."

Sugai, a short but tough, former member of Sato's gang, enjoyed working for Sato in Japan, before his exile. Six years ago, at Tsukiji Fish Market in Tokyo, Sugai was cutting open a fish carcass to remove smuggled weapons when the police arrived. In the rush to escape there was a shoot-out that killed two innocent fish merchants. The police also killed Sugai's two accomplices but Sugai escaped undetected. In the perverse criminal version of the bushido code, Sato punished Sugai for his failed effort by requiring him to endure the Yakuza custom of yubitsume, finger cutting. Sugai lost the end joint of his little finger. In addition, because many of the merchants in the fish market could recognize Sugai, it was impossible for him to stay in Japan. Banished, he now was a minor member of a splinter gang working in New York's Little Tokyo.

Sato returned Sugai's bow with a curt dip of his head. "Where is our associate?" Sato said.

"Waiting in the car. I have the other preparations arranged per your FAX message."

"Good, let's get my luggage and go."

Sugai reached for Sato's suitcase on the luggage carousel. He struggled to carry the suitcase, his stubby finger weakening his grip on the handle.

At the parking garage, Sato saw a tall Japanese man standing next to a white Lincoln Continental. He wore blue jeans and T-shirt covered by a blue New York Yankees windbreaker. His hair was long and freely flowing. When the man saw Sugai and Sato approach he opened the Continental's trunk. Sugai placed the suitcase he was carrying on the ground next to the car. "Sato-San, this is Tanaka-San."

Tanaka stood by the open trunk. He did not bow but rather stared suspiciously at Sato.

Sato took Tanaka's lack of bowing as a rude gesture. He knew he was in the U.S. yet still he required proper respect from his subordinates. In slang Japanese he said to Tanaka, "What part of Japan did you learn these poor manners?"

"Huh?" responded Tanaka.

Sensing the conflict, Sugai quickly interjected in English "Sato-San, please excuse my mistake. I should have told you. Tanaka-San is sansei, third generation American. He doesn't speak Japanese."

The leader's face cracked for a second in disbelief as if to say, "A gaijin on this job, this is lunacy."

Sugai apologetically explained, "He is my best man. He will be useful to us."

Sato's remain stone faced. Extending his hand, he said to Tanaka in clear but slow English, "It is a pleasure to meet you."

"Yeah, the same here," replied Tanaka defensively.

Tanaka drove while Sugai and Sato sat in the rear. As the car pulled from the parking garage, Sato asked in Japanese "Where are the weapons?"

"In the trunk. I have selected Uzis. They will be perfect," said Sugai with a degree of satisfaction. "At 200 rounds per minute they'll stop anything we may happen to meet.

236

"What about my Baretta?" asked Sato.

"Plus a Baretta 9 mm pistol for you Sato-San"

"Fine, now here are your directions. Sugai-chan, you and Tanaka are to drive to Detroit. You must leave immediately. Take this car. You have one day to meet me there with the weapons and supplies. I will fly out later tonight. We can not risk taking the weapons on an airplane."

Sugai gulped, "Be in Detroit tomorrow. We would have to drive all night."

"Hey, no problem dude, I'll pick up some reds and drive the whole way there myself," Tanaka blurted from the driver's seat.

Sugai ignored Tanaka's comment. He turned to Sato and in a lower voice said "Sato-San, why such a rush?"

"We have to complete this job as soon as possible. I will scout the situation and develop a complete plan. When you arrive in the Detroit area, meet me at the Townsend Hotel in Birmingham, Michigan. Here is a map and the phone number. I will give you further instructions when you arrive at the hotel."

"Is that all?"

"Hai."

"Now, have dinner and then take me to the airport. My flight to Detroit leaves in two hours."

Upon arrival in Detroit, the long hours on the plane wore at Sato's eyes but he pressed gamely with his effort. He rented a Lincoln Town car at the Avis counter on the lower level of the Detroit Metropolitan airport. Once in the car in the airport parking garage, he studied the Detroit map for a few minutes. He decided on his route and pulled away reminding himself to drive on the right hand side of the road. Thirty-five minutes later, Sato turned off Townsend Street into the Townsend Hotel Parking lot. He adjusted his tie and strode to the registration desk. The evening clerk cheerfully greeted him.

"I am Sato. I have a reservation."

Punching his name into the hotel computer, she said, "Yes, it's room 202. Oh, it says here you have two messages." The clerk turned and pulled a manila envelope from the pigeonhole wall unit behind the reception desk. Clipped to the envelope was a plain white envelope with Sato's name and room number handwritten on it. "Your room is on the second floor, west wing."

Sato nodded and put the two envelopes under his right arm. He grabbed his key and lugged his bag to the elevator.

In his room, Sato dropped his suitcase on the bed and went to the window. He gave a quick glance outside. Seeing nothing out of the ordinary, he pulled the curtains closed. He studied the two envelopes in his hands. "Why two?" he asked out loud. The manila piece was sealed and the little clasp pushed through the hole. The plain white envelope was also sealed. Other than Sato's name and room number, neither envelopes had any writing on them. Sato opened the manila one first. Inside, he found photocopies of the entire FBI file on the Sunon bombings. Despite bleary vision, Sato reviewed the papers. Reading the English reports was difficult and slow for him. After forty minutes he could barely stay awake. He put the papers down and drank a cup of water. Then he remembered the other envelope.

Ripping off one end, he found no letter. Instead, he shook the envelope and a business card fell out.

Cannon Cadillac-Buick-Sunon, Inc.
2301 Auburn Road, Suite 2001
Auburn Hills, Michigan 48321
(313) 852 -6660

Bob Cannon
President

Sato considered the information for a few moments. He then undressed, took a sleeping pill and went to sleep.

Chapter 20

EASTLAND MALL, MICHIGAN

Chuck parked his truck near Eastland Mall entrance 7. They drove straight from Grayling to the shopping center without stopping at the apartment.

"Debbie, wait here while I make this call." Since Alex's death, Chuck was hesitant to leave Debbie alone.

"Okay."

Chuck walked inside and used the familiar phone. He dialed Cannon's number.

"Hello?"

Chuck recognized Cannon's voice, "Hey, Bob. This is Chuck. How's it going?"

The line was silent for several seconds. "Bob, are you there?" Chuck did his best to sound cheerful.

"Yeah. Yeah I'm here."

"We need to talk. Do you want to call me back?"

"Umm, Yes. I mean no. I guess I don't know. I can't talk now."

"Why don't you call me back like we planned. I have a proposition to discuss."

"I'd rather talk now."

"No. Call me back. We need to talk openly."

"It's ten o'clock at night. How will I explain..." His voice tailed off. "Never mind, I'll call you in ten minutes. Sit tight."

"I'll wait." Chuck hung up the phone and began to pace. He reviewed the plan "It can work," he thought. "No backing out now."

During the past few days at Grayling he put together a plan. He was going to sink a Sunon ship full of new Sunon cars.

239

The irony was unbelievable. Not only could he destroy millions of dollars of Sunon cars, but also they could disrupt the arrival of Sunon's most important new model. Sunon invested a lot of money and advertising on the introduction of the 500GSX. They probably didn't count on the first batch rusting on the ocean bottom. Now, in retrospect, he felt the answer was obvious. We can nail them! The ring of the pay phone shattered his thought.

"Hello? Bob?"

"Yeah. I'm here."

"I have an idea."

"Chuck, answer me one question. What has gotten into you? I am scared shitless. I thought we had a little deal going. I didn't want anyone to get hurt. Now this. Man. I don't know what to do."

"It wasn't supposed to happen that way, man. We had some trouble."

"Did you have to," Cannon stuttered, "to kill both of them. I didn't want anybody to get hurt."

"It's worse than that man. We lost one of our people."

"What?"

"Yeah, man. Don't worry. We took care of him."

"Oh, my god," Cannon yelled, " Chuck..."

"Look man, chill out. You got nothing to worry about. I got a plan. I need you to finance it. We want to get out of the country for awhile."

"Hell, that's the best idea you've had yet."

"We need money."

"Alright. How much?"

"Three hundred K."

"Whoa," Cannon let out a deep breath. "I don't know if I can come up with that kind of money."

"You don't have a choice, man. We need the money. You're good for it."

The line was dead for a moment, then Cannon said "Last time I offered you fifty thousand to stop. What did you do? You went and killed two, no three people. Now you want three hundred K."

Chuck flared, "I didn't kill anyone. You're in this as much as anybody. If you want to blame someone, blame yourself. You better

240

come up with the cash."

"I don't have that kind of money laying around. I'm not even sure I can get it in a couple days."

"You will. Look, I'm heading out of town for a while. I'll call you in seven days. We can make the arrangements then to send the money."

"What if I can't raise it?" Cannon's voice had a panicky edge to it.

"You will. You really have no choice."

"Where can I reach you?"

"I don't know yet. I'll be in Baltimore. I'll call you from there."

"Baltimore?"

"Detroit is too hot right now. Don't worry about it. I'll be in touch. Have the cash ready in seven days."

"I'll try. God I wish I never got you involved in this."

"Seven days, Bob. Seven days." Chuck hung up and headed out the now deserted mall. He found Debbie sitting behind locked doors in the truck.

"What did he say?" she asked.

Chuck climbed into the driver's seat. "He said it's a go. He'll have the money ready for us next week. If we pull it off we're done. No more missions."

Debbie let out a sigh of relief, "Thank god for that. I don't know how much more of this I can take."

"You wanted revenge, right?"

"Well, yeah."

"Well, then you're going to get it. If this works like it's supposed to, you'll get revenge in spades."

Cannon hung up the phone and began to pace the carpet muttering to himself, "What should I do?"

Finally, as if to reassure him, he opened his wall safe. He withdrew a small box and opened it up. Inside were stacks of crisp, one thousand dollar bills. Slowly counting the stacks without removing the bank wrappers satisfied him that there were two hundred and twenty notes left. "Easy come easy go," he mumbled as he placed the money back in the container and returned it to the safe. "Chuck will have to settle for two hundred K."

The telephone rang again. "Hello," Cannon answered.

"Good evening. Is this Mr. Robert Cannon?" The voice had a Japanese accent.

"Yes." Cannon raised a bushy eyebrow while he tried to place the voice. "Who is this?"

"I am Sato. I would like to meet with you as soon as possible. Is tonight convenient?"

The politeness in the man's voice did not disguise the seriousness of the request. Despite the late hour, Cannon agreed. "I'll meet you at my office in thirty minutes. Do you know where it is?"

"Yes. I will be there."

TIMONIUM, MARYLAND

"Brian, keep Debbie company. I'm going to go for a look around town.

"Don't you want some company?" Brian asked.

"No. Not yet. I want to take a look around the area. You two look pretty tired from the drive. I'll be back at the hotel in a couple of hours. Get some sleep."

"Yeah," Brian replied with a sigh. "I could use some zees."

Debbie exited the bathroom, "Gosh, I'm beat."

"Get some sleep," Chuck suggested. "Brian's going to stay with you. I'm going for a little drive."

"Aren't you tired?" Debbie asked.

"Nah. I'm too keyed up to sleep. You crash. I'll be back in a couple of hours." He kissed Debbie lightly on the cheek before walking out the door.

Their hotel was on the north side of town, inside the Baltimore beltway. Chuck sat in the front seat of his truck and studied the map. Although he drove most of the way from Detroit, he wasn't tired. Instead, he was anxious to check out the details of his fledgling, and as yet secret, plan. In Michigan using Google Earth he made a thorough map study of the harbor area and had fleshed out a basic concept. The details would require reconnaissance. Until he saw the actual area and answered some of the nagging detail questions he would be too excited to sleep.

He drove around the beltway toward Sparrow's Point. As he

passed over the Key Bridge, and exited the highway on the bridge's other side, taking side streets through Brooklyn. Wandering through deserted alleys flanked by rail yards and oil tanks, he finally ended in Fairfield. There he found the Sunon auto terminal.

A ship was unloading. Over a hundred men swarmed around the ship. From three ramps that sloped from the ship to the dock spewed Sunon econoboxes one after another. Protective pieces of Styrofoam and tape gaudily decorated each car making them look like Christmas presents for their new owners. Periodically a small bus would pull up to the ship and a group of drivers would exit to jog up the personnel ramp and back into the ship. The bus then returned to the sea of imports that was forming in the parking lot to round up more drivers.

On the other side of the lot, more workers processed cars for shipment further inland. A stream of tractors with auto transport trailers and locomotives with specialized auto rack rail cars moved in and out of the lot, each time withdrawing a fresh load of new Sunons for the U.S. market.

"If I didn't see this I wouldn't believe it!" Chuck said aloud as he stood transfixed by the endless stream of new cars.

A knock on his truck window startled him. Chucked turned to his left to see a security guard standing next to his truck.

"Can I help you?" the guard asked after Chuck rolled down the window.

"Oh. Uh, I was watching the ship get unloaded."

"Oh yeah, they'll have that ship unloaded in about four or five hours. Depends on how many cars they have on board. Anyway, you know this is private property?"

"Oh, I'm sorry. I didn't know that. I didn't see any signs. I was curious about these ships. I was thinking about writing an article about the car import business. So I wanted to get a closer look."

"Is that right. Are you a reporter?"

"Nah, a freelancer."

"My son, he's a reporter for Stars and Stripes in Germany. He's a sergeant in the Army."

"I used to be in the army, Special Forces."

"Is that right. You know, nobody else is around tonight. Why don't you come over to the gatehouse. You can get a closer look at what's going on."

"Are you sure? You won't get in trouble, will you?"

"Heck no. We only got one guard on duty to cover this whole lot. It can get pretty lonely out here sometimes. Especially when they aren't unloading. Leave your truck here. We can walk over together."

They reached the guard shack. The guard held the door open for Chuck. "Want a cup of coffee?"

"No thanks. So, how often do these ships arrive?"

"Sunon ships arrive about two a week. Some of the other car companies also use the terminal on a subcontract basis."

"Do they follow a schedule?"

"No, they don't. I never know when the next ship is coming in. The terminal crew is all under subcontract. The agent gets a call when the ship is about five or six hours out. The agent hires the terminal crew. They show up and unload the ship as fast as possible. Then they leave. My job is to keep an eye on the place. Most of the time this place is fairly deserted."

"I see." Chuck's comment was cut short by the appearance of a slightly built, dark skinned oriental man entering the guard shack.

The man nodded to Chuck and then said to the guard, "Mind if I use the phone? I need to call a cab."

"Go ahead," the guard said cheerfully.

The man started dialing, "Only got a couple of hours in port. We ship out tonight." The man spoke accent-free English.

"Are you from that ship?" Chuck asked.

"Yes, I'm the second officer."

"Where are you going? I can give you a ride." Chuck was hoping to get a chance to quiz the man on details about the ship.

"That's a good idea," the guard offered. "This man is working on an article about car shipping. Maybe you could answer some of his questions while he gives you a lift."

"That sounds fair. My name is Raymond Gomez." He offered Chuck his hand.

"Er, Lance, Lance Powers. Pleased to meet you. My truck is parked over there. Thanks a lot." Chuck said to the guard as he exited the shack.

The two men boarded the truck. "Is that a Japanese ship? I noticed that the name on the back was printed in Japanese letters."

"Yeah, the ship is registered in Japan. It's leased to Sunon but actually owned by one of their shipping companies. Only the captain, first officer, and chief engineer are Japanese. The rest of us are Filipino. I want to visit some of my friends at a pub near the union hall. I only have a few hours."

"Where's that?"

"In Fells Point. I've been making this run for a few years now and I know a couple of people in town."

"Well I'm new here, so you'll have to give me directions."

"No problem, head up the road there. I appreciate the ride. So what do you want to know?"

For the next fifteen minutes, Chuck got what in effect was a personalized detailed briefing on car shipping operations, with emphasis on how they are done in Baltimore harbor.

As Chuck turned onto Calvert Street, he saw the sign announcing the pub. Chuck turned to Gomez. "So if I wanted to watch a certain ship come into port how would I do it?"

"Your best bet is to listen to the Marine radio. Get a marine VHF radio and listen to channel 11. When a ship is off Cape Henry they'll call for a bay pilot. The Cape Henry dispatcher then usually telephones the Baltimore dispatcher. When they're about five hours out they'll radio an updated ETA. Then as the ship gets close it'll be met by a docking pilot for the final maneuvers in the inner harbor. If you listen to the radio and you know the name of the ship you should be able to get plenty of warning that it's coming." Gomez opened the passenger door. "Well, thanks for the ride."

"My pleasure and good luck."

The men shook hands and Gomez left the truck.

The room was dark when Chuck returned to the hotel. He cautiously opened the door and entered. Quietly taking off his shoes and clothes, he crawled into bed next to Debbie. Sighing slightly, she changed her position but did not wake up. Chuck laid next to her with his eyes wide open, while his mind busily digested all the information he learned that evening.

DETROIT, MICHIGAN

Nicca spotted Denzer in the parking lot out front of the Federal Building. "How's it going? " he asked.

There was a glint in Denzer's eye. "Not bad. I've been working the gun list interviews. We have a potential suspect."

"Really?" Nicca held the glass door open for Denzer.

"Yeah, We've talked to all but four of the people on the list. Most are gun collectors. The .44 Automag is basically a collectors' item. We've got solid alibis from almost everyone we've talked to. A couple of them no longer live in the area. There is one, an ex-cop, who has recently disappeared."

"Woah. What's the story on him?"

"His landlady hasn't seen him for a couple of days. She says she hasn't even seen his car. He owes her rent money and she's wondering where he went."

"Great, have the State Police and FBI track down your rent money. Not bad if you can swing it," Nicca dug his hands in his pockets of his Dockers khakis.

"Nah, wait a minute. Listen to this, a guy from his job came looking for him. He hasn't been to work since the last shooting."

"Interesting, it's worth checking."

"I put an APB out for his car. I hope we can find it or him."

"Did you do a background on him?"

"Hmm. That's also interesting. The guy was a regular stud on the force. Great arrest record but lots of complaints about excess violence. Several line of duty shootings including a couple fatalities. He was kicked out after being convicted of assault and battery. He beat the heck out of a guy he caught having an affair with his wife."

"That seems like it would fit the profile. It certainly jibes with the arson cases. Any connection with demolitions?"

"Nothing like that."

"It almost looks too good to be true. If he's a professional, why would he disappear without covering his tracks."

"Maybe he can't. Maybe he's the head wound."

"Have you run this past Gunston?"

"Yeah, he wants to bring the guy in, and fast."

"What's his name?"

"Brian Russo."

TIMONIUM, MARYLAND

"Debbie, wake up." Chuck gently shook Debbie. "I brought you a cup of coffee."

"What time is it?"

"It's house hunting time."

"What?"

"We're going go look for a house to rent. Some place near the water. I got the paper this morning and I've circled some prospects."

"How long was I asleep?"

"About sixteen hours. How are you doing?"

"Tired. Will you let me grab a shower?"

"Sure. We got a lot of work to do in the next couple of days."

Chuck got up to answer a knock on the door. "Come on in Brian. Did you grab a cup of coffee from the lobby? It's free."

"Yeah, I've been up for a couple of hours. I saw you come back. So what's the story? What are we going to do here?"

"I'll tell you what you need to know later. For now we need to find a rental house that has access to a dock. It would be nice if it's private. Debbie and I will pose as a married couple looking for a place to rent. In the meantime, Brian, I want you to start looking for a used boat. It should be about twenty to twenty five feet with at least a cuddy cabin. I don't care how it looks as long as it is runs good. Here's two thousand dollars. That's all we got"

"That won't buy much of a boat." Brian frowned.

"We won't need much of a boat. Tell 'em, it's a down payment." Chuck tensed his biceps and forearms, seemingly annoyed with Brian's questioning. "We won't be making any payments."

"All right. I'll call around. Are there any in the paper?"

"Probably, take a look."

It took most of the day, but by the afternoon, Chuck and Debbie found a trailer park near Cedar Beach that had several vacancies. Chuck selected the most isolated one, a furnished unit, and paid the rent for two months in advance. The owner seeming pleased to find renters this time of year, asked few questions.

Brian spent most of the day on the hotel phone calling numbers listed in the classified ads. He had a few good prospects when Chuck and Debbie returned.

They moved into the trailer the next morning. Debbie stayed there, trying to get it in livable condition while Chuck and Brian went to look at the boats. An hour later, Brian returned alone.

"Where's Chuck?" Debbie raised her eyebrows.

247

"He's coming," was all Brian volunteered.

About a half hour later, Chuck arrived at the back door. "Come and check out our latest acquisition."

Tied to the dock behind the trailer was an old, but racy looking twenty five foot Sea Ray cuddy cabin cruiser. It wore its fifteen years well despite its dull, sun bleached gel coat and weather-beaten fittings.

"It's worn but it will work," Brian said with his hands on his hips and his chest sticking out.

That night Chuck made several lists of supplies to purchase. Then he studied maps of the area thoroughly.

"So what are you working on? When do we get to know what's up?"

"I'm ready to tell you two. Debbie, come in here if you're done."

"Be right there," she replied from the kitchen.

When they were all seated on the used furniture of the rental, Chuck began, "First, let me tell you that this is our last job. We'll each get paid one hundred thousand dollars for pulling this off."

"Really!" Debbie face lit up.

Brian pursed his lips but his tilted head revealed his skepticism. "So how do we get it?"

"The plan is to sink one of Sunon's car transport ships next week. But not any ship. It will be carrying the first load of Sunon's newest 500GSX cars. There's been a lot of press about these cars. Sinking this ship will have as big an impact as anything we can do."

"Are you sure we can do it?" Debbie asked. "It sounds impossible."

"Not impossible, Debbie. It will be risky, but with the right plan we should pull it off."

"So why did we buy the boat?" Brian ran his hand through his black hair. "I thought you said we didn't have the manpower to board the ship."

"We won't have to board. We do the same thing we did with the vans, except that we'll use the boat." Chuck motioned toward the Sea Ray.

"What are you going to do, blow it up at the dock?"

"Maybe. But I'd rather try to hit it while it's on the move. The ship might not sink if we hit it at the dock. I want to rig the boat with a remote control. Then we can steer it in from a distance."

"Can you do that?" Brain said.

"Sure. When I was on the line I worked in the maintenance section for a while."

Chuck rose and paced in front of Brian and Debbie, staring at his too accomplices, searching for clues of dissent or disagreement, and perhaps to confirm his own plan. "I fixed all kinds of actuators and servo controls. If we can't get it to work, we'll rig it like the van and hit it at the dock."

Chucked paused in front of the window. When he turned Brian's and Debbie's serious faces told him he had their consent.

Chuck nodded. "Afterwards, we'll skip town. I figure the best bet is to catch a flight to Mexico. We won't need passports to get into Mexico. We lay low there for a while. If things are cool, we can come back to Detroit. If things are hot, we stay there."

"That sounds flaky Chuck." Brian rose from the couch. "I'd as soon stay in the States. They ain't going to find us."

"That's your call, Brian. Debbie and I will head to Mexico like I said. Is that right, Debbie?"

"I don't know Chuck. This all sounds so dangerous. What will happen to the crew of the ship?"

"What do you think is going to happen to them?" Brian sneered.

"Who cares? They'll get what they deserve. We owe it to Alex. We owe it to America."

"Bullshit." Brian jumped from his seat. "We don't owe anybody anything." The veins in Brian's neck strained like taut ropes. "You said we'll get one hundred gees. To me that's all the money I need." Brian stood still but his eyes bounced back and forth.

Chuck said nothing.

Brian turned his back to Chuck and moved toward the kitchen. "Man, you're way too into this."

"Damn right." Chuck raised his voice and took a step closer to Brian. "Those bastards deserve it after what they done."

"Chuck! Brian!" Debbie stepped between them. "Stop yelling."

Brian twisted his head and squinted at Chuck. In a calm voice he said. "Are you sure we'll get paid?"

"The money will be here in five days. The ship should be arriving about that time. I don't know the exact time for sure, so we have to listen to the radio. The ship we're looking for is called the Honshu Prince."

"You have done your homework," Brian said. "You seem confident."

"I am, but we have a lot more work to do. Are you in?"

"Yeah," Brian said.

"Debbie?" Chuck asked, looking at her.

Debbie glanced at Brian and then for a long time at Chuck. "Yes. I can do it."

DETROIT, MICHIGAN

Joe Nicca was finishing off a cup of coffee in his apartment before heading off to the FBI building when the phone rang. He held it between his neck and shoulder while he adjusted his tie.

"Hello, Nicca here."

"Joe, we got one of them," he heard Laura Snell say.

"What do you mean?" Nicca's neck tingled. "I was getting ready to head to the office."

"We got Russo's car. The city police found it. Abandoned in Hazel Park. Near the race track." Snell's voice raced. "No plates. VIN destroyed. NCIC Id'ed it based on a description. My automated queries picked it up this morning." Snell paused to catch her breath.

"Denzer checked it out. Found apparent blood stains on the front and rear seat and in the trunk. The lab tested it and they match the unidentified blood samples found at the Sunon Headquarters murder scene. Russo is our head wound."

Nicca grabbed the phone off his shoulder and leaned against his door jamb. "Don't jump to conclusions. It could have been someone else in the car. Can we link Russo to any of the other leads?"

"Not that I can see. He has no past association with Sunon. As far as we can tell he never even owned a Sunon car."

"I wonder if Kessler knows him." Nicca said.

"Why don't we ask her?"

"Do you have a picture of him?"

"His official police picture. We've submitted a warrant to search his house. It should be approved later this afternoon. Maybe he has

250

some pictures there."

"The police photo should be good enough. I'll call Kessler and schedule an appointment. Then I'll call you and you can meet me there."

"Right."

"Give me ten minutes." Nicca hung up the phone, nodding to himself. Snell's computer did good, he thought.

Nicca met Snell in front of the Hudsons Department Store in Pontiac Mall, waiting for Liz Kessler to finish a meeting with an account.

Nicca spotted Kessler as she emerged from the double-glass doors of the store. She smiled weakly at him when they made eye contact.

"Good morning, Ms. Kessler. I appreciate you seeing us on such short notice." Nicca stuck out his hand to greet her.

"Good morning. How can I help you?"

"Could you tell us if you know this man?"

Snell handed her the picture of Brian Russo.

Kessler stared at the picture for several seconds. Her lower jaw tightened obviously not recognizing the man. "No. I don't know him."

"Are you sure?" Snell asked looking into Kessler's face.

"I meet a lot of people in this business and remembering faces is one of my talents. I don't know him." Kessler pointed to the photo. "He's wearing a police uniform. Maybe he is a cop. You could ask them."

Nicca smiled at the naive suggestion but it convinced him she was telling the truth. "Well, then. Thank you for your time, Ms. Kessler." He reached for the photograph. "You have my number. If anything else comes up, please give us a call."

CEDAR BEACH, MARYLAND

Chuck closed the boat's engine hatch. "Come on, let's test this remote control. Brian you stay on the boat. Take it out about two hundred yards and then let me see if I can control it from here. If it doesn't work drive the boat back."

251

The boat eased out of the slip with Brian at the controls. When he was far enough he waved his arm.

"Here goes," Chuck winked at Debbie. He flicked the lever and the boat reacted smoothly. Then he began a series of right and left turns each bigger and harder than the previous. "It works pretty well. Want to try Debbie?"

"Sure," She took the controls from Chuck and made a tentative turn. "This is pretty cool. It works great."

They could see Brian waving his arms from the boat.

"I think he wants us to stop," Debbie observed as she handled the control stick.

"Better bring it back before he gets seasick," laughed Chuck. Debbie manipulated the remote and the boat obediently returned toward the dock.

"Brian, cut the throttle," Chuck yelled when the boat neared the dock.

"That was far out. I was getting worried you guys were trying to get rid of me," Brian said as he tied on the bow line.

"How did it look from the water?" Chuck jumped into the boat.

"The controller banged against the side a few times but overall I'd say it looked fine."

"Maybe I can adjust that." Chuck crouched by the boat and fiddled with the hardware. In a few minutes he rose. "Well, that was the toughest part. Tomorrow we start with the bomb. I've got enough TNT for five kicker charges left. We should be able to get four drums in the cabin. That will be almost one thousand pounds of explosive. That will make a big hole."

"So how do we get so close to the ship." Brian crossed his arms and leaned against the transom. "Do we steer it from the dock?"

"No, that won't work. The remote doesn't have that much range. We'll drive the boat close to the ship. Then we'll board a dingy and zip off while the boat goes in empty. Let's go inside and I'll go over the plan with you two. Once we get the dingy we can rehearse."

Inside Chuck got out his charts. Then he placed a piece of clear plastic over the top. On it were drawn a series of lines and symbols.

"This here is the course the ship will take," Chuck pointed to a series of lines on the chart. "It will dock here with the help of a tug boat. I want to hit it before the tugs tie up to it. The ship will be moving slowly at that point. Plus if it sinks here, it will block the dock. That means Sunon's terminal will be out of action until they clear it." Chuck took a deep breath, "Debbie will ride with me on the boat. Brian, you'll take the truck and meet us at the rendezvous point, here. There is an easy slope and a deserted field near the coal facility, I've been up there and nobody said anything to me." He paused and retrieved a beer from the refrigerator, "After we sink the ship, we'll drive to BWI airport. Our best bet is to get on a plane before they get to react. Where should we go?"

"How about Cozumel? I hear it's supposed to be nice," Debbie suggested. Her voice tailed off as she whispered, "Liz went there last year."

"A vacation spot would be good. We'll blend in with the other tourists."

"I say let's return to Detroit. They ain't going to find us."

"What about your car?"

"I'll get a new one. That one's probably been stripped clean by now."

Like I said, that's your call man. I don't recommend it, but if it's what you want to do, then go for it. You'll go back alone though."

Brian considered his options, "I guess I'll stick with you two. No sense taking any more chances. I pretty much burnt my bridges back there."

Chuck smiled, "Tomorrow we'll put the bomb together and we need to buy the dingy. I'm getting a little short on money. I'll call the boss man tomorrow morning and arrange for the money transfer. The ship should be here in two days. When he overnights the money, we'll pick it up and hit the ship." Chuck looked at Brian, "What's wrong, Brian?"

"Oh, I was thinking. Do you think they'll be able to trace us to this house. The landlord and maybe a couple of others saw us around here. I'm wondering if they start to piece it together they might snoop around here."

"Do you think they could find us if they check out the trailer?"

"Maybe. Hell, our fingerprints are all over this place. If they connect this house to the bomb we could be an easy make."

Chuck looked around the room, "So we'll torch the house. We'll make it look like an accident."

"Yeah, but we want it to happen after we leave. We don't want to tip off the locals."

"I got it covered. I'll rig up the last cap and dynamite to the gas line with a timer. We'll leave the gas on when we leave. The TNT will blow the timer to smithereens and they'll think it was a gas explosion."

Brian sighed, "I guess it's the best we can do. I wish so many people didn't see us hanging around. We'll have to keep a low profile."

"Not that many people have seen us," Debbie offered. "I haven't seen anyone outside at all and I've been here more than both of you."

"Yeah, we got nothing to worry about. I'll rig the bomb and this whole place will be history and no one will be the wiser. They'll be too fixated on the ship sunk in the middle of their channel." Chuck smiled.

"You are one sick puppy. That's why I love you," Brian laughed.

Chapter 21

Chuck alone returned to the hotel where they stayed when they first arrived. He told the clerk that he would be staying for two nights. After paying cash he took the key but instead of heading to the room, he walked to a private phone booth in the lobby and dialed Cannon's number collect.

"Where the hell are you Chuck?" Cannon yelled after accepting the charges.

"I told you man. I'm in Baltimore."

"What are you doing there? I've been trying to get a hold of you for a couple of days."

"Why? Do you have the money?"

"Yeah, I got it. I had to really scramble to get it. There ain't no more after this. Where are you so I can send it?"

Cannon's voice sounded tense. "Chill out, man. Here's the plan. Send it by FEDEX to Lance Powers at the Chariot Inn in Timonium, MD. I'm registered there under that name. You need to make sure it is here by tomorrow. Can you handle that? I'll pick up the money tomorrow."

"Are you staying there?" Cannon's voice cracked.

Chuck sensed a sharper edge in Cannon's voice. He decided to be cautious, "You don't have a need to know, old man. Remember, keep information compartmented, like in the SF."

"Don't give me that shit. Where are you staying?" Cannon was almost panicking.

"Chill out, man. You don't need to know where we're staying. Make sure the money is here tomorrow. Got it?"

Cannon took a deep breath, "Okay, okay. I'll get it there. The Chariot Inn in Timonium. Where are you heading?"

255

"Ditto, man. You really don't need to know, but it will be somewhere out of the country. Don't worry. We'll be out of your hair soon enough."

"I can't wait," Cannon paused. In a reconciliatory tone he said, "I never thought it would come to this. I'm sorry for both of us that it had to turn out this way. You were out of control, Chuck."

You ain't seen nothing yet, Chuck thought but said instead, "Yeah it's been real. Make sure the money is here tomorrow. I wouldn't want to ruin a great friendship over money."

"Don't worry. It will be there."

"I'll call you to confirm once I get the delivery." Chuck paused, "Bob, don't fuck with me on this."

Cannon paused and gulped some air. Then his voice cracked, "Nobody's going to mess with you Chuck. It will be there. I'll wait for your call."

"Right, bye."

On his way out Chuck stopped by the hotel desk, "I'm expecting a package tomorrow. Will you please hold it for me. When does the FEDEX delivery usually get here?"

The clerk said, "Sometime around two or three in the afternoon. We can hold it for you."

"Thanks. Someone will pick it up tomorrow afternoon. I'll call before we pick it up."

"No problem," the clerk said.

Before departing Chuck went into the room and messed up the bed and towels, "Might as well make it look like we've been here today," he said aloud.

The next morning, Brian and Chuck sat in the kitchen listening to the marine radio.

Debbie entered the room and asked, "Anything yet?"

"Not yet," Chuck stood and kissed her. "I made a call to the agent's office and they said the ship was due this evening. We have to keep listening to the radio."

"Is there anything we need to do?" Debbie poured a cup of coffee.

"No. The boat is ready to go. We got all four drums rigged up in the cabin. I need to make some adjustments to the triggers. I had some trouble making sure that the contacts will touch when it rams the ship. You might want to practice getting into the Zodiac. Are you sure you know how to start the outboard?"

"If I have any trouble, you can start it when we get in," Debbie replied.

"I guess that covers it. Brian, can you think of anything?"

"Yeah, we need to finish rigging the bomb for the trailer."

"Right. I'll work on that when I'm done with the boat triggers."

"If it's okay, I need to go to the grocery to pick up some stuff for this afternoon," Debbie voice was weak, "Anybody got any requests?" Her wane smile betrayed her concern.

"Get some coffee and donuts," Brian said.

"I'll be back in a little while."

"Don't take too long. I'm expecting to pick up the money this afternoon."

"I won't. See you in a bit."

Debbie left the trailer and drove the truck to the local grocery. Taking a spot in the lot she shut the engine and stared at the wheel. She glanced up and noticed a pay phone by the entrance to the market. At the sight of the phone she knew she was lost and lonely like a stranger in a foreign city. She wondered if she would ever see her friends and family again. Then there was Liz. She had to know about Alex. Cars pulled in and out of the lot and shoppers purposefully walked by but Debbie sat in the car trying to muster the courage to call Liz. Finally, she abruptly opened the door and stepped to the phone.

She dialed her home number, dropped several coins in the slot and hoped that Liz was home.

"Hello," Kessler answered the phone.

"Liz. Hello."

Kessler recognized Debbie's voice, "Hi. I wondered when I'd hear from you. How is Florida?"

"I don't know," Debbie was barely whispering.

"Debbie, is something wrong?"

"Liz, I don't know how to tell you this. I...I'm sorry."

"Debbie, what's wrong? Are you all right?"

"I'm fine. It's Alex."

"Alex. Alex? I haven't heard from the jerk in over a week. What's wrong Debbie?"

257

"I don't know how to say this, but Alex is dead."

"What? "

"It was an accident."

"Oh my god. How? How do you know?"

"I can't explain it any more than that."

"Debbie. Where's Alex? What is going on?" Kessler's voice sounded panicky. "Where are you? I need to talk to you."

"I can't Liz. I'm leaving the country. I wanted you to know. He loved you Liz. He was a good guy."

"Wait. Where are you going? Debbie, what have you gotten into? Debbie, talk to me. I'm your friend. You can trust me."

"I'm sorry Liz. I can't say more. I miss you. I'll miss you." She hung up the phone. Climbing back into the car, she began to sob.

NORFOLK, VIRGINIA

Shane was pacing the floor near the gate at the small terminal at Norfolk International Airport. Finally, a small turboprop plane taxied to the gate and began to unload. Shane's face broke into a wide smile when he spotted Fielding stepping through the aircraft's door. She was wearing a pair of stirrup slacks, with a stylish sweater both of which complimented her excellent figure. She carried her jacket over her sleeve, a small overnight bag, and a soft briefcase.

She greeted Shane with a big hug. Shane returned her embrace and kissed her cheek. "Boy, you look great," he said.

"So do you. And you feel great," as she wrapped her arms around his muscular torso.

"Come on, we've got to hurry. The ship is early and we need to be at the pilot's wharf in ten minutes. We'll grab a cab."

The pilot boat was ready to leave as Shane and Fielding arrived at the pier. They boarded the forty-foot powerboat and it shoved off.

"We should be just in time," the skipper said.

Shane and Fielding settled in at the rear of the launch. They watched the Norfolk skyline shrink behind them. "I never knew this was such a large harbor," Fielding gestured with her hand towards the bewildering array of warehouses, piers, container cranes and ships docked along the bank of each river and bay.

"Newport News and Norfolk do make up the biggest harbor on the East coast. Heck, the Navy alone keeps this place hopping."

"Why do you ship the cars all the way to Baltimore?"

Shane answered, "Sunon decided that. It turns out that it's cheaper to transport cars by ship. It's actually less expensive to sail up the Chesapeake to Baltimore than it would be to unload here and then ship the cars by rail. Baltimore is also closer to the densest East coast markets, like New York and Philadelphia. Plus Baltimore gave us a great deal on the pier facility. Which I'm sure the Mayor and Governor will undoubtedly mention a hundred times Monday."

"Baltimore is the busiest vehicle port on the East coast. They handle over three quarter million vehicles per year. I get plenty of work driving these ships back and forth," the pilot added.

The morning haze made visibility difficult and the pilot went forward to check the radar.

Fielding looked at Shane and said, "Gosh. This is so exciting. I'm like a little girl on a field trip."

"You certainly don't look like a little girl," Shane said with a smug smile.

"You haven't seen anything yet."

The pilot returned and said, "You should be able to see the ship over the port bow." He pointed in a direction toward the front of the launch.

"Where is it?" Fielding squinted across the choppy bay.

"I don't know," Shane replied and cupped his hands over his eyebrows.

"You're looking right at it," the pilot chuckled. "It's that big black box floating over there."

"That?" Shane said pointing to the indistinct shape on the horizon. The black unmarked shape did not resemble the image of a ship that Shane had in his mind. "I thought that was a warehouse on the shore. It certainly doesn't look like a ship."

"You're right about that," the pilot replied. "These RoRo ships aren't much to look at. They can haul some cars and they move right fast. Under the waterline they're all business. It's their superstructure that is so funny looking."

"I wouldn't have guessed that was a ship either," Fielding volunteered. There was a hint of nervousness in her voice.

"Don't worry, ma'm. Aboard that ship is the latest in everything. There's only a crew of twenty or so aboard. Everybody has plenty of room. They have VCR's, a swimming pool, though it's a little cold for swimming today. You'll have a great time on board."

After several more minutes the little pilot cutter approached the side of the RoRo. Looking up, both Shane and Fielding marveled at the size of it. "I can't believe how big it is. And straight up," Fielding commented pointing to the flat sides of the ship. To them it appeared like a gigantic floating shoebox with only the faintest nautical paraphernalia to suggest that it was a ship. Near the waterline was an open portal. A stairway extended from the portal to the waterline. The cutter tied up alongside with the help of two of the crew. The three passengers grabbed their bags and nimbly stepped onto the gangway. The crewmen went out of their way to insure that Fielding boarded safely. The pilot waved to the skipper of the cutter and it pulled away.

Shane, and then Fielding, craned their heads back and gaped at the sheer sides of the ship. Then they quickly followed the pilot up the stairs.

As they entered the portal, Captain Izumi greeted them, "Good morning Mister Shane and Miss Fielding. Welcome aboard." He bowed deeply. "If you will pardon me, I must accompany the pilot. Mister Santos will show you your cabin and give you a tour of the ship. I will see you on the bridge after you have had a chance to freshen up." The captain bowed again.

"Thank you very much, Captain. Please don't let us interrupt. We will stay out of your hair," Shane offered.

"You honor us with your presence." The captain bowed again and said, "Now I must be off." He turned and walked aft.

"This way Mr. and Mrs. Shane," Santos said with a heavy Philippine accent.

Shane and Fielding smiled at the mistake but neither made an effort to correct him.

Mr. Santos took them to an elevator. They rode up eleven decks. "This is your deck. The captain's quarters and bridge are one deck up. You can take those stairs. Your cabin is here." He opened a highly polished wood door and entered the owner's cabin.

Fielding held her breath as she glanced around. The cabin's furnishing and appointments would be at home in any first class hotel.

"You may want to put your clothes in here," he opened a surprisingly large closet. "Here is your wet bar. The head is in here. Lunch will be served in the officer's wardroom at 1300. Captain Izumi will see you on the bridge when you are ready. You may take as long as you want. If you need anything, please don't hesitate to ask."

Santos closed the door on the way out.

"Wow, this is nice," Fielding spun her body with her arms outstretched like a ballerina. "Look here, Waterford crystal on gimbaled mounts. Boy, Shane, you know how to rough it." She approached Shane and wrapped her arms around his shoulders. She kissed him on the lips.

"Let's go see the captain and get a tour of the ship," Shane whispered as he kissed her lips.

"Right now?" Fielding protested.

"We just got on board. It would be the proper thing to do."

"Oh, darn. I hope we don't have to be proper the whole time."

"Nah, we'll have plenty of time to be naughty."

DETROIT, MICHIGAN

The telephone on Nicca's temporary desk in the FBI field office rang twice before he could answer it.

"Hey, Joe. This is Harry Grove."

"Hey Harry, how's it going?"

"Fine. Hey, remember a couple weeks ago when you said you were working on a case involving Sunon car dealerships?"

"Yeah. I'm still working it."

"I figured that, especially when your office told me to call the FBI field office. Well, I don't know if it relates to your case but we had a murder up here last night that I thought I should tell you about."

"Murder, huh. Who was it?"

"A local big shot auto dealer named Cannon. Robert Cannon. We found him in his office late last night. A couple of nine millimeter slugs in his head."

"Oh yeah, I heard about it on the radio. How do you figure this ties in to my case?"

"Well, he is involved with GM dealerships in the northern suburbs. Sort of a family business. He also has some dry cleaners and a construction outfit. What I didn't know until this morning was that he was also a minor partner in several Japanese car dealerships. He has those dealerships under a different name. Mostly Sunon lots here and in the Ann Arbor area. None of the ones that were torched. When I saw the Sunon connection I remembered our conversation a couple of weeks ago when you were asking about word on the street, so I called you."

261

"Where did you find him?"

"Up here in his office. It's in Auburn Hills, but he lives in Grosse Pointe. His wife called us and said he was late getting home and no one answered at his office when she called. We sent over a black and white but they found everything secure. The next morning, his secretary found him dead inside his office."

"Sure it was murder?"

"Pretty sure. No weapon was found on or near the body. No suicide note. No sign of forced entry or theft. Plus he had two bullets in his head. Looks pretty much like homicide."

"Hmm. We'll probably want to send a team up there to help with the investigation. I'll check with Gunston here and see how he wants to work it."

"So what's it like working with the Feds? You getting into it?"

"I'll tell you. It's real interesting. Sure ain't like the arson squad. I'm even thinking about signing up when this is over."

"For the FBI! Ah, come on, Joe. You're too old."

"Maybe they'll make an exception."

"You'll never leave Detroit. You stuck it out this long. Anyway, if you send somebody up here, use my name as a point of contact. I'll make sure your boys get all the cooperation they need."

"Hey, I might come up there myself."

"Not you, Joe. You're a big time investigator with an office in the FBI. You wouldn't want to be seen hanging around with low life cops like myself."

Nicca laughed, "Just for that I'll make sure I get up there personally."

"I'd be honored by your presence."

"Say, wait a minute. Did you say Cannon owned a construction business?" Nicca's mind raced.

"Yeah. I did."

"What kind of construction do they do?"

"I don't know, but I can find out."

"See if they do any blasting work."

"No problem. I'm going to interview the widow this morning. I'll give you a call back."

"Harry, if this connects, you'll be a hero."

262

Grove laughed, "That don't pay the mortgage."

"Ain't that the truth? I'll call you when I find out when I can get up there."

"Right. I'll call you when I find out about the construction company. Take care."

Nicca hung up the phone and stood up stretching his back. The office was quiet. Most of the agents were out chasing down leads. Nicca walked into the conference room and stared out the window thinking about the latest wrinkle. Gunston burst into the room to interrupt his contemplation.

"Nicca, we got a hot lead. Get ready to go to Baltimore."

"Baltimore, why there?"

"Our tap on Kessler's line hit pay dirt. She received a call from a woman in the Baltimore area. It was from a pay phone. I contacted the Baltimore field office and they've sent a team to check out the phone. We're the Originating Office and I want our team on site to coordinate the investigation. You, Snell and I will fly out ASAP. Beverly's taking care of the reservations right now. Call Snell and fill her in. Here is a copy of the phone transcript. Read it over and stop in my office. We should have the travel plans ready by then."

"Right. I got word from the Auburn Hills Police that there was a murder there last night that might connect to this case."

"Last night. How does it tie in?"

"The victim was a minor partner in several Sunon dealerships."

"I see. It might or might not be related. Have Denzer check it out but right now we have a live suspect in Baltimore. That's where the action is. That's where you and I should be. I want to bring Laura along so she gets some arrest experience."

"Something doesn't seem right to me. I mean, why did they go to Baltimore? To lay low? Maybe to do another job? What's in Baltimore?"

"I don't know."

"I'll check with the Sunon execs. See what I can find out. Then I'll call Laura."

"Right. Meet me in my office when you get through."

Five minutes later Nicca entered Gunston's office.

"Joe. Here's the plan. We're on Northwest Flight 129 at 3:10 this afternoon. That should give us enough time to pack a quick bag and head to the airport. We'll have a Bureau car and driver take us there.

263

Baltimore has its SWAT team ready to go in. Plus the Hostage Rescue Team is on alert in Quantico. They'll chopper up if we need them. They'll have a car waiting for us at Baltimore Washington Airport."

"How much do we have?"

"The Baltimore office managed to lift some prints off the phone. So far no one has been able to ID the caller. She said they're leaving the country so we've put a watch on the airports for Russo. It's a long shot, but it's worth taking. They're combing the area with Russo's picture to see if they can get a nibble. It won't be long."

"Yeah, but I hate going to an arrest without my gun."

"What do you mean?"

"I can't bring my gun on the plane."

"We, that is FBI agents, can. Don't worry; we'll issue you whatever you want at Baltimore.

CHESAPEAKE BAY NEAR BALTIMORE, MARYLAND

Santos knocked on the ornate teak door of the owner's cabin. After waiting a full minute he knocked again.

Shane finally answered the door while fumbling with the belt on his bathrobe. "What is it?" Shane asked with obvious displeasure.

In the suite, Santo could see the tousled sheets on the bunk.

"Sorry to bother you, Mr. Shane. The Captain said to tell you we are approaching Baltimore harbor.

If you wish you might like to watch from the bridge."

"Oh," Shane paused. "Sure. Tell him we'll be right up."

"Thank you sir," Santos said before turning away.

"What was that all about?" Fielding asked from the door to the sumptuous marble-trimmed head after Santos left. She was standing with a blanket from the bed wrapped around her torso.

"The captain wants us upstairs on the Bridge. We're approaching Baltimore. I told him we'd be right up."

"What's the hurry?" Fielding said, dropping the blanket and wrapping her arms around Shane.

"There isn't any hurry..." Shane's last words were blurred as Fielding kissed his lips and pushed him toward the double bunk.

264

Debbie returned to the trailer and started to unpack the groceries. She went to open the refrigerator and was startled when she noticed a bomb on the floor. At least it looked like a bomb with two sticks of dynamite, a car battery and various wires. Careful to avoiding touching it, she placed the milk in the icebox. Out the kitchen window she could see Chuck and Brian working on the boat. She decided to wait in the bedroom with the hope that the signs of her crying would fade.

After an hour or so Chuck entered the trailer. "Hey Debbie, can you come here? I need to talk to you," Chuck shouted from the kitchen.

Debbie left the bedroom where she was packing their clothes. "What's up?"

"I'm busy with this circuit..." he looked at Debbie and noticed that she had been crying. "Are you okay?"

Debbie sniffled, "Oh yes. I'm a little sad."

"About what?"

"I don't know. Alex. Everything, I guess. "

"Don't be bummed, Debbie. This is exciting." All his energy was focused on completing the task at hand. "Everything we've worked for, everything we wanted will be taken care of today. This is your chance at revenge. You wanted revenge, right? Well, this is it."

"I'll be fine. What do you need?" she said without vigor.

"I expected a package today. I called and found out that it arrived at the hotel where we stayed. Can you go pick it up for me? I can't 'cause I need to finish rigging this circuit and then I need to check the boat."

"Sure, I think I remember where the hotel was."

"Take the truck. Come right back here."

"The package has the money right?"

"Yeah. That doesn't make you nervous does it?"

"No. Maybe Brian should come with me."

"No. I need him to help me here. We'll be ready to go as soon as you get back. Don't worry. You can handle it. Come straight back here."

Debbie drove to the hotel by the only route she knew. It took forty-five minutes, she missed a turn but she finally found the hotel.

Parking in the front carport she entered the lobby.

"Excuse me sir, I'm here to pick up a package."

"What's the name?" the clerk asked.

"Powers, Lance Powers."

"Let me see. Yes, it arrived this afternoon. He called to say you would be picking it up. Here you are." The clerk handed over the orange, white and blue envelope.

"Thanks." She took the package and walked toward the exit.

Akira Sugai sat on the couch on the far side of the lobby and watched her walk to the door. He withdrew a cellular phone from his jacket and dialed a number. "Sato-San, a woman picked up the envelope. It was not Holzer. What should I do?"

"Wait," was Sato's curt reply. The information that Cannon gave them before they killed him did not include the names of Holzer's accomplices. He had hoped that Holzer would pick up the package. But he was not worried. This woman would undoubtedly lead them to Holzer. "Hai, I see her. We will not be able to finish it here. Come quickly, we will follow her. She thinks she has the money. She will take us to Holzer."

Akira followed Debbie through the door. As he walked he cradled the Uzi machine pistol against his chest under his jacket. He remembered the Tsukiji Fish Market the day of the shoot out. Concern that this plan would also go wrong and that Sato would be upset filled his mind.

"Quickly, get in. She is leaving." Sato ordered from the passenger seat of the Lincoln. Tanaka sat in the back. Both men had weapons drawn but out of view.

Sugai sat behind the wheel and followed Debbie in the truck. In the gathering darkness he turned on his headlights.

"She suspects nothing," Sato said with confidence. "She will take us to Holzer. Then we will strike quickly and leave no trace."

The early winter sun was a large disk on the horizon when Gunston, Nicca and Snell arrived at BWI airport. Two agents from the Baltimore field office greeted them at the gate. "If you would follow us this way sir, we have a chopper waiting." The two local agents led the three visitors through a door in the jet way and down a flight of stairs to the tarmac. There they met a third agent with a bureau car. He drove them to the far side of the field where they saw an unmarked Jet Ranger helicopter that had numerous antennas and other protuber-

266

ances extending from its fuselage. The effect made the helicopter appear unaerodynamic, almost bug like.

"Hello, I'm Special Agent Stevie Akin. I fly this beast. The bird is at your disposal while we're running this operation. It's set up as an airborne command post. It's equipped with thermal viewers for searching, secure radios and telephone, a hundred thousand candlepower search light. I'll give you a quick safety briefing on some emergency procedures. Then we'll fly over to the field office to meet our SAC. We've set up a crisis center there, but we can duplicate most of its command functions from the chopper."

"What does a thermal viewer do?" asked Nicca.

"It allows us to see at night. It works by detecting temperature differences, which the eye can't see. It's handy for tracking people or vehicles without the use of searchlights. We also have night vision goggles which the passengers can use but they are image intensifiers and sometimes they don't work as well as the thermal."

"Sir," one of the agents that met them at the gate spoke to Nicca. "Are you Officer Nicca? I understand you'll need a weapon. I have a standard issue 9-millimeter pistol with an extra magazine. Is this acceptable?"

"Yeah. That's fine." Nicca replied.

"If you would please sign this receipt, it's all yours."

"Thanks." Nicca scribbled his name and then boarded the chopper. "This is what I call getting the red carpet treatment," he said as he donned intercom headphones and buckled his seat belt.

The helicopter turbine began to whine slowly. After several seconds it spooled up to normal power. The pilot radioed the tower and after a brief wait they were airborne heading the short distance to the field office. The pilot's voice came over the headsets, "The field office is over there," pointing to the west. "We're working that area now," he pointed to the northeast across the harbor. "That's where the call originated."

Nicca had never been in a helicopter before and he marveled at the view of the Baltimore skyline in the setting sun. Under different circumstances he could have enjoyed the ride. To the east a fog was forming, but through the mist in the harbor he could see ships moving about. The size of the harbor surprised him. There were numerous docks, piers, and rail yards with large container gantry cranes spread around the periphery of the large bay. Off in the distance he could discern the Francis Scott Key Bridge that glowed orange in the reflected sunset. He glanced at Snell and she smiled back.

Over the intercom he heard the pilot say, "After we visit our SAC I'm scheduled to take you to the phone site, unless of course you want to do something else." The pilot glanced at Gunston.

"That will be fine," Gunston said.

CEDAR BEACH, MARYLAND

Debbie retraced her route and returned directly to the trailer. Afraid to open the package she put it on the kitchen table. Brian was putting coffee grinds into an electric coffee maker. Brian noticed the envelope but he didn't say anything.

"Where's Chuck?" Debbie asked.

"In the boat. I'll meet you there after I make some coffee."

She left out the back door and walked to the boat slip. Chuck looked up from his work, sweat beaded on his forehead even though it was cold.

"Did you get it?" he smiled broadly.

"Yes."

"Was it all there?"

"I didn't open it. The envelope is in the kitchen."

"What! You are something. Let me finish here and we'll go get the dough. We can count it later. We have to hurry. I heard on the scanner that the ship is in the harbor entrance Baltimore." Chuck was visibly buoyant. "Why don't you keep me company."

Debbie climbed in the boat. She put both arms around her torso to fend off the chilly night air while she watched Chuck finish with the arming device.

Chapter 22

CEDAR BEACH, MARYLAND

Akira Sugai slowly drove the white Lincoln past where they observed Debbie park. Then they watched her enter one of several trailers parked in a row along the water's edge. Tanaka scanned the porch of the trailer, and nodded to Sato. Sato said, "Drive down the street. Turn around and park around the corner. We'll wait a few minutes there. Sugai-San and I will go to the front door. Tanaka-San, you go around the back. Stop anyone that tries to run."

"No problem."

Sugai stopped the car in front of a trailer. Tanaka jumped from the passenger seat and walked to the back of the building briskly but not enough to arose anyone's suspicion. Sato and Sugai got out of the Continental and looked around to see if anyone was visible. The street was as dark and deserted as a lunar landscape. Sato put his hand underneath his coat to grip his Baretta 9 mm automatic pistol and followed Sugai to the front of the house. On the porch, Sugai stood his with back flat against the wall of the house next to the door while Sato rang the doorbell.

Brian was in the galley kitchen making coffee when the door-bell rang. "Huh, who could that be?" he wondered to himself. He subconsciously reached down for the handle of his 44 Automag. Walking through the dining room, Brian looked out the front window as he passed by it. He could see the back of Sato's head on the porch. "Who the hell is he?" Brian cracked opened the door and looked at the visitor. "Yes?" He said with an annoyed expression.

"Mr. Holzer, we would like to speak..." Sato replied.

Brian instinctively slammed the door shut before Sato could finish his sentence. "Shit, how do they know Chuck's name? Chuck gave an alias when renting the trailer." His mind raced about what to do, but he was too late. Several bullets from the automatic Barreta sliced through the door and shattered the silence inside the trailer. One of the bullets, slowed by the wood in the front door lodged in Brian's hip. Brian screamed in shock. Dropping his gun he stumbled to the short hallway between the kitchen and the living room. Meanwhile, Sugai smashed one of the living room windows with the butt of his Uzi machine gun. He saw Brian stumbling across the room. Sugai opened fire. Four of the first five rounds hit Brian in the back. He fell flat on the floor, his punctured lungs gasping for air.

Sato started kicking violently on the front door. The lock held. Seeing that the door was not budging, Sugai smashed the remaining window glass with his Uzi and climbed through the jagged opening.

Brian crawled into the kitchen. The sound gurgling in his chest told him he didn't have long to live. "Got to take the mother fuckers with me" he swore to himself. His vision faded and he struggled to stay conscious. With extreme effort he fought the temptation to let go and fade into the darkness. Instead he seized the wires to the booby trap on the gas line with trembling fingers.

Sugai followed Brian's bloody trail into the kitchen. From the entrance he sprayed bullets from his Uzi machine pistol across the room. The bullets zipped past Brian and smashed wildly into the cupboards and harvest-gold refrigerator.

Brian looked up. He saw Sugai come round the kitchen counter. Brian screamed and connected the leads to the car battery.

The kitchen erupted into a ball of flame. The shock wave blew out the remaining windows and doors. Sato was on the porch when the front door came off its hinges and smacked into him. He and the door went flying backward twenty feet.

Chuck and Debbie looked toward the trailer when they heard the Uzi machine gun fire.

"That's gunfire. It's up in the house." He turned to look at Debbie who was standing next to the pilot console. "Debbie, where's Brian?"

"He is in the house making coffee."

The gunfire continued.

"Something is wrong. Start the motor. I'm going to check it out."

Chuck climbed out of the boat onto the dock as the house exploded. "Holy shit, the bomb." As he said this, Chuck saw Tanaka fall to the ground in the backyard.

Chuck turned round, "Debbie, we got to get out of here." He undid the bow and stern lines and pushed the Sea Ray from the dock. "Let's go."

Debbie screamed, "Chuck, what's happening? What about Brian?"

"I don't know. Someone was shooting. Somehow the bomb got set off. There were people in the backyard. Brian's probably dead."

"Oh no, no, Chuck," Debbie lowered her head in her hands.

"Stop it, Debbie, we got to get away. We got to finish this job. We lost too much already."

"What are we going to do?"

"You drive the damn boat to that buoy. I'll get the Zodiac ready."

"Okay, I'll drive the boat, but who was shooting? How did they find us?

"I don't know. Maybe the police? But they're too late to stop us."

Sato landed in the side yard with the door crashing next to him. He was unhurt except for the severe ringing in his ears and numbness in his head. The front door had shielded Sato from the full fury of the explosion. Shaking his head back and forth, he stood up and looked back toward the trailer. Vivid orange flames engulfed the structure. Fire seemed to be shooting from all directions from where the now totally demolished kitchen had been.

Debris from the blast started to crash around him. Sato ducked instinctively but not quickly enough. A two foot long piece of wood spinning through the air hit him on the side of his head above his right ear. The blow knocked him backward, his head hitting the soft ground. Although the blow from the wood was a glancing one, it ripped a deep gash into Sato's head. A stream of warm blood ran down the side of his face.

Sato lay motionless for a minute. When he tried to stand, the ground swirled around him. He lowered himself to his hands and knees. Blood from his head dripped onto his hand. He tried to shake his head to clear the pain but his head only throbbed more.

From the backyard, Tanaka came running to his leader, "Sato-San, Sato-San, are you all right?" Tanaka helped Sato to his feet.

"Yes, I'm fine" he lied. The stinging pain in his forehead was almost unbearable. He was seeing double.

"Where's Sugai?" asked Tanaka.

"I don't know, he was, ... was in the house, He was right there, next to the explosion." Sato was shaking. The pressure from the blast still echoed in his chest. Sato tried to hyperventilate to recover his composure.

"What happened? What exploded?" asked Tanaka.

"Those bastards," Sato yelled, "they set a booby trap in the house." Yelling made his head throb like it was in a vice being tightened. Sato doubled over, clutching his knees.

"We must stop that bleeding," said Tanaka. He ripped a sleeve off his shirt and sopped the blood on Sato's temple.

Recovering momentarily, Sato brushed away Tanaka's hand. "Never mind that, let's get away from here before the authorities arrive."

"Sato-San, right after the explosion, I saw someone leave in a boat from the dock behind the house." Tanaka pointed to the small dock behind the trailer. The flames from the fire clearly lit the dock.

"Someone escaped? Who was it?"

"I'm not sure. It was a man. The boat left in a hurry."

"It must be Holzer. We must catch that bastard. We must complete our mission."

"He left in a boat. What are we going to do?"

"We'll follow him."

"How?"

"We must get a boat."

To Sato's surprise, a small cuddy cabin fishing boat approached the dock. Two fisherman returning from an evening of blue fishing noticed the explosion and steered to the dock to see if they could help.

The pilot of the boat yelled, "Ahoy there, is everything all right? Do you need help?"

Sato saw the boat nearing the dock. He reached down and picked up his pistol. As he bent down, blood rushing to his head almost made him loses consciousness. He concentrated to overcome the pain. "Tanaka-San, wave that boat over here. Tell them we need help."

Tanaka ran down the dock waving both arms over his head. "Help us, there's been an explosion. We need help."

The fisherman could see Tanaka's silhouette against the flames of the house. They also could see Sato stumbling toward the water.

"Hey Jim, pull up to the dock. Those guys look hurt."

"Yeah, you grab the first aid kit," said the pilot.

While the pilot pulled into the slip, the fisherman tossed a line to Tanaka. Tanaka grabbed the line and pulled the boat closer. As he did this, Sato came from behind him. Sato was careful to make sure that Tanaka's body hid the fisherman's view of his pistol. When Tanaka secured the line, the fisherman on the front of the boat jumped on the dock.

"Man, what happened here?" said the fisherman looking up at the burning house. "How did the ..."

Before he could finish his question, Sato raised his gun and shot the man in his chest. The impact of the 9 mm parabellum slug knocked the fisherman backwards off the dock. His body hit against the side of the boat before splashing into the water.

The pilot of the boat saw the muzzle flash and heard the thud and splash of his friend's body. He yelled in panic "What the hell!" He ran back to the steering console under the cuddy cabin. Sato turned and fired. The bullet missed the pilot, smashing into the windshield in front of the steering console and sending a spider web of cracks through the safety glass. The pilot grabbed the gear lever. He jammed it into reverse while pushing on the throttle lever. The 160 horse power inboard motor growled into action; the propeller churning up brown muddy water as the boat strained against the line tied to the dock.

Sato crouched to get a better aim. The pilot turned and looked in terror at the line taut on the bow of the boat. Sato fired again. The slug smashed into the back of the pilot's head and blew his face off as it exited toward the front. His body crashed forward, pushing the gear lever back into neutral. The motor raced wildly. Sato jumped on the boat, pushed the pilot's body aside and lowered the throttle to idle.

"Get on," he yelled to Tanaka, "And release that rope."

Tanaka released the line and jumped on the bow of the boat.

"Can you drive one of these?" asked Sato, his head pounding from the gash on his temple.

"Yes, it's easy."

"Good, let's go."

Tanaka backed the boat from the slip and pointed it into the harbor. The fire lit the water and amplified the luminescent plankton and foam in the remnant of the wake of Chuck's boat. The eerie light left a trail as if Chuck was saying, "Here I am. Come and get me."

"Just follow their wake and go fast," ordered Sato.

Tanaka goosed the throttle and the sporty cuddy cabin raised on plane. After traveling for a few seconds, Tanaka reduced the throttle.

"What's wrong?" demanded Sato.

"I can't see the wake from inside the cabin. I can't tell where to go. You'll have to direct me."

"Hai, hai, go." Sato climbed onto the gunwale of the boat so he could get a view of the wake. When Tanaka gunned the engine, it almost threw Sato overboard. Slipping on the fiberglass, Sato struggled to regain his balance. When he pulled himself up, he could see that Tanaka was veering to the right.

"Hidari, hidari" shouted Sato, his anxiety making him revert to Japanese. "I mean left. Go left."

Sato scoured the horizon for a glimpse of Chuck's boat. A quickly forming fog made visibility difficult. All he could see was the faint wake. With each wave of the crashing quartering sea, the salt spray rose over the bow of the boat and struck Sato in the face. The salt water in his gash stung viciously. The pain made it hard to see, yet he stared ahead, trying to glimpse his prey.

"There, masugu. Straight, straight ahead." About a half mile ahead was Chuck's boat. Sato could barely discern it between wisps of fog that steady grew thicker.

In the Sea Ray, Chuck connected the wires for the final firing circuit. When he finished arming the bomb he went aft and pulled on the line tied to the Zodiac. He brought the rubber boat along side the Sea Ray. He looked back and could barely see the burning house. Shaking his head he said, "This is for you Brian ... and for me."

"Okay, Debbie, let me take over. You get ready to get out. When we get close to the ship, I'll slow down enough for us to get in the Zodiac. I'll use the remote control to drive the Sea Ray right into the side of that mother fucker."

"Chuck, are you sure? Should we do this?" Chuck could not see the tears in Debbie's eyes, but her quivering voice gave her away.

"What? Damn it. Debbie, we have to finish this. We can't let Brian and Alex die in vain. We have to even the score."

"I can't Chuck, this is too much. I can't. What if the police catch us? If they found us once, they'll find us again."

"Shut up, shut up."

Debbie dug her face into her hands.

274

Chuck stared intently at the flat side of the RoRo ship while he mentally calculated when he should jump into the Zodiac. He sighted along an imaginary line along the water between the Sea Ray and the ship trying to estimate the distance. He knew from his plan that he should be at least 500 yards from the explosion, but he didn't count on the visibility being so poor. The large hull of the ship was also making it difficult to accurately estimate the distance. "Just a little closer, a little closer and it will be fine."

When the Sea Ray hit the remnants of the Honshu Princes' bow wave Chuck cut the throttle, "That's it." The Sea Ray lurched forward as its momentum transferred and the hull lunged backward off plane. "Jump in the Zodiac Debbie. Now."

"I can't Chuck, I'm scared."

"Damn it. Do it. We don't have time." Saying this, Chuck grabbed Debbie and they both flopped over the side into the inflatable boat. It was half full of water. Chuck started the small outboard motor and steered away from the Sea Ray. He then undid the remote control unit from the wooden seat top and pushed the remote throttle control unit. The Sea Ray surged forward. Watching the stern of the Sea Ray, Chuck steered it away from the Zodiac and toward the center of the RoRo ship. "Debbie, steer the Zodiac that way. Head for those lights," he said, pointing to the west. "We have to get away from the blast."

The fishing cuddy cabin with its 160 horsepower motor was gaining on the heavily laden Sea Ray. With each crash against the quartering sea, the cuddy cabin closed the distance but the salt spray would cover Sato's face burning the gash in his scalp, making him more determined to finish his mission. He would kill Holzer. He would make the barbarian pay for this.

Tanaka yelled to Sato "Where? Where? Is this good?" He could still not see the Sea Ray.

Sato yelled back into the cabin. "Yes, go straight, we're gaining on them."

Sato was so intent on catching the Sea Ray, that he never noticed the dark hull of the RoRo ship in the distance. Nor did he notice Chuck and Debbie in the black Zodiac inflatable boat. All he could see was the stern of the Sea Ray.

He reached inside his jacket pocket and grabbed another 10 round magazine for the Baretta. Quickly, he replaced magazines. The pleasure of thinking about killing Chuck caused him to temporarily forget about the searing pain. "When we get close to their boat, pull

275

along side. I'll shoot at the driver and then jump on board. I want that bastard to feel the pain."

"Ah yes, I can see the boat now. They must be slowing down," replied Tanaka.

Gunston, Snell and Nicca met in a small conference room adjacent to the Baltimore SAC's office. Gunston had finished briefing the details of the case to date when a local Special Agent burst into the room and said, "We got contact in Cedar Beach. There have been reports of gunfire and an explosion."

"Where is that?" Gunston asked.

"It's near the area we've been working. How many agents do we have up there?"

"We have six teams with two agents each so that makes twelve."

"Good. Get the SWAT team up there now. Activate the crisis center. I will join Gunston's team in the airborne command post. Let's get up there now."

The group wasted no time heading to the helipad behind the field office. The pilot handed Nicca and Snell sets of PVS-7 night vision goggles as they boarded the chopper. "Take these," he said. "This knob adjusts the brightness and this one focuses them. If you have trouble seeing put them on."

Nicca strapped in next to Snell. The pilot made some last minute adjustments to the thermal viewer. Then he fired up the turbine and the chopper was airborne. They took a course directly over the newly renovated inner harbor. Although excited about the upcoming action, both Nicca and Snell enjoyed watching the harbor pass underneath the low flying helicopter.

Chuck finally noticed the fishing boat closing on the Sea Ray. "What? A boat is following the Sea Ray."

"What did you say, Chuck?" Debbie didn't notice because she was steering the Zodiac toward the distant lights. Her composure seemed to have returned.

"There's a damn boat following the Sea Ray."

"Oh my god, a boat," Debbie turned to see and the Zodiac swerved as she inadvertently pulled on the steering arm of the outboard motor.

"Debbie, stay on course," Chuck yelled at Debbie. "Don't worry about that boat. By the time it catches the Sea Ray it will be too late."

Debbie straightened the control arm while Chuck used the remote controls to steer the Sea Ray.

"Almost there Tanaka-San. Turn to the right." Tanaka turned the boat but he made too sharp of a turn. The fishing boat bumped against the Sea Ray and bounced apart. Sato had grabbed hold of the Sea Ray's gunwale with his left hand but the bounce jerked his grip free.

"Again, turn to the right. Now," Sato screamed.

Tanaka struggled to match the speed of the Sea Ray to avoid bouncing. He was not proficient enough with the controls of the boat and was a fraction of a second too slow in making the course correction. Again, the fishing boat approached right alongside the Sea Ray and again the boats bounced apart. This time, Sato only grasped a handful of seawater.

"Goddamn Tanaka, get alongside that boat," Sato yelled in frustration. He was so close that not being able to get on the boat was almost too much for him to bear.

"I'm trying, I'm trying." He adjusted the throttle to exactly match the speed of the Sea Ray. With a twitch of the steering wheel, he neatly brought the fishing boat alongside the Sea Ray.

Sato didn't hesitate. When the two boats were exactly adjacent, he jumped. Landing with a crash in the rear compartment of the Sea Ray, Sato's back hit against the far gunwale. Despite the sharp pain in his back, Sato bounced up and blindly fired a burst of bullets from his Baretta into the bow cabin of the Sea Ray. Steadying himself, he moved toward the front of the boat in a crouch. Seeing the back of the console, Sato fired again. The bullets ripped into the empty seat. "Where are you?" he said, seeing the seat was empty. He then noticed the steering wheel move by itself as Chuck tried to correct the trajectory of the Sea Ray to account for the fishing boat pushing alongside it. "What the hell is this?" Sato looked down at the remote control servo mechanism attached to the steering well. Something was wrong. He ran to the back of the boat and motioned to Tanaka. As he did, the RoRo ship sounded a blast of its horn. Sato and Tanaka simultaneously looked toward the bow and saw the hull of the Honshu Prince only twenty-five yards away.

"What's that?" yelled Sato pointing to the black side of the Honshu Prince, towering like a wall in front of the two pleasure craft. There was no time for an answer as the bow of the Sea Ray rammed the steel plates of the ship's hull. The fender trigger mechanism collapsed with the impact energizing the firing circuit. Six amps from the car batteries flowed through the firing circuit igniting the first in a series of the TNT booster charges. The first drum of ammonia nitrate slurry exploded with a vengeance. The remaining three drums following in sequence separated only by a few microseconds. To an observer, the separate explosions happened too fast to discern, all one could see was a large blast.

The fireball from the blast consumed the Sea Ray, fishing boat and the occupants. Buckling from the pressure wave the outer plates of the RoRo ship's hull cracked open as if a child were ripping paper. In an instant, water was flowing into the main cargo hold where all the new cars were densely packed.

On the bridge Captain Izumi felt the shudder and saw the light from the explosion. He immediately glanced at the pilot who was steering the ship through Baltimore harbor. "Are we on course?" Izumi jumped from his leather captain's chair and yelled into the microphone, "Engineering is there a problem with the engine?"

"No Captain, it sounds like something happened towards the bow," replied a voice from the intercom.

"We are on course. We did not run aground," shakily replied the pilot, obviously shocked that something he had done hundreds of times had gone wrong.

At the hole in the hull, thousands of gallons of fuel stored between the inner and outer hull gushed onto the water and flowed against the burning remains of the Sea Ray and fishing boat. The secondary fire created a wall of flame up the side of the Honshu Prince.

"My god, we are burning," yelled Izumi. "Sound fire stations!"

The fire grew, backing the intense heat into the partly full fuel tanks in the bilge and causing a massive secondary explosion that ripped out the bottom of the ship. The tremendous blast reverberated throughout the car carrier throwing Captain Izumi and the pilot into the plate glass windows of the bridge. The design, which made the ship so efficient in loading and unloading cars, proved fatal when water flooded the car decks. There was nothing the crew could do. Only 30 seconds after the initial blast the Honshu Prince started listing heavily to port. The momentum of the sideways motion catapulted the crew and cargo from the decks of the ship. Hundreds of shiny 500GSXs broke loose from their fastening devices and smashed into each other and the cargo compartment walls.

As water barreled into the ship, it continued to roll to port. Within a minute, the Honshu Prince was on its side. Inside the cavernous cargo hold, the new cars bounced wildly into each other. Some already loose floated violently on the water filling the compartment like kayaks in steep rapids.

Shane was shaving in the owner's suite head when the blast first shook the ship. "What was that?" he said.

Fielding stopped putting on her hose, looked at Shane and said, "I don't know."

Shane turned to finish shaving when the ship's emergency Klaxon alarm pierced the air.

Dropping his razor he said, "We better get dressed."

The second blast sent both he and Fielding to the deck. Shane fell backwards from the head into the cabin while Fielding landed flat on her back and was knocked unconscious. Shane got to his knees and could sense the ship starting to heel to port.

"My god, something happened, we're tipping over. "Mary are you all right?" he yelled to Fielding. She didn't respond.

Scrambling across the pitching deck, Shane reached Fielding as her limp body slid across the floor and hit the cabin bulkhead. With difficulty, he lifted her under her shoulders and dragged her to the cabin door that was now almost below his feet. Loose furniture and knickknacks from the cabin slammed into the bulkhead next to them and blocked the door. Shane shoved the furniture aside and pulled open the cabin door as a wall of water rushed down the passageway. There was no time to escape. The torrent pushed them back into the room quickly filling the luxury cabin with cold seawater. Shane hugged Fielding as the winter water surrounded and claimed them.

In less than two minutes the Honshu Prince went down. There was no time to orderly abandon ship. The crew, passengers and its prized cargo sank to the bottom of the ship channel. The only evidence of a ship was a burning oil slick and the tip of the bow, held afloat by a trapped air pocket.

Chuck looked in awe at the explosion, too dumbfounded to speak. The violence of the blast surprised him, as he had not witnessed the prior explosion.

Debbie started to cry. "My god Chuck, what have we done?" She pointed to the fire.

Chuck didn't respond amazed by the fury of the blast. He had no idea the bomb would work so well.

As his astonishment wore off, Chuck began to realize what happened. "Do you see that? Do you see that?" he yelled. "We did it. We did it. I can't fucking believe it. It worked."

"No Chuck, it's wrong. How could we do that? What about the innocent people?"

"Fuck. Nobody's innocent," Chuck scoffed. "We have revenge!"

"There's no revenge, Chuck," Debbie sobbed. "Only death and destruction. We had no right doing what we did."

"How could you say that? You wanted it as bad as me."

"No I didn't. I couldn't." Her eyes were puffy and remorseful. "I didn't know it would be like this."

"The hell with that. I got what I want. Now let's get the hell out of here." Chuck reached for the tiller and pulled it from Debbie's hand.

"Let's head to the rendezvous point."

"Brian won't be there..." Debbie screamed but Chuck ignored her.

"Whoa! Look over there!" Nicca pointed to a bright flash in the harbor, clearly visible in spite of the fog. He put the night vision goggles up to his eyes to get a better look.

"Should I investigate that sir?" the pilot asked.

"Yes," replied the SAC. "See if you can make anything out with the thermal. Call the crisis center and see if they know about this."

"We should get a little closer sir," the pilot suggested.

"Do it. If there are survivors we might be able to help. Put out a Mayday on the emergency Coast Guard channel."

The chopper banked and quickly closed in on the sinking ship.

Through the Nicca vision goggles Nicca could see the ship listing and sinking quickly. "That's a ship going down," he bellowed. Then he saw the name on the hull of the ship. "Oh my god. It's Sunon's!"

"Sir, I think I see some survivors." The pilot cut in. "They appear to be heading east in a life raft."

"Can you see anyone else?"

"No sir."

"Check the other side. See if there is anyone else."

The pilot circled the burning wreck but found nothing. "Sir, if

280

there was anybody down there they'd show up on the thermal. I can't see anybody."

"I can still see a lifeboat," Nicca offered looking through the night vision goggles. "They look like they might be having problems."

"Fly to the lifeboat. See if we can help them," the SAC ordered. "Then we'll come back here to check for other survivors."

"Roger." The pilot flew towards the lifeboat and intercepted it about two hundred yards from shore. As the helicopter reached the boat it slowed and hovered. The pilot switched on the searchlight and aimed it at the boat.

"Looks like a man and a woman," Nicca said stretching his neck.

Chuck twisted the outboards throttle to accelerate when he recognized the helicopter was headed at them. Then realizing that they would be caught, he slowed down and drew his .45 caliber pistol from his shoulder holster.

The chopper hovered over the Zodiac raft. The rotor down wash kicked up water soaking Chuck. Then a blinding shaft of light shone down on them. Under the glare Chuck felt naked.

"Let's give up, Chuck," Debbie pleaded. "They have us."

"Fucking A man," Chuck shielded his eyes with his left hand, he aimed his pistol and fired four shots.

The chopper was barely twenty feet away and an easy target. The first bullet smashed through the cockpit and hit the SAC in the leg. The second shot shattered the search light before lodging in the fuselage. Two more shots hit the chopper, cutting power cables, and hydraulic lines before passing through the windscreen. Shrapnel sprayed across the pilot and SAC followed by sparks and smoke.

"They're shooting at us," Nicca yelled.

"I'm bleeding," the SAC moaned over the intercom.

Nicca heard the pilot mumble, "I can't see. Need to back off. Get some altitude. Instinctively he pulled up on the collective to make the chopper climb. The chopper swayed back and forth barely obeying the control inputs. "It's not handling right. Something is wrong."

"We better get to land," Gunston said as he undid his seat belt and struggled against the jolting helicopter as he looked at the wound in the SAC's leg."

"Where did the boat go?" Snell shouted.

281

There, toward shore" Nicca looking through the night vision goggles shouted to the pilot. "Can you follow it?"

"I'll try. She's not responding to my input." The helicopter shuddered as Akin applied power and pitched it forward to pick up speed. The change in attitude made it unstable. The chopper began to yaw back and forth, losing altitude.

Nicca saw the ground rapidly approaching outside the window. He readied himself for the impact by grabbing the handrail of his seat then looked over and Snell fumbling with her seat belts, her face locked in a dreadful grimace.

Quickly he undid his seat belt, bracing his foot against the handrail and grabbing the seat on the side of Snell, making his body into a restraint. "We're going down."

Snell nodded grimly.

Nicca looked into her blue eyes and for an instant saw his wife's face. How did she look right before the impact? Like Snell now? Just as quickly the image passed and he saw Snell now smiling holding his hand.

The helicopter dropped rapidly, passing right over Chuck and Debbie as they beached the inflatable boat. One hundred yards further, the chopper slammed into the shore gouging a ditch in the gravel before pitching sideways and coming to a stop on its side. Spinning rotors sliced the ground and rebounded wildly, dirt and rock flying everywhere.

As they hit Snell's body weight pulled Nicca forward. His wrist strained on the aluminum seat restraint before he could no longer hold it, sending him careening into the Plexiglas window of the side door. A momentary blackness passed him and then a sharp pain crossed his forehead. He looked up into the dust and smoke filling the cabin.

"Got to get out of here," he mumbled into the now inoperative intercom.

"Is everybody all right?" the SAC yelled.

"I'm okay," Snell shouted and looked to Nicca her face wrought with concern.

After a moment Nicca mumbled "I'm, I'm all right." He put his hand to his forehead. "I banged my head."

He felt a hand on his shoulder. Snell climbed over Gunston's limp body and hunched over next Nicca. "Joe, are you hurt?"

"I don't think so..." His head spun. "Just dizzy." He tried to stand but the movement made him lightheaded. He slumped backwards. Snell caught Nicca before he could fall. She grunted under his weight.

"Joe, can you hear me!"

He saw Snell's eyes. The image flickered as his eyebrows went up and down. He fought to keep conscious. Nicca made a small nod.

Snell lowered him onto the helicopter's door.

Akin climbed from his harness into the rear of the compartment. "Is he okay?"

"Joe is conscious. Gunston looks bad. He's knocked out and bleeding."

"Let me get the first aid kit."

"Can you take care of them?" Snell asked.

"Yeah. After I find the first aid kit."

"Good, look after Gunston. I think he's the worst off. I'm going after those bastards."

Snell grabbed Nicca's night vision goggles. Placing them on the aircraft skin she climbed out of the door, which now faced up. Standing on top, she scanned the area.

Nicca watched her through blurry eyes. "Laura wait for me," he whispered through parched lips. She didn't hear him and jumped off the helicopter.

The helicopter crashed in an open area near the Curtis Bay coal export pit about a 100 yards away from where Chuck beached the Zodiac. Coal cinders crunched under foot as Chuck and Debbie sprinted across the yard toward railroad tracks. In front of them was a line of coal cars slowly moving under automatic control to a rotary dumper. There, the whole hopper car rotated, emptying its coal into a pit, which funneled the jet-black material unto an endless belt. A noisy conveyor dropped the fuel into a waiting bulk carrier ship.

Chuck stopped when he reached the line of moving hoppers. "Come on Debbie, we need to cross this train."

"No, Chuck, I can't. I'm afraid." She was doubled over puffing heavily.

"God damn it." He scanned the area. "Over there. We can cross by the building."

He pulled her up and ran, this time out-distancing her. He reached the grungy building and stopped. The string of cars extended through the rotary dumper building and continued on the other side. Debbie caught up, panting and slumped against a beam that supported the shed roof of the open structure.

"We've got to cross here," Chuck pointed to the string of slowly moving cars.

"We'll get killed Chuck. There's got to be another way."

Chuck looked around. He noticed an access ladder led to the top of the shed roof. "This way. We'll cross the roof." He began to scale the ladder.

Debbie started to follow. She made it up five rungs when her hands slipped and she fell backward. Her foot caught in a rung and she twisted as she fell. She landed head first with a thud, her arms barely breaking her fall. She laid there stunned on her back, her leg twisted in an impossible manner.

"Debbie, Debbie," Chuck screamed. He could see her in the dim light crumpled at the foot of the ladder. He started down the ladder toward her when Chuck heard a yell.

"Halt. FBI. Stay where you are."

There was a figure moving along the train about fifty yards from Debbie. Chuck crouched like a linebacker on the top rung while he stared at the moving figure. "Debbie's going to get caught," he grimaced. "Shit." He pulled out his pistol and steadily aimed it down the ladder at Debbie's head.

"Debbie, I have to do it. You'll tell them everything." Slowly, he squeezed the trigger. Debbie's body bounced as the round passed through her head.

Chuck looked up and saw the figure take aim at him. He jumped onto the roof and ran across the sloped surface.

"Stop or I'll shoot."

Chuck continued to scale the roof. Snell fired once and the bullet ricocheted off the metal siding. Chuck dove behind a chimneystack. From behind the brick he could see Snell creeping across the open area toward Debbie. He raised his pistol and sighted Snell in the reticule. It's a long shot, he thought. Make it count. Holding steady, he held his breath as he placed the cross hairs just below her neck. The gun turned smoothly as he tracked Snell slowly crawling across the rail bead. Chuck deliberately stroked the smooth steel of the trigger before he squeezed it.

"Drop the gun," bellowed a voice from his right.

Chuck turned quickly. There was a man standing on the roof

pointing a pistol at him.

It took a few moments, but Nicca's head cleared. He saw Akin applying a bandage to Gunston's head. The SAC was sitting sideways against the front seat wrapping a tourniquet to his leg.

"Where's Snell?" Nicca yelled rubbing his temple,

"She went after the guys in the raft." Akin barked.

"That darn gung ho agent," Nicca cussed. "Akin, let me have your night vision goggles?"

Akin pulled them from his head and handed them to Nicca. Nicca grabbed the sides of the helicopter and struggled to lift himself out. He slid down the side of the aircraft to the ground.

Where did they go?" he muttered as he adjusted the night vision goggles.

In the eerie green light he could see the raft but no sign of Snell or the others. The rail cars rumbled in the distance. "They couldn't have crossed those trains. Must have gone through the culvert. He ran up to the culvert crossing underneath the tracks and glanced inside. It was clear. Hunching, he darted through the culvert, placing him on the far side of the hopper cars. As he ran alongside the moving trains, he saw a flash of motion on the top of a building spanning the tracks. Fighting a pounding in his head, Nicca sprinted to a ladder on his side of the building. Sticking his gun in his belt, he scaled the ladder two rungs at a time. While climbing he heard a gun shot, then he heard Snell shout and another gun shot.

"Snell, where is she?"

At the top of the building, Nicca had a clear view of Snell creeping alongside the tracks. Then he saw a man jump behind the chimney. Nicca crept forward as the man raised his gun toward Snell.

"Drop the gun," Nicca ordered.

The man turned quickly whipping around the gun.

Nicca didn't hesitate. He fired.

The round hit Chuck in the shoulder knocking him down sideways. Impact with the sheet metal roof knocked the pistol from his hand. It slid down the pitched surface. Chuck dove for it, his wounded arm flopping by his side. He grabbed the gun and pounced up to return a shot but his foot caught a seam in the roof. Losing his balance he fell backwards. Chuck groped wildly for a handhold as he slid down the slope. At the eaves, Chuck bounced over the edge. His

285

good elbow snagged the top of the fascia plate as his legs swung freely over the side of the roof. Chuck let go of the pistol and grasped the protruding aluminum of the fascia. Down below he saw the coal cars sliding into the building.

Nicca watched Chuck slide. Using his free hand for a third balance point, he carefully worked his way down the roof. When he saw Chuck dangling over the edge, he quickly holstered his weapon. He locked his foot against the fascia and reached for Chuck's arm.

Chuck looked up through eyes glazed with hate and venom. In that instant, Nicca understood the crimes.

"Hold still, I'll pull you up," Nicca commanded.

Chuck's face darkened. "Not so fast copper. I'm taking the short cut."

Before Nicca could grab his arm, Chuck let go. He landed roughly on a pile of coal in a hopper car that was next to be unloaded in the rotary dumper. The fall knocked the wind out of him. Sucking for air he thought he was dizzy from the fall when he felt as if he was being turned upside down. Then, in horror he realized that he was about to be dropped into the pit along with the load of coal. He scrambled for the side of the hopper car, but his feet and hands sifted through the coal. As the car began to empty he screamed. His cries were muffled by the roar of one hundred tons of coal crushing him at the bottom of the pit.

Nicca watched Chuck fall into the hopper car as it entered the building. He ran across the roof to the other side and saw the empty cars stringing out from the building. There was no sign of him. He peered into the pit but saw only coal black darkness.

Nicca descended the ladder. A railroad worker ran up to him and asked, "What's going on?"

"FBI," Nicca said as he flashed his credentials. "Where does this pit lead?" Nicca pointed to the pit underneath the rotary dumper.

"The conveyor starts there. It leads to that loading dock by the bulk carrier ship over there. "

"A suspect fell in that pit. Can we follow him?"

"Ain't no place to go except on that ship and it leaves first thing in the morning for Japan. If he's in that pit I suspect that he won't be in any shape to go anywhere. We're loading over forty thousand tons of coal on that conveyor tonight. He's going to be buried under a big pile of coal."

"Can you stop the loading."

Err, I can, but it will take a while. I'd have to get back to the control tower. By then, a bunch more cars will dump on top.

Nicca looked toward the ship. "Forty thousand tons." He thought for a second. "I need to call an ambulance. We have two other wounded people back there," he said pointing to the crash site.

"I already called the police when I saw the helicopter crash. They're on their way."

Nicca let out a sigh of relief

The worker led Nicca across a gantry to the other side of the dumper. There he saw Snell huddled over Debbie's body at the base of the stairs.

"Laura," Nicca yelled as he tore off his night vision goggles.

Snell looked up, her grimace turning to a smile.

Nicca ran to her and without thinking pulled her to him. He squeezed her like had never squeezed anyone.

"Are you all right?" his voice quivered.

"I'm fine Joe. How about you?" She reached for his face and rubbed a smudge from beneath his eye. Her touch sent a jolt of electricity through him. He saw the image of Chuck taking aim at her.

"Laura, I want to be with you."

"Me too, Joe."

"You think the FBI would accept an over the hill Fire Marshall."

"They better," Snell smiled back. "Or I'm history."

Nicca pulled her into him, closing his eyes.

SHIZUOKA PREFECTURE, JAPAN

S unon's Parts Fabrication Facility fit harmoniously into its rural setting. The outer buildings and main structure, while modern in architecture, looked like a Zen architect had placed them. The concrete columns crisply framed the glazed windows. Behind the copper-tinted glass the factory was quiet this Sunday.

Yasuhiro Hara looked out the window of the factory's lobby. The bare boughs of the Sycamore trees leading up to the front entrance of the Shizuoka Parts Fabrication Facility arched over the tarmac like silent sentinels watching all who entered. Underneath the trees walked Takahashi wearing an overcoat over slumped shoulders. Hara's dark brown eyes followed the old executive as he slowly paced to the factory's front entrance.

As Takahashi entered through the automatic doors, Hara bowed as deeply as he could. From the corner of his eye he saw Mizuno also bow reverently. The old man nodded then headed to the stairway that led to the fourth floor viewing room. Hara glanced at his watch and tried to settle the uneasiness in his stomach.

Mizuno seem to wait a few minutes before he motioned toward Hara to follow him up the stirs. Hara compiled. On the fourth floor, Hara unaccustomed to taking the stairs was glad to wait while Mizuno stopped at a kitchenette to collect a tray with a pitcher of green tea and three small ceramic cups. After catching his breath Hara followed Mizuno as he opened the door to the viewing room.

Takahashi was facing the robots. His face twisted in macabre smile like a kabuki actor as he appeared to contemplate the mechanical work force.

"Some O-cha for you sir," Mizuno said warmly.

"Thank you."

Takahashi took the cup offered by Mizuno. He gingerly sipped

288

the tea, avoiding the traditional slurping sound, betraying his sullen mood. Hara sensed it immediately. No one said a word while they slowly drank.

Takahashi, cradling the empty cup in his two hands like a priest about to make an offering, turned to look out over the factory floor. In formal and traditional Japanese he said in an even, almost eerie tone, "Look at those magnificent machines. Each performing its job. Together a team creating a masterpiece." He directed his words to the robots below, but the Hara heard him clearly.

"Only in a perfect society can man hope to attain the efficiency of those machines. No complaints. Diligent sacrifice. All for the benefit of our way of life. These robots would make our ancestors proud. Like the farmers planting rice, these machines work for the good of us all."

Mizuno nodded, "Takahashi San, we do not yet have machines that do all of man's work. Humans are not replaceable yet."

"That's it. That's the problem," thundered Takahashi. "Loyal workers must be designed and manufactured like a machine. Everyone must operate together to secure a satisfactory result. It is our tradition, our heritage; a heritage that must endure. The society must come first, we all must work hard to assure success of the whole."

"This is true, Fuku Sacho, but times have changed."

"Times have changed, but these values must endure. These values are the crucial ingredient to our society's success." Takahashi glared at the robots.

Hara struggled to understand what the two men were saying. He knew Takahashi had a reason for bringing him to Shizuoka, but he wasn't sure what it was. Their roundabout talk had to be for his benefit. What did it mean? He shook his head. Takahashi's talk was too hard to understand. They had to be talking about Kondo's situation. How Kondo had seemingly lost his mind when he learned the ship sank. How an alcoholic binge brought about psychotic depression. Silence was a good course of action, but soon they would expect him to say something. Hara shifted in his seat. Finally, in desperation he blurted "Kondo was wrong, he was not a team player. We are better off without him!"

Takahashi raised his voice. "Don't be harsh Hara-San. The success of any team depends on it ability to take advantage of the unique talents of all its members."

Takahashi turned, staring directly at Hara. "Kondo-San was a special case. He had many irritating habits, but it was those habits that made him so successful in the United States. During his tenure, he oversaw the miraculous growth of Sunon's American market share. This was no fluke."

"I don't understand," stammered Hara. "If we needed Kondo, why did we plot against him?"

"When it came time for change, Kondo lost sight of what is good for us all. He became too comfortable with the status quo. He could not understand that it was time for change."

"Yes, I see. That is why we had to oust him. It's unfortunate he must be locked away in a sanitarium."

Takahashi's eyes glowed like a lantern about to explode. Yet, his voice remained calm. "Kondo made his own choice. I had no plans to oust him. In fact, once Kondo had agreed with our plan, I expected to put him in charge of the joint venture in the U.S. Now he will rot in a padded room. His mind wasted by alcohol."

"What?" Hara nearly screamed. "If Kondo was to be in charge, then why did you have me arrange the burning of the car dealerships. Why did we force him out?"

Takahashi paced to a desk as he seemed to recall some distasteful memory. "The fires were only to help convince Kondo that the political situation in the U.S. was growing untenable. Only when Kondo perceived the grave political problem in the U.S. would he have agreed to alter his North American development plan."

Hara rubbed his head. "Why? Why burn our own dealerships?"

Takahashi crossed his arms. "Progress sometimes requires a few backward steps. We were running out of time. The board wanted action and we could not reach an agreement. We had to help Kondo to see it our way. A few cars and buildings of some below average dealerships were a small price for continued market penetration with the joint venture."

"Why use terrorists? Why not overrule Kondo?"

Takahashi slammed his hands on the desk. "We did not use terrorists! We gave you a simple mission. Pay that slovenly pig Cannon to arrange a few fires at some of our Detroit dealerships. What did you do? You hired madmen. You let the plan get out of control. The arsons that you arranged were to be simple diversions at the few car dealers. Instead these madmen destroyed millions of yen of our property. You created a monster."

The words came from a face taut like a carnivore about to strike.

"Then you allowed Kondo to make an arrangement with disreputable gangsters. A move that cast an international pall on our company. The media and the American politicians demanded action. Even the politicians publicly questioned Sunon. You put Sunon in a difficult position." Takahashi threw his head to toward the factory. "Itoh-San, the honorable man that he is, resigned this morning as Chief Executive Officer. Our leader has born the responsibility for the action of his company - the action of a few outrageous employees. Our leader has done what he had to do to save the honor of our company."

Hara sat motionless a rivulet of sweat running down his forehead. The CEO of his company resigned because of his actions. What was Takahashi going to demand from him?

"I assumed the duties of CEO. I will lead this company into the next century. It will be my job to clean this company of those who do not work for the common good." Takahashi again made a stinging glare. In a blinding flash, the brilliance of Takahashi's plan became clear to Hara. Itoh gone. Kondo replaced. The company was Takahashi's.

Takahashi lowered his voice. "The American FBI submitted a request to the Japanese National Police. The Americans want to know how those vile gangsters pursued the terrorists. It seems that the FBI has only a few isolated clues about the identity of the gangsters. They have evidence of some phone calls. A rented car."

Hara reached for a chair trying to steady himself. Takahashi was acting as if he had no knowledge of the Yakuza, but surely Takahashi knew. Why was he saying this? Hara's head spun. It was he, Hara, who met with Cannon and arranged the arsons. Cannon burned a few dealerships; he gave him money. It was he who gave the information on Cannon to the Yakuza. He was following Takahashi's orders, wasn't he? No. Wait. I understand. I am the only one directly related to the crimes. I am to be sacrificed. His arms started to quiver.

"Orders, orders, I was following orders." Hara choked back tears.

Takahashi's eyes turned red. His stern face squeezed even tighter. "What do you mean orders? We told you to arrange the arson of three dealerships. We did not expect to lose a ship and its load of brand new cars!"

Hara trembled. He could not control himself and started moaning and coughing. Takahashi was blaming Hara for the disaster in the U.S. He did not know how to defend himself. Between coughs he stammered. "No, no. I know nothing about the Yakuza! Kondo arranged them. I left them the information about the Americans so they could find them easily. Those were your orders." He clutched his face in his hands."

Turning his back, Takahashi changed his tone. His voice sounded like that of a priest blessing a condemned man. "In the days of my noble ancestors, such treachery and malfeasance required only one solution. You have caused our company much dishonor. Many a man more capable than you slit his belly to retain his family's honor."

Hara stopped sobbing. He bent over even more, burying his face in the tatami mat. He surrendered. He knew he had no choice. Like the many Japanese after World War Two, to whom surrender meant certain death, his submission would bring his ultimate destruction.

Takahashi glanced at Mizuno. The junior nodded suggesting that the job was done. Turning back to the sobbing Hara, Takahashi said "Hara-San, settle yourself. Mizuno is right. Times have changed. You have been a loyal Sunon man. We reward loyalty."

Hara could not look up, his body still trembling violently. Takahashi motioned to Mizuno. Mizuno reached down and grabbed Hara by the arms. He pulled the prostrate man to a small couch.

"Hara-San listen. All the information on this case is in this file." Mizuno handed a manila folder to the new CEO. "The file will be kept in a secure place. The FBI will learn nothing."

Hara looked up, still disconsolate. "Huh?"

"We have arranged an assignment for you and your family at our Singapore electronics plant. There you will be safely away from any investigation. You and your family will be well cared for."

"I don't understand?"

"We have contacts in the National Police. The investigation, if there is one, will never leave the shores of the United States. You will be safe."

Hara shook his head meekly, still not sure how to absorb what his superior was saying. "I don't understand."

"It is simple. You are with Sunon. Sunon will take care of you. You are with us. We are with you."

"Singapore, huh." He paused to wipe away tears with his coat sleeve. "Oh . . .I understand. Oh thank you, thank you," Hara bowed low to the floor.

Takahashi nodded and glanced down at the robots. He said, "It's December. The rice paddies and steep hills of Shizuoka prefecture are dull brown. Each field lies dormant anticipating the next frantic planting and growing season. In only a few months the perpetual cycle of rice harvest will begin anew. Now, it is time to rest."

End

Robert Kempinski and Bernard Kempinski are identical twin brothers and modern renaissance men.

Trained as mechanical engineers at Georgia Tech and MIT respectively, they have had careers as US Army combat engineers, submarine designers, defense analysts, rocket scientists, photographers, business development consultants, government officials, model train entrepreneurs, bonsai artists and authors. As twins one can finish the other's sentence, a good trait for collaborating on a book.

LaVergne, TN USA
15 June 2010
186270LV00004B/20/P

9 781452 854496